The Great &
Calamitous Tale of
Johan Thoms

Ian Thornton

The Friday Project
An imprint of HarperCollins*Publishers*
77–85 Fulham Palace Road
Hammersmith, London W6 8JB
www.harpercollins.co.uk

First published by Simon & Schuster Canada, 2013 Canada
First published in the UK by The Friday Project as in ebook in 2013
Paperback edition first published 2014

A catalogue record for this book is available from the British Library

ISBN 978-0-00-755149-1

Printed and bound in Great Britain by Clays Ltd, St Ives plc

MIX
Paper from
responsible sources
FSC™ C007454
www.fsc.org

To Heather, Laszlo and Clementine

Contents

Part Four

The Great &
Calamitous Tale of
Johan Thoms

Prologue

A Refracted Tale of Two Wordy Old Gentlemen in a Blue Prism

A rural cricket match in buttercup time, seen and heard through the trees; it is surely the loveliest scene in England and the most disarming sound. From the ranks of the unseen dead forever passing along our country lanes, the Englishman falls out for a moment to look over the gate of the cricket field and smile.

—J. M. Barrie

2009. Northern England

I sat with my grandfather Ernest in a very comfortable, spacious ward in the hospital in Goole. The doctors had said that he would not live for much more than a week.

Goole is as Goole sounds, a dirty-gray inland port in Yorkshire not far from England's east coast. More than one hundred years earlier, Count Dracula might well have grimaced as he passed through, en route from Whitby to Carfax Abbey. Most foreigners (and some southerners) think it is spelled *Ghoul,* especially after their first, and invariably only, visit. This is where Ernest's final days were to be spent, though at least the hospital sat at the very edge of town and his window faced the more pleasant countryside.

It had been a rapid decline for a man who, well into his nineties, on the eleventh day of the previous November, had walked the three and three-quarter miles to the train station before daybreak. He had traveled south on three trains of varying decrepitude and two rickety tubes to stand by the Cenotaph on Whitehall with thousands of others. Many were bemedaled, some wheelchaired, but each had a shared something behind the eyes and a similar thought focused just above the horizon, as the high bells of St. Stephen's in Westminster struck eleven and the nation fell silent. Then, with only tea accompanied by Bovriled and buttered crumpets from the Wolseley on Piccadilly as fuel, he had made the return trip the same day, pushing open, with untroubled lungs, his unlatched door way past the time that saw most decent folks in bed. He had told me that it was the only day he could ever remember when he had not conversed with a single person. He had had his reasons.

Now he tugged at a length of clear plastic tubing, which disappeared under sterile white tape and into the wattle of his forearm; an artificial tributary into the slowing yet still magnificent deep red tide within. He did not appear to be uncomfortable. On the contrary, he exhibited a strong and urgent desire to speak.

He gestured toward the clock above his bed with his right hand. "In the story I am about to tell, please bear in mind the possible minor defects and chronological leaps in the memory of a dying man or two. Exaggeration is naturally occurring in the DNA of the cadaver known as the tale. This is important." He looked straight at me in the way that he always had, in order to let me know that this part of the game was not to be taken lightly.

I do not paraphrase, for my grandfather spoke this way from as far back as I can recall. His deliberate and florid verbals had always transformed the planning, execution, and completion of what for a young lad might otherwise have been everyday chores, into marvelous adventures of joyous nonsense. He turned tuneless whistles into lush arias effortlessly.

He had been my mentor and teacher, instructing me on how to hold a fish knife, stun a billiard ball. He taught me the subtleties and implications of en passant on the chessboard. He knew whether to introduce the team to the Queen or the Queen to the team. He taught me that the correct answer to "How do you do?" is indeed "How do you do?" Of his early life, I vaguely recall references to his days as an emetic, vicious, ear-tugging martinet of a schoolmaster; his inherited connections to and shares in the Cunard shipping line, gained through an ancestor's good fortune in a Cape Town card game over ever-cheapening rum with bothersome (but luckily pie-eyed and wobbly) pirates; his junior partnership with Sir Thomas

Beecham,[1] England's greatest-ever conductor and founder of both the Royal and the London Philharmonic orchestras; dinners with royalty, with Niven and Korda, Gielgud and Fonteyn, Olivier and Churchill. I remember framed monochrome photographs of him at that time, as a young man in a Savile Row tuxedo, Jermyn Street cuff links, well-heeled Bond Street shoes, a heavily starched shirt, and a head of black hair expertly topped off with a light Brylcreem.

This did not seem to me to be the same person who, from the boundary rope on summer afternoons of my boyhood, taught me the lengthy names of Welsh railway stations, chuckled at cricketers being struck in the groin or on the backside, and joyously read to me Kipling, Barrie, and *The Captain Erasmus Adventurer's Book for Boys, Daredevils and Young Kings*. And he was far from the man who lay before me now, though from the neck up, at least, he appeared unchanged—his matinee idol's widow's peak proudly silver, his eyes active and mischievous. The sunken contours of the bedsheets, however, suggested that much of the man I had known all my life was already gone.

I suspected that it was right to remain silent. I thought it misplaced to counter his statement about dying men, for we knew each other too well. He would indeed die, in this bed constructed for such purposes. He would soon be not breathing. And cold. I knew I must simply listen.

I had always loved my grandfather's stories. At first, I believed them absolutely. Later, I tried to distinguish between truth and fairy tale. I often got this wrong. Of course, I had been spoon-fed cynicism from an early age by Ernest's wife, Betty, my dear late grandmother, who had told me repeatedly, "Lad! Never believe anything of what you hear, and only half of what you see."

But of all the stories he ever told me, not one compared to the one he now told me in the last hours of his life. I believed him then. I still believe him.

* * *

It was during a stint as the mayor of Goole that Ernest, a very sprightly eighty-eight, spent two weeks in the hills outside Sarajevo in the sublimely warm and cloudless April of 2003, attempting to find a twin town for his parish. Sarajevo had been chosen for personal reasons; Ernest had recently read his father's wartime diaries, in which the old city had featured heavily and whose characters had enthralled him.

Very early one Friday morning, Ernest stumbled across a shack in a village destroyed by war, a hermitage surrounded by a sea of flowers, a prism of blues, azures, cobalts, teals, and beryls. Of lilacs and violets.

Ernest recalled with absolute clarity the fine sapphire haze through which he walked. Peeking through a grubby, splintered pane, he saw a small, square room, with unsure blue light leaking in from another window on the opposite wall. An old man was moving slowly within, declaiming loudly enough for Ernest to hear from outside.

"I am the Resurrection.
And I am the Life . . ."

Ernest tapped on the window. The old man stopped moving and turned slowly to him, seeming to beckon him in.

Ernest entered the shack hesitantly. The door opened slowly and required the help of Ernest's upper arm to overcome the resistance, though there was neither lock nor latch. There were minimal signs of a woman's recent presence: a tray with two plates, cutlery and an empty goblet, a jug of water, a vase of yellow roses. By them he saw an exquisite old man, with a mournful, creased countenance and worldly-wise eyes that appeared a youthful blue.

"Welcome to my humble abode," the old man said in a superb English accent. "You might be in a position to help me. The alignment of events is quite remarkable, and I see now perhaps necessary. Are you fond of mathematics, my friend? Symmetry? Patterns? The Laws of Physics? I suspect you think I am a madman. I always proudly confess this to be true. For what is the blasted point otherwise?"

Ernest chuckled, and then chuckled again when he realized that the old man was being totally serious.

"And what about time travel?" the old man continued. "I think I may be about to crack it. Johan Thoms is the name," he said.

Ernest moved cautiously across the worn boards into an area less cramped by relics and reminders whose relevance he was soon to understand. This old man's collection appeared to him to encapsulate a life, and to fill his nostrils with a poignant aroma, a scent of a moment in time.

He watched as the man edged forward, barefoot. Barely keeping his balance, he shuffled to a stop. Ernest continued to observe the solitarian.

"These things you see here are my vortex, my portal, a wormhole in the space-time continuum, my passage back in time."

They heard a noise in the corner of his shack.

"That bastard thug of a rat is back to ruin my day!"

He started to reach for a rusty old fork that lay on the stained sideboard beside him. But before he had managed any back lift with which to propel the missile, the toothy rodent was gone.

"One of these old friends shall allow me to slip through, slip back. My escape route."

The old man waved at a handful of aged objects, nestled around him in his makeshift hermitage; a trilogy of aged books, some sepia photographs, a wireless radio set, a crystal paperweight within which a bit of paper seemed to float, a battered typewriter, several bound manuscripts, an empty bottle of cologne, a remarkable open sea chest filled with yellowed, crispy letters and powder-blue ones written in the same tidy feminine handwriting. "If I concentrate hard enough at the right time, when the stars are in the right constellation," he explained to Ernest, "I'm sure I'll be transported back through history." Back to the time when the paper was new, without words. To when the ink was royal blue, fresh and wet, still on the nib hovering above the top left corner of the sheet and about to leave its indelible and permanent message.

Johan picked up a handful of the blue sheets, inhaled deeply, a trace of a smile on his lips, and then passed them to Ernest, keeping his eyes on them. Some were addressed in identical fine calligraphy to Miss Blanche de la Peña.

Johan continued. "I shall now glide back to our belle époque. I shall balance the books and save mankind. And *this* time around I shall perhaps allow myself the small luxury of being *with her*. I know where and when to find her. Even if I did not, my pulse should be drawn to her conductivity." Here he paused, closing his eyes and gathering his breath. "*This* time I shall bathe in her. *This* time she will be my perpetual banquet of roasted delights and also my scarlet Bacchus with which to wash her own self down. I swear it." His diatribe gathered momentum and volume, reaching a crescendo. "As a youth, I shall keep one eye on the white June night when we shall meet on the lawns of the Old Sultan's Palace, but I shall glide there and not burn my precious days en route. I shall bask in the knowledge of devilish, God-given treats ahead to be devoured over decades. She will feel a *vampirus* coming through time. She will demand it and recognize it when it comes with uncomfortable, pleasurable consternation. Lorelei!"

He paused, and tilted his head back to speak to a higher power.

"Dionysus! Inform those spirits to clear the way, for my dry run is over, and what sort of cretin does not learn by his mistakes, particularly ones of the magnitude and the severity in which I infamously deal?

"I have attempted to cultivate the mythical and elusive Blue Rose of Forgetfulness to erase my memory forever and to therefore discover the ecstatic state of knowing no pain, but I have merely succeeded in shrouding and blanketing the landscape around this hut in a mass of flowers of varying hues of azure. Indeed, the shades of the flora only haunt me more, reminding me of my pivotal summer almost ninety years ago. Time is so short. I have to escape this scabby quod, this jail, this grimmest of prisons which I call my mind, which is right now closing in on the remnants of my consciousness and the shards of my sanity. If only I could find that portal back. For the sake of all mankind.

"I am the Resurrection
And I am the Life."

He repeated this until his deluded mantra was broken by his own words.

"I have afflicted every soul on this planet. Believers and infidels. Heretics and blasphemers. I defy you to find a life I have not changed or ended. The twentieth century was mine. Just the final Apocalypse to welcome in. Should I have the politeness, should I display the etiquette to die first?"

My grandfather Ernest did nothing all Easter weekend but sit in one of Bosnia's most dilapidated chairs, in an excuse of a dwelling, with another old man. He did not budge except to urinate and to move his bowels. Uncharacteristically, Ernest hardly said a word himself. He just sat and listened. It was one old gentleman's story to another; that of the host, a tale which covers a life of over one hundred years; the other not far off, and therefore (as in many biographies and autobiographies) one where a day may seem to last an age and where a decade may slip by within a sentence or paragraph.

According to my grandfather, Johan claimed to have changed—actually to have destroyed—the twentieth century.

Ernest had hoped to keep the story for a time when we would have an adequate number of days together to record the magnum opus of Johan Thoms. There remained within him a discipline to do things correctly and with due process, though this was marvelously mixed with a sense of the romantic and the truly delicious. My grandfather, the ordered musician, the headmaster, the recounter of fine and giant fables. Time, though, would have her wicked way. And so it was my task, my solemn duty, not only to hear the tale of Johan Thoms, but to complete it. Ernest pleaded with me, "Glide gently, my dear boy. In buttercup times. Down country lanes. Never forgetting to fall out from the ranks, look over that old gate, and to smile."

Part One

I should like to bury something precious in every place where I've been happy and then, when I'm old and ugly and miserable, I could come back and dig it up and remember.

Evelyn Waugh, *Brideshead Revisited*

One

Around the Time
When Adolf Was a Glint in
His First Cousin's Eye

*Give and it shall be given to you. For whatever measure you deal out to others,
it will be dealt to you in return.*

—Luke 6:38

February 1894. Bosnia

Johan Thoms (pronounced *Yo-han Tomes*) was born in Argona, a small town twenty-three miles south of Sarajevo, during the hellish depths of winter 1894.

His family was not overly religious. They were, however, surrounded in the village by enough Catholicism to expose Johan osmotically to the curse of guilt.

Johan was an only child, and had been lucky to live through a worrying labor. He was a breach birth, and arrived a month early, on the twelfth of February. He had jaundice and coughed up blood. The umbilical cord was wrapped tight around his neck. Thick black curls crowned his large head. The cause of his parents' worry was that another boy had been born to them four years earlier in exactly the same manner. He'd shared the same characteristics: the yellow skin, the breach, the cord, the blood, the hair. Carl had not survived. Drago and Elena feared a repeat. It was probably from this fear that there developed an extra-special bond between parents and child.

Johan pulled through. Within three months, he shed his sub-Saharan curls, and he appeared less yellow by the day. With his now fair hair, the blue eyes of his mother, Elena, and the surname Thoms, there was more than a hint in Johan of Aryanesque lineage from Austria and the north. He became almost normal looking.

Johan was happier than most boys, alone with a soccer ball in the street, or a chess set in front of the hearth. Even if he was only playing against himself—usually the domain of the autistic and potentially schizophrenic—he would remain occupied for hours.

He was a smart child, and he went about his boyhood business with a minimum of fuss. If it had not been for the food disappearing from his plate three times daily, his underclothes getting a weekly scrub, and his bedclothes marginally disturbed each morning, his parents might have sworn that they were nursing nothing more than a friendly poltergeist. He was ordinary and unobtrusive. If he was two, three, or even four hours late home from school, he was not missed. Maybe it would have been better for all involved if his lateness—due usually to his error-riddled sense of direction—had been noted.

Maybe then, things would have been different.

*   *   *

Johan's father, Drago, was also an only child, born on his parents' isolated farm near the Serbian border in 1854. He was forty years old by the time young Johan appeared.

Drago resembled a mad professor (which was convenient given that he was one, albeit a fine one). His unruly hair looked like it was always ready for a street battle, and he lacked full vision in his right eye. He loved to don an eye patch, but equally enjoyed switching the patch from one eye to the other, or even to remove it to see people struggle to know into which pupil to look. His poor vision meant he only did this when stationary, to avoid accidents. This was one of his many ideas of fun. Yet his strong, handsome features outweighed his quirks. He was a strapping six foot three and boasted a lean jaw, olive skin, mocha eyes, and a regulation fashion sense. However, he always donned at least one distinctive, unforgettable item on any given day. This might be a solid silver pocket watch (engraved, chiming, charming), or bright red socks; or, to complement a handlebar mustache, he would loop around his sinewy neck a gold chain with a miniature comb attached. He christened the comb "Jezebel" and would run her through his hirsute top lip.

Drago had flat feet and a tendency to waffle on about absolutely nothing for an age, often to complete strangers. But he had a huge heart. The whole town knew it, as he teased and trundled through his daily life without setting their world on fire.

Two

Pawn to Queen Four

Chess is a fairy tale of 1001 blunders.

—Savielly Tartakower

May 1901. Near Sarajevo.

Most adults fell in love with Johan's deep blue eyes, but his contemporaries at school preferred to concentrate on the size of his ash-blond mopped head, which was larger than average at best. At worst, he resembled a fugitive from Easter Island.

Johan walked with that six-year-old's nongait, which, accentuated by the size of his head and pipe-cleaner legs, verged on a cute stagger.

Of his two passions, soccer and chess, he was far better at chess. With a ball, his will was strong, but not his art. His feet were way too small to keep his head from overstepping his center of gravity, and down he would come. His stock answer whenever some clever clogs informed him that he had fallen over was to slowly get up, dust himself off, and say that he was merely trying to break a bar of chocolate that he had in his back pocket.

On the chessboard, however, he could be nasty. His innocent blue eyes and waifish body masked a killer instinct. In front of the sixty-four squares, he was closer in spirit to Attila the Hun than to Little Lord Fauntleroy.

It must have been the size of that head.

In Johan's ninth summer, Senad Pestic, the Bosnian grand master and stooping old Arab, came to a school ten miles away from Johan's, on the southern slopes of Mount Igman, to play against all the best boys in the area. It was an annual event and Johan's first time. The matches were scheduled for four-thirty, after school and at forty tables set up in a circle in the main hall.

One of Johan's uncles, Toothless Mico, usually ferried him to chess meets, but tonight Johan wanted only one person to be there: his mother. She would be so proud of her only child, and the little boy always wanted to please her. But she was too busy selling the fruit of (and for) her feudal boss from a makeshift hut in the town square. He comforted himself that if he continued to progress at the game, before long he would be beating grand masters for fun.

The grand master would play games against all the boys simultaneously. The honor in being the last to lose was immense, and legends could grow around boys who had come close to victory. No one from the area had ever beaten the old genius. Each board had a rudimentary clock to the right of the set, on the old guy's side, consisting of oversized hourglasses, egg timers, and abaci. Each board had a different-shaped bean counter, loaned from the classrooms. Every time the sands of time ran out on a player, a bean was shifted.

Heads! Johan won the flip of a coin and chose white.

Good versus evil, Johan chanted inside his skull, as if the future of mankind depended on him. *Good versus evil.*

After twenty revolutions, some boys had been humiliated and were back in the schoolyard kicking their heels or being herded home by their shamed parents. Not Johan Thoms. His stubborn little legs did not even reach the floor from his seat. He pulled his socks up to below his bare knees every ten minutes or so and waited for his enemy to approach. He left one shoelace untied, for that, to the superstitious boy, represented Pestic—"the one Johan Thoms would famously undo."

The grand master spent more time at Johan's table than at any of the others, and Johan's confidence grew as he realized he was at least doing better than his contemporaries.

The little boy (white) had adopted the Oleg Defense. Pestic (black) was wide-eyed at this feisty approach; one had to know the play in depth, its history, its options and permutations, if one were to succeed.

Johan made the crusty old codger scratch his manky head. That, though, could easily have been a flea, causing some bother at the funeral of one of his thousand or so relatives whose ancestors had made this genius their home a decade before.

Johan heard the vile twin curses *idi u kurac*[2] and *tizi pizdun*[3] for the first time that day, as Fleabag glanced up to look at Johan's eyes, right, left, right, left, as if to double-check that the boy knew what he was doing. Young Johan rolled his eyes.

Johan had placed his knights centrally, to offer control of the whole board before a forced exchange from Pestic. Each player was now left with only one.

Pieces were now traded at a steady pace. Johan felt that if he had the choice of either position—his or Pestic's—he would take his own.

Queens made their way into the action.

Pestic surveyed the battlefield, from a lofty height, in a scabby gray suit with bobbles of worsted around the elbows and collar. His chin shoved through white whiskers. His mouth was uneven, his lips were badly chapped, and his teeth leaned erratically, like brown tombstones. Greasy wisps of gray-and-silver hair grew randomly across his skull. His crown generously shed itself onto the back line of his pawn's defense. This tall, bent, skinny wretch had clearly thrown his lot into the game he loved. His shirt looked as if some poor soul had tried to scrub it clean. His mauve tie was badly knotted, and was no longer at the apex of his collar as he returned again to Johan. He looked like he had lost a love, and had never recovered. His brown eyes, however, were clear and youthful, and did not hide the fierce intelligence behind them.

* * *

Only half a dozen boys remained.

Old Fleabag now had to pull up a seat for each visit to Johan's board.

Johan sneaked in a castle maneuver. Fleabag followed. His clock ticked. Both clocks ticked, but Johan's seemed to him to move in slow motion.

Hmm, thought Johan. *Flea by name,* flee *by nature . . .*

Johan's neurons were firing as he offered an exchange which, when accepted, left the boy a pawn up.

Johan consolidated with a centrally placed queen covering his outlying pieces.

Everything was now under the cover of a compatriot piece. He had never before lined up such a defense (which by its very nature, was morphing into an attack).

Cometh the hour, cometh the urchin.

Johan spotted a trap, revealing an undiscovered check which left him a major piece up, as well as his pawn advantage. He then eagerly exchanged queens, to whittle away any remaining leverage from Fleabag.

If the game had been halted now, Johan Thoms would have been crowned champion. He was way ahead. He (white) held a centrally placed rook, a white-squared bishop, a knight, and five pawns.

Pestic (black) had four pawns, a black-squared bishop, and a rook.

* * *

Evening had arrived. Old Busic, the lazy school janitor and gardener, could be heard whistling out in the entrance, threatening to do his shoddy mopping tasks once the battle was through.

The whistling broke Johan's now iron concentration, and he looked up to notice that the gathering of parents off to one side had dwindled.

Yet the crowd had added one to its number. *She* now stood next to Toothless Mico.

It was his mother, Elena Thoms.

Tears almost came to Johan's eyes as Fleabag once again came to his table, the number of combatants down to just one, Johan himself. Another boy slunk off into the dusk.

Her sparkling blue eyes were damp with tears—"wetter than an otter's pocket," she later admitted—which made them twinkle even more. Lazy old Busic, standing by her now, put down his mop and urged on the little lad with a slowly pumping fist.

She had made it after all, Johan thought. She'd had enough confidence in him to know that he would still be alive on the board.

Johan quickly regained his composure, but it was too late. Old Fleabag's eyes were focused. He had to produce something remarkable. This he did.

Black (Fleabag) played an inspired and sacrificial rook to h3, in a move that would have initially appeared like suicide even to seasoned professionals. Johan, left with no choice if he was to avoid a checkmate at h6, took Fleabag's rook at h3, aligning his pawns on the outer flank. It was a price worth paying for Fleabag, who advanced his pawn to h6 for a check. Johan was forced to pitch his king back to h4, whereupon the ruthless old genius slid his now proud, erect bishop to f2 for an inspired victory.

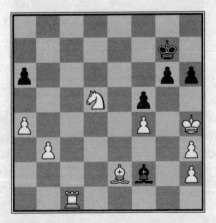

The unbeaten grand master never came to any of the schools again. He shuffled off to the hills to be fed on by fleas until his death, hastened by a malicious Kaposi's sarcoma, whereby the fleas passed on the baton to their counterparts the worms.

Elena had been there long enough to see the grand master crumple in turmoil as the game slid away from him. Her own flesh and blood had sat opposite, shoelaces dangling inches from the dusty boards. Johan had ratcheted up the old man's misery with remarkable nonchalance. As the minutes had passed by, the old guy had stooped lower and their respective caricatured outlines had become more pronounced against the yellow light at the far end of the hall. Elena witnessed a swift exchange, a change of posture, and, ultimately, a handshake.

Johan did not want to let his mother know how close he had come to winning. She must not think her presence there had put him off. (It may also have been a hint at an almost frantic desire to please his parents, which some might have seen as unhealthy and perhaps even pathological. The frenetic nature of this adorable trait led Johan to miss breaths when he saw his parents' smiles.) And anyway, if Pestic could pull off a victory from that position, Johan realized, perhaps nothing would have prevented his own brave defeat. He had, however, lasted longer than any other boy; and he suspected that she loved him as much as he loved her.

At checkmate, Johan jumped down from his chair, and discovered that he had left the wrong shoe untied. He landed, leaving the old guy scratching various parts of his fading cadaver. The lad tied his lace and staggered toward his mother and Toothless Mico. An overexcited Busic tried to meet him halfway. Johan sidestepped him almost with grace, and stumbled on toward Elena, who picked him up and squeezed him.

Toothless Mico took them back to Argona. The boy later remembered being happy as he fell asleep in the cart on the dirt track. He woke from time to time with images of a chessboard on the lids of his eyes. When he opened them, the image was transposed onto the stars in the clear night sky.

Mars was his rook, the moon his queen.

He saw an army of a thousand pawns in the celestials, which made him wonder why *he* was allowed only eight.

Three

Serendipity's Day Off

It's too soon to tell.

— Chinese Premier Zhou Enlai, when asked by Henry Kissinger if he
thought the French Revolution of 1789 had been of benefit to humanity

It was serendipity's day off," insisted my grandfather Ernest. "By all
rights, Johan Thoms should have been blinded, if not killed, as a seven-
year-old."

June 1901. Near Sarajevo.

Johan's boyhood nightly routine had been an odd one.

First, he would close his eyes and mentally check off each of the continents on his father's huge ancient globe, which Drago had requisitioned
from the school where he worked. The spherical atlas held center stage in
the living room, its pink, yellow, and red landmasses enveloped by the blue
oceans. The globe also held special status for the boy, as it was larger (however marginally) than his own head. He would spend hours in bed remembering its countries, its capitals, and its seas. As time went by, he increased
the difficulty of his nocturnal examinations, testing himself with the capital

of Ceylon, the neighboring bodies of water to the Yellow Sea, or the longitudes of Costa Rica's coastlines. His spongelike brain soaked up everything.

After this initial task, he would transport himself mentally to the side of a deserted rural road. In his reveries, a leaden sky threatened a premature dusk. In a lay-by sat an empty mustard-yellow carriage. The horses had been released. This abandoned cart marked the part of the forest where he would meet his friend. Young Johan then had to stand absolutely motionless next to the wood, and stare in until his pal arrived. This would complete his nightly duties.

His chum was a stag deer, and possessor of the land's largest antlers—fourteen blades, to be exact. Some nights Johan would lie there for hours, staring at the vivid canvas on the inside of his neuronized eye, awaiting the appearance of the friendly, beckoning deer thirty yards or so into the thick forest. Other nights the deer appeared within minutes, even seconds. Johan had no control. He could only get there and stare into the dense green and brown. But after a glint in the eye and a nod from his imaginary buddy, he would be allowed to enter a restful, deep sleep. If he did not obey these rules, he believed, the world would be nudged off its axis.

* * *

Johan had been visiting the same spot in his mind every night for a couple of years when his parents sent him on a holiday to the countryside. Rudimentary tents; appalling food with grit and burned grass, cremated on campfires; mildly disgusting ditties sung around the campfire every night by the older boys.

On the final afternoon, the group was taken to a local landed estate, where various wild species roamed. It had been a tinderbox of a summer, the hottest in living memory. Ten minutes after arriving, the group was led off to a crumbling canteen at the edge of a lake to hydrate themselves before the afternoon's exertions. That is, everyone apart from one melon-headed, blue-eyed, stick-legged youth who had spotted one of the most common species in the park, a deer. Johan was in a trance. It was his friend!

At last, he could meet him and talk to him, as he had wished for every night since he could remember.

No one saw the boy stagger off in the opposite direction to the rest of his group. He stumbled in the field's divots and potholes, like the town drunk leaving the tavern at midnight, toward his buddy. Mothers the world over would have picked him up, wrapped him in cotton wool, and stolen away to the hills with him.

His target was minding his own business, eating grass in the clearing with several other deer. Johan had never been so excited. How come they had not told him he was going to see his friend today? He reached the beast with unusual confidence and speed, and greeted his pal.

"Hello you. I have come to see you. They never told me I was coming; I don't know if they told you."

The deer stopped munching for a few seconds and eyed him with mistrust.

"I'm on holiday. I guess you're on holiday from the woods, too. Sometimes I wait hours for you, but I want you to know that I do not mind," Johan said.

A couple of the other deer had now raised their heads.

"Do you like it better out here than in the woods?"

No answer.

"Your antlers are bigger than usual.

"It's so hot today, though. Aren't you hot under all that fur?"

No answer. Johan moved closer to try to pat the deer but had to delve between his huge antlers to reach the promised land of the beast's fuzzy forehead. This was permitted for all of two seconds. Johan felt a rush of love, then something else inside his brain. The deer had raised his head back and taken Johan part of the way with him. The antlers ripped deep into the young boy's head. Johan had whispered the words *I love you,* as near the deer's ears as he could. From the canteen, the group gasped as the creature lifted Johan clear of the long grass and catapulted him like a rag doll into an expanse of nettly gorse. Wads of blood caught the light of the sun. The deer volleyed back six feet from the human debris, calmed himself, and carried on grazing. Johan was left facedown, rapidly leaking rhesus positive from his temple. The last thing he remembered thinking before a blackness overtook him was, *What have I done to upset my friend? Should I have let him know last night that I was coming?*

He did not cry.

* * *

He regained consciousness swaddled in bandages that magnified his large skull. He was in a crisp sterile linen hospital bed, stitched up, wrapped in white, and as high as any seven-year-old could be.

Over the coming days, he started to piece together what had happened. His friend Deer had butted him, punctured his head, and put him firmly on the seat of his little blue shorts. Friends can be so cruel. Every night for almost two weeks after, Johan would return in his mind's eye to the side of the forest, to the lay-by, next to the mustard carriage, to wait for his friend and forgive him. He needed to apologize for turning up at the park without warning; it had just not been polite. If there was one thing he was learning from his parents, it was the importance of manners.

Johan did not want to lose his best friend. However, over the coming weeks, no matter how long he stayed awake, no visitor came from the woods to tell him everything was all right. Some nights he would not sleep. No deer appeared. The only time he would drift off without Deer's permission was after the administration of another batch of opiates.

He had been a lucky lad. The antler had entered the skull in that tenderest spot to the north by northwest of the temple. He had come within a fraction of an inch of losing his eye, of permanent brain damage. (This would perhaps explain his tendency later in life to don a pirate's patch.) The doctors proclaimed it a miracle that he was not dead. While he was being lifted clean off the ground, Johan's medicine-ball head had acted as a buffer, and so he lived to tell the tale.

* * *

The anguish of Johan's parents was outweighed only by the relief they felt when it became apparent that this had been one very lucky escape. They battled through all the obvious parental horrors: thoughts of burying him, of no life in his corpse; of his wispy blond hair and tiny fingernails still growing underground, his lips turning green before fully decomposing; of him rotting in a tiny coffin while the world went on in the marketplace and the classroom around their absolute hells. Of placing favorite chess pieces on a fresh mound of earth as they returned each day to stand Johan's figurine soldiers back up on the sinking turf. Parents are not supposed to put any of their kids into the ground; to have two out of two dead would probably have been too much for Drago and Elena.

The hospital staff adopted Johan Thoms as their mascot. This was the same precocious child who had also almost defeated, and hence retired, the local legend of a chess master. As the story of the weird kid who talked to deer spread, so did the young boy's influence. This fleeting fame meant he received the best care possible, and was given precedence over the old guys down the hall who could not stop defecating themselves during the day or trying to hump each other during the night, and over the mad old crones on the ground floor, who yelled for the return of infants lost forty years ago, for husbands lost the previous week, for items lost from their stubborn-stained, chin-hugging underwear drawer the previous day. One resourceful *lunatica* had been stealing these panties with ever-increasing cunning and throwing them in the duck pond in the orchard, at the hind-quarters of the hospital.

The ducks soon left.

* * *

When the owner of the estate with the deer park returned from philander-ing, pinballing, and buggering his way around the gentlemen's clubs of London's Soho and Mayfair, a generous donation was made to the hospital.

Of Austrian extraction and a distant cousin of Franz Joseph and the Hapsburgs, Count Erich von Kaunitz XV enjoyed decent relations with Vienna. He was not so sure that this status would be maintained if his nocturnal activities in London were known. He had been well acquainted with the Oscar Wilde crowd. He yearned to be stunningly handsome. As a younger man, Kaunitz had turned a few heads, but the side effects of his excesses could not be masked over à la Dorian Gray. He wanted to have a young maiden swoon at fifty paces, even if it were merely to keep those wagging tongues still. It was, however, the love that dared not speak its name that was the Count's allure.

Without siblings, the Count had inherited the family fortune. He was ludicrously rich, and was considered by the Hapsburgs to be one of their less formal social bridgeheads in Bosnia. His estate of over three thousand acres was home to hundreds of grazing fourteen-bladed deer, and its palatial castle of white neo-Moorish splendor, all verdigris, garlic-headed domes and proud spires, was superior to any other in the Balkans. Though he tried to pass himself off as one of them, the Count was considered by the locals to be very much part of the well-oiled imperial machine. This he would take any opportunity to rectify. Within days of the Count's return from England, therefore, the hospital duly received its benefactor at a renaming ceremony attended by the press from Sarajevo and a lone photographer.

As for the young lad, who stared through the small gap in his bandages with the bluest eyes, it was announced that he would receive the antlers of the guilty deer, to have them mounted on a wall. It would be the beast's turn to be the spit-roasted guest of honor at the Count's next royal banquet. Johan nearly relapsed when he heard this. He did not want his friend punished, never mind killed for dinner. His insomnia was fueled, and he would lie awake wondering how Deer slept with such an awkward appendage on his head. Johan waited by the forest in the lay-by beside the deserted mustard-yellow carriage to warn his friend, but it was no use. He believed that his pal must be consumed by guilt and must have made his way deep into the forest to pay his penance.

His be-antlered buddy never came to see him ever again.

* * *

The Count told Johan that he was free to visit the castle when he was well again, at any time, although he privately pointed out to the boy's family that he would require at least four days' notice. Even more privately, the Count pointed out to his small (yet dependable) circle of servants that this lead time was necessary to clean up the debris of his notorious sodomous gatherings, which lasted for days and covered many acres.

The Count promised that Johan's family never would want for anything, though he was not writing them into his will. As it turned out, his promise was more of a renewable, inexhaustible as-needed job offer. It really did not seem like much of an offer at the time at all. Yet as the cameras clicked away at the posing Count and a bandaged but standing Johan, the photographer was disturbed by something in his view. He moved around the awkward camera on its clumsy tripod to investigate whatever had landed on his apparatus. He shooed it away.

There was a click, a puff of smoke, and all was done for the day.

It would be about a dozen years before Johan saw his benefactor again, and longer still before it dawned on Johan that Count Kaunitz was one of the most generous and beautiful human beings any one of us could ever wish to meet.

Around the photographer's head, the butterfly which had briefly rested on the lens flapped its wings and slowly headed toward the pollen-flecked hospital orchard before taking flight on a slow, winding thermal toward Sarajevo, to the north.

* * *

The hospital was sparse. Paint peeled from the walls and the smell of bleach only briefly won its perpetual war over tobacco, vomit, and feces.

One little boy lay there, with a gaping hole in his bulbous head. He was the most grateful recipient of the nurses' toil and of the generosity of spirit which is unique to their calling, the selfless act of giving care to the injured, sick, and dying. Johan spent many hours watching them as they scurried through the hospital injecting, chatting, and joking to a beat, in order to overcome the horror of their tasks. He would catch them yawning after marathon shifts, or crying after a particular old guy had rattled his last breath. While his friends were being force-fed Catholicism, Orthodoxy, or Islam, it was these women whose impression began to form in him a worldview based on everyday experience.

Johan had started to piece together his own proposition for the nature of things. He had learned at school that humans breathed out just enough carbon dioxide to feed the trees, which in turn returned just the right amount of oxygen for humans. Then there was the sun, which was just far enough away to keep him warm and to grow crops, and to give the world light for enough time to do work and have a bit of play before proffering the night, which loaned just enough darkness to allow sleep, for tomorrow's energy. If the sun were any closer, life would not be possible; any farther away, he would freeze. There was just enough food on the table for when he was hungry, and if he was thirsty, there was stuff he could pour into his mouth to quench his thirst. If he was cold, there were clothes or a fire, and there was ice for a hot day. He had a soccer ball or a chess set when he was bored. There were those injections and white tablets for when his head hurt. There had been horses to take men around, and now there were engines and automobiles to do it as well. There seemed to be someone for every job. Everything just seemed to work, but was its sheer brilliance by divine design? Or, more likely, was it just too marvelous to have been designed? He started to suspect, with increasing evidence, the latter.

And here were these wonderful women in starched white who would give love and comfort to those with little love and no comfort. He presumed that there were just enough of these generous girls, spread around the globe the right distance apart, that he would never be alone with his pain and would always be clean, surrounded by caring faces and by loving hands, which would put him back together again. The scattering of these angels meant that everywhere had just enough and they were not in excess or shortfall in any one location. The pieces of life's jigsaw seemed to fall into place, so well designed that there could not possibly be a God who could be doing this. It was just too big a job.

He considered infinity in the other direction, to the smallest particle. If x was an atom, y, cosmic vastness, and z, time, it was just too much. It was miraculous in its nature, in its randomness, in its nondesign. Just one huge coincidence that all seemed to work. From the nurses and their love, he extrapolated a theory that explained everything. It was naive and juvenile (he was just a small boy), but also incredibly neat and real.

The Universe (and everything in it) had been arrived at simply by a series of coincidences—good luck and bad luck, and nothing more. He was convinced of what Caesar had once suspected: that the skies had endured for whatever reason, but that his own future was yet to be determined. His path was in the palm of his own hand. Johan gave God zero credit for life's canvas and no credit for the oils, which he dreamed of using sometimes liberally, sometimes sparingly, to create a busy yet beautifully arced masterpiece. He would attempt to be measured in his decisions, for he knew that statistics would always be lurking, and would likely kick the fool in the shins. So, having thanked coincidence for delivering him to his current coordinates, Johan would now aim, within the parameters of reason, mathematics, and statistics, to be the Caesar of his own fortunes.

He pondered that he had used up so much of his good luck in surviving a bladed antler in the skull that, if he were to ever again have such a close scrape with death, he would have to run and run and run. He imagined it to be the equivalent of having used up eight feline lives in a single incident. Right now, though, he was grateful to be alive, for he knew that there was no one waiting for him on the other side of that white light.

And so Johan Thoms became Europe's youngest atheist.

"Does all that God nonsense make sense to you, Dad?" he groggily asked Drago.

"I know, son. It's like a blind man in a dark room looking for a black cat which isn't there, but still finding the thing!"

Johan explained his theory of the Universe, which he had dubbed the Immoral Highground, to his father. Drago was proud.

Four

The Butterflies Flutter By

Happiness is like a butterfly, which, when pursued, is always beyond our grasp,
but, if you will sit down quietly, may alight upon you.

—Nathaniel Hawthorne

My schooldays! The silent gliding on of my existence, the unseen, un-felt progress of my life, from childhood up to youth. Let me think, as I look back upon that flowing water, now a dry channel overgrown with leaves, whether there are any marks along its course, by which I can remember how it ran."

"*David Copperfield*?" Ernest asked.

"But of course. Who else?"

* * *

September 1901. Argona.

For a few weeks, Johan lived out the role of minor local celebrity. The bandages came off layer by layer, ultimately revealing a rather normal, if not very lucky, stitched-up young boy. After the interminable summer holiday, he returned to school.

Clusters of children flocked reluctantly to the crumbling schoolyard each morning—less like bees to honey, and more like a hefty trawl of kicking fish. Their uniform khaki trousers and steel-gray shirts sensibly replaced the bleached white of the spring term. With the gray shirts came the unmistakable September nip in the air, and the butterfly nerves of the new term.

Johan had to endure a barrage of teasing about his talking to animals rather than the respect he might have thought he deserved for cheating death, saving the hospital, and becoming friends with European royalty all in one fell swoop.

He would tag along with groups of other boys in the local park, invariably in their wake. The comforting ringing of sublime church bells nearby was enough to send Johan into a deep trance. By the time he would come around, he would find his supposed friends a distant memory, just a small puff of dust where they had stood. He would hear the distant echo of muffled laughter disappearing into the labyrinth of back alleys before he wandered off by himself, seemingly untroubled but still breathing too fast for his own good.

In his solitary walks, he got to know the town by heart. He became a flâneur. Argona was an archaic wonderland, and a safe place in which to grow up. Even the stray dogs bounced around worry-free. Side streets and alleyways, where the bells squeezed and resonated, were wedged between buildings which looked as if they had been there forever. The gargoyles, which seemed to have come straight from a tale by Edgar Allan Poe, glared and spewed not just from towers and eaves, but on door knockers, too, and were carved into the white stone itself. Though supernatural, they lacked any sort of actual threat. Even the abundant ghost stories carried no horror, nor bore any malice.

Argona's centerpiece was a church dating back to the fourteenth century. Although the cloisters had been destroyed by fire (allegedly during an almighty scrap between God and Lucifer in the fifteenth century), the church had made Argona an important trading center, and it remained a magnificent structure. The rest of the town's architecture slipstreamed in its former glory.

Old men, when they were not riding through town on trusty, rusty bikes, waited for the last train in faded suits with small trunks. Others sat on the benches around town, considering the club of other old guys doing the same for thousands of miles in every direction. They sat alone, or with a contemporary or a grandson, to whom they repeated exaggerated tales.

In the mornings, the smell of the town's two bakeries pervaded avenue and nostril. The smells of the late afternoon were of steaming vegetables, infused with roasting meats and paprika from open windows. The Pavlovian clink of cutlery made the children's mouths water.

The long Argona days gave way to nights of dimly lit taverns, couples kissing in the alleys, and wet cobblestones, to be steamed dry by the morning sun. There was none of the danger of the big city, and if that left the locals a bit naive, then they were more than a little happy. There was an honesty and refreshing plainness to the people, and pretentions were spotted sooner than a degenerate, hungover Austrian count with his fly down.

February 12, 1907

It was his thirteenth birthday, and in the morning he had been playing chess against himself, thinking of talking to deer real or imaginary, and pressing his nose into English literature. Yet he had been unable to fully relax.

He spent his birthday afternoon on his language homework, a thousand words on any subject he chose. He was racking his brains for inspiration, and repeatedly kicking his ball around the garden, when two turquoise butterflies playing tag flew past his nose. He went inside, picked up a pen, and began to write.

> One amazingly beautiful creature, many different, unrelated names in different languages, words, all equally charming in their ability to describe it, and all so VERY different.
>
> Mariposa, papillon, *butterfly*, Schmetterling, borboleta, farfalla, babochka, kupu kupu . . .

The butterfly may well be unique in this characteristic on the planet—not just in the animal kingdom, but in the sphere of the spoken word, Johan Thoms said to himself. He said many things to himself, for his father had taken him to one side as a boy, and with a seriousness Johan could measure in his mind, told him that the man who shows off his intelligence without justification is the same braggard who boasts of the size of his prison cell.

A trawl of Johan's university library years later would reveal that of the four hundred languages sourced there, no two words for "butterfly" bore any resemblance to each other, not even in such close cousins as Spanish and Portuguese.

"The only commonality is in repeated syllables, meant perhaps to display the symmetry of that fine creature. In Ethiopian, he is the *birra birro,* in Japanese, the *chou chou,* and among the Aborigines either the *buuja buuja,* the *malimali,* or the *man man.*" (A very young Johan Thoms made this observation way before a certain Mr. Rorschach thought about boring us rigid with his diagram.)

Johan noted, too, that butterflies always seemed to be around whenever he thought of them. He entitled the essay "The Butterflies Flutter By."

He was a weird little lad. And, without doubt, a time bomb.

Part Two

Remorse, the fatal egg by pleasure laid.

—William Cowper

One

Fools Rush In

The feeling of friendship is like that of being comfortably filled with roast beef.
—Boswell's *Life of Johnson*

September 1912

Johan Thoms packed up his books in Argona. At the age of eighteen, he had been accepted at the University of Sarajevo with the help of a scholarship—a major shaking of the kaleidoscope for young Johan, one might think, but not really. In Sarajevo he was only an hour from his childhood comforts, and he went rushing forward into dusty libraries while clinging to the past, returning at every opportunity to the Womb of Argona (a phrase he also used jokingly to refer to his mother). His determination to enjoy the present seemed to be dogged by his worry about the future and, more specifically, his desire to please his parents. He tried repeatedly to remind himself of his own theory of the Universe, and to live in the present. He tried to tell himself that what was done was done, that what *will be* was within his own control, and that there was no God to punish him for present, past, or future deeds. Within these seconds, he found peace of mind. However, it would take only somewhere between a fragment of a conversation and the distraction of a passing sparrow to lead his mind astray, and he would have broken his calming promise to himself.

* * *

Chess and soccer finally conceded to books.

Johan's love of literature had been grounded in summer afternoons in the school glen reading Dickens with his favorite teacher, upon whom he had developed a crush at the age of ten. The class dissected English classics under the apple blossom trees, which in spring were whiter than the students' bleach-white shirts. Johan was then rarely seen without a scabby novel or a yellowing library newspaper. Often he disagreed fiercely with what he read. When something made sense, he would slowly close his tome, his thumb keeping his spot, and ponder the newly found truth.

In his university years, he adopted the same technique for things with which he did *not* concur. Finally, differing opinions received more of his attention than those confirming his own often-stubborn beliefs. (Conversely, history professors claim that Pol Pot, Stalin, and Hitler read only books with which they already agreed, giving them an even more distorted vision of the world.)

Johan also stumbled upon a method of recording every required academic (and nonacademic) detail to memory. When his brain could take no more, he would stuff his face with vegetables, seeds, and legumes, pass a massive stool, and by this vacuum, create room for new knowledge. His theory was given extra weight when, at the age of nineteen, he read that Martin Luther had invented the Protestant religion while facilitating an extremely satisfying evacuation of his bowels. When he read *The Hound of the Baskervilles,* he was stunned to discover that Sherlock Holmes himself noted (on the subject of his Baker Street flat being thick with tobacco smoke), "I find that a concentrated atmosphere helps a concentration of thought. I have not pushed it to the length of getting into a box to think, but that is the logical outcome of my convictions."

Johan took three seconds out of his life to imagine the fictional English demigod in a tiny fictional WC, a fictional shadow cast by his deerstalker hat, worn at forty-five degrees for the fictional duration of his ponderings.

Johan snapped back to reality as the word *deerstalker* scuttled through his brain. For what was he himself if not an erstwhile deerstalker? He wondered where his old pal Deer was now, and then asked himself if he thought he was normal.

He shuddered.

* * *

Johan Thoms found Anton Chekhov interminably dull and depressing, but knew that the old Russian had every reason to be down.

The French, he concluded, were far too pretentious, but then, like the rest of civilization, Johan didn't gravitate toward them as a people anyway. Victor Hugo and Baudelaire were excused. When Johan read of a trial over the publication of *Madame Bovary,* Flaubert too found favor. He was granted special status when Johan read the judge's summing up: "No gauze for him, no veils—he gives us nature in all her nudity and crudity."

Anything banned or censored found its way onto Johan's dustless shelves: *Ulysses, Huckleberry Finn, The Scarlet Letter, Uncle Tom's Cabin, Moll Flanders, Candide,* and, latterly, *Chatterley.*

Goethe, Kafka, Dostoyevsky, Mary Shelley, Keats, Andersen, Zola, Yeats, Marlowe.

He worshipped Darwin for debunking God's good book. Johan Thoms even shared a birthday with Darwin.

The work of Robert Louis Stevenson amazed Johan. He would enjoy many afternoon discussions of Stevenson with his personal tutor, Professor Tiberius Novac. Their main bone of contention involved *Jekyll and Hyde.* The professor insisted it was a tale of Victorian double standards. Johan found this far too obvious, and (not that he agreed with Stevenson) observed an anti-Darwinist angle to the story, the worrying implications of meddling with nature. When they weren't discussing books, Johan was crushing Novac at chess. Tiberius would close his oak study door upon his student's departure, locking in the magical smell of old volumes, and mop his brow as young Master Thoms marched proudly down the stone hallways.

On glorious afternoons in the fall of '12 and spring of '13, Johan and Novac would billet themselves out on the quadrangle lawn under the monkey puzzle trees. They were shaded, too, by the white berry tree, and enveloped in Moroccan jasmine, early spring breezes, and Johan's budding optimism. In their discussions, Johan reveled in playing the role of Devil's avocado (Ernest assured me that Johan did not mean to be funny here— his English was indeed flawed, albeit very rarely).

Novac tended to just smile and inhale the scent of a young yellow rosebush over his left shoulder.

Johan realized on one of these afternoons that the theory he had hatched in the hospital all those years before dovetailed perfectly with his disapproval of the Church.

"Life is all just either good luck or bad luck. If those idiots needed something to believe in for their afterlife and salvation, it only means that they are hedging their guilty bets. Ironically, they are the ones, their minds clouded with fear and guilt, who are unable to see the real beauty of the most wonderful coincidence in the Universe. And that is the Universe itself. These religious types, perversely, are too afraid to enjoy this wonderful set of moments, too constipated to witness the greatest glory. And so I resolve to make the present my god."

Before the hour was up, he was once again either rushing into the future or pondering the past.

* * *

In the early days of college, Johan saw more of the night than he did of the day, and he discovered the wonder of Bram Stoker's *Dracula*. He did not see only night in it. He also saw the absolute beauty of the love story, and wondered if he would ever experience a love that transcended continents, time, and, indeed, lifetimes. For this he hoped, even though his heart broke for the Transylvanian. He knew that should he stumble across such marvelous misfortune, his own would break as well.

* * *

Johan was way ahead in his schooling. He excelled in languages, and was tutored in Italian, German, Spanish, French, and English. He was soon soaking up literature in all these foreign tongues. He loved how the English refused to compromise with their own translation of *bon appétit*, recognizing thus with irony that their skills lay not in the culinary arena. He loved Germanic word order, and the implications of placing the verb at the end of a sentence. Everyone would have to be polite and to listen to the full statement without the infernal "May I interject?" although it didn't seem to have had much effect on Prussian and Teutonic behavior, hubris, and propensity to war.

On the sports field he started to grow into his body. Girls began to notice him.

He had lost his virginity on a cold November day at the age of fourteen to a beauty, Ellen, from the neighboring village. It had been a sublimely unremarkable event. Near the end of his first term at university, he dropped "The Ugly Duckling" on his study desk and ran off to meet a petite, brown-eyed brunette, who would annoyingly insist on inserting her long fingernails into the unsuspecting youth's urethra. He hoped that this was not normal behavior and that he'd just stumbled upon a degenerate lover, albeit a feisty and infinitely kissable one.

* * *

These seemed halcyon days, although he suffered many dark moments. He lost a series of good friends through accident and illness. The loss of each would, it seemed to his seedling paranoia, follow either a disagreement with Johan, or was bizarrely connected to his reading material at that time.

The news of one friend's drowning reached Johan as he was reading Herman Melville. While engrossed in Thomas Hardy, he learned of two friends' simultaneous end, one in a coal-mining accident, the other ravaged by wild dogs in the hills.

A pal who claimed he was possessed by the devil committed suicide as Johan neared the fulcrum of Goethe's *Faust*.

An ex-girlfriend gave in to the desperate complications brought on by syphilis as Johan waded through *Madame Bovary*.

An English nautical friend went down with his ship when Johan had barely begun *Robinson Crusoe* and was still fifteen pages from the end of Conrad's *The Nigger of the Narcissus*. The statistics were now suggesting to him that this might be more than coincidence: he might have developed a reverse Midas touch.

* * *

Johan's best chum at university was William Atticus Forsythe Cartwright, a confident, ebullient Englishman studying psychology and philosophy. Johan became heavily anglicized in his chum's presence, earning himself an English nickname—"Bighead"—as well as the Spanish "El Capitán," which originated in his choice of cologne, a spicy number with a hint of oak from a local bespokerie.

Johan mimicked his pal, subconsciously adopting his physical mannerisms, his English turns of phrase, and his fondness for filth and crassness.

Bill Cartwright was the son of a diplomat, the right-hand man to the British ambassador to Bosnia. The family came from Huddersfield in the West Riding of Yorkshire. Billy had been a well-spoken youth, but chose to discard his demeanor of privilege. Instead he presented himself as a rough-edged commoner with a broad northern twang and a penchant for the extreme, the hyperbolic, and the damned-right crude. Cartwright was fascinated by the struggles of the workers; he harbored thoughts of revolution. He had been removed from his English boarding school at the age of twelve after one daft prank too many. The final straw involved a bizarre attempt to prove a theorem on probability. Billy had pondered the twin questions of why bread would always seem to fall butter side down and why a cat always landed on its feet. The youth had therefore strapped a slice of bread (butter side up) to a cat's back and dropped the feline from three floors up in his dormitory, to see which prevailed, the butter or the cat's paws. The headmaster's report had jolted Billy's father into bringing the boy within his paternal reach in Sarajevo, where Billy regularly received an eardrum-rattling clip to the skull. Billy wore each as a badge of honor, for he claimed they all just reminded him that he was alive.

Two

A Vision of Love
(Wearing Boxing Gloves)

The female praying mantis devours the male,
While they are mating,
The male sometimes continues copulating,
Even after the female has bitten off his head
and part of his upper torso.

—Tom Waits, "Army Ants"

June 8, 1913. 12:30 P.M.

Sarajevo's Madresa is one of the oldest seats of learning in Europe. Its theology and law faculties date to 1551. They were built concurrently with the Gazi Husrev Beys mosque, arguably the finest structure of its type in Europe, which housed a wonderfully liberal form of Islam. A more recent addition to the university, in 1878, on extra acreage on the western edge of the city, hugged the River Miljacka. This school was quadrangled around botanical gardens of stunning neoclassical beauty, with sunken gardens and Greek pillars. Ancient ornate tombs, graves, plinth stones, and crosses, each unique, finely littered the gardens, alongside a single white berry tree and a perpetually splashing fountain. Thirty-five-foot ceilings, cool, tiled mosaics, and hardwood staircases twenty feet wide adorned the inside of the building. The main entrance resembled the illegitimate child of the courthouse in New Orleans and the Theatre Royal, Haymarket (an admirable ancestry). The western wing was strangely Moorish in design, but integrated well, as the Muslims had integrated with the Catholics and the Orthodox in the city itself.

Johan Thoms and Billy Cartwright spent many a warm afternoon in informal psychiatric session in the quadrangle, their couch the billiard-baize, manicured lawn. Here Bill poked and prodded at Johan's mind, initially for a case study, and then out of curiosity, in friendship, and for fun. Staring up at the swaying blossoms and the monkey puzzle trees that bordered the quad, with the azure expanse beyond, Johan was more than happy to be a relaxed guinea pig for his friend. These sessions went uninterrupted unless a pretty young girl wandered by.

"Simply functional," observed Johan of a girl's pigtails.

"Blasphemers and infidels. Degenerates and heretics. What a joy!"

"You, my friend, are a malodorous ne'er-do-well!"

"Could not agree more, my friend," said Billy. "I'd be like a damned bulldog with its face in a bucket of porridge."

This boy banter went on for most of the afternoon, and well into the summer holidays. Johan reckoned there was nothing wrong with having good friends with whom to mull over the sweetest of subjects in the June sunshine at the age of nineteen, without a care in the world.

"Oh, my word! How would you like to wear THAT as a hat?" said Billy as a heavily pregnant beauty passed by.

"I have a feeling that I would not take it off even for dinner at the dean's."

"I am sure the dean would be quite chuffed about that."

"I am not indulging that old rotter. And at his age, I am sure he would have certain . . . problems."

"Like an oyster in a keyhole."

"You mean like playing billiards with a rope."

They rolled around in fits of giggles.

The early summer sun warmed their young faces and started to turn them an even tan.

Three girls passed within close enough range for their scent of new white soap and the final drops from a dewberry perfume bottle to pique the boys' olfactory nerves. Then it was gone, and impossible to recapture. But that was their intention, of course, and far more romantic than new perfume and old soap. Johan swept blades of freshly cut grass from his sun-faded dress shoe to make his gawping more subtle. For that is what *they* wanted. Subtle was important. Politely doffing the cap to Aphrodite.

"It is a good job I don't believe in heaven, William my friend, because acquainting with you leaves me not a cat in hell's chance."

"By George, you believe in heaven all right. It was in that coffeehouse five minutes ago, still in your nostrils right now. And within a breadth of a cat's cock hair of you five seconds ago. So do not give me that twaddle! They love it. Look at them, and acting as if they had just finished choir practice."

Billy stared at the woman, daydreaming, for more than a few seconds.

"Stop right now!" he said. "I *must* think of something else before I go crazy and they drag me off to the Old Pajama Club to be straitjacketed, drip-fed bromide, and cold-showered all damned summer."

They both knew that Johan was by no means as promiscuous as his pal. It was not for the lack of opportunity, it was for the lack of opportunism. Billy was making the most of his psychiatric studies in a very practical way. He could pick out a girl's desires and needs. He read her body language, and learned which buttons to press in order to achieve his wicked, wicked goal.

Johan, on the other hand, from *his* studies, knew the practicality of the past participle of "to wiggle" in Italian. He knew that the title *Our Mutual Friend* was an illogical use of English; that *Our Friend in Common* was grammatically correct; and that Dickens had indeed made this error on purpose. He knew it was possible to have three consecutive *e*'s in the same word in French (*La femme était créée pour servir l'homme*) and the Time-Manner-Place rule in German (*Ich bin um neun Uhr mit dem Zug nach Halle gefahren*).

Billy knew which chemicals a girl's brain would release to make her want whoever or whatever had given her the pleasure.

"It's called oxytocin, Thoms. A pituitary hormone stimulates uterine muscle contractions. The hormone of love, the sugarcoating the ladies need to reproduce. Oxytocin is Darwinism at work. The desire for inter-course is the *genius of genus.* I heard that in a lecture yesterday. It's been oxytocin that has led us as humans to do it face-to-face for forty thousand years. You know, the only other creature on the planet to do it in the same manner is the bonobo chimp. Adorable little blighter lives in the Congo, apparently, Johan. Did you know that?"

"I am all ears."

"Ha! A bit like the bonobo chimp, then," Bill said. "Where would you be without me, old chap? Hmm? Ignorant about chimps, for one!"

And so they rambled on as another sublime afternoon wound to a close. The sun disappeared behind the wondrous stone palace that was the dean's house. Billy tapped Johan on the shoulder and proposed:

"Come on, let's go have a martini. The burlesque girls start at midnight. Let's get drunk first. How about a sweaty flagon of self-respect for me and a shot of dignity for your good self?"

"It's a deal."

They marched off to cause trouble with total malice aforethought, discussing Chaucer and the genius genesis of the word *fuck*.

* * *

William Atticus Forsythe Cartwright was a strapping six-foot-three man mountain in his bare bear feet. Long wavy hair rested on his broad shoulders. He sported, as usual, a crisp white linen shirt, top button undone, and a claret tie of subtle pattern and (subliminally Freudian) large, fat knot, which just kept his shirt collar from informality. When shirtless, he was identifiable by a tattoo on his thighlike left biceps: a swooping swallow with Billy's name beneath it reminded him of the impetuous nature of youth in general and, more specifically, his own.

It was a short walk of twenty minutes from the university quadrangle along the Appel Quay by the gushing Miljacka to their favorite bar in the old town of Bascarsija, the "marketplace." Thirty minutes after entering the area, they were still cutting a swath through its maze, famed for the spiced aromas emanating from ovens stuffed with tray after tray of *cevapcici,* the local staple of minced beef, potato, and onion wrapped in thick dough. It seemed that Bascarsija was made up of a hundred back alleys, yet was strangely ordered. Each nook and ginnel housed a particular trade, be it the butcher, the antiquarian bookseller (*saffah*), or the dealer in copper, wood, fruit, Turkish tobacco hookah pipes, cowbells, coffee shops, shoes, meats, rugs (kilims) from Persia, Moorish fezzes or apotropaic jewelry, to ward off evil spirits.

They walked through the bohemian medieval backstreets, soaking in the incongruous backdrop of evening prayer as smoke filled the charmed alleys. It was on a similar evening not many weeks before this (Johan was mid–*Dorian Gray*) when Bill Cartwright had first introduced his good friend to *la fée verte,* the green fairy. We all have our favorite vice, which can often be the very thing we should, on all accounts, avoid. The mirth we find may have a quite devilish draw, likely to increase our intake and thereby the chances of ultimate destruction; but she is as alluring as a cruel princess. Johan's poison proved to be the particularly malicious absinthe.

Their destination now was the Old Sultan's Palace, one of the oldest buildings in the city, dating back to the 1500s. Perched on the hills to the east, and of a white Moorish design, it seemed to come straight out of *The Thief of Bagdad.* Sunset gave it an air of the regal, of high society. However, it showed its true colors at about eight in the morning, when the debris and detritus of the night littered its wonderful halls and lush gardens. Prostitutes, clients, deserters, deadbeats, drunks, lesbians, fiends, crazies, vagrants, homosexuals, opium addicts, soldiers, vampires, suicide cases, police chiefs, gamblers, and weirdos. Squadrons of sozzled barbarians. The obese, fantasists, elitists, illusionists, and delusionists. Cheats, frauds, judges, mentals, judgmentals, and fiddlers. The grim of mind and the loose of faculty. The pompous and the snaggletoothed, the bothersome and the prejudiced. All were there.

After a wait of no more than five minutes at the edge of Bascarsija, an omnibus picked the boys up and started its trundle down the boulevard. It was sticky and stinky in the bus, with only standing room for newcomers. It spewed them out at the top of the hill.

The light was fading as the lads approached the Old Sultan's Palace. The Old Sultan of Byzantium was rumored to have been an ally of Kubla Khan himself. Centuries before, he had positioned his harem of two hundred or more nubile women here. Back in 1575, by order of the Sultan (*buyurultus*), the girls lived only with the city's eunuchs, the best physician in the land, and His Highness himself. Here, he decreed his own, albeit slightly less grandiose, Xanadu.

"Pah! It was just a fad and a fashion among these sultan chaps. Bloody show-offs," Bill said.

*   *   *

They walked along the stony driveway up to the mansion. Johan felt they were entering a bygone age, that time was standing still for them, as it does when one is nineteen. The clatter of the loose stones under their Oxford brogues invited them into a different world, and offered the promise of being an adult.

This was *their* time, for *this* was (metaphorically) the Saturday lunchtime of their youth. They cast no shadow.

That evening, the Old Sultan's Palace heaved under a weighty Moorish mystery. Weird attracted exquisite in a perpetual wave of self-fueling cosines and logarithms. The palace remains to this day a venue of staggering beauty, full of time-slip corridors, medieval arches, and cul-de-sacs where amazed visitors' pocket watches stop.

They were drawn to the yellow lights through the grandiose Persian arches on the rear lawn. An energy emanated from there, and given the nature of energies, archways, and lights, boys are duty bound to inspect.

Billy whittled on half philosophically, half rhetorically, in Johan's ear.

"But, Thoms, old bean. If a man says something in a forest, and a woman is not there to hear it, is he still wrong?"

No answer.

On the other side of the arch, a party was in full flow. Black ties and white tuxedos, white and black evening dresses, and waiters. Johan tried to put his finger on the energy as they entered the fray.

"Keep your pecker up."

"Keep YOUR pecker out."

This was their routine as they telepathically divided to conquer.

Johan heard few Bosnian or even European accents. Most of the partygoers, he realized, were Americans. There seemed to be something distinct about this party, something which he could not quite identify. Was it their New World energy, with their modern haircuts, their lack of walrus mustaches and beards?

Perhaps it was the more modern music or a strange dance he had never seen before. Or was it the stench of wealth which pervaded the air?

Or was it . . . Holy Jesus . . . was it the most absolute beauty with whom he found himself faced?

Seconds of silence ticked by. If absolute zero is minus 273 degrees Celsius, then this was an absolute silence. The absolute of that silence was equaled only by the absolute of the blackness in her eyes.

Her lips were a scarlet sofa in an ivory palace.

Johan's embarrassing lack of words was broken by the familiar voice of Professor Tiberius Novac. The rest of the world had continued while Johan had disappeared into his cataleptic trance. Worse than that, the woman had simply stared at this fool.

He sort of heard the prof's words, nudging the stem of his cerebral cortex.

"Johan Thoms! My boy! What an absolute pleasure! What brings you to a party for the American ambassador? Do you know him, my boy? You ARE a dark horse, aren't you!" A gentle tap to the shin from the outside of his tutor's well-polished dress shoe was not enough. The dusky beauty suppressed a laugh.

"But who is SHE?" blurted Johan, totally forgetting his place, stumbling in and out of his body.

"She? She? She? Who is she? The cat's mother?" corrected Tiberius. The same tutor who had been run ragged in a literary discussion by Johan not three days before was now correcting the scholar's usually impeccable manners.

She, it transpired, was an American living in Vienna, the widow of a diplomat who had found a watery grave with the *Titanic* the previous year, one of the unfortunates forced to listen to the band play.

She seemed to be in her late twenties perhaps early thirties, and possessed a hypnotic beauty that would take young Johan tens of years to absorb. The experienced coyness of her initial smile, the way her front teeth half bit into the side of her nether lip, her perfectly measured handshake, revealed everything Johan needed to see, but hid enough to make his deviant blood boil.

"Lorelei, please meet Johan Thoms. Johan, this is Lorelei Ribeiro, with the American embassy in Vienna."

"Yes, errrm, it is, isn't it?" Johan mumbled as he struggled for breath. His member did, however, show signs of life.

He caught himself staring at her small chest. Lorelei Ribeiro caught him and smiled to herself. He felt like he had been struck. It was a vision of love, wearing boxing gloves! (This Venus's grandfather, he would learn later, had been a renowned pugilist back in the States.)

"Ermmmm. Hello, Lorelei," he managed.

"Pleased to make your acquaintance, Johan Thoms, I am sure. And who is your friend?" she added. He glanced down at his tentlike crotch before he realized she was referring to someone else.

"Oh yes, of course, this is William Cartwright," who had appeared at Johan's shoulder.

"Bill, this is . . . ermmm . . . Lorelei, Mrs. Ribeiro from the Vienna embassy . . . in America."

Johan's next fifteen minutes were a blur, and even if he had wanted to (and he had wanted to, he assured Ernest) he could not for the life of him recall the conversation, or even if he had been part of one, or whether he had been in a trance. All he could recall was taking a trip into the noirish eyes of the woman in front of him.

Later, when he asked her to remind him (or, more accurately, to inform him) of the content of their first discussion, Lorelei would giggle, and mercilessly tease him by telling him a completely different version of events every time, with that wicked glint in her eye.

He was aware he had been impaired by a couple of ales. And what does alcohol do, other than have the effect of a truth serum?

He noticed that Professor Tiberius Novac moved slightly to his right to leave these two to their own devices. He could be quite devious (what Bill would have described as "mauve") at times, but he was fond of his protégé. Novac had been grabbed by some desperate old battle-ax from the British Consul, after a bit of Balkan rough in her bed. She clung to him like a barnacle to a tugboat, had eyebrows like a couple of baby raccoons in awkward repose, and danced like a giraffe with the staggers. This had made surveillance on Johan difficult. When his student pressed him afterward for details, he struggled to offer anything really substantial, for he, too, had swallowed some gin, as one had to in order to face the aging beast from London.

("She had a face like a blind cobbler's thumb," he admitted to Johan later. "But, my boy, was she a cracker with the gaslight out!")

* * *

By the time he came around, Johan had lost Lorelei.

He sought Novac, but the English vulturette was circling, craving her pound of flesh—or more, if her luck was in. Novac was inching backward, avoiding her cabbagey breath.

Cartwright staggered toward Johan from the crowd.

"Did you *see* her?" Johan whispered.

His spirit had been kidnapped.

"What are you talking about?" His eyes widened. "Please don't tell me you have been hooked? I thought you were made of finer stuff, old bean!"

"I blew it."

"Oh, Jesus Christ!"

Professor Novac butted in between the two troublemakers and cringed.

"I think you quoted some Shakespeare at her. I am *so* sorry." He winked.

Johan threw his hands over his face.

"Oh, balls! What must she think of me?"

"Do not worry, boy. I am sure it was the 'Happy days seeking such happy nights' line. Not a bad choice, even if I say so myself. There's nothing wrong with a bit of defenseless honesty."

"Yes, but what good is that right now? She's with some fool somewhere. And this is not the first mistaken impulse of an undisciplined heart."

"Johan! You cannot think like that, or you will drive yourself mad. Jealousy is the worst of traits. It may be based in love, but it is never less than ultimate destruction. Leave it at the door, with your cane and your hound. She is a beautiful woman, and attention is bound to come her way. It comes with the territory, my boy. What the hand possesses, the soul never pines for. If it is meant to happen, it will. It's like looking for a fifty-forint note on the floor. *Que sera, sera.* And, my boy, the tone should *always* be set by Caesar!"

Tiberius's words of wisdom comforted Johan. He tried his best to believe him.

"At least mine didn't have a cleft palate and a lazy eye!" he said.

Cartwright guffawed.

* * *

The party was thinning as Professor Novac bade his farewell, with his banshee-cum-gargoyle in tow.

"Oh yes, and one more thing, Johan, that I recall."

"Yes?" said the young scholar.

Tiberius leaned forward and said quietly into his student's left ear, "I think I heard you mumble something to her which doubled me up. I should describe it as a guttural growl."

He leaned in a bit farther and whispered.

Johan Thoms turned June-tuxedo white when he learned of the shocking desire he had expressed. He went to sit down, before he fell down.

He *had* to stop drinking that stuff!

* * *

Tiberius Novac could be a brute sometimes. After his next tutorial, and perhaps to console Johan, Prof gave away a little more of his eavesdropping, and told the boy he had wonderfully, and with blind poise, stopped Lorelei from stepping on and killing a worm on the palace's lawn.

Lorelei had then quoted, word-perfectly, a poem by Dorothy Parker.

> *"It costs me never a stab nor squirm*
> *To tread by chance upon a worm.*
> *"Aha, my little dear," I say,*
> *"Your clan will pay me back one day!"**

Lorelei and Dorothy Parker were great friends. It was Lorelei who made the introduction to Robert Benchley, who gave Parker her first column in *Vanity Fair* and her major break. Lorelei had also first shown Parker through the front door of the Algonquin Hotel, and the two ladies shared many an evening, as well as a wit, a beauty, and a style all of their own.

With a confidence one can often only paradoxically achieve in a gutless trance, Johan Thoms had volleyed back with his own second verse, off a martini-stained cuff. He started with a steadying prefix.

---

* Although published much later, in 1927, the poem had been part of Dorothy's repertoire for many years.

"Yes, but . . ."

He straightened his collar, ran a hand through his handsome hair, and added his impromptu reply.

> *"Yet should one escape by being cremated,*
> *One's respite is just belated.*
> *Some clod will throw one's ashes out.*
> *And frenzied worms shall scream and shout."*

Touché!

He had winked, taken a slug from his glass, and carried on in his trance. Gibbering wreck, to poet genius, back to gibbering wreck. Lorelei had been transfixed, and the deal was as good as done.

Three

Drago Thoms: Pythagoras, Madness, and an Indian Summer in Bed

> *I shall confine myself neither to Horace's rules nor to any man's rules that has ever lived.*
> —Laurence Sterne, *Tristram Shandy*

June 9, 1913

Four hours after Johan's initial encounter with Lorelei and three hundred yards from the front gates of the palace, the heavens opened. It was as if God had turned on a pipe in the ceiling above a film set as Johan plowed on, unsteadily but with a steady determination. He was soaked to the bone, but he pictured Lorelei caught in the downpour, and smiled; when he stumbled ankle-deep into a puddle as he neared the Miljacka, he merely chuckled.

It was almost daylight. Normal people were already rising to go to their work, and bakers had been hard at it for hours already. Soon everyone would be scuttling around in their raincoats, their hats, their umbrellas. It made him feel sad to the pit of his stomach. Their routine, their normality—this was not where *he* was heading in his life. He segued off into a long train of thought on his deep hatred for umbrellas. He had thoroughly despised them ever since during a force-seven mistral, he had witnessed a young couple kebabed by an errant beach parasol while they were harmlessly copulating.

Was the loss of dozens of eyes every year really a price worth paying to avoid a few thousand head colds? What sort of selfish fool would risk others' eyes with such abandon, just to stay dry? (He had recently read in a science journal that every year, on average, sixty-three eyes were lost to umbrella spikes, but by only sixty-two people. Was someone actually unfortunate enough to lose both? If so, was this in the same incident? Or, even more worrying, two separate ones?)

"So little kindness in the world today," he muttered. "So little thought for others."

Then he heard himself repeating, "Bastard umbrellas, bastard umbrellas," and shook his head to clear it.

He was almost at his dorm. He pulled out his key and slunk into the wonderful old building. The birds nesting in the ivy were tuning up for the day.

Five minutes later, Johan Thoms was on his sheltered balcony, dried off, naked on his back, fast asleep.

* * *

Moments after he awoke, Johan found himself watching a lone and final drop of rainwater overstay its welcome on the nearest leaf of ivy.

Johan turned his head away, and saw that an envelope had been slipped beneath his door. He climbed down from his perch in the window, and slid in bare feet across the shiny floorboards, as if he were ice-skating on the River Miljacka at Christmas. It was with far less grace than he wished. He could glide only three feet in his dormroom. Still, for a split second, he could pretend that he was capable of more elegance.

A line came into his head, one that in the past had seemed to leave a deep, unshiftable hollow feeling. He knew he was guilty of trying to live too fast, of wishing his life away. Yet this time the line was not unwelcome, for it reminded him of the beauty of his life right now:

"Glide gently, thus forever glide."

He reached the doorway unscathed and picked up the envelope. The handwriting was his mother's, and an underlying sense of dread and worry made him pause. He could not think why—he often received letters from her.

He hurriedly slipped his letter opener into the right-hand side, and flicked it open with a swish of the wrist.

Dear Johan,

Bad news, I am afraid. Your father has lost his job.
    So, I hate to put this on you, son, but we need your help.
    We all know how important your studies are to you (and there-fore to us) and we love you for this, so God forbid they be affected.
    Your father sends his love. As do I (of course).

                                              With all my heart,
                                              Your Mama xxx

He closed the letter slowly and slipped it back into the envelope, staring straight ahead.

* * *

At night, Johan's father, Drago, used to tell the boy fairy tales. The magical stories of Hans Christian Andersen and Wilhelm and Jacob Grimm would bring each day to a close. Drago then would return to one of his three favorite hobbies: campanology, constructing matchstick models, and collecting pinecones.

Every morning, Drago rose at six minutes past six. He showered in cold water for nine minutes. He ate a bowl of cold salted porridge. He imbibed two glasses of tepid water. He tried to put a comb through his crazy locks after he'd shaved his beard, already heavy after twenty-four hours. Johan used to love rubbing his face against his father's five-o'clock shadow, begging his dad to give him a chin pie.

Drago left the house on the stroke of eight every morning and walked (always without an umbrella, for he, like Johan, suspected them of mischief) the two miles to school. He taught an array of subjects to an array of ages, but his lectures were always met with enthusiasm, for they were delivered at an impeccably high level.

He was a jack of all trades and a master of many: languages to philosophy, sciences to the arts.

He remembered every pupil he had ever had, their quirks and their strengths. He had a private joke with each of them. This endeared him to everyone at the school.

He instilled the love of knowledge into his own flesh and blood, too. Many evenings, Johan and Drago had sat by the fire in the living room of the old house in Argona as Drago set his eight-year-old boy mathematical problems of increasingly tough proportions, and within three years, high-end calculus, integration, differentiation, coefficients, constants, cosines, sines, tangents, and logarithms. Sheets covered by sigmas or dy/dx's would be strewn across the deep red hearth rug, spilling over onto the surrounding mahogany floorboards. Pythagoras's theorem on right-angled triangles followed. Then Drago passed on Pythagoras's lesser-known theorem on beans. It is lesser known for very good reasons, for Pythagoras's better work was—at this stage—well behind him.

Pythagoras reviled beans, for, they say, beans reminded him of testicles. Drago called it *frijolophobia*. Pythagoras developed an acute case of it, and could not even say the word *bean*.

Beans, however, just made Drago Thoms fart like a clogged sink.

* * *

THE BRIEF, YET VITAL STORY OF DRAGO'S OBSESSION WITH PYTHAGORAS

Pythagoras founded his own Orphic cult in Greece in 530 BC. His main and hugely controversial theory centered on the existence of zero. Previously, there had been no concept of zero. Greek digits had started with "one," because who would take "zero" goats, "zero" donkeys to market?

Pythagoras proposed the existence of zero, and with it came its inevitable inverse of infinity. And if one believes in God, then one has to accept that there is a Satan. This, along with the predictable cyclical nature of mathematics, undermined the teachings of the Scriptures and the possibility of any all-seeing deity. It was heresy.

Society became split. Pythagoras and his Orphist followers broke away. They fled Greece and settled in the ancient city of Crotone, southern Italy, where they could live in relative safety from their now sworn enemies within the old order.

They really should have stuck to mathematics. Many of Pythagoras's followers were forced to take vows of silence and to observe bizarre customs, which included the outlawing of beans. Initially, the word *bean* was banned. Later, *all* verbal communication was forbidden, apart from within the higher order.

Birds, particularly male swallows, were never allowed in any house.

Any dropped objects, particularly food, were never to be picked up. This, they believed, was bad luck. They would instead invite Pythagoras's favorite hound, Braco, into the dining hall after each meal, to clean the floor of any tidbits. During thunderstorms, one's feet had to remain on the ground. Any imprint of the body on bedclothes had to be smoothed out.

The pursuing zealots tracked down the heretic to his enclave in Crotone. They were feeling murderous, but in a way that only a lynch mob of very understanding, tolerant religious fundamentalists can be.

Some they slaughtered within the city walls, and they left some others castrated in the dusty streets. Then they chased Pythagoras and the rest out of Crotone. When the castrated victims rediscovered their vocal cords, Pythagoras was well out of town and making his escape. He came to, of all places, a bean field, which he had to cross in order to survive. His remaining trickle of fickle followers trampled through the crop; only Pythagoras had the conviction not to cross, not to make a Faustian pact with the diabolical bean.

And so he was cut down at the edge of the bean field, screaming anti-legume propaganda until his last breath. And THAT was the end of one of the greatest mathematical brains and maddest men the world had ever known.

* * *

It was Drago's obsession with Pythagoras which eventually tipped him into his very own deep-trenched psychosis.

There were those locals who would suggest that in order for Drago to arrive at the front doors of madness, the journey need be neither long nor arduous. It was less a prolonged and tortured ride, and more a popping around the corner for a pint of milk. The effects on his family (and the unsuspecting world), however, would be catastrophic.

* * *

Drago, although fully versed in the hypotheses of Pythagoras, refused to subscribe to any of his teachings. He started to eat beans with every meal.

Before long, he would have bouts of eating ONLY beans, and beans of every breed. He became prolifically flatulent, often attempting traditional folk tunes with his emissions. Pythagoras became his nemesis, his Professor Moriarty.

Drago's physical health began to deteriorate. His face was gaunt and shadowy. He became a bean expert, and grew beans in any spare patch of land or any darkened cupboard.

The vitamin deficiency from his bean-only intake progressed; previous eccentricities were magnified and new ones multiplied by his physical decline. His colleagues, who still had enormous respect for the man, tried to intervene, but the madness was taking over his behavior. He would be found carrying out more of the very acts against which Pythagoras had rebelled.

For example, during a thunderstorm, Drago would be found not only NOT touching the ground, but climbing trees or, worse, sitting on the roof of the house with his arms wrapped around his knees, his chin resting on them. He refused to use bedsheets, for fear of rising with them uncrumpled. He left beans in every room. He laid them out in a circle around the house and wore them on strings around his neck and wrists.

Furthermore, when he was at the dinner table, he would clumsily, but purposefully, knock food and utensils onto the floor, and slowly pick them up with a wide grin.

Johan's mother, Elena, consulted her closest friends and then a doctor. She was concerned, more so when he started to leave all the windows open and, with bread and seeds, enticed into their house birds of every genus.

At school, meanwhile, any kind of quiet was a sign to Drago that his pupils were being tempted into a Pythagorean vow of silence. One member of the class always had to be talking, humming, whistling, or singing. Drago did not sleep night after night for fear of silence.

After many such sleepless nights, Drago began talking to himself on the way to school and around the grounds. This was simply not tolerable, so the headmaster took action. He successfully packaged the move as offering Drago a sabbatical to further his *anti-Pythagorean* studies. He was even afforded a meager pension, sold to him as a "study wage."

For this, the Thoms family was eternally grateful, for during his sabbatical, Drago's behavior was at least predictable.

So what if they had to tolerate swallows (and other hungry birds) in the house? Clarence, the ginger tomcat, was delighted, until, having won many battles, he lost the war. He was slung out on his furry ear for helping himself to one too many feathery enemies.

Because their child had left home, Elena could enjoy bedclothes in the relative sanity of a spare room. She and Drago did remain sexually active, though. Drago's dedication to his research strangely concentrated his libidinal reserves, which were thrust upon and into an initially disturbed Elena. They regressed into humping like street dogs. Drago considered employing a cheap pianist to prevent a lack of noise.

The name Pythagoras was banned from the household, referred to only in *Macbeth* fashion, as "the Greek."

Elena eventually embraced the new Drago, especially as much of his attention was now directed toward her. How many of her friends could boast of exploits such as theirs?

"The older the violin, the sweeter the music," Drago would claim.

Having the house to themselves afforded them luxuries in their sexual deeds. Having her anal area dive-bombed by wild birds searching for crumbs while she fellated Drago was, however, a bridge too far.

Well, at least, at first.

* * *

So when, in June 1913, a letter arrived at the ancient University of Sarajevo addressed to Johan Thoms, it urged the recipient to consider making a small sacrifice for the greater familial good.

Johan considered bar work (he had made plenty of contacts from his time spent on the other side), laboring (but he was too uncoordinated to be of much use, those skinny matchstick legs and small feet), but it would really be more a question of what he could find.

He then recalled a summer over a decade before, when a wealthy young nobleman offered help of any kind should he or his family ever require it. He was still owed by the crazed, philandering, bug-eyed, buggering count whose buck had once almost taken the young lad's eye and his life. It was time for Count Sodom to make good on his promise. Johan went to his old oak study desk, pulled out a yellowed notebook, and flicked through it. He came to a page written in a childish scrawl, very much that of a seven-year-old. Johan Thoms then took out his best writing paper, pen, and inkpot and started to write:

Dear Count,

I hope you may remember me . . .

Four

The *Kama Sutra*, Ganika, and Russian Vampires

Take the Kama Sutra. *How many people died from the* Kama Sutra, *as opposed to the Bible? Who wins?*

—Frank Zappa

June 9, 1913

After he had written his note, Johan Thoms spent the next part of the searing June day that followed reading and rereading a rare copy of the *Kama Sutra,* one of the first ever published in English, part of a trilogy. He had procured the collection by a stroke of luck. The tutor who had lent it to him lost his job at the college for exposing himself to a group of visiting nuns from County Cork. The professor fled the university in shame before Johan could return the books.

The books were to become Johan's lifelong companions, to accompany him throughout his adventures as he traversed the continent and zigzagged his way through a self-induced mayhem. The trilogy (along with a number of other objects collected around this time) would then become the focus for his final whirlpool of psychosis. But I am rushing ahead.

The edition was a beauty, printed on thick paper. Its white vellum binding, trimmed with gold, boasted the original extended title:

The Kama Sutra of Vatsyayana
Translated from the Sanscrit
In Seven Parts, with Preface, Introduction and Concluding Remarks

The inside cover offered further intrigue and mystery:

Cosmopoli: 1883; for the Kama Shastra Society of London and Benares,
and for private circulation only

(Bizarrely, Vatsyayana always claimed that he was celibate.)

The other books Johan had inherited from his nun-loving mentor bore equally intriguing titles.

Ananga-Ranga and the Hindu Art of Love
Translated from the Sanscrit and annotated by A.F.F. and B.F.R.
1885

and

The Perfumed Garden of the Sheikh Nefzaoui
Or the Arab Art of Love, sixteenth century
Translated from the French Version of the Arabian MS.
1886

Johan set about slow foreplay with the books, studying them tantrically. Intrigued by the genre, and knowing that barely a thousand copies had been published of Richard F. Burton's unsurpassed translations, he then scoured the college and the city's secondhand bookstores for a copy of *The Arabian Nights*. He would eventually find a copy under the pillow of the woman who would change his life. In fact, she had already set about this particular task, just hours before, at that hotbed of Oriental debauchery and degeneracy, the Old Sultan's Palace.

Lorelei Ribeiro was currently lying in a cool bath in Suite 30 of the Hotel President, not more than three-quarters of a mile from where Johan was slowly digesting the ins and outs of coitus. Rolling around in the relaxing waters of her tub, this rare beauty would have been a picture for any man (as well as most women, hermaphrodites, and eunuchs) to behold. The bathtub brimmed with scented oils of gardenia and ylang-ylang. The smooth, dark skin of her legs shone with the oil as the back of her knees rested on the rim of the tub, her glistening forelocks and feet dangling akimbo on the outside. Her head lay back, submerged to her brow. The ceiling fan whirred above enviously.

When Lorelei eventually did get out of her bath, with fingers still not crinkled, it was to head to her bed and the breakfast tray of luscious fruits and cold coffee which the room-service staff had left an hour previously. She sat on the white duvet in her bathrobe, towel wrapped on her head, and poured a healthy dose of strong cold coffee into her mouth. She turned on the gramophone and listened. A soothing harp filled the room, from deep shag carpets to palatial ceiling.

* * *

Later, in the heat of the afternoon, Lorelei flounced around Bascarsija and along the banks of the Miljacka, a glorious swathe in white, turning heads all along her route. Wives smacked husbands' arms. Cars narrowly avoided hitting each other; trees braced themselves for a sudden strike from a fender. The early-afternoon temperature peaked and the locals sweated; the day seemed to stand still for a few minutes, as only summer days can. When Lorelei eventually sauntered back into the cool of the President's lobby, the ceiling fans were rotating at full tilt, struggling against the early-evening southern European heat.

She instructed the bellhop to come to her floor, and the lift crawled upward, opening onto the third floor hallway, with its deep cream carpets centrally laid on dark brown oak floorboards. The sturdy white walls and high ceilings were interrupted by grainy sepia photographs of mustachioed young men in all-in-one swimsuits and of bonneted ladies in fields of knee-high daisies. One of the ladies showed just a hint of breast. This forced Lorelei to look twice as she stepped out, for the President did have the reputation of being a liberal spot.

The cage door closed behind her. Lorelei dispensed with her shoes. Her feet enjoyed the luxury of the crushed rugs en route to her suite. Manicured phalanges fingered the cold key into the lock.

* * *

Lorelei observed the evening's arrival from her balcony. The quiet luxury inside the President was at odds with the smoky, squawking city. Both had once been heavily influenced by Islam and by the Turks. The hotel's mystic Eastern design had evolved, however, into lush cream-and-scarlet carpets, deep mahogany pillars, hygienic modern conveniences, and Western ways. These now were juxtaposed with a metropolis still populated with ancient mosques and bearded street traders, apparently stubbornly lingering from the sixteenth century.

She looked at her thin gold wristwatch and involuntarily slowed her pace. Meanwhile, in the lobby, three dark-suited gentlemen removed their hats, announced their arrival, and headed for the bar.

Forty minutes later, in Suite 30, diamond earrings were clipped and cramponned, a sweet musk of Lyonnais *parfum* was pumped at the regulatory nine inches, and long black silk gloves were fixed. The thickness of the deep aqua curtains, twenty feet high, now kept out the evening buzz. An envelope had been pushed under Lorelei's door announcing the arrival of her dinner guests.

Lorelei gathered herself. She headed for the door, head tilted, swaying elegantly.

* * *

The boys walked eagerly over cobbles, but not eagerly enough to prevent Bill from yawning as Johan outlined the theory of the sixty-four practices of the *Kama Sutra*. A woman who gained mastery of all sixty-four crafts was respected, took her place in a male-dominated world, and became known as a ganika. Bill told him to shut up, but Johan kept the word on his lips.

"*Ganika, ganika, ganika . . .*"

They entered a trinket-filled, rouge-lit *taberne,* and Cartwright bought two steins of cold pilsner. Even before he had settled into his seat, he started into a mad monologue. Five minutes passed before Johan realized he had not heard one single word.

"Never mind that, Billy Boy," Johan interrupted. "Come on. Drink up."

Johan was in a rush again. His nervous and sometimes infectiously uncomfortable energy was getting the better of him as he whispered to himself some words that kept repeating in his mind.

Glide gently, thus forever glide.

They soon emptied their glasses and disappeared down a side street, into the shadows of the gathered dusk.

"Bon vivants! Good livers!" Johan yelled as their glasses met in the next bar.

Johan told himself he was feeling happy, and bookmarked it for future reference so that he would not feel guilty about letting such a moment slip by him.

Glide gently, El Capitán! Glide gently!

*   *   *

Mario Srna, Lorelei's closest ally in the embassy in Vienna, hosted a relaxed dinner at a fine Russian establishment, Troika, just two blocks from the President. Besides Lorelei, Srna's guests were two old pals from the consulate. The dinner lasted a pleasant two hours, consisting of a deep scarlet beetroot borscht, heavily peppered, followed by sublime roast venison, locally bred from the grounds of the Count of Kaunitz himself—an eccentric, but owner of the finest beasts in the land.

Srna was even offered the animal's head for his wall as a souvenir, a tradition of the time. He cordially accepted, as he was a gentleman with impeccable etiquette. To turn it down would have been an insult. The head was to be delivered to his town house in Vienna.

Srna was a slight, youthful forty-six-year-old, with clever brown eyes and a peerless generosity of spirit rare among diplomats. He was ambitious, but he achieved what he did through talent, quality, and vision, not Machiavellian techniques. Lorelei looked up to him, yet he was reliant on her as his eyes and his confidante.

The dinner guests were James Whitt and Herb LaRoux, from Boise, Idaho, and Baton Rouge, Louisiana, respectively. They contributed adequate tales from the professional field and above-average insight into the realpolitik of Europe and the raping of Africa. They did a fine impression of homosexual twins who were attached at the hip and dressed like each other for reasons over and above cordiality. Srna suggested this to Lorelei as Tweedledee and Tweedledum disappeared off together for a second time.

"Silly fool!" answered Lorelei. "They are smoking opium in the back."

Srna had had no idea.

"Don't look so shocked, Mario, you big dummy," she said, smiling. "Even Queen Victoria used to do it, you know that!"

"That is German propaganda, Lorelei!"

"It is NOT. *And she was German,* remember! Even Conan Doyle has Sherlock Holmes doing something like it to chase down Moriarty. They say he is addicted. Bram Stoker's *Dracula.* The sucking of youth and never seeing daylight. It's the height of fashion in London, and don't look so prudish! If you want to be shocked, I will tell you what Prince Albert once had done to his *bratwurst*!"

When Lorelei had finished telling him, Mario Srna's eyes nearly popped out of his head. He announced that he needed another vodka. The other two dinner guests meandered back from behind a thick curtain in lazy unison. *"Na Zdarovye."*

"Vodka is always best tasted at a healthy distance from Moscow!" announced Srna philosophically. "Vodka tasted in Moscow means an imminent visit to the ballet, lurking around some ridiculously icy corner. And endless dishes of potatoes. And Chekhov. Don't even get me started on Chekhov. Anton, the Darling of the Criminally Depressed and the Champion of Suicidally Dull Birds."

"Here's to Anton! *na zdarovye,* everyone!"

More of the iced firewater thawed any remaining inhibitions. The waiters turned a blind eye to the mild anti-Russianisms around the table (for they themselves were there in Sarajevo for a good reason, and it was not the love of their motherland).

The maître d' and his tuxedoed crew had started to resemble a *cape* of vampires. As more vodka was ordered, they gathered at the exits of the large, ancient banqueting hall, now serving only the diplomats' table. Each had the obligatory widow's peak and a stare that concentrated somewhere through the eyes and fifty feet beyond the skull of the person he was addressing. Any one of them could have been two hundred and fifty years old while appearing to be fifty. They served everything with a worrying lack of garlic and generous helpings of gloopy Romanian Cabernets. The maître d' had them all under his control, though his well-practiced misogynist focus was on Lorelei. And to hell with tradition. If, back in the land of his forefathers, the Mad Monk Rasputin could have made passionate, unholy, and hairy love to his queen, and in turn, his queen, Catherine, reputedly died under the weight of an eager, yet somewhat intrigued, copulating stallion, then certainly this beauty might grace *his* tables and imbibe *his* vodka. The clear liquid reappeared from an inexhaustible source behind the bloodred curtains.

Srna's imaginings were elsewhere. *Why had Prince Albert done THAT to himself?* he thought.

* * *

The fuel from the fine vodka had led the foursome out of the clutches of the polite vampires and into a den of vice. The Cellar sat three meandering city blocks away, and down a side street.

There they took their place around a circular table and ordered overpriced champagne. The conversation swayed pendulously between world politics and a cheaper form of prostitution—the one on offer not twenty feet away. The Cellar also hosted a shockingly untalented, overmaquillaged French cabaret chanteuse, called Dorithe, who croaked a ghastly libretto. According to Herb, her tone resembled that of a goose farting in the fog.

* * *

Meanwhile, more absinthe was firing up the boys as they headed back toward the palace. The streets were quiet.

They pondered the wisdom of their trek to the Old Sultan's.

"I know! Follow me." Johan pulled his friend to the left, away from the empty boulevard.

* * *

A fine and fragrant lady of the night muscled in between the twins and whispered in Herb's ear. He looked interested.

A burst of laughter echoed as Srna gave them all his best impression of the perpetually furious, energetically uncomfortable, and supremely crazy Indian diplomat from Vienna, Mr. Rajee. It was his party piece. It was a good one.

* * *

The door opened. The boys entered the Cellar.

There, at the first table they were set to walk past, were three smartly dressed, drunk men and a girl whom Johan recognized, her pupils as black as the Earl of Hell's riding boots.

Oh God! Concentrate! Johan, concentrate!

Johan moved directly toward the table from where the laughter came.

Aphrodite had surely seen him.

Five

We Are the Music Makers.
We Are the Dreamers of Dreams.

Oh! Pleasant exercise of hope and joy!
For mighty were the auxiliars which then stood
Upon our side, we who were strong in love!
Bliss was it in that dawn to be alive,
But to be young was very heaven!

—William Wordsworth

Early hours June 10, 1913. Sarajevo.

Lorelei Ribeiro indeed recognized Johan Thoms straightaway.

She motioned him forward, gesturing to Herb to make way for the two strays.

Introductions were made in English. This time it was Bill's turn to play the drunken fool as Herb announced;

"I'm 'merican."

"You are a *merkin*?"[4] Bill spluttered. "He's a fucking *merkin*!"

He had tried to whisper this in Johan's ear, but everyone had overheard. None of the men knew it referred to a certain kind of hairpiece. Lorelei, however, smirked. Johan and Bill took their places at the table, glancing around at the assortment of female detritus scattered around the Cellar.

"It's like the bloody Crimea in here," Bill said.

The boys nodded their heads in appreciation to the host, Srna, who remained as well groomed as a cat, and as well preserved as black-currant jam.

Johan was no longer the gibbering wreck of the night before. He held the ensuing conversation with his elders in the palm of his hand, moving it skillfully to include each present. He inquired politely as to James's home state of Idaho, engaged Mario on the family tree of the Srna clan in Sarajevo, and delved for details of New Orleans from Herb.

"The French Quarter is one place I would truly love to visit one day."

"It's one mad place, son," Herb agreed, with heavy eyelids.

"I have an invitation from the owner of the Napoleon House to stay whenever I want. His son is in the same faculty as I. Do you know of the place, sir? It's on St. Louis and Chartres, I think." He pronounced the street names as a local would have.

"Every one in the quarter knows the Napoleon House. Best bourbon sours this side of the Mississippi, and the other side, too, I'd hazard a guess. I've climbed that crooked old staircase myself on a couple of occasions, to untold treasures above," Herb said, with a weary bullishness.

"And are there really vampires there?" Johan attempted to rerail the conversation in front of the lady. Lorelei squirmed in her seat.

"There's every sort of vampire and weird creature of the night in the Easy. Odd critters from seaboard to west head to N'awlins for their crazy antics. It's why I left, sir. They'll get you in the end," Herb said. "You should take your friend up on the offer. There ain't nowhere like it."

"And the black magic?"

"As I said, those weirdos get up to everythin'. Voodoo shit is just the start of things. Snakes and skulls make 'em live forever. But make 'em look like they eaten' nothing but bones for a year a' Sundays."

"I prefer the Garden District," interjected the beauty to Herb's right. "Those mansions are haunted, for sure." Her features lit up, and the reflection of a candle danced in her black eyes. Herb took this distraction as his chance to excuse himself and headed toward a darkened arch. James followed him, slowly.

Cartwright and Srna were discussing the rights and wrongs of duels and satisfaction, and Johan was left face-to-face once again with Lorelei.

"So, we meet again," was Johan's opening gambit. At least it was in English and the words were in the right order.

"A pleasure." Lorelei advanced her metaphorical pawn forward one space.

"May I excuse myself for last night? I don't know what came over me,"

Johan said, but with enough confidence so that she might think he was not a complete moron. So far so good.

"That's all right. It happens," she answered in vermouth tones with a tilt of the head which implied that it was not the first time she had had such an effect on man or boy, but it also suggested that she quite enjoyed it.

They had the next twenty minutes all to themselves.

Soon the American boys were meandering back to the table, stopping to ogle young ladies and engage them in a confused dialogue. Lorelei leaned forward and, with her left hand under the table, grabbed Johan's crotch.

An awkward pause followed. Lorelei grinned.

"What *is* that perfume?" was all that the youth could manage.

"It is called Chance." With her right hand, she twisted his shirt collar and top buttons a half turn, and with her black eyes she glared deep into his dilated pupils.

"And *YES*, Johan Thoms. You have one."

She bit her bottom lip, just to the left, and slowly blinked.

Johan was reduced to rubble. Luckily, his groin also felt like a chunk of masonry.

Herb yelled for more drinks and asked the new guests if they would care to join him. Johan pondered, for the sake of his performance, whether he should further imbibe. He wanted to file this in his memory for later perusal.

"Yes, please, actually. I'll take a bourbon sour, Herb. Thank you," said Johan.

Bill yelled to a passing waiter, "Make that two, please." He glanced to the right to see Lorelei removing her hand.

Perfect, Bill thought, and he winked at his pal.

Generous to a fault, Srna demanded more champagne, and then he continued his tête-à-tête with Bill on Serbian expansionist policy.

Meanwhile, there was a more important agenda on a different Eastern Front. To Cartwright's right, Lorelei was twitching in her seat. She rubbed Johan's bare shin with her warm foot.

Later, Johan only recalled noting his own gratitude toward Srna for allowing the obvious frisson to flourish.

The next thing he knew, he was alone with Lorelei. He was kissing her, up against giant wrought-iron gates leading to a darkened courtyard. Darkened, but for the softest of yellow lights coming from two or three windows on different floors.

Fade-out.

The next thing he recalled, they were in an elevator, black trestle closing behind them.

Fade-out.

A knock on the door and two glasses of champagne, with a strawberry in each flute, entered on a solid silver platter, followed by the night porter, all beady eyes and a center parting. The room was luxury.

Fade-out.

A relaxed, naked Lorelei facing him on her back on the bed, head nearest to him, as he staggered off to urinate. She smiled at him as he left the room. He recalled that he had remembered to raise the toilet seat before he'd peed.

(His father had drilled it into him to put the seat back down afterward, in case the female in question were married. For if she were and the seat were left raised, then there would be one malicious, vengeance-seeking husband hiding in the closet for his next visit, clutching a saber—precisely the one thing one would not want to meet in a state of undress and/or arousal.)

In the bathroom, his erection had posed a problem. He did not want to miss the bowl and piss all over her floor, though it was more likely to hit the back of the wall six feet up right now.

He considered doing a handstand and giggled to himself.

In his dorm he had perfected the art of knowing exactly where to stand with a full-blown one (adjacent to the gray-cracking porcelain sink). As he started to urinate and turgidity decreased, he would slowly inch forward, shuffling, in order to maintain bull's-eye into the center of the bowl. Now, he would have to replicate this skill in a bathroom of untried dimensions.

"Bang on!" he whispered.

Not a drop even touched the porcelain as he smiled at the splashing: he had been a real success in the bathroom. But he could not recall much about what had happened in the bedroom.

These were his main recollections of his first evening with Lorelei Ribeiro. Johan Thoms was still very much a boy.

* * *

The following three days, Lorelei's last in Sarajevo, were spent in the confines of her suite. Lorelei and Johan ventured into the old town for just one dinner, into an unseasonably chilly evening.

Their venue that night became their restaurant of choice whenever Lorelei would return to this, Johan's city. Taberne Parioli—named after the hamlet in Italy where the owner had met and fallen in love with his wife in the winter of '89—was, it seemed, a place for young chaps looking to impress their belles. It had only six tables. Three of these adorned the ivy-covered balcony, from which the patrons were able to acknowledge some of their fellow burgers of the old town and ignore the rest down a long unwelcoming Balkan nose. The owners loved their cuisine and never looked down any sort of nose at anyone. Johan recalled fondly the owner's wife, her generosity, her love of providing for her extended family of satisfied guests, bringing out the desire-fused dishes created by her beau, who perpetually and profusely sweated away in the back of the establishment.

"Are you frightened of me?" Lorelei had asked out of the blue.

There had been a split-second pause before Johan offered, "No, why?"

On their first anniversary, back at the same spot, equally out of the blue, he would admit, "Yes, of course, I was."

She laughed at him. She had, of course, known.

Back in the President, supplies of food, coffee, and other liquid refreshment were delivered to the vast mahogany writing desk in her suite.

This was a novel experience for both of them. Johan was not used to spending the next day, never mind three days, with a conquest, though he hardly saw Lorelei as a conquest—more as a monumental work in progress.

For Lorelei, this was the first time since her husband had perished that she had slept with a man. A woman, yes, but not a man.

These details had come to light as Johan had gradually wound down over the days to talk at ease with her and had become *almost* himself. As his nerves had dissipated, Lorelei had found him increasingly charming, funny, and intelligent. She had laughed.

It would be twelve months, however, before she actually realized that Johan had not been circumcised, for she would never see anything but a turgid member. In her presence it would always be thus. They say the Queen of England perceives and therefore believes that the world smells of fresh paint, for there is always some poor sod twenty yards in front of her with a brush and a large pot, slapping it on at velocity. So it was (sort of) with Lorelei and Johan.

* * *

Srna was to have accompanied Lorelei back to Vienna, but he had gone back one day earlier than planned (but only once he was convinced that Lorelei had wanted to stay in Sarajevo). Always the gent, Srna reassured her that none of this would be mentioned in Austria. She trusted him implicitly. He had prepaid her departure with a bank draft from the American embassy, allowing her to simply stroll and saunter out of the President as she wished. This she knew how to do.

Johan accompanied her to the station and threatened to get on the train with her. She joked and called him "a stupid boy," though she was confident that he could be groomed—and that soon they would share a great love (which, according to the hyperbolic Cartwright, was "to make Krakatoa look like an abbey candle").

The train door closed, the whistle blew, and she was gone, to the north.

Six

A Sweet Deity of Debauchery

Moreover, the Lord said, because the daughters of Zion are haughty, and walk with stretched-forth necks and wanton eyes, walking and mincing as they go, and making a tinkling with their feet.

—Isaiah 3:1

June 16, 1913

Johan lay horizontal on his favorite window ledge in his chambers, with a hefty Egyptian cushion behind his bulbous head, soaking in volume three of the *Kama Sutra*. The sun turned his face a soft brown.

Three slow, light, effeminate knocks landed on his door. It was not the day for the cleaner to mop his floors. Johan jumped down and glided gently to open the door. He was met by a vision of shocking-pink cuffs, pale skin, thinning reddish hair, and bulging green eyes.

The Count stood five foot eight in his stacked-heeled, perpetually new shoes. He was just months from his fortieth birthday, and his most time-consuming pastime, aside from learning Eastern religions, was attempting to maintain his youth. Sadly for him, his hedonistic lifestyle did not dovetail with his efforts. ("My *ying* is outweighing my *yang* again," he said.) This did not stop his being pampered by an array of bemused stylists and fledgling pedicurists more suited to Cleopatra than a Teutonic twentieth-century count.

The visitor held out an elevated and angled hand.

"The Fifteenth Count of Kaunitz. I think it's fifteen. To the rescue."

Johan had hardly expected this when he had written to royalty for help.

Johan held out a hand to shake in the normal fashion. For a few seconds, neither moved, and an impasse looked inevitable. They met in the middle.

"Johan Thoms, but then I guess you know that." Johan showed neither airs nor graces, allowing Kaunitz not an inch in his attempt to foist his lofty social position upon him. "A pleasure to meet you, and a bit of a surprise."

"Ah yes, it sounded like you were in need, so why not do away with convention? I have made a living out of doing away with convention! Did you know that, young Johan?" The Count's arms flailed and his eyes flirted.

Johan did not know whether it would be rude to laugh, but he almost could not help himself.

The Count, for his part, was delighted with what he had found. Firm young student, almost touching six feet without shoes, with possibly a brain to match his looks, and piercing blue eyes that reminded him of the North, of the *Vaterland, die Heimat.*

O Sweet Deity of Debauchery. I owe you! The warmth of an unblemished and virginal young boy. He silently began to formulate a strategy to corrupt the (perceived) pureness of his newly acquired charge.

Rather than keep the Count in his small dorm, Johan suggested a stroll round the grounds to discuss their business. The Count tried to keep a lid on his flirtations. Johan, for his part, was keen to point out that it was not charity that he sought, for the work ethic instilled by his father, Drago, would not allow this.

"Well, I have odd jobs around the estate, but your being here at school sort of excludes you from those."

"What about anything here in the city? You must have some contacts?"

"I have many, but I am not sure what they would require." The Count paused. "I will summon Wilfried and have him contact his Man Servants' Union, put the word out that way. Come!"

Fifteen minutes later, the angular Wilfried departed from the front of the university in the back of a chauffeur-driven car, commandeered from the dean, with a list of addresses in his hand.

"And don't come back until you have good news for Johan!" the Count shrieked after him.

"Come! Let's have some lunch. You must be starving to death, look at you." He prodded the young man under the ribs. "You are all skin and bones! I know the perfect place. Let us get some *real meat* into you, boy. Follow me."

Johan had no real choice in the matter. They marched off together in the direction of the Town Hall, Johan praying he would not be spotted by Bill Cartwright.

Every few yards, the Count could not resist a skip.

All his still-illegal dreams were perhaps coming true.

* * *

The city's main artery, the Appel Quay, which hugs the river, was quiet, and seemed to move at slow motion in the heat of the afternoon.

The Count was parading his prey along the quay, though it was unlikely that any of his degenerate cohorts would be seen alive in daylight.

They entered the restaurant. The Count's family had known the owners of Troika for generations, as the family had supplied the venison to the kitchens. This entitled Kaunitz to the royal treatment he always craved but failed to achieve in a land notoriously homophobic and increasingly anti-Prussian.

As for Johan, it had been many years since he had last been so close to a deer. Various heads of the beasts were mounted on the walls.

"It's good I no longer count them as friends," Johan said.

"Yes, I'm sorry. I was wondering about that. We *were already* on the way."

They discussed Drago's mental issues (Johan was quietly proud of them), Johan's studies (they were thoroughly enjoyable), and the activities of the Black Hand (as individuals, they were not to be crossed at any time of day anywhere, even with a bunch of pals around, but Johan dismissed them as a serious political force, which surprised Kaunitz; the Count thought for a moment of delving further, but his mind wandered).

Johan had his food ordered for him by Kaunitz, in a limp display of authority. The borscht, which took an age to arrive, was the deepest beetroot red and gloopy. The inside of the venison was a soft pink, but still oozed a scarlet spill on its first tender cut. Kaunitz moved in his seat.

"What an age to wait! Not that I am complaining!" the Count said. "I think they must have been to my place to catch it." Leaning toward Johan, he added, "Talking of my place, you MUST come visit."

"That would be nice." The Count, Johan thought, seemed to be over-looking the reason for their relationship, which was business, not pleasure.

Kaunitz changed the subject.

"It is called Troika here, because *troika,* as well as meaning 'three,' is also the name of the most famous bear in Russia, a bear of great strength, a bear of great wisdom, and we all know the Russian Bear is not a speedy sort when it comes to turning itself around. A bit like Chef, clearly! So, it is superb *essen,* but equine cries to Catherine the Great, they make you wait for it."

Now, the Count, thankfully having shed his pink jacket, preferred not to eat, but to sit and watch his new friend, as if, it seemed to Johan, he were fattening him up for market.

As Johan masticated the second-to-final chunk of finest heavily-peppered venison, Wilfried entered holding a stack of notes and messages.

The sweat on the butler's head was rapidly mopped away by both Wilfried himself and an eager-to-please waiter, who received a quick bony jab to the midriff and a minitorrent of mumbled, clipped abuse. The waiter backed off.

"Well, what do we have?" Kaunitz demanded.

"Various situations, yet many are not in Sarajevo and others are for skilled staff. Some are not available for a couple of months. Some are probably below your, erm . . . Herr Thoms's requirements."

"Well, don't waste our time with those. What do you think there *could* be, so we may actually *help* this fine young man, as opposed to simply have my brutal beasts try to kill him. I am quite, quite positive that he would rather be wandering by the Miljacka with a bunch of jocular young chums and a fine bottle of rosé. Come on, man!"

Wilfried bit his tongue and mopped his brow again. "The municipality needs three police officers."

"Yuk!" yelled Kaunitz. "Horrible and ignorant brutes who only want to stop people's fun. *Untermensch!* Next."

Wilfried turned to the next note in his pile. "Your old friend, General Oskar Potiorek. Very, very good pay. All I know is that it is something to do with the council . . . or, more specifically, their ladies."

This final word changed Kaunitz's look of joy to one of disgust. Johan turned to the Count. Kaunitz had no *real* choice but to agree.

"Very well, what would Potiorek prefer us to do?"

"He has invited you to his mansion house at the Konak for six this evening to discuss the duties."

"Excellent. We will be there for six-thirty," the Count said, and motioned to the waiter for two shot glasses to be filled.

He glanced at his pocket watch. It was almost four.

"You will need to dress for this, Johan, but regulation is adequate. *Na zdarovye.*"

"*Na zdarovye* and thank you, Count."

The waiter was still on hand to yet again refill the eggcups with clear liquid. Wilfried frowned. After the shots were gone, his disdainful brow creased even more deeply.

Johan was pleased with the sound of the work.

With school now over for the summer, he was rid of the burden of college examinations. His only scholarly duty for the summer came in the form of an extensive reading list, which he could complete with one eye closed over a rainy weekend in late August. If his theory was right, the vacuum created by his lack of activity the rest of the summer would require commensurate mental stimulation.

The potential drawback was how it might encroach on his planned sojourns to Vienna to molest Lorelei, or on his availability to be pestered should she come to him. Lorelei's movements were at least less inhibited than his. The cost of travel was to her negligible, given her connections through the embassy and the railways of Southern Europe. He now had his own high-up connections and was hobnobbing with royalty, though he sensed that any favors from Kaunitz were dependent on what was in it for Kaunitz. A limp slap on his back jolted him back from his daydreaming.

"Come, chum!" Kaunitz said. "Let's make you presentable for the General. You look like an unmade bed, my boy."

Johan was taken off to the Count's personal tailor, Schneider.

"That's more like it," announced Kaunitz an hour or so later. "The General can be a bit of an old stick-in-the-mud. Nouveau Austria! But, oh my! You do scrub up like an absolute dream, Johan Thoms!"

*   *   *

In 1913, Oskar Potiorek, General of the Austrian Army, was billeted in Sarajevo. His mansion, the Konak, nestled in the upmarket district of Bistrik, south of the central Miljacka. Johan had heard of the majesty within the Konak, but had never dreamed he would ever be behind its forty-foot walls as a guest of the General. It was all the more bizarre that he was going there because of his father's psychosis-inducing obsession with Pythagoras. The Konak, a haunt of extreme beauty, was the fourth Saraj. The Saraj (the genesis of the name Sarajevo) were constructed by the Turks from which to rule the city in the sixteenth century. The first three were destroyed before or by the Great Fire of 1879, leaving in isolation the bewildering Renaissance allure of the Konak. It remained for many decades the only three-floor building in the city, which underlined its authority. It became the residence for royal guests to the city, until Potiorek commandeered it for himself.

On the stroke of six-thirty, the dean's car entered the grounds between the two stone lions on either side of the front gates, and through a small squadron of Austrian infantry.

It was well known that no one should keep General Potiorek waiting.

Johan tried his best not to look intimidated by his surroundings.

He first saw the General's gargantuan walrus mustache from forty yards as Potiorek prowled the grounds at the back of the Konak. The old soldier spun around.

This could be interesting, thought Johan as he pondered the contrast between count and general. But then there was probably more sodomy in the army than anywhere else in Austria.

"Kaunitz! Late!"

An awkward silence.

"General. I am grateful that you were able to see me. How are things with those dastardly Black Handers? When are we going to swat them, like the pesky flies they are?"

The General mumbled into his hairy top lip some Prussian inanities that seemed to lack verbs of any kind. Johan understood the morsel-like clues because his German was excellent, perhaps better than Potiorek's.

"Him?" The General finally gestured toward Johan while looking at Kaunitz.

"Johan Thoms, sir," Johan replied confidently on his own behalf. The General seemed taken aback by the boy's initiative, for his eyebrows were raised and his mouth open.

"Let's make brief." This was his most constructed sentence. "Need man. Do not like . . . kept waiting by . . . by . . . by certain . . . [mumble mumble something homophobic]. You? Drive?"

He spoke, Johan thought, like he was sending a telegram with a limited amount of coins in his pocket.

"Yes, sir," Johan replied. The General already seemed to like Johan infinitely more than he did the Count as he eyed him up and down with nodding approval.

"Good. Your lineage? What?"

"Excuse me, sir?"

"Bloody Slav, bloody Serb. How much? In you?"

"Great-grandmother knew one once. Not for long, though."

"Good. Turk?"

"She would not speak to them at all."

"Even better. In! Friday six A.M. Report. Müller front gate. Ninety-five forints* month."

"Kaunitz. Müller now. State room."

"*Danke,* Herr General. You simply must come visit the estate soon for some shooting," Kaunitz replied, flouncing into the shade of the mansion's splendor to meet Müller, who, Johan later learned, ran the Konak's nonmilitary affairs.

Potiorek did not acknowledge Kaunitz's invitation.

Johan's eyes were semiglazed from the thought of the money and his family's relief, their pride. The political intrigue thrilled him. So did the surroundings.

---

* There were roughly two English crowns and just over two American dollars to a forint in 1913. The inflated pay was a reflection of Masonic-like machinations, and also of a possible level of responsibility Johan may not have been expecting.

Gastronomically, sociologically, sartorially, and financially, it had been a damned fine day.

*   *   *

Johan slumped onto his bed that night delighted with himself. He had never felt more powerful.

He would attend the Count's estate the following morning to discover the full nature of his duties. A car would be waiting for him at seven A.M. by the Registrar's office. He would take breakfast with Kaunitz and discuss the General's job.

Bill knocked and entered his pal's dorm, and Johan filled him in on the day's proceedings, and on the impending doom of the next day.

"Just don't wash your old chap," Bill suggested.

"He is NOT going to have his way with me. And anyway, I have the job now. I could just turn up on Friday at the Konak, ask for Müller. Kaunitz could put the kibosh on it, though. Those Austrians are all lodges and *Gesellschaften*."

"You have no choice. You go. You fulfill your obligations, and you do not let him sodomize you. Simple."

"I fear it won't be *that* easy. I mean, he can't rape me. But that does not mean it is going to be a relaxed day in the country."

"It rarely is *that easy,* el Capitán. And you could do *Wurst.*" Bill laughed.

Johan scowled and narrowed his eyes.

"Funny. I hate it when people laugh at their own very poor jokes. And at the expense of a friend."

"*That's* what makes it funny. Because you're hardly on your knees, are you? If you'll excuse the phrase. You're working at the Konak, for ninety-five forints a month. A tab at the President, and your friend in Suite Thirty. Driving for the Walrus. A sugar daddy buying you new clothes at Schneider's; eating at the best restaurants in the city—Troika, for God's sake. Private drivers. Country estates. You *deserve* to be laughed at, you rotter! You deserve to be rogered, and damned hard, too! Just one day with a funny-dressed kraut in the country and you are in the clear, el Capitán! Then you have nothing really to worry about other than to roll around all summer with your very own Statue of Liberty."

Johan dropped a recently received telegram on the chest of the prostrate Bill and paced the room.

"She is back in on Wednesday," he said. "Weird times, Billy. Weird times."

"From the ridiculous to the sublime. Wonderful times, I would say. Revel in them, man. Every single moment. You will look back in years to come and see these as your golden days."

"I am going to, Bill. I am going to try . . ."

He picked up his dorm keys, whispering to himself:

Glide gently, I know . . . Glide gently!

And then, more audibly:

"Come on, I need to go outside. I need some fresh air."

And off they went, Johan wondering what sort of future he was making for himself.

Seven

A Day (or So) in the Country

The first stage is like ordinary drinking, the second when you begin to see mon-
strous and cruel things, but if you can persevere you will enter in upon the third
stage where you see things that you want to see, wonderful curious things.

—Oscar Wilde

June 17, 1913. Dawn.

Johan Thoms rose with the sun. Both had their shoulders back, chests
and chins out.

He did, contrary to William Atticus Forsythe Cartwright's advice,
wash. He put on a short-sleeved white shirt, black waistcoat, beige trousers with black braces, new olive-hued socks, and black brogues. His hair
was side-parted, oiled but showing glimpses of blond from the sun. His
face had an even youthful summer tan, and he added a subtle hint of El
Capitán cologne, merely for politeness. He could easily have been going to
church as he closed the door of his neat dorm behind him. Such tidiness
would soon be a thing of the past.

He was greeted on the stroke of seven by an aging chauffeur named
Helmut Grockenberger, who had white skin and a shock of red hair, and
who exuded the scent of garlic. Helmut Grockenberger was propped up
by a shiny new Packard.

It was a glorious morning. Small boys walked lively dogs, and medical students headed for the dusty shade of libraries, for there was no summer respite for them. Less focused rogues stumbled home with bow ties undone and drooping.

The car rolled smoothly out of the city limits. Johan felt unusually calm, comforted by the beauty of the morning, the luxury of the car, and the good things that were happening to him. The only problem was his father, but as insanities go, Drago's even seemed weirdly wonderful. He noted that he needed to send a telegram to Argona to let his parents know of his progress. Perhaps he could even surprise them with a visit.

The journey was swift. The unusual tranquillity that had descended upon him relaxed him further. The trick would be to feel like this every day. He knew that this was within his youthful grasp.

Glide gently . . .

The car came to a halt on the gravel at the front of the Moorish splendor of the *castile,* the windows of which were taller than his house in Argona. The glass-paneled doors at the top of the twenty stone steps opened and out stepped Kaunitz himself, with a huge, welcoming grin, as if he had not seen his new best friend for three decades. It had been just a few hours.

It was past eight.

"Let us break our fast! Do you like sausage?"

Holy Mary, he didn't take long, did he? Johan thought.

"I do," he said aloud. "And I am famished."

"Superb! Come, follow me. We should eat in the glen. It is simply heaven before nine."

* * *

In the orchard, Wilfried pulled a chair out for Johan. He was almost polite. After a breakfast of fresh fruits, delicious meats, juice, and coffee, the Count and Johan strolled through the grounds, observing the manicured lawns and hedges, the centuries-old stonework. The Count explained the quirks of the manor. As he did, he seemed to calm down. The innuendo dried up.

"I wanted to thank you for all your help, Count," said Johan eventually.

"Kaunitz, please. Less of the formality, now we're friends."

"Fine. Kaunitz."

A comfortable pause followed. And so as the formality was lost, there seemed in direct proportion to be less of the predator in Kaunitz. The Count told Johan the history of the Kaunitz family all the way back to Salzburg in the early sixteenth century. They reached the lake, by the deep forest, where they sat on a recently scrubbed stone bench. Johan glanced into the woods. A deer peered back. Johan decided to ignore this.

At some point, Kaunitz knew that he had to divulge the precise nature of the General's work. He had concealed it so far, to entice the boy into his lair. Johan was there now.

"Right," he began. "I spoke with Müller at length. Here is the arrangement. Potiorek is overseeing maneuvers, as a show of strength to the Serbs. You will be needed to chauffeur dignitaries and their wives around as they come into town, mainly from Vienna and Salzburg, but also from Berlin and Munich. Discretion is vital, and your hours may be irregular. Müller has spoken to your dean, who vouched for you, as did a Professor Tiberius Novac. You really are well thought of there you know, young man. You will need to share responsibilities with drivers already at the Konak. Franz Urban and Leopold Loyka are longtime members of Potiorek's staff. You will be their backup, and you will do as they ask. This Friday will be your induction. Do not arrive even one minute late—you can't imagine what they are like sometimes. But I know you will do just fine there, and you won't let me—or yourself, or your family—down. You have an open account at Schneider's, by the way, where we got the suit yesterday. This is my gift to you. I want you to indulge yourself, so I have instructed old man Schneider to treat you as he would me. God help you." He broke into the previous Kaunitz for a second, arms flailing.

He recomposed himself. It was peeving to him that he could not control himself for more than an hour. He had been doing so well, too.

A lump appeared in Johan's throat. The Count was actually just a lonely man in his ivory towers, desperate to be needed and loved.

"Do you have any questions?" Kaunitz asked.

"None straightaway, but I am sure I will have."

"Good answer. I like that about you. Nothing seems to worry you, and you take your time. You will go far, I think. I cannot thank that grumpy old skeleton with antlers enough for bringing you here as a friend."

Johan smiled, and felt no fear as the Count slapped him softly on the shoulder.

"Come. Let's go relax inside the house. Today is Johan day! I have some wonderful art to show you. I want you to treat this place like it is your own. I would not want you to come here and feel inhibited."

"Well, that's a tough one to turn down!"

"Good. I am glad that this is sorted out, but I do mean it, you know. These are not hollow words. I like to stand by my promises."

"I can see that. I know that. And I appreciate that."

Johan spoke to Kaunitz as a friend and an equal. Kaunitz heard Johan in the same way.

They shook hands and held each other's gaze. Johan spoke first. He was keen to do this, in order to give meaning to the deal they had just struck as friends.

"Tell me about London!" he demanded, with not a "sir," nor a "Count," nor a "Kaunitz."

"Crazy, crazy place. Especially right now. But not as crazy as Marrakech, or Constantinople." Kaunitz rolled his eyes as Johan tried to imagine the bacchanalia being replayed on the Count's inner eye.

"What is it about London?"

"The history, the writers, the power, the architecture, the people, the freedoms, of a kind."

They disappeared toward the manor, walking as relaxed friends would.

* * *

By noon, Kaunitz had expertly opened a bottle of Dom Pérignon without the help of Wilfried. He and Johan sat in the shade at the front of the southern wing, on deep-cushioned chaise longues.

"Tell me about you!" Kaunitz inquired, though it did not make Johan feel uncomfortable. Quite the opposite. He spoke for an hour, relaxed as could be, until (while on the subject of Bill Cartwright) Kaunitz couldn't take it anymore.

"Oh, I DO love English boys, so very proper," he said. Kaunitz had not before approached the taboo of his homosexuality. They laughed.

They were soon on the third bottle. Kaunitz was proving to be wonderfully independent in chilling and pouring the Sekt without Wilfried.

"What sort of girls do you like?" the Count wondered as he refilled the glasses.

"Blondes, dark girls. Whatever. Right now an American. Why do you ask?"

"Never you mind, you nosy scoundrel. Can't a new pal be curious? *Prost!*" Their glasses chinked.

"What sort of boys do you like?" Johan found himself saying. Then he waited like a bullied boy, expecting the full weight of his opponent upon him in seconds. He cringed.

This would be the litmus test of their new friendship.

The Count spat out a palateful of finest Dom, choking. He looked in Johan's eyes for a second, then exploded into raucous laughter.

"You are *the* best! Oh, my boy. If only, if only!"

Johan breathed a deep sigh of relief. The friendship had found its equilibrium.

"You stay here. I need to talk to Wilfried about a couple of things." Kaunitz patted him on the back, shaking his head, still in disbelief at the turn of the conversation. "Oh, and I will answer your wonderful probings when I return, Johan Thoms."

Kaunitz disappeared into the cool of the vaulted banqueting hall, laughing. Johan entered a daydream, thinking how he and Bill might spend their days if they lived in such a place.

Kaunitz had been gone for ten minutes before he swept back out exuding a sense of expectancy.

"Now, where *were* we? Ah yes, your naughty probings. Well, to be honest, I like boys like you. But fear not. You are my friend, and I hope you feel I am yours. So, let's get that out of the way. I also like many other types of boys. I am a bit of a brute, when it comes down to it. 'East is east and west is west, and this is where they meet.' They gather here from Chicago to the Ottoman. It is the scourge of the idle class, I am afraid. But I never venture to zones where others do not want to venture. I am a *polite* brute."

He reached for a gold cigarette case.

"We have some crazy parties. Wilde was always invited and continually threatened to accept. But alas, that never happened. God rest his harassed soul, the poor, poor genius."

Wilfried appeared and gestured to the Count.

"Everything is arranged, sirs."

Johan noted the plural with intrigue. "Anything of which I should be aware?" he asked.

"All in good time," the Count answered. "The impatience of youth. Life should be savored, for there is no going back at the end of the journey. Relish the trek, for destinations can be so dull. Just look at Belgrade, for heaven's sake. Glide gently, thus forever glide, my boy!"

Johan shuddered, as if his grave were being danced on by the future.

Kaunitz lit a long pipe, which exuded a sweet-smelling vapor that made his eyes roll and glaze. He explained how the vessel was made from bamboo, rimmed with silver, stuffed with palm slices and hair. It was fed by a bowl of clay, in which Kaunitz had melted globules of opium, held over an oil lamp's flame.

He was midflow, extravagantly quoting an English poet, slowly and thoughtfully pacing imaginary boards:

> *"On with the dance!*
> *Let joy be unconfined,*
> *No sleep till morn,*
> *When youth and pleasure meet,*
> *To chase the glowing hours with flying feet."*

Thus he announced his love for the world, madly puffing on the pipe and flailing more slowly now.

Johan interrupted with an involuntary blurt. "Do you have some of that stuff for me?"

Silence.

"I mean . . . Please?" he added.

"OH MY GOD!"

I've done it this time. I have crossed the line, Johan thought.

"OH MY DEAR GOD!"

Johan began to apologize, but had little chance of getting a word in, even considering the Count's influenced condition.

"I am so rude. I just thought you didn't . . ."

"Erm . . . I don't. But I am not stupid!"

"I want to have your children, Johan Thoms!"

Pause. Long pause.

"But I haven't got any!"

A further second passed, before they both folded into uncontrollable laughter. When this had subsided, Kaunitz rose to enter the shelter of the hall, beckoning Johan to follow. "Are you sure about this? Feeding you this was really not on my agenda," he said over his left shoulder, now with the caring attitude of an elder brother.

"I am not stupid, but neither do I want to die stupid," Johan said.

"My word! What a delicious surprise you constantly are. And I don't want you to die stupid either. This has to be of your own volition."

"If the Queen of England, Byron, and Sherlock Holmes smoked the stuff, then I shall take it in my stride." Johan realized that the champagne was making him slightly giddy.

"There is no such person as Sherlock Holmes, Johan."

"*That,* Count Kaunitz the Fifteenth, is *not* the point!"

"I guess you are right!"

"Now, you'll have to show me how."

"Easy." Kaunitz opened a silver snuffbox and emptied a pile of its brownish contents into the contraption. He cackled to himself as he lit it for Johan and passed it over.

"Just don't tell your mother, please."

The smoke hit Johan's bloodstream and he felt his eyelids grow heavy. The Count produced a fine cigar and a cool, sweating flute of Dom.

"Willkommen, mein Freund."

When Johan felt the initial nausea pass, it was then his turn—his facial musculature lax—to babble, which he did, for fifteen minutes, mainly on the subject of bonobo chimps. The Count felt it only fair to sit back and indulge the youth. The monologue continued until Johan heard car engines in the distance. The noise closed in until the clatter of the chip gravel was louder than the hum of the cars. Several doors opened, feet on loose stone, several doors closed, with a *clunk,*

clunk, clunk. Voices, foreign voices, those of women, girls, laughter and giggles.

Wilfried appeared from out of the sunlight, and introduced their female visitors. Kaunitz was keen to see who had been summoned. Two beautiful creatures, touching six foot each, with shocks of blond hair, porcelain skin, and the clearest blue-green eyes paraded past Johan with saucy smiles. They stopped and kissed each other. A dusky-skinned vision from Persia then approached Johan and placed her full lips on his, leaving them there. Her eyes half opened as the rest of her frame remained still, then her lids fell again. A narrow gap in her front teeth pulled Johan's lip toward her. She confidently revealed a gold ring containing a sapphire stone in her right nipple as she pulled away, glancing down at Johan's bulging lap.

An ebony duo inspected Johan as they marched by his flank together. They were perfect specimens, with high cheekbones and taut rare eyes, suggesting a skin wound drum-tight, making them susceptible to being pleasured.

The Count nodded. He clapped and signaled a start to the festivities. The girls turned their starved desires along with their hands and mouths on each other, and the two ebonies turned to Johan.

"This is Johan Thoms," the Count said. "Please him, ladies, for he is my friend. If you please him today, you please me. He is now your friend. I will return shortly," he announced, with an impressive authority, as the harem set about their wonderful duties.

"And you enjoy, Johan, my friend," he added. "I love you, like a brother. *Bis spaeter.*" He clapped his hands again and retreated, now closer in spirit to a revered, respected Caligula.

The thrum of a harp approached from down a hallway, and a table had appeared, holding a large tray, lined immaculately with row upon row of small glasses of absinthe.

Billy would never believe this.

*   *   *

The bacchanalia continued until, as a naked, happy group, they met the next sunrise outside the great hall. Generations before, carnivores had here torn into flesh at banquets celebrating ancient customs. Now it was the sweat from lithe nymphomaniacs that stained the knots of the tables, to a mystical backbeat of Sanskrit and Aramaic yelps. The party cosine twisted back to sine.

Kaunitz appeared once more, to lay an asexual and avuncular tender kiss on the forehead of each of his guests, including Johan, before retiring once more to Lord knows where, to do Lord knows what, with Lord knows whom.

Johan felt a glow of happiness. He was untouchable, for this is what his life had become.

* * *

Throughout the proceedings, which had seen daylight disappear and return, nothing had felt grubby or shameful. Johan now rested upon a plateau on which he was indestructible. He was in a true state of glorious joy. Nothing could touch him other than a dozen groping hands, including his own.

More importantly, he had a new friend: a lonely soul who had just needed a pal and an equal.

Three of the girls made their way to their chambers. One duo, however, had won a toss of a forint piece to take the grinning bigheaded boy with them.

They all climbed the twelve-foot-wide staircase slowly to the first floor. Two of the girls pulled Johan into a huge room with high windows. They were protected from the day's glare by thick cream curtains as they collapsed onto what seemed to be the world's biggest and softest bed and drifted, intertwined, into a blissful slumber.

* * *

The next thing Johan knew, it was late morning once more. All three seemed to stir at the same time. Their bodies had taken pleasure and slept in synchronicity, why not wake together?

So they all bathed together, tumbling just once back into fucking with the slow pace inspired by the laziness of the approaching noon. They en-

tered a vortex, into the realm of outer-body experience. The rest was an
ecstatic blur with no concept of time; an ancient version of the Blue Rose
of Forgetfulness.

* * *

A naked Johan, sated and bathed, looked out from his baroque balcony to
see the lone figure of Kaunitz down by the lake, on a stone bench. Johan
threw on a heavy robe and headed down, without a rush but with a defi-
nite purpose.

It wasn't until Johan was ten yards away that Kaunitz spun round. He
bore not an ounce of the sadness his posture had suggested, merely a huge
grin.

"Well?" he said.

"Not what I expected when I left town!"

"Not what I was expecting to provide. If you were not such a relief, a
revelation, a breath of fresh air in my life compared to the idiots whom I
once called acquaintances! I am glad it turned out this way. As long as you
are all right and promise to continue to be you, I will always be here for you,
Johan Thoms.

"But now," the Count said, "we need to get you back to civilization.
You have a date, my friend." He winked wickedly. "It's a good job you are
such a slip of a lad with potent powers of recovery! Let's not make *such a*
habit of it, but please come back soon. You are always welcome."

"It's a deal."

"And now, tell me more about this Billy friend of yours."

They laughed. Then they hugged and wandered back slowly to the
manor, where Wilfried had prepared the Packard.

Thirty minutes later, after one last cup of coffee, Johan, in his civvies,
climbed into the back of the automobile to leave paradise to return to the
city.

He turned around for one last look, to see three balconies of nymphs,
some seminaked and scrubbed, some still naked and sweating, but all wav-
ing to their new chum.

"Well, I guess Ahab got his fish." Kaunitz smiled.

Johan nodded (pondering what life must have been like *all the time* for Kubla Khan and the Old Sultan, over in the decreed pleasure dome of Xanadu, or down the road and up the hill at the Palace).

"We hope we welcome sir again soon," said Wilfried as he closed the car door. He afforded himself a half smile.

*   *   *

Alone in the back of the Packard, Johan blurted out, "Johan Thoms! You lucky bum! You bloody lucky bum!"

They were just a mile from the campus. Johan was still organizing his thoughts, when another verbal volley left his lips.

"Thank Christ. Am I glad I washed my old chap!"

The driver sprayed spittle onto the windshield.

Did I just say that or think it? Johan wondered. Then he smiled to himself. If he *had* said it, it would have made the driver's day.

Johan bit his lip to suppress a giggle. He thought of the last twenty-four (or so) hours. With a whole solar revolution in the company of five rabid, rampant nymphomaniacs, each seventy-two degrees of rotation had brought him fresh honey and a heavenly creature of diabolical desires.

"Balls to the outbursts, you rotter," he reassured himself, loudly and carefree. "The madness suits you well."

Looking only marginally disheveled from his exertions, and as yet unruffled by guilt (for he still did not know that he was in love with Lorelei), he observed from the car window elbow nudges and sly looks from the throngs of curious eyes around the faculty. He alighted from the Packard, spoke briefly with the driver, who was seen to doff his hat in Johan Thoms's direction.

Johan Thoms marched off toward his dorm and yelled to the skies:

"Blasphemers and infidels. Degenerates and heretics. What a joy!"

These were turning out to be strange days indeed. That same day, William Atticus Forsythe Cartwright, discovered that he had inadvertently become a father back in Yorkshire. The child was a boy. Bill Cartwright's only son was to be called Ernest, and he would take his father's surname nine months later when he left his mother's bosom for the idle comfort of the Cartwright family and their ancestral home in Huddersfield.

Ernest Cartwright. My grandfather.

Eight

Just a Lucky Man
Who Made the Grade

*The exquisite art of idleness. One of the most important things any university
can teach.*

—Oscar Wilde

Easter Saturday 2003. Dawn.

The stuff about a twin town served a purpose. I had other ambitions, of
course. I chose Sarajevo with a very clear objective in mind, though that
is not to underestimate the difficulty of the task and the extremely unlikely
eventuality of finding *him*," said Ernest. "But by God, it was worth a shot!"

* * *

In the azure light of the hermit's shack, an old, stooping Johan Thoms
was urinating. Billy did not grow old as he, Johan, had grown old. He was cut
down in his prime before breakfast on July 1 of '16. It was just three years and
a handful of days from the morning when he had reveled around Sarajevo,
the quadrangle, the Old Sultan's Palace, Bascarsija, the Cellar, and the libraries, his huge and friendly heart bursting with pride, to the morning when he
was unceremoniously spread across a muddy French field between trenches.

It was a terrible waste.

When Johan spoke of his old pal, he twitched. He saw in Ernest's Anglo-Saxon features what Bill might have looked like had he grown old like the rest of them. He willfully transposed Bill's voice onto Ernest's, for it was uncannily similar. Had Bill really died? Was he, Johan, being haunted by his spirit? Was Bill asking for an apology from the other side?

Poor old bastard.

Ernest flicked through the erotic pictures in the second volume of the *Kama Sutra,* bound with cracking, but still-fine old vellum. Then Johan Thoms continued with his story, and my grandfather closed the book, his thumb marking a page.

"Over the next twelve months, we fell in love," Johan said, his eyes on the volume in Ernest's hand. "When she could be, she was with me in Sarajevo. We spent three weeks in Vienna in August of '13. In September, we met in Split and barely left the hotel room for five days. In October, we pretended to be strangers in Dubrovnik, much to the chagrin of the jealous patrons of a scummy bar where I'd sat smoking French cigarettes and drinking cheap schnapps until she came in—my blaze of beauty, my welcome enslaver, exhibiting a certain conductivity toward her center and seducing me in front of them. For some reason she took a photograph of me. Their sarcastic comments about the size of my head stopped.

"November saw us in Bucharest, planning a trip to the Carpathians. The letters came in her handwriting every other day. The days in between, I reciprocated. Often more than once, either side of luncheon.

"In December, she came to me. Usual room, usual service. As she did for nearly all of January and February. The winter was a bleak one, but not that bleak, given I spent most of it in the President, ordering room service and liberally helping myself to her. My tasks for Potiorek were menial, but for ninety-five forints I didn't complain. And on top of the decent money, I was given hours, even days, off at a time."

This dovetailed perfectly with Johan's libidinal demands, as well as his studies.

"In March and April, we reunited for lengthy weekends in Belgrade and then in Zagreb. On one of those two trips—Zagreb, I think—she warned me for the first time that if I did not calm down I would be dead of a heart attack by the time I was thirty-five. She worried for me. That's how she was. She gave me a glass paperweight containing a scrap of paper, five words. I read these words, which were in the tiniest of prints and the most immaculate font, and I knew that I need never look any further than her."

In May, Johan did not see her. He was busy coming top of the university in his examinations. This delay, his hiatus, just meant that June was going to be as sizzling as the previous year. For a full month he used his penis for urinating only, in preparation for her reappearance, for now he understood from the *Kama Sutra* the power of tantricity.

"It was a Friday. It was late in the month. All of June '14 was hot, lending a backdrop of craziness," Johan said. Ernest sensed a fulcrum approaching in the old man's tale.

"Lorelei was to be at the Hotel President for at least another fifteen days and nights. We would be spending very little time if any in my college dorm, though she had put in a special request to have a private hour there together one afternoon."

*   *   *

That Friday morning Johan had a 6 A.M. appointment with Müller. He rose at four-thirty, using his own alarm-clock system of drinking a glass of water for every hour under six he wanted to sleep. This would guarantee his bladder would wake him, asking to be emptied.

He wetted an impudent and belligerent cowlick, checked his teeth, including the slightly crooked ones on his lower set, hissed through them, and slapped his cheeks to hasten the blood flow.

Twenty seconds later, after having taken a mental picture of sleeping beauty, he kissed the warm skin on her cheek, declined to roll her over and molest her in her (initial state of) sleep. Subconsciously he stepped backward. He could NOT be late.

"I'm going to get you later," slipped out.

"Stop doing THAT!" slipped out next, and he was forced into shaking his head like a crazed soaked dog to rid himself of another attack of the blurts.

Five large strides and he was out the door.

He marched down Musala Street, Franz Joseph Street, across the Appel Quay, over the river via Kaiser Bridge, and into the plush neighborhood of

Bistrik. As he reached the militaries, puffing at the front gates, he checked his pocket watch, chained proudly to his houndstooth waistcoat.

He approached the chattering bunch, coughed lightly, and announced his arrival.

"Guten Morgen."

It was a new bunch of soldiers, whom he had not seen before. The atmosphere had changed.

One soldier, who clearly held himself in some sort of authority, stepped forward, checked out Johan, and upon seeing his blue eyes gestured with a single neck-and-chin thrust to proceed through the gates. The crowd parted.

The mob of gray uniforms, peaked caps, rifles, and mustaches watched the boy. He swaggered toward the Konak, past the shade of an unusually pissy sentry box. His upright confidence, his perfect Hanoverian German, and his bespoke tailoring gave an impression of wealth and breeding, belying his status as a (once) near-penniless student from Argona.

As he approached the Konak, a tall, wiry, bent figure appeared in the entrance. It eyed Johan and stepped into the morning sunshine. It was Müller, Potiorek's right-hand man.

"Thoms?" he hollered.

He looked Johan straight in the eye—with one of his eyes, anyway. The other, his right, jutted off at forty-five degrees over Johan's left shoulder, giving the impression that he was able to weep down his back. Müller seemed permanently bent at the waist at a curiously similar angle to the strabismus of his eyes. An angle at the corner of his mouth offered a permanent smile. It was an odd combination, but Johan found it a most disarming and pleasant permutation. Whether the crooked smile was there by birth or through injury, it seemed fortuitous, as it fitted the official's general demeanor and mood perfectly. It told no lies. Müller's bony hand patted Johan on the shoulder in a further gesture of familiarity.

Johan was now ushered into the Konak and its true interior, which previously had been out of bounds to him.

"Thoms, come with me, let's have a chat. You seen round this place properly?" Müller asked, gesturing loosely to its Renaissance splendor. It looked fine in the light cast by the early sun, framed by an early-morning silence, save for a few birds. The air carried a ribboned raft of honey from a nearby abundance of tuberoses. "Come, you will need to know your way around here like a rat in a drainpipe before too long. I will tell you the rest as we go. It's all pretty simple. But first take off that tie, jacket, and waistcoat. Mmm, rather nice, I must say, young man," he said as he fingered Schneider's cloth.

"Save that for when *they* arrive on Sunday."

Nine

The Accusative Case

The dance is a poem of which each movement is a world.

—Mata Hari

Easter Saturday, 2003. 4 P.M.

Müller opened the fifteen-foot-high iron gates to the compound housing thirty sparkling Packards, the fleet for the Hapsburg military hierarchy. The loose gravel rattled below, scraping the bottom of the entrance.

Johan observed the exquisite cars. He had never been interested in their machinations, their whirring, combusting, blowing, and chugging under the bonnet. He focused on their practicalities, their path from *A* to *B*. His favorite case in German was the accusative, that involving movement. The car allowed him movement. Time allowed him movement.

Overeager, impatient, and optimistic as ever, Johan Thoms had never considered moving backward.

*   *   *

He looked at my grandfather.

"If only I could go back now in Time, and correct my single mistake, which has led to hundreds of millions of deaths!" he said to Ernest in the nervous blue light of the hut. "If only I had gone back then, in Space. Reversed that blasted car outside that damned café! Then I could give Billy another chance! Maybe he would then have to face the ignominy of growing old and weird, like everyone else."

He thought again of Cartwright and he was enveloped in remorse.

"The accusative case . . . *den, die, das, die* . . ."

I digress. Back to 1914. Back to June the twenty-sixth.

*　　*　　*

Müller and Johan strolled along the row of cars, admiring the workmanship, smelling the newness.

"All ready for *his* visit on Sunday," Müller proudly announced.

Then the forint dropped. Johan knew who *he* was.

"*They* will be staying here at the Konak, after the maneuvers have been inspected by His Highness. Everything must run like clockwork, my boy. You will be transferring some of the vehicles to the railway station tomorrow. Everything goes by the Miljacka along this route." He handed Johan some folded papers.

"Urban and Loyka will be driving on the day. You will do as they say. We are having a briefing for all at two this afternoon. Any questions so far?"

"Yes, lots, sir."

Müller grabbed the papers back out of Johan's hands before he could examine them.

"All in good time, son. All in good time."

Johan frowned.

*　*　*

Meanwhile, in the luxury of her room, Lorelei slept. When she stirred, she pulled from her embossed trunk a copy of *The Arabian Nights*.

Turkish expansionism had left an indelible mark of the Orient in every nook and cranny of ancient Sarajevo. This made it the perfect place to immerse herself in the eroticism of this Eastern classic. For here, she heard morning prayers from her hotel window and breathed the smells of the East. Boring, rigid Vienna held no such mysticism. She yearned to delve deeper into the Orient, through Constantinople, over the Bosphorus, across the Silk Roads to India, Rangoon, Malaya, and China. But for now, this would suffice: to observe, smell, and listen from the coziness of her hotel window, to be absorbed in the pages of her tome.

Sixty pages in, she dozed off. The vellum-bound masterpiece nestled itself under the pillow, later to be charged inadvertently with the massive responsibility of propping up Johan Thoms's skull. Much, much later, a trio of similar books would become (in his crooked mind) a possible portal, a potential wormhole in the space-time continuum, to take him back in history on his solitary magic carpet ride to change the world.

Ten

The Black Hand

Decency is indecency's conspiracy of silence.

—George Bernard Shaw

Johan held up his hand to Ernest in apology. "Please tell me if I am tell-ing you facts of which you are aware. I am no history teacher. Did you know that if one kills a man, one is an assassin; if one kills millions, one is a conqueror; but if one kills everybody, one is a god." [5]

What he told of then was the terrain of myth and legend. And of hard and menacing men.

Narodna Odbrana (National Defense) recruited and trained young men to fight for its anti-imperialist cause. Indoctrination was minimal, as hatred for the imperialists in Vienna was tangible from a young age. It was as innate as it had been once inert, and saboteurs and agents provocateurs were rife throughout the territories as well as inside Austria itself. The mis-chief of this fifth column increased with the passing weeks and months. They—Narodna Odbrana—had become so effective that the government in Vienna recognized their work, openly asking diplomatic Belgrade to curb the terrorists' actions. Belgrade's old ally of Moscow was in no position to back up the Serbs at this point, given the Russians' recent exertions against the Japanese. So Serbia relented to Vienna, but with reluctance. Whether the Serbs continued to encourage more covert operations is difficult to determine. That a blind eye was turned is probably closer to the truth.

Johan was keen to point out to Ernest that the insurgents were not all of the same level of experience.

"Yes, there was a conspiracy," he said. "But you know that the literal translation of conspiracy is 'to breathe together.' These *café conspirateurs,* these ragtag, epistatic assassins, could hardly breathe individually, never mind together. This is why they were chosen. Each had developed tuberculosis, and so could be recognized from forty yards by a chest-rattling bloody cough. Each carried Cabernet-stained handkerchiefs. The ugly splutter of infection means that the illness's victims can identify one of their own in a bar or on a tram. The cough is that of a peeved sea lion. It is one of nature's sicker versions of the wood pigeon chatting on a sweet April morning to his mate, or a whale's haunting moans from a thousand miles. The grubby body would jackknife; the burgundy cloth would be produced almost immediately, invariably from an old gray jacket, shredded down to a hessian sack. The hand would cover the mouth in a spasm of the whole torso and chest. Veins would protrude on the neck, the eyes crossing and watering. A blob of spittle dropped into the manky rag, which was then checked for its blood content. The victim knew already that there was blood there. It was one more ratchet to his last day, his last breath, yet he would always open the cloth to check its contents, in the infinitely optimistic hope that it might be clear, just a mouthful of gob. As if it were just a summer head cold he remembered having had as a six-year-old. He would pray for a palmful of yellow dribble with snotty green islands. Yet he knew what to expect. Death, or more precisely *Mycobacterium tuberculosis,* now known as *bacillus tuberculosis.* A little parasitic beggar which attacks the mucous membranes of the lungs. It forms nodules called tubercles, causing rampant bleeding. It was angry enough in its own distant youth to occur elsewhere on the geography of the body, including the balls and even the unsuspecting hip. The fungus then became saprophytic. This meant that it digested the organic matter which it had destroyed before moving on to the next course. A cancer mutates and grows as a tumor; TB simply eats the cells away."

Johan broke off for a minute. Ernest thought better of speaking.

"I knew little of it at the time," the older man continued. "I was busy having fun. If I had read newspapers like I read books, I would have known. If anything, some militant Serbs were perceived dangerous individuals and thugs in alleys and bars with razors and broad fists."

With the potency of one's strength reduced by the entry requirements of either youth or tuberculosis, one's level of proficiency is likely to be far lower. One such boy had been charged with the assassination of the Hapsburg military chief, General Potiorek. The murder weapon of choice was a poisoned dagger. The venue was Vienna. He had botched that, even leaving his tool back in Belgrade.

And so, a dedicated faction of the National Defense was founded: Ujedinjenje ili Smrt (literally Union or Death) was born.

For the fear of underusing vowels, may we from now on refer to Ujedinjenje ili Smrt under their usual anglicized name of the Black Hand?

This was their seal:

On that same founding night, a sick young man called Gavrilo Princip was inducted while spluttering vile germs from his lungs. He had a lazy eye and he wore a hard-pencil mustache. His would be a special task.

The Black Hand was a dark and multiplying cell of nefarious intentions, and its appetite for destruction was growing.

Eleven

The Day Abu Hasan Broke Wind

Murder is born of love. And love attains the greatest intensity in murder.
—Octave Mirbeau

Sunday, June 28, 1914. Central Sarajevo.

At dawn, an airless and stifling heat blanketed the ancient citadel. The city was ready for the royal visit.[6]

June the twenty-eight, was St. Vitus Day, a day celebrated by Serb nationalists.

As he left suite number thirty of the Hotel President, Johan noticed a sign hanging on the inside of the door. It read:

DO NOT DISTURB

If only he had read the sign differently and left EVERYONE on the planet alone.

* * *

The child beggars gathered around the fountain in Bascarsija. Out of pride, they would take money but never food.

Down each alley, a coffee dealer buzzed around, shuttling shiny trays of extra-rich *kavna* (strong coffee) back and forth to his foot soldiers in their rattling bazaars which held enough copper to melt down to arm a huge battalion. These men needed to keep their energy levels up for their days were long. It was easy to nod off at the back of their establishments, hypnotized by the constant whir of the charmers of Arabia. There the chiming trinkets from Gilgamesh and marmites from Babylonia gave way to an array of pipes, able—they say—to raise a hundred snakes to dance. Old men with folded miens leaned over chessboards. The verdegris of every mosque roof seemed greener than ever against the bluest sky.

Crowds had started to line the route along the river early in the morning. For the sake of image, only a meager local police force of one hundred and twenty were scattered along the thoroughfare. The army had been given the day off. Policemen lackadaisically chatted among themselves or sucked on rolled-up cigarettes. A couple of them looked seriously hungover. Some were unshaven. Peaked caps (kepis) were atilt. The men wearing them exuded an air of disinterest and boredom. Early clouds had burned away. Little children held flags of the Hapsburg royal crest, breathing in the pipe-tobacco smoke of uncles and fathers.

Drago and Elena Thoms had already walked the length of the route by the river, the Miljacka. Drago completed the distance in roughly half the number of Elena's strides, avoiding any large cracks in the pavements. Using his symmetry gland, he noticed the same hacking cough at equidistant intervals along the banks of the river.

It was rare for them both to get to the city these days. They used to love it in the olden days when they were first in love, their stolen evenings at an old spot called Parioli. He would always preorder her favorite bisque for her; "with the lobster on the side," he would add, knowing she found this adorable.

They were now back, proud that their boy had bailed them out of their temporary crisis, eager to see him in his smart new suit, shiny dress shoes, and Sunday haircut, and in the company of royalty. Along the ceremonial route, two hours before the Archduke was expected, a solitary Packard swept by. In the back, a balding pale-skinned character with bulging green eyes and a mustard-plaid jacket waved his arms extravagantly, with instructions for his steady, angular driver. So angular that Drago almost thought of Pythagoras, but instead simply queried, from his lofty position:

"Who the hell is that idiot?"

"Don't know, darling. But he looks very familiar." Elena grimaced. The murmur of the crowd calmed Drago, but Elena still tried to place the Germanic face in the car. She had narrowed it down to a face in a sepia photograph, maybe a decade earlier.

A whiff of ylang-ylang took Drago's nostrils as a creature of rare, foreign, and wild beauty in white strolled confidently past them. She held a fine copy of *The Arabian Nights*. Drago could not take his eyes from her as Elena's elbow met his ribs, followed by a wry, loving, knowing smile. He admired this stranger's full lips, as plump as Amalfi figs in June, and wondered how her skin would look with goose bumps.

Billy Cartwright, having gained a foothold from a brick outhouse (which he resembled) at the side of the college steps, had climbed a nearby tree outside the Madresa faculty for a better vantage point. He had scaled the wall with a cold drink, a banana, and a giant doorstep of warm bread in his large paw.

The lung-hollowing cough was back. Someone was ill, Drago thought. "Give them a year at best," he said.

"Kaunitz, Count Kaunitz, of course! Remember the deer? That was him with the popping eyes. The deer! The deer that nearly popped out Johan's eyes!"

Another cough. Someone close by would be checking his handkerchief.

"They really shouldn't put others at risk," Elena pointed out.

"Probably a Serb. Poor bastard."

Fezzes of swollen-glans mauve and chunky Turkish mustaches mixed in with homogeneous Western dark suits, the clipped and oiled haircuts. This did not help the identification of their boy.

Ylang-ylang walked back in the opposite direction. Drago closed his eyes, enhancing the olfactory pleasure, believing too, that this would dramatically decrease the chances of a second bruised rib. He didn't know that his son had bought the fragrance and that his own flesh and blood had fallen in love with its wearer.

* * *

Half a mile away, at the train station, the platform clock ticked toward eight. Johan stood on the side steps, elegant and handsome in Schneider's finest. He was keeping an eye out for his parents, for his belle, resplendent in white, and for his crazy best pal.

He soon met Kaunitz. The Count admired his friend's latest purchase from the tailor and they embraced.

Johan's fellow chauffeurs, Leopold Loyka and Franz Urban, eyed them with suspicion. Johan believed he heard the word *Upstart!* muttered. Was there also a homophobic comment?

The drivers smelled of booze, and had not bothered to shave. Slovenly, they paced the steps of the station. Their old shoes lapped, dusty and unpolished.

Urban was a mustachioed, grubby Prussian, perhaps fifty years old, a mere five feet five. His eyes were way too close together.

Would not trust a marsh hound with eyes so close and so beady! Johan thought.

Loyka was even shorter, and looked like he would snap an ankle if he fell off the curb. His greasy hair was slapped down to the right, the parting more crooked than the Carpathians. He had cabbage in his mustache. Their level of interest in their duties seemed worryingly low.

Urban and Loyka expelled sickening guffs of wind in a nauseating tournament. From time to time, one of the shocking creatures would strike a match to extinguish the vile odor.

They would not ordinarily have bothered to get rid of the stench. Müller, however, was on his bent, wonky-eyed prowl, for even a seemingly tolerant gent had his limits.

Repulsed municipal officials, train guards, and cops alike kept their distance from the perpetrators, who meanwhile delighted in their own antics.

Johan had been keen to wish them both a good morning at seven A.M., as agreed in their briefing, but they had been nowhere to be seen. Müller had appeared shortly after and checked out Johan's immaculate appearance through his nystagmus. When Müller asked if he had seen Urban and Loyka, Johan could only tell the truth, but he attempted to leave things open-ended.

"I have not, sir, but I have not been here that long. And I was reading some of the notes, so they could easily have, you know . . ." And he trailed off.

Müller had shaken his head, resigned to more incompetence from the pair. When eventually the duo had stumbled in, they were followed by a distinct smell of stale urine. The hum was exacerbated by the heat of the morning and the lack of any fresh air in the old stone station.

At seven minutes to nine, Loyka was in the process of cupping his hand to his behind and aiming the offending rancidity toward a giggling Urban like a six-year-old when Müller turned the corner with General Walrus. Whether the General's presence swayed Müller's decision is impossible to determine and can only now be a matter of conjecture, but he was left with little choice but to dismiss the two aging scalawags for the day. They were placed on a disciplinary charge on the spot, and, later in that momentous week, were fired for good.

In the background stood Johan, their antithesis. Erect, smart, polished, eyes hinting at intelligence, someone in whom one might almost trust! He was revealed to Müller and Potiorek as the ghastly pair scuttled away. Müller sensed where Herr General was looking as he barked, "Yes, do it . . . Good lad . . . Him . . . Like."

The General's telegram-speak was becoming neither more expressive nor more expansive.

General Potiorek headed back into the station, leaving Müller to approach Johan.

"Thoms, my boy. You are now on driving duty. Stand by for further orders. I am counting on you!"

"Yes, sir." Johan beamed, fully confident that it was not tough to perform better than Urban and Loyka.

Billy, Lorelei, Ma, and Pa were going to be so proud. Whether he was to drive a car for junior officials or simply signal the start of the royal convoy, it really did not matter to Johan. He might even get his picture in the newspaper!

"Imagine THAT! My picture in the paper. I could be famous!" he said.

*　*　*

Billy Cartwright recognized the fine swagger of a figure in white and smiled to himself. It was Lorelei, of course. He was still up the ash tree. He had heard of Johan's father's tendency to climb trees, but seemed to recall that it was related to thunderstorms. He decided to check the trees along the route anyway for Thoms Senior. He picked out only a policeman, who appeared to have dozed off in a sturdy oak by the promenade along the Miljacka.

A shuddering cough broke the soft murmur of the crowd as numbers slowly gathered. Cartwright was spending equal time searching for his best pal, his best pal's mad father, and pretty girls.

Back at the station, Johan heard the unmistakable chug of a steam engine heading toward the central platforms.

A minor brouhaha surrounded the arrival of the train carrying the royal party from the leafy western suburb of Ilidza, where the couple had overnighted at the Hotel Austria.

Billy was still high in his tree, hair flopping over his tan face, playfully whistling at passing girls or pulling faces at young children. If they did not give this bonobo chimp his rightful fill of attention, he pretended to fall, banana still in hand, half peeled. When there was no one there to wind up or annoy, he yelled, in a friendly tone, at a small Turkish-looking boy passing beneath him, "Hey you. I know you. I never forget a fez!" The boy looked confused and embarrassed. Bill smiled to himself, and moved on to pondering the actual differences between his twin heroes—heresy and blasphemy.

* * *

Among the crowd, Drago and Elena waited, eager and proud.

* * *

Urban and Loyka trundled themselves through the alleys of Bascarsija to a nearby bar, buffered from the searing sun by a cloud of flatulent filth, growling obscenities to each other through manky green and gray teeth.

* * *

Lorelei had just been learning from *The Thousand and One Nights* how the ruler of the lands, Caliph, had planned to kill his new wife, Scheherazade, as he had slaughtered all his previous wives, after just the one night of passion. Lorelei glanced up from time to time from her comfortable seat at the front of the crowd to try to catch a glimpse of her beau.

Caliph Harun al-Rashid was not able to kill Scheherazade, though. Each night, the clever beauty would tell him another installment of an ancient tale of murder and revenge. The tale captured the Caliph's imagination. Each night, Scheherazade's life was spared, for her story was unfinished. By the time one thousand and one Arabian nights had passed, Scheherazade had borne the Caliph five beautiful children, and his love for her was real. They lived happily ever after. (Well, until they died.)

Scheherazade was now embarking on the ancient tale of "The Day Abu Hasan Broke Wind.

* * *

THE ANCIENT TALE OF ABU HASAN

In Arabia of old, as today, the breaking of wind was a much-frowned-upon activity. Abu Hasan was a respected and learned man of many qualities. He prided himself on his etiquette.

However, one day while at lunch with the Sultan, he accidentally farted. Such was his shame around the palace that he banished himself from Baghdad to China. He mounted his camel and rode off in the direction of the Orient.

After many years, he yearned for the city of his youth, so he decided to return. Many months he rode from the end of the world to the ancient city of Baghdad. He reached it late one night. He decided to stop outside the walls of the city, which he would enter at dawn in full daylight. As he tried to fall into a slumber that night beneath the cold stars, he heard the wailings of a young girl next to his tent. When he listened at her door, he discovered that she was to marry the next day. The only reason, however, for her weeping was that she wanted to know her exact age. Her mother could not tell her this. The only thing the old crone could tell her was that her beloved daughter had been born in the year that Abu Hasan had farted. Abu Hasan was overtaken by grief and embarrassment. He mounted his camel once more, and cursed the people of Baghdad as peasants who kept track of time only by his flatulence. He disappeared off toward the horizon, never to be seen again.

* * *

— Lorelei giggled. She thought of reading the story to Johan later, in a park, cooled from the sunshine under a tangerine tree.

* * *

Potiorek took his position with the other dignitaries, numbering fifteen in total, on the dusty station platform. The Walrus's military uniform, laden with medals, stood at the group's apex. A grim shadow of black suits and top hats flanked the General symmetrically, like a formation of geese heading south.

Elena, who also possessed an osmotic sense of symmetry, asked Drago every thirty seconds if he could see anything. He offered to lift her onto his shoulders. She considered accepting his unconventional offer.

With a burst of black, grubby smoke and genteel applause, the train pulled into the station.

Archduke Franz Ferdinand and his adoring, pregnant wife, Sophie, disembarked from their plush carriage to a fanfare of buglers, one of whom was distinctly off-key, much to the Countess's amusement. She politely half smiled to herself, which brought a rouge blush to her porcelain cheeks. The note actually deserved more of a belly laugh, but Sophie knew that they had left the womb of the Hapsburgs and were in the provinces. Franz noticed her snigger, and smiled happily to himself at her wonderful ways and at the bugler's inner turmoil. He placed a reassuring royal hand in the small of her back. Instantly she became unaware of all else, only of the secure touch of her (if not yet Austria's) emperor.

The Walrus Potiorek stepped forward to welcome the couple as Johan watched from a distance. He felt a presence at his side and turned to see the friendly face of Müller.

"Thoms. You are to drive the first Packard. You will be driving *them*."

Johan felt a rush of adrenaline surge to his extremities.

"Simply drive to the City Hall, straight along Appel Quay. The reception and luncheon will be held there. I trust you more than those other clowns."

"No problem, Herr Müller," Johan said before striding purposefully to the vehicle, the first of eight.

Minutes later, Walrus approached, leading the royal pair. Johan already had taken his seat and had the engine idling. He looked straight ahead as the three dignitaries climbed into the rear seats, the Walrus facing the back, opposite Ferdinand, resplendent in a light powder-blue military uniform and plumed cocked hat, and his radiant lady, Sophie Chotek, Her Serene Highness, the Princess of Hohenberg.

The couple smiled, radiating warmth and humanity. This belied the local propaganda, which Johan had weighed (and largely discarded) during his time at college. Radical ideas permeated the colleges there, as they did almost every European school at the time, but Johan tried to sidestep the egos of those who ranted at rallies, waved pamphlets, and grew self-important beards. If Cartwright had been political, then Johan might easily have been more exposed to an ideology, dragged along, and soon swayed. Cartwright, however, opted for mischief, girls, and mischievous girls; and for now Johan suspected it smart to follow his pal's wisdom.

Johan was so relaxed now that he even felt he should be in the back with them, especially as he had started to quite *like* them. There was a magnetism in them, and certainly between them. He even found himself slowly nodding his approval.

He overheard Potiorek outlining the timetable to the couple, and then some giggles and laughter among the three. The first car, driven by Johan Thoms, then pulled off, steady speed, smooth clutchwork, low revs.

They left the station compound. Johan could hear nothing now above the sound of the engine and the low din of the crowds. They left the shade and drove into the full glare of the midsummer's day.

* * *

Elena Thoms fainted when she saw her son driving the Archduke Franz Ferdinand, Countess Sophie, and General Potiorek. Drago didn't know what to do. Johan was not quite sure whether he saw the broad grin of the world's proudest father in the corner of his eye.

Out of character, Lorelei became slightly flushed when she saw Johan. She slid off her chair and headed toward her hotel, in order to prep herself for him with a chilled bottle of brut. She kept her thumb in *The Arabian Nights,* on page one of "The Tale of Kafur the Black Eunuch," which she would relish in the cool of her chambers.

* * *

Several assassination attempts had been planned. Belts, braces, belts. The dangerous figures who made up the vast majority at the menacing gatherings of the Black Hand bore absolutely no resemblance to the *café conspirateurs* who had been handed this important task. No, these were young, inexperienced boys in a hard man's world. And it would show.

Nedjelko Čabrinović, Cvjetko Popović, and Danilo Ilić were charged with the responsibilities for three of the contingency attacks, but only if the first assassin, one Muhammed Mehmedbasic, failed. Mehmedbasic lost his nerve when the cars approached along the Appel Quay. Even though he had been drilled thoroughly, he forgot to count to ten after pulling the pin on his grenade. Johan saw what he thought was a bomb rise up out of the crowd. It was about to land in the back of his Packard, but he accelerated. The device hit the back of the car and exploded on the road to his rear, seriously injuring the two people in the car behind. One was the Count of Mancini, a close friend of the Archduke's.

Other attempts were made by the Black Hand, equally disorderly. Unsteady hands fired bullets wide; a lunge with a bayonet from behind the lines only scratched the paintwork of the Packard; a backfiring handgun was knocked from a would-be assassin's hand by a teenage girl. The others in the gang of seven did not even have the courage to attempt their duties. As for Gavrilo Princip, the captain of the crew, he fled, and sloped away to his shame. The three members of the Black Hand who had had the courage to at least attempt their duties were apprehended.

First, though, came further ignominy. They had planned to swallow their phials of cyanide and jump into the rapids of the Miljacka for a glorious martyr's end. (Or, if they were lucky enough to be in a position to flee, the entrances to the sewers on the south banks should have led them to safety.)

After the indignities of malfunctioning weapons, unexploding devices, and abysmal marksmanship, each of the coughing, spluttering trio of failed assassins had stormed, at distances a furlong apart, through the crowds. They then swigged their poison and, from the walls by the river, faced the crowds and declared, "Greater Serbia until Eternity!" They each then turned and leaped into the river.

However:

- According to the municipal physicians questioned later in the afternoon, their cyanide capsules were over ten years old. This lapsed time made the otherwise lethal liquid very unlethal. It was, however, toxic enough to make an already weak man throw up, a vomiting so violent that it could make the subject believe that he was about to throw up his own pelvis.

- The tide was out. There would be no death upon impact in a fast-flowing river, bodies swept away to oblivion in a romantic swish. Instead, sick skinny wretches in hessian sack suits, bad mustaches, and greased side partings, dripping with vomit, infested with lung blood, manky vegetables, and possibly shards of pelvic bone in their wiry facial hair, stood up to their waists in a shitty mud bath, surrounded by a politely baying mob (politely, for there were children present).

The cops, excited by an event of any kind in this backwater, dragged the men out of the sludge and carted them off for questioning.

* * *

The convoy reached the City Hall, a stunning design in the style of the ancient Mameluks. There, the local dignitaries acted as if nothing untoward had happened, and attempted to carry on with all the scripted details in their itineraries. Officials darted around in the mayhem. This all may seem incredible given the attempts on Ferdinand's life. It would be so easy to edit those grainy Keystone Cops flicks of the time into the footage that still survives of Sarajevo on June 28, 1914. One would never know where slapstick Hollywood ended and the day that changed the world began. The footage of the steps of Sarajevo City Hall might suddenly include a young Charlie Chaplin, a spazzy-eyed Mack Sennett, or deadpan Buster Keaton. In the midst of a Fatty Arbuckle scene would appear two drunken, flatulent grubsters staggering to a bar, Bill Cartwright in a tree eating a banana, or our innocent young hero, Johan Thoms, looking bemused but serene as the day's crazy events unfolded around him. Inside the City Hall, however, the talks started as planned. Ferdinand was dumbfounded.

"What is the good of your speeches?" he asked when he had recovered his ability to speak. "I come to Sarajevo on a visit and I get bombs thrown at me. It is outrageous."

Kaunitz's arms were in full windmilling mode.

News filtered through of Mancini's serious injuries. Ferdinand insisted on visiting him in the hospital. "We must. Come on. Drive me. Sophie, you please stay here, my dear."

Potiorek butted in. "Your Highness. Do you think that Sarajevo is full of assassins?"

Now it was the pregnant Sophie's turn. "As long as the Archduke shows himself in public today, I will not leave his side."

And so it was settled. But Johan had received other instructions: to head to the military inspection outside the city; also others: to drive back to the train station.

So it was that Johan drove the Packard off from the City Hall with his passengers, into a void.

The city had settled into a surreal calm. If you have ever been in Baton Rouge, Biloxi, or Key Largo after a hurricane, then you have witnessed a similar stillness, under silent skies of deep azure. The drive toward the military camps (or was it the hospital? or the train station?) began in such a still, queer silence.

Heading west, Johan reached the crossroads by the Miljacka, opposite the right turn north into Franz Joseph Street by the Latin Bridge.

Johan Thoms turned.

The confused orders and the silence had disoriented him. Now, alone again with Ferdinand, Sophie, and Potiorek, he took a ninety-degree turn away from the river and trundled forward into the city. The reason would remain a mystery for decades.

There on the corner (and still there today) was the *parfumerie* where he used to refill his El Capitán.

* * *

In the blue-lit shack, Johan tilted his head back and seemed for a while to be meditating. He lowered his gaze until he was staring into Ernest's eyes.

"A single whiff from that damned fine store sparks an involuntary memory in me. I know that I am a full eight hundred and forty-one miles from Paris. Even further from Proust's madeleine biscuit. I know these facts, but I am more lost than I can ever tell. This captured aroma leads me to imagine an errant act with my belle, involving the powder-blue plume feather which has blown from the Archduke's military headgear in the earlier furor and has settled on my driving seat.

"I turn right and head in the direction of the old Hotel President. This is what the history books say.

"I am in love. What can I tell you? How fragile we are. How fragile we ALL are.

"True to form, I am half in a reverie of last night's degeneracy and half in the evening to come, when all I need to do is to drive a car in a straight line by the river.

"However, the scent of that cologne is soon to be replaced by the pungency of burned gunpowder, and I am no longer elsewhere. On the opposite side, there stands the old café—Schiller's. A hacking cough emanates from within.

"Old Potiorek is still comforting the Archduke after the earlier attempts on his life, and paying particular attention to Sophie; she is quite the lady, after all.

"As before, Ferdinand and Sophie are sitting in the back facing forward, with the Walrus facing them. The car comes to a slow stop. My passengers gasp, seeming to realize that we are penned in, in an otherwise silent side street, by high, close, grubby walls. Ahead is a cul-de-sac, a temporary dead end, blocked off for the procession.

"From an open window above, I can hear the calming strains of the *Gymnopédies* from a pianist of some talent. Does this cause a pause? It certainly seems to.

"As I try to put the car in reverse gear (which I have never done before, but have also never imagined would be either required or difficult), we again hear a death-rattling cough from within the coffee shop. As the splutter grows louder and more frequent, I look up to the pavement outside. There stands an incredulous Gavrilo Princip, scabby sandwich in his wretched hand, gob open, half-chewed fatty pig covering his graying incisors. In slow motion (if slow motion can pass in a split second), a revolver that started its life in Russia is pulled from a jacket resembling a hessian sack, and three, four, five, and then six bullets are shot into the back of the Packard.

"On this somber and dangerous corner, my destiny and that of the twentieth century and beyond are decided. The unearthly consummation of my happiness has started."

Johan held up his hand to beg for Ernest's continued silence, and then looked away from him. They sat for almost an hour before Johan continued.

* * *

Franz Ferdinand took a soon-to-be-fatal shot in the neck and four more across his torso and arm; the pregnant Countess Sophie, one in the abdomen.

Franz and Sophie declared their undying love for each other as they bled and died slowly in each other's arms. They implored each other to stay alive to look after their offspring. One of Princip's few comments after his arrest was that his only regret was the love he had destroyed. He had had no idea that Franz Ferdinand was such a humane man, full of love for his family, full of love for his wife.

Later, between coughs, Princip would speak of his remorse far more articulately and with far more humanity than he had ever spoken of a Greater Serbia. It was as if some thing, some soul, had transmigrated from the back of the car that day into the creature who had destroyed it. Sophie and her unborn were dead within minutes.

* * *

Johan found himself repeating, blurting out loud just one word:

"*Zuruck . . . zuruck . . . zuruck . . .*" (Backward, backward, backward.)

He was still whimpering this an hour later as the royal physician covered the Ferdinands' drained, bloodless faces with a unifying death shroud. They lay on their luxurious bed in the Konak, where they should have slept soundly that night.

* * *

Bill Cartwright was heading back from the riverside through the park to his dorm. He approached two young boys, of maybe nine and fifteen years old, playing chess under an oak tree of biblical proportions. The concentration on their faces was almost as intense as the muck. The younger scruff, in graying white shorts and blue shirt, played black and faced his teenage counterpart, in khaki shorts and canary-yellow vest, shoeless, holding white. Cartwright hovered above them for ten seconds. The scenario did not look good for the older boy as the endgame neared. Bill tapped khaki and canary, no shoes, with the outside of his tough reddish brown leather Yorkshire brogue and announced, with a deadpan delivery, in English:

"If you need the answer, kid, just ask my girlfriend. She's got the answer for bloody everything! And if you don't take that damned castle soon, the bloody Prussians will!"

The kid just frowned, understanding not one word.

Cartwright waited for an answer, out of bloody-mindedness, though he knew none was forthcoming in a month of such Sundays.

"Speak up or forever hold your chess piece," he said.

Then he was on his way, leaving in his slipstream his unique version of harmless confusion.

"Some folk are as thick as ten thousand shithouse doors nailed together," he bellowed, shaking his head. Then in the distance, in the eerie lunchtime silence, he heard three, four, five, and then six gunshots. Thirty seconds later, he was being deafened by birdsong.

There were no camels, and this was not Baghdad, yet Abu Hasan had indeed farted.

Twelve

A Microcosm of the Apocalypse

If people would only read the Book of Revelations,
They would really turn around and straighten out.
It's all we need to do is get the Good Book,
Read it, put it to everyday life . . .
Sistas, Niggaz, Whiteys, Jews, Crackaz,
Don't Worry! If there's Hell below, we're ALL gonna go!

—Curtis Mayfield

June 28, 1914. Later on.

Oh my God! What the hell have I done?"
He slammed the door of his dorm room.

He reached for a bottle of clear liquid, which made him retch as he glugged it. His eyes watered and then the whites turned scarlet.

He put his head in his hands and staggered to the mirror, blindly.

When his hip crashed violently into porcelain, he took his hands away and examined his face. Diverging veins stuck out on his neck, resembling a Vienna tram line. He still had splats of royal-bluish blood on his face—a face which no longer bore the innocence it had when he had washed it that morning, kissed his girl, and bade farewell for the day.

"Sweet Lord!" he screamed. "Noooooo! What the fuck have you gone and done? By Christ, you will pay for this!"

He took more of the clear liquid, coughed most of it out onto the floor. He heard voices in his head.

* * *

Two old ladies in their toothless seventies were cleaning the college dorms when they heard screams. One knocked on his door, and she dropped her metal bucket onto the clean corridor floor. The clatter echoed in his skull.

An ample matron of a woman squeezed into the frame of the door before she was pulled back by a woman who could have been her twin. They found an unblinking boy, crumpled against the far wall, saying the same words over and over. The two now took up a perfectly framed position in the hallway, completing a symmetry that seemed to mock Johan's own mental state, for his previous desire to rush into the future was now met by a wish to return to the womb and the serenity of *yesterday*.

"It's a microcosm of the Apocalypse. It's a microcosm of the Apocalypse. It's a microcosm of the Apocalypse," *ad infinitum*.

"Has the poor dear gone mad?" the first woman wondered.

"No, no. Listen! I think he has a point," said the second old crone with a nodding wisdom as she slowly closed the door.

"He may indeed have trodden in more than he can chew."

* * *

Kaunitz, who had lost all his theatrical fluster, found Johan in his dorm after a brief search of the hotel. He sensed that Johan was itching to bolt, like a thoroughbred hoofing the turf with its front pins. For Johan, the path of least resistance would be to flee. The only option he had was to make Johan as comfortable as possible wherever this wonderful would-be *disparu* were to go. And the key to that was to protect his identity as the one whose error had led to the assassination, while still offering freedom of passage, food, shelter wherever he went.

Over the next day, Kaunitz managed to gather together a huge wedge of cash, some official-looking papers which would usually be months in the waiting and which had been hurriedly signed in Prussian and French scrawls, and a list of addresses pulled from a desk in the General's office by a compliant assistant.

The papers bore no date of expiration. They allowed unlimited travel and guaranteed a welcoming ear at embassies and consulates across the continent. Kaunitz had even procured Müller's help in requisitioning an embassy stamp, as well as the help of the visiting French diplomat, François Durand-Baudrit. Monsieur Durand-Baudrit, a stroppy, ignorant, short-tempered, garlicky, sweaty, stumpy Frenchman, and the Count were "acquainted" in their still-unholy version of the Masons. The love that dared not speak its name put its stamp on Johan's passport to a geographical freedom.

Kaunitz also set about spreading the story that a drunken Franz Urban had been the driver. For those with an eagle eye who have been there to deny this, a second myth was circulated, that Leopold Loyka was to blame. Only an old Pathé newsreel offers any alternative theory.

An Austrian bankbook, offering access to an account laden with one hefty and recent deposit of an amount with six zeros, appeared by late Monday. With the collusion of the dean, the Count had obtained a spare latchkey to Johan's chambers to prepare a kit bag for his pal, with its contents of paperwork, cash, bankbooks, valuables, a paperweight from Lorelei, his vellum-bound *Kama Sutra*, his letters, a cigarette case, and his El Capitán eau de cologne.

* * *

Johan knew he had used up eight of his nine lives already. He knew that his next, single brush with death would leave him with no further chance. He told himself, with some justification, that bullets flying past him by inches into the back of a Packard should be perceived as a near-death experience. He foresaw more bullets flying, and handcuffs clicking tightly onto his wrists.

"They will think I was in on it. They will think I am Black Hand, for how could anyone make such a dumb move and then be so unlucky as to meet the assassin?"

His mental machinations were given extra weight by his verbalizing them, clearly and at volume.

More calculus, more dy/dx's, more sigmas. The odds were too long, given the constant volume k of the authorities' paranoia.

He alone had been in charge of that car and (according to his own theory of the Universe) was directly responsible for the death of that wonderful couple in love and for the fact that their children were now orphans. There had been no fate, no master plan; just his huge error. He had spent his luck on surviving a fight with fourteen-blade antlers, and his brain had been further scarred by the reality-shifting devil absinthe.

His desire to love each moment on its merits (and to glide) had been more than pincered. It had been ruined—at least for now.

It was true; both his animal instinct and his highly tuned mathematical brain concurred:

"I am fucked. I have to run."

* * *

On the way back to his dorm, Johan had stopped at the Hotel President, and there consumed a bottle of vodka under the watchful eye of Herman, the bartender, who had presumed a lovers' tiff. Herman had been nearing the end of *Anna Karenina* when Johan had disturbed his calm. Johan scribbled on hotel notepaper, screwing up each leaf after a few seconds.

After an hour, tears almost in his eyes, he left.

Lorelei, not a hundred feet away, up in her suite, eagerly awaited his return, aching in a pair of his pajama bottoms. At around six o'clock, she came down, hoping to find him in the bar, all proud and full of tales. She was met by a sheepish Herman, dreading the sob story of a breakup. Herman was surprised to find a perky and cheery Lorelei, and, unable to marry the duo's moods, he asked her about her beau.

"Is everything *sehr gut* now with Herr Johan?"

"Herman?"

"Well, he was in a bad way. I thought that you two must be, you know . . . I see it *alles* the time . . . I see everything from here, ma'am."

"I'm here to meet him. You mean he was here before?"

"Yes, fräulein, since a couple of more hours ago. He was traumatized . . . Yes, this is the word . . . traumatized . . . *Scheisse,* my English is get good, *stimmt?*"

Lorelei turned on her heels to find Billy Cartwright in the doorway. He checked her face, which had lost its usual look of composure and confidence.

"Oh my God!" he said. "You have not heard, have you, lass?"

"Heard what?"

"Oh! Come here, girl." Bill took Lorelei's hand in both of his and came close to her. "He drove the car. He took a wrong turn. Ferdinand and Sophie were killed. I've been looking all over for him. Christ knows where he's gone, but there was an empty bottle smashed on his floor . . . and blood."

Lorelei's dark skin turned a shade of pale.

They were about to leave together when Lorelei stopped and asked Herman what time Johan had left.

"When he ran out of paper."

"What paper?" Bill said.

"All in *die Mull, mein Herr,*" and he gestured toward the waste bin behind his polished mahogany bar.

"Show me all of it," said Bill.

Herman pulled up the bin. He emptied the contents on the floor.

Together they started to uncrumple sheets, most of them illegible or stained with olives.

Bill stopped when he found one addressed to him.

William Cartwright,

> *My best friend . . .*
> *Always keep yer pecker up.*

For the first time in his life, Bill looked embarrassed.

Lorelei found one to Johan's parents, which simply read:

Mother, Father,

> *Thank you for everything.*
> *I am so sorry. I love you both.*
> *Always have; always will.*
> *Please do not imagine that you are not going to be daily visitors*
> to me.

> *Your loving son,*
> *Johan*

* * *

There was one left. Herman picked it up, unscrewed it, slowly read it, and passed it to Lorelei.

"I think this must be for you, fräulein."

She turned the paper toward her. It was a short note.

To my delicious fire!

> *By George, have I messed up!*
> *Cue frenzied worms.*
> *Adieu. Adieu. Remember me.*

Lorelei's dark eyes welled up.

"Stupid bloody idiot!"

* * *

Insult was added to injury when she discovered that he had charged the vodka to her room.

Adieu indeed.

Thirteen

A Farewell of Scarlet Wax and Gardenia

At least the Inquisition was about keeping something together. Analysis is only about taking a person apart. I would rather die than see an analyst.

—Werner Herzog

In the watery yellow light of the late afternoon at the Konak, the Count stared from an open upstairs window. He wondered if he, too, should leave the city, for if Johan was to blame for the events of that pivotal Sunday, then Kaunitz should bear some of the burden. However, he was several degrees of separation from the epicenter, and it was not he who had entered a daydream on the topic of Lorelei's undergarments and a feather, or entered a Sarajevan cul-de-sac without the skill to get out the way he had gone in.

But Johan had become the son Kaunitz had never envisaged. Besides arranging for Johan's safe passage, the Count had arranged for a delivery to the Thoms residence in Argona. A bouquet of gardenias addressed to Elena, with a small note in a lemon-yellow envelope, quill-addressed and scarlet-wax-sealed with his ancient forefather's royal ring.

Frau Thoms,

I am so sorry to hear of Johan's disappearance. I am sure he will be all right, for he is made of stern stuff, your boy. As I feel partly responsible for the unfolding of events, please allow me to be of any assistance possible. The work I had arranged for Johan was well paid. As you are no longer likely to benefit from your son's employ (for the immediate future), I have taken the liberty to furnish a private account with a little something for the two souls who gave the world something delightful and exquisite in your son and my friend, Johan Thoms. Do accept this to comfort your blow until that marvelous boy reappears to illuminate this barren and glum time. Please continue to be as proud of him as you always were. If you had seen him last Sunday morn, you would have burst. My, oh my, how smart did he look! If you did see him, just hold that thought, that image. And know that if it had not been for his quick thinking, there would have been bloodshed aplenty on the drive from the station; many more innocents, even children, could have been hurt.

If there is anything you need as a family or personally, of any nature, at any juncture, I would consider it politely hurtful if I were not the first to be asked to help.

Yours,
Count Erich von Kaunitz XV

Drago and Elena held each other as together they read the Count's letter.

Elena seemed a foot smaller and twenty pounds lighter already. Drago just stared ahead. The thought flashed through Elena's mind that there was something more than friendship or patronage in the relationship between the Count and her boy, but she dismissed it as irrelevant. The offer of help brought a tear to her eye. But it did not even register with Drago. He went into a lengthy episode, his hair twanging north, south, east, and west like the arms of some mad Hindu god he had once seen in one of the saucier of Johan Thoms's tomes.

* * *

Johan's feet hurt. He remembered embracing Kaunitz and taking a bag from him. He recalled talking to Herman on a road in the dark. He remembered not looking back. He tried to remember how long he had been walking. He could not.

He now felt a hole in his sock, and a burning blister. He wasn't sure where he was and why. He was wearing his suit, though it was in far from good condition. The newness of his shoes had rubbed his heels raw. He hopped from leg to leg to check the extent of the injury, peering down the side of each brogue in turn. He felt sandpaper stubble on his face. His hair felt oily and gritty, and his shirt hung below his waistcoat. His loose tie exposed two open buttonholes above the knot. Though Johan did not know the day, he could gauge it by his facial hair. It was Tuesday. Apart from a couple of involuntary shrieks of pain up to the celestials in the balmy summer sky, his chin felt as if it had been pointing groundward for hours. He instinctively headed west, toward his lone compass of the setting sun. It would lead him to the Adriatic, the sea, and into Italy—a buffer from a reality to which he was currently myopic. He had been grabbing on to his kit bag, with far too much gusto, he realized. He stopped in his tracks, pulled the army satchel from his dusty shoulder, and opened the bag. Good old Kaunitz!

Then he remembered, hazily, Kaunitz pleading with him to stay at the estate. He knew that the Count himself knew that his request was useless.

The topography of the landscape suggested he was tens of miles from the city. He could see no signs of life in any direction. He was walking country roads, over hills. Other than a pair of carefully mating hedgehogs, he'd seen not a living soul. He had walked far, then. He must have slept a few hours since leaving. He sat on the verge under a pine tree. His thirst became intense, hunger in its slipstream. He went into his kit bag and pulled out a cigarette from a gold case. He had seen the case before, when he'd spent a day in the country. He checked through the papers, and he then lit his smoke and studied the forms more closely. They were all extremely official looking, with stamps in different languages, illegible, spidery paw prints from Lord-knows-whom. They appeared to offer him a certain lofty status, which his current appearance belied. Yet it was not as much status as was offered to him by a bankbook from the Bank of Vienna, with one solitary entry in the first column, as well as a beautiful hide-leather wallet, made all the more beautiful by its stuffed contents—at least forty, maybe fifty one-hundred-forint notes.

Dizzy relief overcame him. He recalled a similar feeling from his childhood. He took just one of the notes and dropped it into his inside jacket pocket, where he saw Schneider's label. This dislodged his blocked memory: two corpses, professing their undying love in the back of a shiny Packard; gaping red holes in a neck and a pregnant belly. He puffed hard on the remnants of the cigarette, in a vain attempt to repress his memory. Dropping the butt to the dust under the tree, he closed his eyes tight. The pressure on his temples became immense. He tried to beat down the pain, but it only grew more intense. Now he was reminded of a different sensation from his early years, that of an umbilical cord, tight around his neck, images flashed cinematographically onto the screen of his inner eyelids: of his parents, shamed, in darkened rooms and behind closed doors; of Lorelei, wondering why he had abandoned her; the returning corpses.

How could anyone have turned such a dream of a situation into such abject horror?

How could anyone have grabbed so much notoriety from the jaws of notability?

How could anyone have fucked up so badly?

His head felt like it would implode. Eyes still closed, he took deep breaths to rid himself of the agony crushing his skull. He felt as though a hot knife were gouging out his left eye. He could not walk on in this heat. Franz and Sophie stared at him inquisitively, with their bullet holes pouring out a generously thick Merlot. He half prized open his right eye.

The pain notched up on the dial. He slipped toward unconsciousness, trying his best to think of smelling the Blue Rose of Forgetfulness. He tuned in instead to a personal showing of his worst nightmare:

Lorelei packs her things into the trunk. It has been delivered up by the sweaty porter, whom she had met previously under clearer skies. The manager has reserved her a sleeper cabin on the train, courtesy of an open check provided by Srna. She would enter the carriage from the same platform where the plumed Archduke had stepped several fateful days earlier.

She ponders how everything was as it had been before in the railway station. The hotel hall clock still ticked, the trains were on the same tracks, the same city hugged the structure in its womb. Everything is the same, but everything has changed: all the constants in the world could not turn back time. She is smart, she knows this. (Johan did not; he was about to start his lengthy search for portals and wormholes in the space-time continuum.)

And with the sounding of a rude horn, a station is full of choking warm steam and the din of a rumpus caused by a rabble of drunken Gypsies. Her time in this ancient city would now end. On the train, she stares straight ahead, typically stubborn, unblinking. The train hits a new daylight, within minutes it reaches the countryside. The carriage heads north through a Europe still green.

Johan's vision switched to mean and vengeful brows in uniforms, carrying revolvers and handcuffs, searching for the turncoat–agent provocateur–traitor who had ruthlessly sacrificed the Archduke and his princess. But none of them would think to look for *that* man in the still contours of a slumped figure beneath the branches of a tree in a field late in the day to the west.

Part Three

Here lies the body of Ezra Pound,
Lost at sea and never found.

—Ezra Pound

One

And the Ass Saw the Angel

Angels can fly, because they take themselves lightly.

—G. K. Chesterton

Early July 1914

A smell in his nostrils reminded him of his childhood. He felt like a piece of his brain had been removed, but he still knew that if it had, he would not know it. It was not just the smell that brought back a memory; it was the numb state behind his eyes. It was also the clinking and clanking of metal objects, the girls' chatter and the rapid, clipped sound their shoes made on the tiled floors.

"Hospital," he managed.

"That's right, precious. Just relax."

It was that same angelic tone he had heard as a child after the deer had impaled him. He felt clean, crisp linen up to his chest. His large head (the unstoppable force) sank into a concrete slab of regulation hospital pillow (the immovable object).

He dared to squint one eye open to see the bleach white of a hospital ward for the second time in his life. It seemed as if no time had lapsed in between. The truth was that things could not have changed more radically;

he would soon discover this in a report in a week-old newspaper. Ambassadors from Moscow, Paris, and London were making noises, echoing those of Belgrade. From Berlin and Vienna, Teutonic gutturals countered. Johan's brain was not too fuzzy to forget the principal Law of Physics, half confirmed by the headline EUROPE DAYS FROM WAR. Every action has an equal and opposite reaction. What the physics professor omits is that in real life, opposite reactions are rarely equal.

On an inside page, diplomatic releases from consulates around the continent were backed up by pictures of the state funeral. Johan recalled the death rattles. Boys from Frankfurt, Lyons, and Glasgow were now preparing to mobilize, all because he had been thinking about his (and/or her) nether regions.

The debut of a storm lightly tapped, with little rhythm, on the window behind him. A porcelain-faced angel in white appeared at his side.

"Your things, your jacket, your bag—everything is safe, my dear," she whispered. Johan remembered the kit bag and started to sweat. He reengaged his brain to focus on what the nurse had actually said.

"You're a lucky boy." Her breath touched his ear. "The farmer's lad who brought you in thought not to check your satchel or your pockets. People would smother your pretty face in the night for a lot less than that, you know. So, you behave and do as I say, and I will not tell them. Hmm?"

The angel's accent had a heavy Croatian clip to it. This confirmed that he had indeed been trekking west. She dried his frowning brow, slowly.

"Thank you," Johan said. He fell back into a slumber, relaxed by the cocktail of heavy opiates in his veins and the now rhythmic pentameter of a matured summer storm, finger-drumming on the cracked pane behind him. The nurse's sublime Gregorian mantra delivered him deeper, to near-coma.

You need to sleep, my sweets. You need to sleep. Sleep. Sleep, was its generous refrain.

* * *

The rain still battered the window when he stirred the next day, and the horror to which he opened his eyes possessed the breath of a blowtorch. Mickey was his name. A deranged, degenerate Irishman. Wild-eyed and near toothless, he was intent on finding out where his daughter, who he seemed to be convinced was frolicking with the devil, had hidden the whiskey.

"That bitch has horns under that hat! She-devil!" Mickey breathed into Johan's nostrils, and halitosis from hell made Johan violently retch from the deep south of his solar plexus.

"For God's sake, let me be." This was no time for his usual politeness.

"But it's not your grog she's taken, you selfish little arse. It's not right!"

"It certainly is *not* right!" Johan said, referring more to the Irishman's breath.

He had now stumbled back into full consciousness.

"You'd think Irish butter wouldn't melt in her mouth, but Mickey knows the truth. She is the dark one, all right. I'm no fecking idiot!" Johan shifted to the far side of his narrow bed as Mickey retreated upon hearing a nurse's footsteps in the hall.

Johan breathed again.

"Argh, by Jesus! You do know that this is the halfway house to hell? You can tell that by the way all the nurses talk to her, or I should say to *him,* Mephisto. What's your name, lad?" Mickey stood still, looked directly at Johan, and pointed with a gnarly digit.

"Please leave me be."

"Aye. Maybe I will do that. But I have to see if I might beat the Dark One, that I do," Mickey said, winking madly in time with his Irish lilt as he came closer again, working himself back into a froth. Johan reeled as far back as he could and raised his left knee to prevent any further encroachment.

Johan's main concern was now that he had perhaps been committed to a mental asylum. He glanced around the ward. There were two other beds, but one just revealed a bump under the covers, and the other was concealed behind a graying curtain, beyond which emanated the squelches of bodily ablutions and various moans.

Mickey's face was sunken, sullen, his eyes set deep, his cheekbones sharp and angular, like wrenches in a thinning sock. His green irises, their pupils dilated into black saucers, sat on yellowy whites with thin pink-veined corners. He was maybe five foot ten, but as he was crooked down toward Johan's bed, it was hard for the poor lad to judge. Mickey's bony hands had raised blue veins resembling pencils, and alabaster, yellowed fingers. They could have taken out an eye at two paces. His hair was thinning and curly. His eyes were off center. He had seen this in other drinkers. The long-term effects of his booze intake had permanently loosened his retinal musculature. His pajama top was unevenly buttoned and exposed a sunburned neck like a turkey's wattle. His earlobes sprouted fluff, which was lit by the daylight struggling through the grubby windows. One hirsute ear was significantly larger than the other and seemed to be erect, which, allied to his angular and sunken features, gave the impression of his having swallowed a coat hanger.

Mickey threw his arms toward the high ceilings of the Victorian ward to illustrate the size of the alleged horns on his daughter's head. His stained dressing gown fell open, and Johan spotted the weeping sores collected around his groin.

Johan tried to look away, but he had already seen that a green slime had collected at the tip of Mickey's urethra. It had coagulated into a teasing gloopy drip toward the sterilized tile. The wad fell with a splat onto the floor and formed its very own Emerald Isle. Mickey took his time in pulling the unfortunate robe together and knotting the belt.

The shameless Irishman blushed not as he continued on about his lot with Mephisto-Syphilis.

"Did I tell you that I am in love with a pretty one back in Ireland? She's a belter."

And with that, he pulled out a picture of the most angelic, pretty-featured Irish market girl. Even in sepia, one could make out eyes greener than Mickey's used and gonorrheal towels. Mickey got close again. In his bed, Johan shuffled away from the hot, dry, beastly winds from Mickey's back teeth. If the devil did indeed exist in Mickey's head, it was behind his crumbling teeth and on his crusty, felty tongue.

Johan turned onto his right side, hoping Mickey would get the hint and leave him be. He thought of his own girl, Lorelei, and where she would be right now. He needed a cigarette to forget.

"Damned lunatic!" Johan blurted in a tight spasm, a tic now in his left eye. Fortunately, Mickey was well out of radar.

As the madman trekked off to his corner, diagonal to Johan's, in swept the disinfected angel. The ridiculous deferred to the sublime.

"Nurse, where am I?" Johan asked with slight panic.

"Do not worry, my sweet. They are not all like our Irish friend. His daughter works here. My best friend. He followed her here from Ireland. Mad. As for the others, the poor boy over there has rare cancer or something." She gestured to the corner of the ward to his right.

"Only a kid. Maybe only has two months. Opposite is Gabriel. Lost his foot in the farmyard, silly lad. Though we were a bit concerned about your babble and nonsense when you came in, you are not in Mickey's league. Not yet, anyway. And to answer your question, you are about ten miles to the east of Mostar, Johan Thoms."

He did not feel surprised as she addressed him by his full name.

His body, however, filled with adrenaline.

"Does my name mean anything to you?" he asked.

"Should it, my sweet? Are you famous?"

Johan looked away. "No, no. Forget it. Am I all right? What happened to me? Am I allowed to leave?"

"Slow down, handsome. You only have headaches, on one side. You are free to leave at any time. Unless you are on the run from the police? Is that why I should know who you are? Is that why you have all that money in that kit bag? Did you kill someone? Did you rob a bank?"

Johan was clearly nervous. He felt his heart racing. "No, no, no . . ."

"Joking, my sweet." The angel smiled.

She was in her late twenties, and her angelic features hid the kind of wisdom, which is easily learned in a hospital ward. She leaned forward to plump his unplumpable pillow and breathed in his left ear. "Though robbing a bank would be very naughty, handsome boy. It's not often we get your type in here. We have Mickeys to deal with. Or poor souls like him next to you. Nothing we can do, they say. Parents don't even visit him. No one does. He was abandoned. He's riddled, we think. Or like Gabriel, village idiots not keen on holding on to their limbs. What does the village do without its performing monkey? But you . . . you make a girl want to come to work in the morning." She straightened his bedsheets, adding extra tension to those which covered his pelvic area.

"Headaches? Are they dangerous?"

"Relax, my sweet." She touched his cheek. "You have headaches, that's all. They are a rare kind, though. Sometimes it's a tumor, but the doctor thinks you're all right. Headaches like these do start around the solstices, though, apparently. Now, isn't that weird? You been having them for long?"

"Don't know. What day is it?"

"It is July the thirteenth, handsome. You have been here ten days or more, I guess. You used up nearly all our morphine, you selfish brute. Still, fewer bedpans for you! I am teasing, love." She mopped his brow with a cool hand towel.

"I remember I got a headache when I was still in the city. I thought nothing of it then. It was about the last week of June."

"There you go. I'm just a nurse, love. I clean up Mickey. Do what the doctors tell me. We girls, we obey the moon. Johan Thoms, you go for the sun, it seems, my special one."

"Will they go away soon? I feel like my eyes will pop out."

"They will, but you need to look after yourself. Get to the Adriatic. Go swimming. Stay out of the city and be nice to yourself. Get some sun on you. Eat lots of oranges. Some fish. You looked good when they brought you in. I checked you into your pajamas myself." She stared deep into his eyes, one side of her mouth fractionally raised with an accompanying eyebrow. "Perk of the job, handsome. Though you are heading toward looking like a ghost right now. You seen yourself?"

"Not for a while, not since . . . God knows when."

Angel clipped across the tiles with her heels and returned momentarily with a mirror, which she held to his face. Dark rings had developed around his young eyes, he saw.

"I look like death."

"Don't say that, Johan, my angel! Look to your right sometime soon. When that poor creature emerges from those sheets, you will see what death looks like. And in a boy probably not yet ten years old. And unlikely to reach it."

Johan blushed. Changing the subject, he asked, "Do you have a newspaper, please, Nurse?"

He feared his mug shot and the words *wanted* and *reward*.

"Maybe from Zagreb, two days ago. Anything in particular?"

"No, no, no . . ." he said, way too keenly, he thought.

"Well, I will have a look, my sweet, and sometime soon, we need to think about getting you well and out of here. When you read the news, you will see for yourself. This place is going to be full to the rafters by the end of the month, they say. It is a sad, sad world. Why do you silly men insist of spilling guts, for us poor girls to run around and clean up?"

Two

It Only Hurts When I Laugh
(Part I)

No war is inevitable until it breaks out.

—A. J. P. Taylor

He had been unconscious for forty-eight hours, they told him. Each time he picked up a paper, he saw news of the assassination again. This led to a vicious circle of headaches, terror visions, and sedation. The nurses were unaware of the link, and so the local newspapers with their sketchy, biased news kept coming. One time when he woke, he was met by a second and a third angel. The second stood to his left, another vision in white, with pale skin and an Irish lilt, soft and generous. This beauty introduced herself as Josephine. It appeared that Mickey, the sick, confused wreck, had been carrying a picture of his own daughter—not his beloved.

The third angel looked at him from behind a curtain to his right. He was a tiny, hollow boy who had risen from his own hospital bed for the first time in weeks. The boy smiled an incongruous smile. Then he shuffled weakly back to his bed, where he clambered onto the mattress. He lay down on his left-hand side. His head (like Johan's too big for his body) faced Johan, his sick eyes holding the softest gleam, trying to say something.

"Calm yourself, love," came the smooth Irish voice, with the same dialect as the degenerate Mickey. That accent was all the Celtic duo had in common other than their current coordinates to the east of Mostar.

Johan shifted his legs and felt as though a weight was about to drop from his bed. The nurse leaned over and held something out of Johan's view under the lip of the covers, to prevent its falling to the floor.

"How are you feeling, my love? Here's a newspaper for you."

Johan picked up the crispy rag from the bed and, finding it at page twelve, set about returning it to its rightful front-page first state, which was not easy given his current lack of coordination.

There he saw talk of ultimata to the Serbs from Vienna, which, the commentators seemed convinced, could never be accepted by Belgrade. Vienna demanded the dissolution of the Black Hand, and that the group renounce all Serbian claims to Bosnia and turn over all suspected Odbrana members, including Major Dragonivic (aka Apis), for trial. Johan feared seeing his photograph or his name each time the Black Hand was mentioned.

There was more fighting talk from the British, the French, and the Russians. Bullish noises from Wilhelm II.

Johan scanned for talk of the assassination. There were a couple of pictures on page ten of Franz Ferdinand lying in state, and a mug shot of Princip. Johan needed a cigarette but remembered that the only one he was likely to find would be currently resting on or adjacent to Mickey's diseased prick in the Irishman's dressing gown. Princip's rakish face stared out of the paper, mad bug eyes. A caption beneath pondered his likely fate.

Johan lay back on his pillow. He felt like crying, but caught sight of the skeleton boy to his right, who had not taken his eyes off Johan. Johan did not cry. But then neither had Gavrilo Princip.

The boy nodded, seemingly down to where Johan had felt the heavy weight. The weight was now in the hands of Josephine, who, coming round the other side of his bed, placed the object in Johan's hand.

"He said you were going to need it," she said, gesturing over her shoulder to the sick youth.

"Lord only knows where he got it from, but he said it's yours now."

Johan looked down. In his right hand, he held a crucifix.

Three

The Die Is Cast
(aka *Les Jeux Sont Faits*)

Destruction cometh; and they shall seek peace, and there shall be none.
—Ezekiel 7:25

Late July 1914

Johan daydreamed of Lorelei's long journey back to Vienna. She stared from her sleeper carriage into the early dusk. Her copy of *The Arabian Nights* sat in the bottom of her trunk, never to be opened again. It nestled next to a bottle of ylang-ylang, which would not be sidelined for nearly as long. This need not have bothered him, for—as he would discover one day—her fidelity to him, as sturdy as a lover could ever wish for, would never be breached.

Miles to the west, Johan Thoms sat in a wicker chair on a patio of the hospital. He stared out into the incessant summer rain, toward a fuzzy horizon of forest and hills, and clutched a kit bag to his snug sky-blue-and-white striped pajamas. He scanned the bag's contents. Nurse One, Angelface, had brought it to him that morning at his request. For days now he had continued to scan the newspapers for any mention of his name, or his picture, but there had been none. To inquire into the matter, however, would be tantamount to revealing his identity. He had gauged the full extent of the bag's contents and the opportunities they afforded him. He had formulated a plan to leave the hospital as soon as he was fit and take a boat west to Italy, where anonymity was more likely. Late July was upon them. Vienna's declaration of demands had been made. Belgrade's response, despite being conciliatory beyond any expert's expectations, had been rejected out of hand.

All bets were placed. The die was cast.

The Russians waded in with their Serbian bedfellows.

When he read of this development, while on the toilet with his pajama bottoms around his ankles, Johan crumpled. He was found there in an unsightly, unholy mess an hour later by his own ward mate's unfortunate daughter, Josephine. More feces followed. Wilhelm II's bowels unloaded over the Russians. France's pact with Moscow brought them in. This process was accelerated and magnified by alleged Gallic-led activity in a neutral Belgium and by accusations of subterfuge and bombings on Teutonic soil. It was, indeed, silly season for the agent provocateur. The fifth column thrived like a virulent summer flu.

By early August '14, the British had prevaricated for weeks. The Germans had presumed that this would end in an abstention from Westminster. London tossed a coin.

Heads!

"Heads it is, old boy. Jolly hockey sticks! What what! Get kitted out, Tommy. Let's go bash the Bosch!"

Johan was found twitching and writhing under his bed in a deep psychotic ditch. He was pulled out (from under the bed, not from the psychotic ditch) by two burly, unshaven, square-jawed, stale-breathed orderlies. He clutched a cross and a newspaper, drooling, much to the delight of the syphilitic, deranged Mickey, who victoriously yelled, "He's coming to me in the Old JimJam Club!"

Les jeux étaient faits. You've made your bed, young man. Want to lie under it?

* * *

In the black of night, Johan felt a cold hand on the side of his temple. The owner of the tiny, bony paw said nothing. Johan started to mumble, as if speaking in tongues. He knew little afterward of the subject matter of which he spoke to the owner of the small, cold mitt. The hand dried Johan's brow, and then positioned the silver crucifix centrally on his chest. Johan thought he felt an arm stretch out halfway across him and give the softest of hugs.

* * *

The frail, shy young bag of bones in the bed next to Johan continued to watch his only friend. He was as sensitive as a Sicilian seismograph, and his agile young brain pondered a next move.

Four

The Unlikely Bedfellow

Arithmetic, arithmetock.
Turn the hands back on the clock.
How does the ocean rock the boat?
How did the razor find my throat?
The only strings that hold me here
Are tangled up around the pier.

—Tom Waits, "Alice"

August 1914

Johan woke up. He was holding the weighty silver cross. The shape of the item mattered less to him than the fact that it seemed to have come from some caring soul.

Haunting screams came down the dark corridor. Mickey was having his latest treatment. The mystery remained as to which skanky unfortunate had passed the ailment on to the Irishman. And which self-respectless and repugnant monster had given it to her? There must have been some *Untermensch* members' club whose sole membership requirement was to be vile and rotten. *Oh well, I guess there's someone for everyone,* Johan thought. Silently he saluted Mickey's state of mind, for he suspected that it demanded quiet respect.

Johan peered over the mound his feet made at the end of his near-concrete, yet disinfected bed. Gabriel's bed lay empty. The only time Johan had seen one-legged Gabriel was on an afternoon when the farmhand (who, as a child, was renowned for sleepwalking, sometimes miles at a time with his black Labrador) had slid himself from his bed, fast asleep. He had hopped in ever-decreasing circles before arriving back at his place of rest. He then fell facedown onto his pillow, to continue his snoring.

Johan glanced at the silent corner to his right. The other young lad was sitting on the edge of his bed, waiting. He was not more than five feet in height and a skeletal eighty pounds, in a grubby grayish dressing gown and bare feet. The boy smiled a quarter smile which suggested that he was capable of not much more. Johan returned the gesture, and in a local dialect spoke to the urchin.

"I'm Johan Thoms. Pleased to meet you, young man."

"And the same to you, sir. Cicero is the name." His impeccable manners belied his appearance. "He was a famous Roman, you know."

"Is that so? And do you have a surname, Cicero?"

"No, sir. Just Cicero. Cicero has no family. None worth mentioning, anyway. The other Cicero had no family and no surname. Cicero was born alone." He puffed out his meager chest. "And Cicero will bet you all the money in your dressing gown that this is the only Cicero you know, so why would he need a surname, Johan Thoms?"

Johan pulled the corners of his mouth down and tilted his slowly nodding head to the right in agreement.

The lad was as bald as a kettle. Deep shadows circled his dark brown eyes, and sharp bones stuck out from his shoulder blades.

"I have been watching you," he said. "You need to get out of here."

"Why? What do you know? Have *they* been here asking about me?"

"No, I mean that they give you injections, and you will never leave if they keep on showing you newspapers."

Johan realized that this pattern was true. He needed a cigarette. Cicero went on.

"The nurses are nice, and they like you. More than they did anyone else who has slept or died in your bed."

Johan was taken aback by the scamp's forthrightness. He told himself it must be the only way to be when one stares death in the face so cruelly young.

"You have a way with words, Cicero."

"I don't know what you two are talking about, but it sounds like nonsense to me," Josephine announced in English as she came marching in.

She fiercely scrubbed her hands on a towel which reeked of bleach, even from ten yards.

"We have a bright young spark here," Johan said to her, nodding at Cicero. "Nobody warned me."

"True. That young lad was not behind the door when balls were handed out, if you'll excuse my French."

Johan winked at a puzzled, monolingual Cicero.

"She likes you, Emperor Cicero," Johan whispered (in Serbo-Croat).

The screaming from down the hall abated.

"How did you know he was emperor?" the boy said. "I never told you that. You must be smart to know that. And to speak to the lady nurse in that other language."

"Not as smart as Cicero. And not as smart as you, when I was your age."

Cicero looked marginally less pained, his features ever so slightly less gray. "I want to leave. The madman drives everyone crazy, and the nurses could give my bed to someone who needs it more. I could come with you, because you need to leave, too. Can we?"

"That is madness, Cicero. We cannot do that. We need their help. You especially."

"I need to get out. If I have six months or six years to live, what's the point of spending them here? I love the nurses, but if I see something of the outside for six days or six hours, it will be worth it."

"It still makes no sense."

"Of course it does, because I know what you see in those newspapers. These beds will soon be needed. Or if I go alone, maybe I'll die before Dubrovnik, then you'll be to blame."

The little blighter had located Johan's Achilles' heel. Could he really take firsthand evidence of his stupidity here in this very ward? Soldiers bleeding, bawling for their mothers, dying feet away from him?

Could he take another death on his conscience?

The boy was not done. "Imagine if you were a young boy left to die in a hospital. Wouldn't you want someone to help you?"

Johan's memory darted back a decade or so. He saw the symmetry. And it was time to move on, in case *they* were indeed looking for him.

"All right, you damned scamp. Tell me more."

* * *

By midnight, after having taken advantage of a Last Supper and having raided the stores for some opiates, they were gone.

An unlikely pair, with very different troubles, they headed out at Johan's command:

"Let's rusticate!"

* * *

Less than a mile down the road, Johan had Cicero on his shoulders. This went on for an hour or so until they freed a young donkey from a cruelly tight chain. The poor beast had not even been able to reach water. So, after drinking liberally at a nearby creek, he—the mule—was more than happy to take Cicero's minimal weight.

On they marched, with Johan using the light cast on the moon as a guide to the sun's position. Cicero leaned forward after ten miles or so. He rested his head, initially on the fuzzy nape of the donkey's neck and then on a pillow which they had liberated from the ward.

Johan was back in his Schneider's suit, which had been dusted down and pressed by one of the angels. His shoes were clean. His socks, which had been darned and cleaned, were now on Cicero's feet. Cicero was in his own pajamas with Johan's over the top of them, then the tent of Johan's dressing gown. It would have been comical if it were not so tragic.

Cicero slept with a smile on his face.

Johan tried to take deep breaths and to put his troubles into perspective.

Before long, Angelface or Josephine, starting a new day of loving and giving, would find the empty beds. On Cicero's pillow, she would see a note. She would open it, read its contents, and run from the ward, to find the other. Not to raise an alarm nor to set out a search party, not to tell the police of a petty thief or two, but to hug her colleague and probably cry with joy. Johan and Cicero were on their way, as friends, to show the sick and ballsy lad the tiniest bit of life. It was moments like this that would give the nurses the fuel they would doubtless need to get through the horrors ahead.

Their beds would be stripped and made ready for more unfortunates. If *they* were looking for him, *they* would not find him there!"

* * *

My dearest J.,
Where the hell are you, you silly boy? You know where to find me!

Yours, L. xxx

Five

"Ciao Bello!"

While stands the Coliseum, Rome shall stand;
When falls the Coliseum, Rome shall fall;
And when Rome falls—the World.

—Lord Byron

During the night, they slipped through the slumbering medieval beauty of Mostar, two-thirds of the way from Sarajevo to the Adriatic, and over the ancient bridge of Stari Most. Around daybreak, Cicero slowly stirred. Unleashed from the confines of their hospital beds, released from the effects of stifling narcotics, and focused by their need to run away, Johan and Cicero had managed to be twenty or thirty miles away from the ward by dawn. Cicero could hardly contain his excitement at the thought of reaching the land of his namesake.

"Good morning, sleepyhead." Johan greeted the bleary-eyed child as he lifted his scrawny head from the rhythmic comfort of the donkey's neck.

"Where are we?"

"We just left the Land of Nod, where there is no God. And you can't see a thing for monkeys!" Johan joked. It was a clumsy ad hoc translation from Yorkshire English, one of Bill's favorite revised lines for waking Johan up.

(Bill's version was:

In the Land of Nod,
Where this is no God,
And yer can't see nowt fer nettles.

It had always made Johan giggle.)

Cicero shook his head and accepted a flask of water from Johan, putting it to his cracked and parched lips.

They pushed on in a comfortable silence. Their path drew a straight line from the rising sun in the east. Given it was midsummer, the sea would soon come. Cicero had never seen the sea. A crumbling shack at the side of the road served up day-old coffee, white cheese, and a fatty wurst, the skin of which got stuck in their teeth. When it became time to settle the account, Johan realized he had no small change. The proprietress, a toothless old hag with endless creases on her face ("More than Leeds has tramlines," Bill would have said) rolled her generous eyes. Then she stared deep into the dark wells of Cicero's pupils as if they were her crystal ball, and mouthed to him an informed and silent "good luck." Johan lifted Cicero into his seat on the beast's back, then Johan yelled back to the bag of bones in the doorway:

"Thank you for your kindness. How far to the coast, madam?"

"One hour, past the next peak. Just keep going," she said, and she slipped back into her dark shack. That night Johan dreamed of how she had then pondered things yet to come, which from the depths of Cicero's eyes had become exponentially clearer to her.

* * *

The boy's illness seemed to be of little concern or consequence to Cicero himself, so why should Johan involve himself unnecessarily? He asked the young lad to make him aware of how he was feeling, and if he needed anything. They shook on it as Johan briefly entered Cicero's wise slipstream and tried to enjoy each emancipating breath.

They soon reached the port of Split. Johan purchased two passes for the crossing to Ancona, bribing the old guy on the desk with a shekel to allow the boy on board without papers (it happened all the time and was considered to be an unofficial sales tax by the scruffy bureaucrat). The donkey was not to be allowed on the boat, and Johan released him into an adjacent pasture.

Cicero the Senator took Johan's hand with his cold, bony paw.

They walked the plank together.

They showed their tickets and boarded an old wooden boat, powered by the filthiest of engines. Maybe fifty were able to sail in her, although on this day, there were only an old deckhand, Johan, and Johan's physically frail but mentally feisty young Roman soldier.

The old boy waited an extra hour to see if anyone else would show, making excuses for their tardiness, but Cicero and Johan cared not. They were on no schedule.

Finally, the grumpy young skipper arrived; the deckhand departed and let the ropes loose from the jetty. They reversed gear (this led Johan to chain-smoke for half an hour) out to the depths of the bay before chugging to a stop and heading west toward Italy.

Soon the warm Adriatic wind was blowing in their faces. And for the first time in weeks, the first time since the morning of June the twenty-eighth, Johan Thoms felt almost unburdened. Cicero's smile dislodged osmotic endorphins from within Johan and released them into his system.

Cicero lay down on one of the two benches that ran the length of the boat. He rested his head on his new hero's lap, while Johan, delighted to be putting a deep, watery buffer between himself and any of his pursuers, looked out below the tide line at his own wavy reflection. His hair had grown, his face had thinned, and the words of Shelley came involuntarily into his mind:

Rarely, rarely, comest thou,
Spirit of Delight!

When Cicero awoke, they were within sight of Italian soil.

Rome's finest was returning!

*   *   *

Ernest watched as Johan reached into the trunk, disturbing its thousands of letters in their small powder-blue envelopes. In his nostrils, Ernest caught a wonderful, invisible ribbon of released ylang-ylang, gardenia, and sweet Himalayan tuberose. The envelopes he saw first had been addressed simply to *Johan Thoms, c/o The Count, Sarajevo*. Others bore the words *Johan Thoms, Argona*. The trunk appeared to have spent time at the bottom of the ocean, for there were fish scales around the seams, though when Ernest ran one through his fingers, he swore that it smelled of warm butter. The trunk had a large letter *P* painted in lilac on the side, and it was the type in which you'd expect to hide a fortune in Spanish gold.

Sarajevo, July 14, 1914

My dearest J.,

I am still in Sarajevo. I will stay here at the President for you. Oh Christ, I miss you. Tomorrow, I will see Novac. I don't know what to do. Should I visit your family? Please come back to me, you fool. I am afraid that your ghost is not good enough!

These days are dragging. Though in many moments I fear the worst, I truly believe that you are out there, and that deep down you would love to return; if not to here, then at least to me. I wish we were again drinking schnapps in Dubrovnik, or once more in that Bucharest orchard. Please come to me the second you receive this, and let's disappear together. I need stay neither in Vienna nor here.

And nothing is your fault. Please return. I swore to myself that today I would not be driven once again to the point where I write words and lines to force Caligula to blush, my brutish darling.

I love you, and I don't care that I feel so selfish. There are greater machinations at work.

Yours, madly,
L. xxxx

*   *   *

Among the letters, Ernest noticed several written on a different paper stock. These sheets were also a different color, and when he leafed through them, he saw that they were also in a different handwriting, that of a man.

There was another pattern too: these were unfinished, often ending in the scrawl of an unstable person. Ernest held in his hand one of the letters Johan had tried to write to Lorelei, and looked at the elder man, who nodded slowly, looking away and to the floor.

"I know," he said. "I know."

Six

The March of Don Quixote

Heaven goes by favor. If it went by merit, you would stay out and your dog would go in.

—Mark Twain

Summer 1914. Italy

The beach was purple-stained with the ejaculated protective sepia ink of a panicked school of marooned cuttlefish.

The boat pulled up adjacent to a jetty only slightly less dilapidated than the one they had left in Split. No one welcomed them, other than a bouncing, barking shaggy dog. Judging by its appearance, it was descended from a rare mélange of scraggy, easily pleased hounds. The mutt appeared to be enthusiastically awaiting someone it knew well. It wagged its tail feverishly until it took a swift head count of the strangers on board. Its excitement abated, but only marginally.

Cicero's sunken features rose toward the horizontal.

The captain threw a rope to the deck and leaped over onto the wooden slats, which looked like they were about to give way. He aimed a flying left leg at the animal, offering a crude curse: *"Idi u kurac,"* and threw the loop over an erect plank. The dog backed off, but only slightly. It seemed used to abuse from the natives. Yet there were still two humans on the boat who had not yet tried to crack its ribs, and its instinct told it to persevere.

Johan sensed what was coming next. Cicero was first off the vessel, the skipper being kind enough, albeit begrudgingly, to offer a helping hand to the feeble lad who was still in pajama bottoms. Johan was left to find terra firma himself, which he was especially careful to do, given the price-less contents of the kit bag. Cicero was face-to-face immediately with the hound, having his chops licked and already talking as if he owned the dog.

"He's hungry, Johan. And look at him, he has different-colored eyes."

Johan was outnumbered, six legs to two.

The mutt's faithful head, that of a sheepdog, reached as high as Cicero's knee. His scruffy, fuzzy coat (and torso) was a terrier's. He had one wise and tolerant eye, like that of a retriever, and one argent silver, as keen as that of a husky. Despite the goo and the gunk collected in the corners of these eyes, they pierced Johan's. The dog's immediate future was assured. Johan knew Roman history and was not going to enter into a scrap with a determined Cicero.

"What's his name, Cicero?" he asked.

Johan was now embracing the spirit of the adventure. He had made Cicero (and now a mutt) happy. He was encouraging every cell in the young scamp's frame to forget his woes, and by transference, perhaps self-ishly, the same of his own cells. For despite his curriculum vitae, Johan Thoms was still very much a boy.

"His full name in royal circles, in the European courts, is the Fre-quenter of Tree Trunks and the Master of a Thousand and One Fleas, but I shall call him Alfredo!" Cicero checked under the creature's groin to see what hung or did not hang there.

"Yes! His name is Alfredo! And he likes you, I can tell."

Johan gently rubbed his pal's crown, now grown to the texture of an old tennis ball.

"Come on," he said, "we need to get you some shoes! And your *new* best friend needs some lunch."

Cicero reached up, grinning, and tapped Johan in the midriff, in rec-ognition of his teasing.

The gruff skipper of the boat had turned his back on the pathetic sight by the tiny breakers and puffed on a rolled cigarette.

"How far to the first town, please?" Johan asked him.

"Maybe an hour for you."

The pair, with their new canine pal, headed toward what looked like a road to the hinterlands.

Johan thanked the skipper for the journey.

"Don't flatter yourself," he replied. "You would still be on the other side had I not had thirty to take back tonight."

Johan chose to ignore the gibe.

Cicero, however, piped up. "Thank you, sir. And Alfredo says thank you, too."

The skipper grunted and stubbed out his butt end.

"Bad man," said Cicero. "So little kindness in the world today. So very little thought for others." Johan racked his brains as to where he had heard that line before.

* * *

Cicero (the First) had lived in the century before Christ in Rome. He was a self-made man, born penniless and without family connections. He had no soldiering abilities, only a burning ambition to succeed.

He also had a magnificently intelligent and fiery wit, and had overcome the massive hurdle of a debilitating stutter as a child to become one of the finest orators ancient Rome had ever known, if not *the* finest.

He strove, against all odds and conventional wisdom, toward a life no one who had seen him as a young boy would ever have believed. Cicero had put this down to the power of his mind, which he was convinced, and later proved, could not just overcome his own mental doubts and physical ailments, but convince dozens, hundreds, thousands of men to act upon a single word of his.

Even as a newcomer to the Senate, he would weave his magic around politickers and the most Machiavellian of old brains. He was a performer, a showman, feeding off the adulation of his admirers, who, either willingly or begrudgingly, ended up as one, united at his feet.

Cicero, the original *Homo politicus,* was a survivor.

* * *

On they marched toward the town, with Cicero on Johan's shoulders again, more because of the boy's lack of footwear than because of tiredness. Cicero was energized, and would far rather have had his new furry pal within the easy reach of his undernourished mitt. Next to them, at a polite heel, Alfredo dressaged proudly, eyes checking left, then right. If any of his canine buddies were watching, they would know that he had new mates and was about to get a dishful of offal or some bones. Much like Johan pulling out of Sarajevo station in his new Schneider's garb, eager to be seen by all who knew him, Alfredo, too, could be pompous.

They wandered into the town to a series of suspicious looks, for they were an unlikely trio:

- An overenthusiastic, proud, scraggy hound.

- A handsomely disheveled young man in a Schneider's suit minus his socks, clutching a kit bag, with a twisted facial expression that made him look like he was trying to shit a sea urchin.

- On his shoulders, an escapee from a juvenile asylum on the point of death in chain-gang pajamas, which, when he removed, exposed a rib cage with freshly scratched paw marks, making his torso resemble the sheet music for *A Requiem for a Street Urchin*.

They sat at a café, which looked closed. If it was indeed closed, Johan would have the opportunity to find footwear, even some clothes for the boy. If it was open, he would do the same, but leave some food in front of his new pals and have some waiting for him upon his return.

It was open.

After ordering eggs, bread, and water for themselves and bones for Alfredo (for it was all the café had to offer), Johan left. He returned within fifteen minutes with a bag of improvised clothing, which Cicero gladly donned in a bush. He came out in sandals, an old school shirt, and blue shorts, with a slightly too large kepi tilted on his head.

Once sated with food and drink, they sat by the roadside, waiting for a ride to somewhere, which took its time in arriving. Ever the compromising politician, Cicero maintained a perfect balance of attention to Alfredo and Johan as they waited. This made Johan smile once more, which he realized he was doing more than he had for a while; but this in turn then only made him remember. He reached for a cigarette and lit it. In the town, he had given the newspaper seller a wide berth, and even sang to himself (avoiding silence, as his father was doing at the very same moment) when within earshot of any updates from the world. If his mug shot had appeared in any edition, then it had not been matched to his guilty face, which was a relief. He took another drag of his smoke and sucked down into his lungs any thoughts that were thinking of ruining his day. It was the reality of the repercussions of his actions on June 28, 1914, that made him leave, he reminded himself; his stupidity, shame, and guilt when the world was at his feet, not on his shoulders. This was not just self-preservation; out of sight, out of mind; delusional.

Sometimes madmen know things. Johan Thoms sensed that he was being hunted, that he was a wanted man. This was very true, but not quite the way he imagined. He knew he had to keep moving, but as he sat by the roadside, Johan noticed patches of marigold[7] growing wild in the field opposite. He recalled the long summer days ten years before, when his father and he would walk for hours through the lush countryside around Argona, collecting brambles and berries for Elena to make into sugary jams and pies. Drago had then been a keen botanist and naturalist, always testing his young lad on the names of plants on their treks.

Rosebay Willowherb, Burdock, Teasel, Comfrey, Rosehips, Horsetails, Feverfew, Hawthorns, Evening Primrose. Poplar, Maple, Pine, Oak. Johan always struggled to recall these. But Marigold, *Calendula*, Johan had always remembered.

He picked himself up from the rock on the side of the road.

"Where are you going?"

"Something for us. In that field." Johan recognized he had just spoken in the manner of Potiorek. He was taking control.

Cicero took a couple of weary steps. The hound feigned polite curiosity by raising one eyebrow, then the other.

"You see a girl you like, boss?" Cicero yelled, joking.

Johan picked buttery orange flowers and returned in less than ten minutes with his kit bag stuffed.

"Are you all right?" Cicero asked.

"Bugger me! Will be soon. Look! My old man used to swear by this stuff. It is magical."

"You need it," was the lad's only response.

"But, Cicero! Your pals the Romans used this stuff for medicine, for cosmetics, you name it. My father used to go on about it all the time. Probably is doing so right now. Probably boring the pants off some poor unfortunate in the village, telling him how it is not only a flower, but pretty damned useful, too. It's really called calendula, because it flowers on the first of every calendar month. It *must* be the first today. You may set your watch by this stuff. He used it for cuts and bruises, headaches, as an antiseptic, an anti-inflammatory, and for his nerves! Even helps to stop bleeding. He would take bags and bushels of it to our school for that poor old nurse to heal warts, scrofula, fevers. Doesn't need good soil either. As tough as old boots."

Johan now seemed convinced it would save both Cicero and himself. Cicero had not inquired into the reasons behind Johan's mental problems. He knew his friend should be kept away from newspapers. He came to the conclusion that he was either wanted by the law, a deserter, or delusional and avoiding the one story that was engulfing Europe. The first shots of the Great War in Europe had already been fired, a few days earlier, on August 21, 1914.

The deeper they meandered westward into northern Italy, the less likely it was that Johan's identity would be revealed, or so Johan believed. He calculated the precise statistical permutation required for those chasing him to track him down (from the rear, at least), and with each crossroads or split in the road, the length of those odds increased. However, his fear declined in inverse proportion to his guilt. Every silver lining had a cloud for him, in those days.

The dubious-looking triumvirate soon found themselves trundling in the direction of Milan in a pickup truck driven by a young married couple on a carefree honeymoon. Their only company in the back of the vehicle was the couple's suitcases, an old trombone, and some straw. The groom resembled Rudolph Valentino. His Latina bride was a creature of rare natural beauty in a scarlet-and-white dress to the knee, charcoal hair to her shoulders, and wise ebony eyes.

Johan tried not to think of Lorelei as Scarlet spent most of the journey tucked into Rudolph's torso in the driver's side.

(Ernest was reminded of Clark Gable in *It Happened One Night*.)

"We will stay in a hotel tonight," announced Johan, much to Cicero's delight. Alfredo looked up into Cicero's eyes, whining, somehow able to decipher Serbo-Croat. Cicero's expression fell.

"Yes, him, too. Of course!"

"Can we get our own car as well? Then we can go where we want and when."

Johan choked. The thought of sitting behind a steering wheel, using a gear stick, made him shake ever so slightly.

"What is it?" Cicero asked. Johan was already lighting a cigarette, quite a task as the truck was struggling with potholes and hardly out of a raw second gear. The awkward clunking change of gears further frayed Johan's nervous system.

Cicero changed the subject. "Will we be in Milan today? Will we be in Milan today?" He kicked Johan's shin.

"Milano? No, no way," Johan said, shaking his head and catching up with himself.

Cicero searched his friend's face.

"What's wrong?" he asked.

Johan took a deep breath and decided to face his fear.

"Yes, we will buy a new car in Milano. Or in the next big town."

He turned to face Cicero.

"I'll need a damned map. I do know that much for sure!"

Cicero dropped off to sleep within minutes of putting his head on the straw. Alfredo did not need a second invitation to join him. Johan watched over them both, his new family. Before long, he was away, too, the odor of the marigold filling his senses.

When they awoke, it was to the slowing of the vehicle and the din of a crowd. Johan and Cicero peered over the side of the truck. They were in a small dusty market town. This was Forlì, forty miles to the southeast of Bologna, past Rimini and the tiny principality of San Marino. They were still 180 miles from Milan.

Alfredo stretched himself and seemed to smile up at his new owners, happy that his earlier adoption hadn't been a dream. Cicero scratched the hound's back, which made him stick his tongue out with each rub, much to the lad's amusement. It was approaching dusk as Rudolph Gable-Valentino let down the back flap of the truck for them to exit. He was keen to disappear with Scarlet, but offered the use of his truck and straw as a bed for the night.

"Thanks, my friend," Johan managed in his north-of-basic Italian, "but I made a promise. This little guy needs some comfort tonight." He gently ruffled Cicero's ever-fuzzening crew cut.

"No problem. Good luck to you both. Sorry, *the three of you.*" He smiled before skipping off to the nearest hostel with his bride in tow. This made Johan sad and lonely to the pit of his stomach. What would Lorelei be thinking right now? He did not know if it was his shame or hers that was fueling his flight.

Johan felt a tug at his shirt. Two dark eyes stared up at him.

Johan struggled a smile to feebly chase the memories away, and they headed off toward the market square in search of a bed.

* * *

When they found a spot to stay (Rossi's of Forlì) with a decent rate and an owner who welcomed the hound (whom the proprietor called Poochini), Johan asked for hot water and some old glass jars. The clean-shaven, dapper owner, Signor Rossi, kindly obliged the odd request and invited them into his kitchen, despite mutterings from his wife, who was house-sized, with the physique of an unfinished sculpture.

"Fatta beech. Blood-a typ-a, ragu!" Rossi muttered. "She would-a even-a make-a a bloody boa cona-stricta choke-a." This made Cicero weep with laughter when Johan translated.

They all sat in his kitchen, darkened by the glare of the low sun. It had cool tiles, and colored glass in the windows. To Johan it felt of a different age. Cicero just watched wearily now as Johan got busy. He boiled water and added sugar to some, and cut the petals and flowers of the marigolds into different proportions and piles. He marked some of the jars with a symbol foreign to Cicero. The boy fell asleep with his head on the table in the middle of the kitchen, as Signor Rossi watched Johan silently in amazement.

Johan nudged his friend awake. A range of finished jars stood in front of the boy.

"This one is for you," he announced, pouring the contents of a particularly first-piss-of-the-day-colored jar into an eggcup, then a different one for their host.

He knocked back one from a third jar for himself.

"O! Nectar of the Gods!"

Cicero slugged back the potion. Alfredo leaped up and licked the sugary remnants from the corners of Cicero's slightly less gray lips.

* * *

They spent a luxurious night in clean sheets with four pillows each.

When Johan woke, he told himself that there was no going back. Neither in time, nor in a brand-new Packard down a cul-de-sac. When a madman turns a corner into a dead end, there is no reverse gear.

They would head west into the sunset. On the outskirts of Forlì, Johan bought a car.

* * *

The potion was working. Given that he had not yet found the elusive Blue Rose of Forgetfulness or experienced its supposed wondrous properties, Johan had considered the other options, of soaking himself in booze or in the comfort of women's bosoms. He had sampled, too, the cushion of a hospital ward and its narcotic escapes. It was, however, in an innocuous garden plant, once adored by his father, that he found a major element of Cicero's physical salvation and at least a dulling of the side effects of his own guilt and shame. Wherever they stopped, the natives no longer eyed Cicero as a freak or a dying wretch. The boy was finally afforded the lack of stares that most of us take for granted. Johan's nerves improved marginally and he slept more soundly. He twitched far less, and began to turn to the potion when he felt an episode of his dark madness looming.

They became marigold experts. They knew what each combination of petal and stamen did, in what measures, taken orally or externally. Whenever they saw any in a field around the first of each month, they stopped and collected all they could. They administered each other's doses until Cicero knew more than Johan. They filled the backseat of the car, which

Alfredo gladly used as a bed. The flowers cured his fleas, but not his cute insolence nor his dog breath.

Cicero had the idea of selling the excess, when they had one, to local apothecaries, disclosing very little of its makeup, merely its wondrous healing properties. It was a good business, and although they did not need the money, Johan encouraged the boy. It was a fine diversion, and self-reliance was a great lesson.

They continued their journey to the west, out of Italy, past Marseilles and into Spain, skirting the majestic Pyrenees by Port-Vendres and Cerbère. They made slow progress in the cool of the morning and in the early evening, avoiding the heat of the day.

They ate like Spanish kings and overnighted in comfort in Gerona, Lerida, Zaragoza, and then the elevated cool of Soria. Each night they devoured their favorite dish of roast piglet. Cicero tasted wine for the first time—a delicate number from Bilbao suggested by a one-eyed, three-toothed waiter named Jesús.

That was until they reached Segovia, an exquisite and crumbling citadel to the northwest of Madrid, in the middle of September 1914. Johan spent a night drinking local grog and dangling his pipe-cleaner legs from the immense first-century Roman aqueduct that ran through the ancient hill town. He enjoyed the company of a frisky Spanish *rascalita* who had taken a liking to him. As he walked back to his digs in the early-morning light, he stopped for a coffee. It was there he found out about the gruesome slaughter of the Battle of the Marne. The newspaper headline (accusing emetic negligence on the part of those in charge of a brave body of men) read:

LIONS LED BY DONKEYS

Johan sat down on the steps of the medieval cathedral. For the first time, he considered the possibility of the salvation that he might find over either shoulder, in the church. He remained with his wonderings until he felt the (weirdly comforting) tongue of Alfredo traverse the diagonal of his face, which had been warming in the glare of the morning sun, catching them up from the east.

Sarajevo, August 28, 1914

My dearest J.,

I will be leaving the President tomorrow. Novac has insisted that I stay at his town house, which is most generous. Srna has agreed, of course.

I will find you, Johan Thoms. I do promise you that, for there is something you need to know; something which would certainly bring you to me without delay. Please make it so, and soon, you lovely fool. I shall remain that sweet syrup to the vampire's lips.

Yours, with all my love,
Lorelei xxx

Ernest finished the next brief letter in the stack and observed old Johan. He slipped the note back into the aged, powder-blue envelope.

"You *must* have gone to her! You *must* have replied!"

"It was not that easy, though I wish it had been. I did not see these letters for a long time. And not before this world was to take an even more vicious turn . . ."

Seven

In No-Man's-Land

He had a persistently troubled frown, which gave him the expression of someone who is trying to repair a watch with his gloves on.

—James Thurber

They collected their belongings from the hotel, hung the crucifix on the rearview mirror, filled the tank, and found the warming open road out of Segovia and toward the ancient walled city of Avila, their next stop. Here among magnificent churches, and fine examples of Gothic, Renaissance, and Moorish architecture, they found a peaceful sanctuary, fresh paella, and fine vino.

They did not stay long. Johan planned to take Cicero and Alfredo as far west as they could possibly get, away from the turmoil across the continent. They trundled on, though at no great pace, and soon entered Portugal at the historic citadel of Badajoz. They then headed toward Lisbon and the Atlantic, before veering off to the south to avoid civilization.

On a windy day in early October '14, they reached the last outpost of Europe. Their Land's End. From here, there was no "going over the top." These lucky bastards had found a safe trench.

The fishing village of Sagres, the End of the World, hugged the most southwesterly tip of Portugal. To the south baked the warm refuge of the

Mediterranean. Beyond were the deserts and the Moors, the myths of Morocco and North Africa.

To the west swelled the steely, gray depths of the Atlantic, destined to become a nautical tomb for many in the next three months, the next three years, and the next three decades.

* * *

One early evening shortly after their arrival, they enjoyed a bottle of port and fresh sardines in a local café. There, Johan struck a deal with a local joiner-fisherman-shepherd-lothario in his early thirties by the name of Pedro. From Pedro he rented, for pennies, a small farm holding on the edge of the village. He had trusted Pedro's fun-loving and uniquely green eyes from their first meeting. No deposit had been required.

"Let's break bread and shake hands on it," said Johan outside Pedro's single-room dwelling by the harbor. For Cicero, any friend of Johan Thoms was a friend of his.

For Alfredo, it was easy.

"Oh, him!" said Johan. "Two tomato-laced sardines and a bowl of icy water and he is anyone's."

Their new abode was on the dorsal fin jutting into the Atlantic, less than a quarter mile from the village in the direction of the sleepier hamlet of Vila do Bispo.

Pedro spoke a few words of English, but not many. The village had seen its fair share of friendly, often wrecked (in both senses of the word) fishermen from the British Isles and their navy cousins over the years. To speak in English was acceptable; to mutter a syllable in Spanish, however, was punishable with a good hiding and a dunking in the Med. The hatred for the Spanish ran deep after centuries of torment. The British held disputed Spanish land in nearby Gibraltar and therefore shared a common enemy with the Portuguese. So Johan and Pedro decided that Anglo-Saxon was to be the newcomers' conduit as they adapted to their new locale. Moreover, Pedro, a philandering, testosterone-soaked, swashbuckling, fish-hunting woodworker, knew of a local maiden, Ismeralda, a schoolteacher of magnificent proportions yet sadly unholy looks, who kept an English-Portuguese dictionary on her mantelpiece. Pedro had seen it while making love to her from behind (for it was the only way with her) one balmy night the previous year. He would arrange a haphazard meeting with her outside the school (which he had avoided for twelve months), knowing full well he would be made very welcome indeed in her roomy dwelling.

Within a week, and with malice aforethought, the gang had their book, and their group's communication flourished.

Cicero later noted to Johan, in fine English and with utmost seriousness, that Pedro's conquest had been "quite, quite ghastly."

* * *

Johan coped well enough in company. Lonely moments, however, brought on episodes.

An old lighthouse sat a mile from the harbor. Its solitary purpose was to guide ships in and out of the world's busiest shipping lane. There, way above the deserted Zavial Beach, Johan sat watching many sunrises and sunsets. He often stared down at the raging waters, wondering if he would be in less pain should he join the murk two hundred feet below. Would he be settling some Faustian debt? Or would he become one more unnecessary statistic, which into the bargain would leave a young boy and his dog alone in a foreign land? He was, of course, a coward. This is why he was where he was. So he would return to his car and take a swig of marigold or, if the mood took him, some local port of supreme quality. Port was in ample, cheap supply and would often soothe him more than the marigold, which Cicero and Johan had decided now to grow.

Cicero's health had continued to ameliorate at a remarkable rate. They made an effort to speak the local dialect of Portuguese, initially with blunt yet worthy efforts of *obrigadinho, peixe,* or *vila*. Their spongy young brains soon wrapped themselves around the tongue. With the help of the dictionary and the notorious Pedro, they were made increasingly welcome by the traditionally wary village folk. These were fisherfolk, who survived on the trust of their comrades, their solid collective at sea, and not on outsiders from Lisbon, who invariably shafted them on roads and taxes, military drafts and schools. An outsider would, and should, and often did have it tough there in Sagres. However, as Johan had a sick young child and a dog in tow, the locals, with their uniform of weather-beaten faces, fishing caps and bleached shirts, sagely nodded their approval. This was all despite Johan's relative wealth and the nice car, which he made an effort never to clean nor to drive too fast. He left the crucifix safely on show. It worked well with the locals, especially when man and boy made a show at church every week, with a well-trained Alfredo sitting politely outside in a bow tie. The villagers thought them mad, but that was all right.

When Johan did utilize the car, he would pick up locals on the side of the road. Before long, even full canteens would find two extra seats for the strangers and some bones for their canine sidekick, who, oddly, received a similarly courteous welcome from the mutts of the village.

Pedro put the word around that if there were any sickness, his friend from the east (for this is all the locals would understand) had a potion, which he would happily administer for free. The plant was now flourishing in pots around the foreigner's shack. Far from this upsetting the local medicine man, the local quack welcomed the respite, though the sturdy village folk rarely complained of any ailment anyway.

Every day they would see Johan up on the top of the cliffs staring out to sea. They kept their distance to start with, unable or unwilling to communicate. They knew to leave him to his wanderings, though they still did not know that the horror engulfing the world, with millions of lives soon to be lost in a previously unmatched inferno, was, in his mind, all his fault. While Johan's state of mental void continued, the rest of the continent was caught up in a kaleidoscopic cataclysm that afforded to no one else the luxury of any such limbo. The word *limbo* meant nothing to the poor sods in the Highland Regiments, the Welsh Fusiliers, the Bedfordshires, the King's Cavalry, the Green Howards. Nor, come to that, the Landsturm Batterie, the Bayerische 6. Landwehr, or the Pionier-Kompanie.

"All *my* fault."

Soon there would be the horror of the Eastern Front, which would deliver more corpses to the mud, and more telegrams back to wives and mothers, sisters and lovers, than its western twin.

"All *my* fault."

Then there was Turkey. Its apocalyptic slaughter ravaged lives and left widows by the thousand weeping, from Gallipoli to Wagga Wagga via Yerevan.

"All my damned fault."

It would soon be impossible for Johan to hide from news coming across Europe, news of tens of thousands, then hundreds of thousands, of youthful casualties. Huge swathes of Northern France and Belgium became quagmires of trenches, littered with twisted biplanes, bullet-holed helmets of all hues, corpses, and dead horses among the deadly green whiff of mustard gas. And was Bill in the middle of all this?

"God, it is all *my* fucking fault!"

* * *

One night, as the sun dipped once again to the west, Johan decided that he would not move from his spot until the sun rose from over his left shoulder the following dawn. Cicero and Alfredo found him by the lighthouse, shivering from the harsh Atlantic freshness.

After putting the orangey cure to Johan's muttering lips, Cicero decided to finally, fully broach the subject.

"What is it, boss? Isn't it time you told me what is wrong with you?"

Johan slowly turned round to see his young pal, who appeared quite alive these days. Considering Johan's silence until now, and the silence that he would resume, a verbal release of perhaps five or eight minutes of one day, of one week, of one year was not such a self-indulgence rant. There was a silence for thirty seconds.

"I have not your courage, my Roman hero. I do not know where to start. Nor do I know where all this will end. I can see no end. All I see is death. All I see are the mistakes I have made. I see the faces of the people I have loved and who have loved me but who now must hate me but whom I still love. I see strangers' loved ones lost, rotting somewhere in a blasted field. The children asking where Daddy is and when he is coming home. Sweethearts slumped on benches at railway stations with handkerchiefs, hoping each day, every day, for some lost moment, for a lost love from some sunny summer to return. Mothers waiting in cold kitchens for their flesh and blood to come home, but their flesh is now in one part of Belgium and their blood spilled across another. And it is way too late for them to replace the irreplaceable. The mothers' wombs are barren and their time has gone. The unimaginable grief of one poor mother multiplied by a number beyond comprehension, Cicero."

Cicero, unable to understand what Johan was talking about, indulged him, for he knew that this was more important for the moment. Johan spoke more calmly.

"I had everything a young lad could have wanted. Everything was just perfect. And yet I managed to transform it not just into *nothing*, like some sad fool would do, but into death, destruction, horror, and hell on the vastest possible scale. If there is one single thing to give me some sick solace, it is that I am the best at what I do, Cicero. I am the master of my dark domain, the ruler of my black art."

Cicero was trying, but he was still not getting it.

Johan looked into the boy's concerned dark eyes.

"This war is all my fault. You want to know why newspapers send me crazy, or the sight of a soldier or an old woman crying? Because *I* was driving the car when the Archduke was shot. *I* took the wrong turn. *I* could not reverse the damned car. *I* drove them into a street where those blasted Serbs were having a sandwich. A sandwich, for Christ's sake! It was all over in less than a minute."

And he snapped the middle finger and thumb on his right hand.

"If only I had followed the simple instructions, the world would be at peace. Hundreds of thousands of lives not wasted. I'm a mass murderer, but I didn't mean to be. Mass manslaughter is not on any statute books in any constitution, for the obvious reason that no one would be guilty of such a ridiculous crime. One can kill someone without meaning to once. But a million deaths cannot be accidental. The lawmakers cannot square that particular circle. Yet yours truly did *just* that on their behalf! Congratulations, Cicero. You are friends with the world's most prolific mass murderer."

Cicero sat in stunned silence. Alfredo, too, lay motionless, his eyebrows twitching from left to right.

"I have tried to be good, to *do* good. Instead? Bloody mayhem. And now what is there for me to do, other than run? You have been the best thing to happen to me since. That day in the hospital when you befriended me has saved my sad excuse for a life so far, and for that I thank you. But this remains *my* burden and *I* must live with my actions. I have no one to blame but myself. I was surrounded by people who gave and gave, and I rewarded them with disappointment and shame. This is the way things are; nothing can change them now. They just become worse and worse in a maelstrom of shed blood and lost and sawn limbs. Tens of thousands of nurses hearing a million and more screams. Death rattles in foreign fields, boys and grown men in sludge. On piss-, shit-, and bloodstained mattresses, they yell their last breaths for their mothers across borders. They implore their help, beg their presence as they regress to infancy in the moment before they recognize the advent of their last miserable second. All my bloody fault, my young friend. Now do you understand?"

Tears streamed down Cicero's still face, and he made not a sound.

Alfredo lodged himself under the urchin's loose shoulder in a show of solidarity, a vain attempt to comfort.

"In towns and villages and isolated farmhouses for thousands of miles, doors remain open throughout the night, in the dumb, forlorn hope that a uniformed, unshaven figure will stumble through them in the depths of the night, and a mother or wife will find her loved one asleep in his favorite chair the following dawn. Extra places are set for dinner, but each evening, dessert is a lonely wail in the back garden, so as not to upset the young ones upstairs, clinging instinctively to their teddy bears, too young to understand why Johnny is no longer there. I have changed the world! I have touched the lives of millions. Millions of boys and men, whose final word in a trench in a foreign field or in a stinking hospital was 'mother,' which, if you were to see it just once, just once in your life, Cicero, you would think was the saddest thing you had ever seen. Think about it for a second. Well, this is millions. Bloody *millions*. And their mothers were not there for them. Can you understand this, my friend? I still do not think that I fully can . . . or ever will."

Cicero put his bony arm on Johan's shoulder. He moved his still-delicate frame even closer to his mate and held him as best he could. His kepi fell to the ground as its peak hit Johan's burdened shoulder. Alfredo lay on their feet, trying to spread and to share an unspreadable and unsharable burden. Johan only stared out to sea.

They stayed motionless for hours.

Passing strangers would have presumed them a stone statue, a statue in remembrance of a unique friendship, with secrets abounding, of a sadness, a remorse, a loss, a waste impossible to comprehend.

It could be seen in their faces, even from the distant, dusty road to the old lighthouse at the End of the World.

* * *

Sarajevo, September 14, 1914

My dearest J.,

Music, when soft voices die,
Vibrates in the memory;
Odours, when sweet violets sicken,
Live within the sense they quicken.

Rose leaves, when the rose is dead,
Are heap'd for the beloved's bed;
And so thy thoughts when thou are gone,
Love itself shall slumber on.

Yours, with love, as genius unashamedly steals rather than borrows,
Lorelei xxx

P.S. I am pregnant, my darling. We are having a baby. You know that begging is not my business, so I choose my words carefully. Get here soon, my love.

Ernest handed the letter back to Johan, who dropped it back onto one of the large piles of others, for he now seemed oddly disinterested in maintaining their order. He had passed perhaps one out of every ten to Ernest to read. Some envelopes contained photographs, Ernest noted, and some letters were far longer than the ones he was being allowed to see.

There was a knock on the door. A lady of powerful beauty entered. She lived, it seemed, across the expanse of bluish rocks, in the house which was visible from the dusty and cobwebbed window at the back of the hermitage. Ernest thought Johan called her Bandita, which made her giggle. She handed the two old men mugs of coffee and plates of cheese, bread, and cold cuts of pork. She said nothing, but fondly stroked Johan's head. She then closed the door behind her, and the old man continued his tale. Ernest noted that just as a single day in his story had taken many hours to retell, so longer periods of time (months and years) seemed to him to pass by very quickly, which according to his oracle, Johan, was very probably an indication that the days in question were all spent in a very similar fashion and that they lacked adventure, which pleased Alfredo. And Cicero. And, most of all, Johan.

Eight

"A Shadow Can Never Claim the Beauty of the Image"

If you could hear, at every jolt, the blood
Come gargling from the froth-corrupted lungs,
Obscene as cancer, bitter as the cud
Of vile, incurable sores on innocent tongues,
My friend, you would not tell with such high zest
To children ardent for some desperate glory,
The old Lie; Dulce et Decorum est,
Pro patria mori.

—Wilfred Owen, 1918[8]

1916. Sagres, Portugal

Pedro and Johan passed many port-soaked days in the bar at the harbor. The Crazy Foreigner (*estrangeiro louco*), or Azul, as he became known because of the blueness of his eyes, was welcomed there as one of their own.

Short of boarding a liner to the Americas or a boat to Africa, Johan could run away no farther. If he was to be found, then at this juncture, he thought, so be it.

The four of them, including the ever-present hound, who was taking on more human sensibilities by the day, often took a boat out when the sea was calm. They enjoyed English and Spanish lessons, as well as the basics of chess, while they fished for dorado, sardine, cod, and flat dabs with hand lines laced with deep beige mussels. Upon their return, they left the owner of the vessel a chunky white fillet for his generosity.

The car sat under a barn roof, superfluous. Cicero would start it up from time to time to keep her from dying, but never when Johan was around. Almost every day, Johan thought of Elena, Drago, Bill, and Kaunitz.

And Lorelei, of course. But they were now so far apart; they might as well have lived centuries apart. What was the difference? There was none.

He would awake some mornings, or in the middle of the night, and consider making his way to Vienna or to New York to find Lorelei, to surprise her and try again, but he had not the guts to face further ignominy. No reverse gear.

Johan could not even take solace in a religion, which would have left scope for meeting those he loved afresh, in a different life.

He was in a cul-de-sac, a dead-end street, and he never did deal with those very well.

As for Cicero, any hint of death had departed along with the dark rings around his eyes. There was meat on his cheekbones, his lips had developed a pinkish hue, and a sparkle could be seen in his brown eyes. His hair was now a dark and healthy silk.

The boys filled their days with long treks with Alfredo while refining their language. They swam off the many local beaches and climbed the grandiose hills above the coves, which took on strange grainy resolutions depending on the Atlantic fret.

Cicero had bought a soccer ball from a local boy in the street, for he was now earning good money of his own by beating Johan at gin rummy. Each night, they shuffled a deck around the fire in the hearth oven in the sparse kitchen. They would play ball for hours down on the beach, with the mutt sometimes joining in but just as often watching politely from the sideline. The sea mist would come quickly and they would play long after it was feasible, the way kids insist on doing. Cicero would have played until dawn had Johan not suggested a *sopa de peixe* in their favorite café in the village square.

So they would retire to a scabby bench and devour soup and fresh bread, and play chess until Cicero nodded off between Johan's ponderous moves.

One summer night after supper, as they approached the open front door of their dwelling, the reliably tardy postmaster handed Johan an envelope with a familiar red wax seal. It read as follows:

My Wonderful Boy!

You're alive, I hope! I suspect as much from my friend at the Bank of Vienna, but this is not adequate proof in itself for a deeply concerned and dear and guilty friend.

I know what it is to run and hide, for I have built a life on doing so.

So, let's compare notes at the earliest available opportunity, and forget about these cruel and bruised skies under which we find our-selves morbidly lurking.

I would not blame you if you did not return, for there are many places to see and I encourage you to breathe in your exquisite and heavenly youth out there. But please do so with a reassured family, and with a sense of enjoyment, if you might muster up the mind.

Hence Burgundy, claret, and port,
Away with old hock and Madeira,
Too earthly ye are for my sport;
There's a beverage brighter and clearer.

> *Yours, wishing that you are gliding gently,*
> *With the plain inscription,*
> *Kaunitz*

The letter had been cut. Literally. Scissors had been used. The censorship prodded Johan's paranoia, but in the wrong direction. He should not have worried about being exposed as the man responsible for torching a continent. The reason for the intrusions into his friend's correspondence was not Johan but a rampant homophobia that had taken root in Bosnia. The authorities monitored Kaunitz and eyed his every move. They also alerted the equally mean-spirited officials of the postmaster general in Lisbon, whose petty bureaucrats held back or, on a good day, butchered with cuts anything from the Count, whose letters were easily spotted by the red wax seal. As in much of Europe, here was a dark and brooding nastiness which would raise its graceless and vicious head into view soon enough. It was a miracle that one or two letters slipped through the net, but the postmaster's staff were as inept as they were unfathomably mean. The result of their nastiness was that many dozens, if not hundreds, of missives from Kaunitz to Portugal were stashed in a locker marked *Pederastas de Merda,* and would therefore never alert the poor young man that, every day, there landed in the castle a letter to Johan from Lorelei. The banking system, however, remained above such murkiness, though Johan worried that the infrequent but necessary money wires he received from Vienna had exposed him. He thought now of his deep friendship with Kaunitz, with its openness and honesty, and this put him in a mind to ask Cicero a question he had long pondered.

"Why were you in hospital, Cicero?"

Cicero closed the dictionary he had been studying, placed his head on his pillow, and stared at the ceiling.

"For nothing. Literally nothing. I was just dumped there by my mother and was rotting. She never wanted me, never loved me, but I do not blame her. I know nothing else. Your sentimental books might have called it a broken heart, but that is just crazy. I was waiting for my moment. You were part of my plan, Johan Thoms. This Cicero, like all Ciceros before, will always make a habit of outstaying his welcome! I will insist on not breaking with tradition!" He weakly waved a paw, as if ending a speech on the steps of the Senate.

Cicero really did believe his own positivity. Born to an indifferent mother, he recognized just how lucky he was to have reached that lonely hospital bed in Mostar in the first place. That he had escaped with a man like Johan, had a fine friend in Alfredo, was learning languages, was breathing the fine ocean air at the end of the continent, and felt the sun on his face and salty water on his feet almost every day of his new life was all a quite remarkable slice of superb fortune. He did not, like Johan, have to remind himself of his blessings. And perhaps *this* was his true gift, for his appreciation of beauty was unencumbered by worry or remorse.

Alfredo collapsed on Cicero's feet. Johan smiled and then lowered the gaslight. He then went back out to the porch to smoke a last cigarette of the day, mesmerized by the lighthouse on the rocks above and soothed by the enveloping warmth of the night. He fell asleep in the rocking chair on the porch and dreamed of William Atticus Forsythe Cartwright making him laugh with his vile ideas, his crass theories. He awoke violently in the night from a part of the dream he could not recall. However, as he rose, embedded in his mind were the words

A shadow can never claim the beauty of the image.

He could not reenter his dream, nor even sleep.

It was early on July 1, 1916. Johan knew it was the first of the month because the calendula had flowered. He watched the silent sunrise from his porch, with a mug of gritty coffee in one hand and a lump of floury bread dolloped in strawberry jam balanced on his left knee, unaware that, within three hours, Bill Cartwright's huge friendly frame would be splattered across a field in France.

*   *   *

Sarajeeo, February 15, 1915

My dearest J.,

> *We have a boy. He was born on your twenty-first birthday. Lord knows when you will see this news, if ever. Lord knows if you ever will learn that you are a father, and that he is so very beautiful. I will call him Carl, after your brother. I write to you as if into a void, but I pray that we may soon read these things together, and laugh at my panicked sentimentality. I have a blind spot of deep horror that you will read my daily missives to you far into the future, when I am gone or when we are so old we would not recognize each other were we to meet. I don't think I could cope with that pain. Perhaps an emptiness would be preferable. I remember the lawns of the Old Sultan's Palace, and your face that June night not two years ago. I don't think I would want to see those eyes next in the face of an old man, especially if the regret in them matches mine now.*

> *How dare you rattle my life so wonderfully and then forsake me, you swine?*

> *There are times when I wonder how you can do this to me and to our son. There are lonely hours. There are, however, moments when*

I am convinced we will be together soon. This war will end and my soldier will come home over the hill. These thoughts see me through, as will Carl now. You would, and you will, be so proud of him.

For his sake I cannot put myself first anymore, especially when I consider what you must feel each day, with this damned war. However, you must not blame yourself, my darling. Those bastards always get what they want, and how dare they pin this on you? Next to your return, I wish for five minutes in a locked room with them. They would then know the meaning of bloodshed.

I will get what I want. You know this. I will find you, Johan Thoms. But I would far prefer to be found. By you, and very soon. I will, of course, write again tomorrow.

I love you. Your son loves you.

Yours, Lorelei xxx

Nine

The Birth of Blanche in a Dangerous Ladbroke Grove Pub

There is nothing to writing. All you do is sit down at a typewriter and bleed.
—Ernest Hemingway

The routine of their Portuguese days and nights remained the same over the next two years. Johan kept his hair neatly clipped, but there was always a sandpaper shadow to his chin, which now needed some meat on it, as he otherwise neglected himself for days on end. He needed to bathe more regularly, and not just in the force of the Atlantic breakers. He had been setting no good example to his pal, who now kept a nursing eye over his elder. And there were many days when Johan thought about just taking the boat out by himself at dawn, with one intention. Each time, however, his responsibility to Cicero came back to him. It was at these times, too, that he remembered his family and Kaunitz and Bill and how he had let them down enough already. He began to pen notes to his family from time to time, but always would have them sent from Lisbon or, farther afield, from Spain or North Africa, to mask his true whereabouts.

He received a note soon afterward from his mother, which he carried with him at all times. He constantly reread it, or perhaps (Cicero suggested more than once, and never to a denial) he was soaking in her fine handwriting.

Dearest Son,

I could weep at just writing those words. Oh my, where do I start?

    To receive your letter last week was the most wondrous surprise. Your father and I had dared to dream of such a day. We are deliriously happy to know that you are alive. We immediately contacted your friend Kaunitz, who reluctantly (but gladly, too, if that is possible) gave us the name of your village.

    Please come home. No blame attaches to your name, and certainly none within these walls.

    I shall write more later today, for I have so much to say, but I simply need to get this to the mail right now to send you my undying and unconditional love.

    More later.

> *Your mother, who misses you more than you could imagine,*
> *More later,*
> *Mama*

More letters indeed followed, and after reading them to Cicero and Alfredo, he stored them away. Their tone and their message never altered much, and he was comforted to read that Kaunitz's generosity was not restricted to Thoms Junior. The only things that changed, with a pendulous swing, were his father's bizarre activities. These always made Johan chuckle proudly.

It was around this time that Johan started to write prolifically. He bought an old typewriter from an emporium of weird delights and low ceilings, just by the market square. Later in the afternoon when Cicero arrived back at the hut, he saw the latest acquisition, which had been given a central spot on their kitchen table. He did not expect a large literary output, though, not even when his friend walked in hoisting a stack of paper that went from his belly button up to his jutted-out chin.

"Writing might be addictive," Johan said, "and if I am thinking about my tales, then I cannot be thinking about other things. We are men, and 'tis how we were builded, my Roman pal. And anyway, we've run out of books to read. So, we had better write some! And you know what? I can even control how these stories go. Imagine a life like that!" He smiled to himself while staring at the single lightbulb above his head, until his vision blurred and all he saw were Lorelei's Nubian eyes.

Within a year, he had finished a manuscript. In secret, high above Zavial Beach, Cicero copied the manuscript out almost concurrently as his pal tapped out the subsequent chapters either in the hut or in the small amount of shade offered outside at the front of it. Johan entitled it *The Brigadier in the White Kilt.* He was very proud of the opus, and tucked it away, happy in the knowledge that each page had allowed him a time of respite from guilt. The brigadier in question is a young man called Stanley Rex-Foyle of the Dragoon Guards. He is the only soldier in the whole of the British army who is allowed to wear a white kilt. His unique distinction is that he had saved the life of the Queen in 1895 after uncovering a plot by enemies of the empire. This he did quite inadvertently in a dangerous pub in Ladbroke Grove, but such is life, he supposed later. Our hero, while exhibiting courage and daring, ultimately professes to a pacific leaning, and through the very public confession of this on the steps of the British Museum, he wins his darling's heart.

Johan signed the manuscript with the nom de plume Blanche de la Pena—*blanche* as the French for "white"; *pena,* the Portuguese for "feather."

"The white feather is the symbol of cowardice in the British army, Cicero."

"But you know that *pena* in Spanish means misery, sorrow, regret, penalty, and cowardice? But *peña* (pronounced *pen-ya*) is a rock!"

"Yes, I did, but I had forgotten," Johan said, staring out the window and nodding. Then his laughter took over and left him gasping for breath. When he finally recovered his poise, he announced, "It is therefore perfect, for this stout young wench called Blanche, with the help of her quill and perhaps her marigold, shall overcome her *pena* and become a *peña.* I swear it, my Roman friend."

So, Blanche de la Peña it was. And he, or rather, she, began almost immediately on Stanley Rex-Foyle's next adventure, entitled *The White-Kilted Brigadier and the Exquisite Daring Rescue of Lady Heather Belle.*

Meanwhile, Cicero had stealthily sent his own copy of *The Brigadier in the White Kilt* to a publisher whose name he'd found on the sleeve of Johan's battered copy of *David Copperfield.* Two years later, the sequel followed to the same London address, as did, eighteen months after that, *The White-Kilted Brigadier, the Secret of the Black Hand, and the Powder-Blue Plume,* a fictionalized tale of the events of June 28, 1914. A full confession of Johan's single, yet pivotal, error seemed imminent.

*   *   *

News had constantly filtered through to Sagres of Passchendaele, Verdun, the Somme, and Ardennes. Their full scale was not yet apparent, but what was heard was not far off the mark. The typical sensationalizing process of Chinese whispers did not apply: to exaggerate this Great War was not possible, for there were no words in the lexicon of the time to encompass this horror. Johan considered resuming female company as a diversion, but soon there were hundreds of happy American soldiers in the village, spreading news of victory. The doughboys had arrived in Europe and, with their duties complete, were now infiltrating its corners. (Johan was intrigued as to why they had earned this name and their second moniker of dogfaces. One leggy, pink-skinned youth from Arkansas was happy to explain, over a deck of cards by the harbor: "I don't know where 'doughboys' comes from, my friend, but 'dogface' is easy. It's because of our dog tags; also we sleep in pup tents, we growl at everything we eat, and we try to seduce every female we see.")

The news of victory eased Johan's psychosis microscopically, or at least slowed his lunacy's acceleration. Cicero managed this process as best he could, filtering information to suit his pal's mental health, becoming a microcosmic Ministry of Information for the independent state of El Capitania.

At eleven A.M. on November 11, 1918, over four years after their arrival at World's End, the war was finally ended. Johan Thoms had been sleeping still, but not as soundly as millions of other boys.

When he woke and heard the news of the armistice, he was soon hovering over a pint of port, and he wrote the first of several letters to Bill, cheekily marked thus:

Bill Cartwright
If you, Mr. Postman, do not know him, ask your sister
Huddersfield,
England.

Johan would never discuss the contents of these letters, despite more than one prompt from my grandfather. They were written to Ernest's father after all. Early in 1919, a letter was returned, with a scrawled note in what appeared to be a young girl's hand. The ink was smudged and stained, as if by a tear, and the details were thankfully brief. Johan then knew why his previous missives had gone unanswered.

*   *   *

Johan passed this note to Ernest.

"I sent my best friend to his death," he said, squinting hard at Ernest. "Of course, there are millions of deaths with which I have to deal, but this single slaughter possesses a proximity and represents a regret more difficult than who knows how many noughts after a number. How many more would I have sacrificed to save my beloved Bill! I know I am not in control of any such devilish exchange, but I suspect that if I were, a large number of unknown soldiers would be held up and offered to Faust. The poor bastards."

Ernest had no immediate words, and Johan, too, fell silent.

Ten

Cicero's Fine Oceanarium of Spewed Wonders (1920–1932)

Bones of an impressive romance
Scattered all across the sands
A secret safe with all the world
Too vain to seem so capable.
— Ian George Brown and John Squire, "All Across the Sands"

December 1920

In the chilly winter of 1920–1921 when visitors to the area were scarce, Cicero began cleaning the vast, pebbleless, fine sand beaches around Sagres. The project was to last for many years, and to bring him much joy. He did this not from a sense of neatness, but from a desire to see the contents of the ocean's guts, to nosily sieve through her sputum. (The psychologist in Bill Cartwright would have loved an hour or so with this thoroughly intriguing young man.) Cicero marveled at the briny debris. He would chat to Alfredo while he worked, explaining that jetsam had come from a ship; flotsam was simply stuff that floated, while, like that damned forgotten Musketeer, the most fascinating of the three was lagan—the relieved scrapings of the ocean floor itself, which he suspected by law belonged to the King but which in practice was the sole property of the Emperor of Rome and his dog. Despite everything (or perhaps because of everything), it was rare for Cicero to be found without the makings of a smile on his young face, which, at sixteen, was developing signs of being quite handsome.

Johan preferred to stay up on the hill while Cicero was busy. The boy gathered the more interesting finds of detritus onto the grass banks sloping high above the sand, and after months, these became museums of oceanographic wonder. As he laid out each new salty and slimy discovery, he explained to Alfredo its recent history, rehearsing and honing it to relay later to Johan over soup. He giggled a lot to himself, often for Alfredo's benefit, for the dog possessed a sensitive barometer to the lads' moods.

Some days, when there was little to report from the ocean, Cicero told Johan fanciful tales of the dragoons of mermaids whom he had met that day. He brought home a trunk, which he said his favorite mermaid, called Pandora, had brought to him from the ocean floor. It had a large letter *P* painted on the side in lilac, and it was the type in which you'd expect to find, or to hide, a fortune in Spanish gold. There were indeed fish scales around the seams, and when he ran one through his thumb and forefinger, Johan was sure that he smelled instead warm butter. Cicero enthusiastically went into great detail about the mermaids' affairs with fishermen, sailors, and other nautical types. Ten of our years, he explained, make up a single mermaid year, and so their stories of their mothers and their aunts were rich and wondrous, and trawled from recent centuries. Apparently, Walter Raleigh had gained a reputation for only ever talking about himself; Drake had been a dreadful gossip, desperate to discover which of his contemporaries had made a pass at the creatures in a lonely moment; and Lord Nelson had missed his mother awfully. Columbus, they insisted, had only been trying to find a cure for seasickness, but instead, by marvelous misfortune, had found one for homesickness, and called it the Americas.

"Oh, boss! You should come tomorrow to see what I have to catalog. That big angry sea is keeping me a busy boy. A rocking horse. An aircraft propeller. A herd of sea horses. Last week, ten thousand toy soldiers and a harpsichord, an Egyptian galley and an octopus with a monocle. But our most beautiful piece is a small horse in a glass case, with a fine ivory horn on its nose. I've found a skull ten times the size of yours, and counted one hundred and twenty-eight perfect teeth. He's a giant. The boys and I, we call him Ignatius. If Cicero cannot make or change history, at least Cicero may record it."

He immediately realized that this final statement had been quite a thing to say in the company of Johan Thoms, but Johan waved away his apology and thought instead that in all his twenty-seven years, he had never witnessed (nor could he imagine witnessing) anyone so successfully refer to themselves from time to time in the third person. (Cicero had indeed mastered this, as was the stubborn and determined nature of this Roman hero.)

Cicero told of three viciously carnivorous, venomous, deviously conspiratorial sea anemones, Aztec gold, electric blue, and poppy red, who had been marooned in the breakers after they had pursued a deep-sea crab with a horrendous sense of direction. This, too, had been quite a thing to say in the company of Johan Thoms. The deep-sea crab with a shell of Ascot turquoise had fallen in love with a Henslow[9] swimming crab. They had chased her through the warm Atlantic waters to the vast open sands of Zavial Beach. The crabs had sensed they were being followed, but each time they had spun around, they had been met with a plantlike stillness. The resplendent predators were soon wilting in the Portuguese sunshine, just yards from their intended prey, who happily nuzzled each other and chuckled at the dying trio.

Cicero told Johan that an elderly, beached blue whale had told him her life story, which had made him weep. Her eyelid had thudded as she had died, and the ground had trembled. I imagine her frame may now take up a large portion of the old Museu de Cicero, which back then was rapidly becoming a wonder of the age, and yet was a very well-kept secret.

The boys from the villages would come and visit Cicero to see what he had found from the Atlantic, though oddly they were not able to see many of the marvels described later to Johan, often in front of them. This made them suspect that Cicero was exaggerating the truth to his pal, but they also believed he was doing this to aid the older man's mood. Cicero would referee soccer matches for the boys on the beach, and as he guided them all home afterward, he spoke to them of the preciseness of social etiquette, all of which he had extracted from Johan. Johan was always happy to continue these lessons from the wall at the front of the hut. The boys giggled and grinned initially but, each time, were soon captivated. The sharing of this knowledge (and what he saw as *love*) soothed Johan, and he would remind himself to constantly remind himself of this. He started to teach them how to play chess, too, convinced that the lessons of the board contained strategy and skill, but he maintained that it was a game for gentlemen. He urged his pupils to take the decorum learned from the boundaries of the board into the very soul of their beings.

"Of course, chess is about war, but it is more about living by the rules, striving for success through thinking, and shaking your opponent's hand, should one win or lose. Etiquette, decency, chin up, shoulders back, boys!"

He delighted in dredging up many tips which he promised would give the young scamps a romantic advantage in years to come. The boys would blush, though they knew not why. The impromptu classes in front of the hut became more frequent, until, one sweet-aroma'd evening in May of 1926, when the aiding and abetting air held captive the whiff of jasmine, Johan officially founded the Young Hooligans' Chess Club.

Johan took enormous pride in this distraction, and was soon holding court in the dusty classroom of the village school, thanks to Ismerelda's generosity and a spare set of keys. This allowed the chessboards to be left overnight if necessary, for many of the boys were becoming quite proficient, prompting memories for Johan of a night two decades previous when the scent of an unlikely victory had briefly filled his eager nostrils.

Johan designed a coat of arms for the club. A field of calendula sat below a neo-Moorish garlic-headed domed palace, reminiscent of the fine architecture in Bascarsija, at Kaunitz's ancestral castle and the Old Sultan's. The marigold lurked behind a portcullis, half open, half closed. The stately grille was flanked to the right by a fourteen-blade antler and a butterfly, and to the left by a figure pulling down on a rope, guided by a pulley above, suggesting that the barrier might actually be lifting. One word in a scroll underlined the images: *Deslizar*. In English, "to glide."

Eleven

Suffragettes, Mermaids, and Hooligans (1932)

For art comes to you proposing frankly to give nothing but the highest quality to your moments as they pass, and simply for those moments' sake.

—Walter Pater

The White-Kilted Brigadier found a small but solid market, straddling a strange demographic of *Boy's Own* book-club types and a smattering of romantic young ladies. It seemed the publisher, Tobias Kilz of the Ruben-Wolfram Press, was losing money on Blanche's works, yet he also seemed keen to receive more manuscripts. Johan chuckled when he thought of Cicero's initial stealth. The small proceeds were funneled into a Portuguese bank account in the name of the Young Hooligans' Chess Club, whose treasurer was the dependable, proud Ismerelda. Brand-new chessboards, pieces, books by grand masters, and timer clocks were soon delivered to the school.

Blanche de la Peña became the personal hero of Emmeline Pankhurst, the leader of the British suffrage movement, the Women's Social and Political Union. Despite paradoxically having advocated militancy in her own methods, Ms. Pankhurst had also been famed on the international stage for her pacifist view (as, of course, was Blanche). She was less famed for her shuddering, bubbling, raging desire to meet Brigadier Stanley Rex-Foyle.

Over the next two years, *The White-Kilted Brigadier versus the Laugh of the Spanish Horseman*, *The White-Kilted Brigadier's Search for the Scarlet Grail*, and *The White-Kilted Brigadier and the Strange Hiatus of the Bohemian Blade* were mailed to England. Kilz was delighted each time, read them with gusto over and over again, and almost as an afterthought, sent them to the printer for publication.

* * *

It was now 1932.

Johan, an adult and quite well Cicero, and a very old Alfredo had stayed within a ten-mile radius of the village hugging oblivion for almost eighteen years. In that time Johan had deteriorated.

As the world had slipped into the Great Depression, Cicero had done his best to convince Johan that it had not been his fault. This time there had been no direct causal link back to June 28, 1914, although Johan had already persuaded himself to the contrary. Of course, it *had* been his fault. And hence, more ridiculous behavior followed.

So what if he was found wandering the streets naked on summer afternoons and at winter dawns?

So what if he talked to himself by the roadside, sipping English tea which he had delivered from Southampton via Lisbon (his one extravagance)?

So what if he had started to wear a patch on his right eye for no reason whatsoever? The locals knew it was for no reason, for he had also been seen wearing it on his left eye.

His ever-increasing number of out-of-body experiences did not disturb him. Indeed, he reveled in them, even looked forward to them, doping himself by adding extra nutmeg or mature cheese to the bubbling copper pots on the old fire stove in the scullery, in an attempt to fire the neurons in his finely wayward brain. The hallucinogenic properties of nutmeg are well known.

It was while under its influence in May of '32 that Johan first heard of Pedro's drowning. Then, in the same hour, he saw an old and myopic, yet still mobile Alfredo killed: hit and then dragged a quarter of a mile by a pig truck. The saddest part was that this was not a hallucination. He heard the sickening thud of truck on dog, and then a yelp. He yelled to Cicero, who was showering around the back of the shack. They ran up the dirt road to where Alfredo lay whimpering, his silver and brown eyes still alive but his back end a flattened mess, as if it had gone slowly and surely through one of the village ladies' washing mangles. The old mutt looked at them both, his lids getting heavier each time he switched from Johan to Cicero. The hound's life seemed to be flashing in front of him, and he appeared to regress to a sunny day on a foreign beach. A boat with three figures was coming ashore. They might just be a master and friend like he had seen other dogs have. Why not them? Smart, old Alfredo, with his knowing, graying whiskers and symmetrical *grisé* eyebrows, knew that he was in trouble. Cicero's tears landed on the dying dog's fuzzy face. It would be au revoir in a second, old chum. Then, before the next hurried breath was complete, it was a dead dog's face, with just a hint of the young pup Alfredo. And adieu.

Old Alfredo, who had sired many strange-looking litters around the hamlet, was buried later that day in a hessian sack, deep, deep in the ground, up by the lighthouse, not far (Cicero reckoned) from the bones of a blue whale, a unicorn, and several mermaids. Alfredo was left so deep as to prevent the whiff of a cadaver, and thus prevent being dug up by foxes or scavengers in the night. The spot was marked by rocks and stones, until Cicero could come up with something more appropriate, which, in a spot like Sagres, had to be a cross.

Pedro was afforded no such luxury as a cross, nor a proper burial—just the depths of the ocean.

Two good friends were gone. Johan could not shed a tear. Cicero wept each time he remembered the day he and Johan had arrived in the boat from Split, their inimitable welcome on the pebbly shores of Italy. He cried when he thought of how life must have been for the pup Alfredo, shunned by other dogs, perhaps because his eyes had made him different. Alfredo had been a loner, like Johan, like Cicero himself.

Cicero cried when he thought of a frustrated life, unable to verbalize, to tell his human friends how much he loved them, instead of dumb whines and annoying barks. He cried when he thought of Alfredo being hungry. Or bouncing on the beach like a gazelle. Or falling asleep on Cicero's feet in bed every single night since that night when he, like Sancho Panza, had slept on a donkey's back, somewhere near Dubrovnik. He realized he was crying a hell of a lot.

"It is the deal into which we enter, my young Roman, when they enter our lives. This day invariably comes, unless we go first. To lose them hurts and we have to accept that, for the joy they bring us in one single hour is worth the pain you feel now. Ask yourself why you are crying. Out of joy, I'd hope. He had eighteen years of warm beds, and always a belly never far from being full of meat and gravy; we should all be so lucky."

As much as Cicero did not want to be convinced, he knew his friend was right. Cicero told Johan that Pandora, his favorite mermaid, had comforted him one day, and told him that life can be painful and death may well bring sadness, so we absolutely must seek the magic in the detail and in the moment. Glide, boys, glide.

And so once again, there were just two.

Though not for long.

* * *

New York City, February 12, 1927

My dearest J.,

It's our son's birthday again today. He is twelve years old. Happy birthday to you, too. The years are now passing so quickly. I may sometimes forget your face, but Carl still hears about his father every day. New York City is treating us well, but I miss Europe. Many days, it seems like it was all a different lifetime, or an out-of-body experience, or some recent moving picture which dared to breach my emotions, which I fear have chilled beyond redemption. I could, however, make an exception, if you were to appear to me.

I bloody well dare you, my beloved disparu.

Yours,
Lorelei xxx

Twelve

Let's Rusticate Again

If Hitler invaded Hell I would make at least a favourable reference to the devil in the House of Commons.

—Sir Winston Churchill

If Johan Thoms was guilty, then so, too, was one Henry Tandey (VC, DCM, MM) of the Warwickshires. For it was Tandey who allowed a dispirited, disheveled German soldier to go free during a scrap in Marcoing, France, back in 1918. The private's name was Adolf Hitler, and he had fully expected to be shot. Thereafter, he had become convinced of his destiny as the savior of the German *Volk*.

A failed Austrian painter with one bollock, Hitler was of dubious stock; he is thought to have been the product of inbreeding. This might have given his family tree the impression of being a touch too vertical, lacking in branches. He was miffed by the reparations his neighboring Germany had been forced to pay under the 1919 Treaty of Versailles (coincidentally signed on June 28, the anniversary of Abu Hasan's lingering Sarajevan trump), a begrudging deal intended to neatly wrap up proceedings after more than thirty-six million guts had been spilled.

Berlin's bill of account was a shocking $33 billion. The Germans' precious coal was deemed to be French. Swaths of their precious land, their *heilige Erde,* became Polish. They owed cash to the latecomers from America. Their balls (for not all of them had only one) were firmly in the hands of the British and the Russians. To rub salt into the wound, they were forced to admit guilt for the whole sorry show. (This they soothed somewhat by sinking their own fleet at Scapa Flow off Scotland rather than handing their naval hardware over.)

The Treaty of Versailles succeeded only in engendering a festering, supremely nasty Teutonic resentment. Hitler channeled the anger felt by a nation. He rallied bullies, agents provocateurs, pyromaniacs, murderers, retards, delinquents, and twisted intellectuals. He blamed the Jews for the whole nasty business and zigzagged his way to power through a mélange of Machiavellia and sheer fear. All well documented, all stemming from the outcome of the Great War, and, therefore, all the fault of Johan Thoms.

Or so Johan believed, and that was all that mattered.

* * *

The amateur psychologist in Bill Cartwright might have suggested that Johan's instinct to head west toward the dipping sun pointed to a desire to disappear and, in doing so, to erase the past. He might well have had a case. But it had also allowed Johan to offer protection from the war to both of the lads, for down at the End of the World in Sagres, even the Great War had had a buffer zone: Spain.

Across Europe, however, the dominoes, were now starting to fall. Portugal fell under the fascist wickedness of Salazar in 1932.

"It's time to scram. Once again, we shall be forced to rusticate," Johan said.

So, a very different-looking pair from the ones who rolled into town all those years before packed their belongings together and began their reluctant retreat from the End of the World.

After the Young Hooligans' Chess Club had made a promise to Johan and to Cicero to continue to meet three times weekly until their friends returned, to limit their use of the word *she* to just three times monthly and never in the company of a female, to never use red ink in a letter, and to nurture their younger siblings into the society, the boys (and some who were now fully grown, who had returned for the evening) embraced the men they had grown to love deeply. Johan promised to write to them each year on June the twenty-eighth, which he did until he did not even know many of the club, for they continued to induct young boys each new school term, and apparently still do to this day.

Johan and Cicero spent a few silent minutes at Alfredo's resting place. They then collected the old kit bag from under the floorboards, fired-up the dirty old car, and slipped away from Vila do Bispo and from Sagres under cover of darkness, as they had done once before from a hospital ten miles east of Mostar.

Thirteen

Jackboots, Cleopatra, and the Bearded Lady (1932–1936)

During times of universal deceit telling the truth becomes a revolutionary act.

—George Orwell

Cádiz, Spain. 1932.

For the next four years (from 1932 to 1936) they took refuge in the beauty of Cádiz, on Spain's southwestern coast, between the Iberian border and British Gibraltar. Cicero was in his late twenties, a handsome man, with dark Slavic eyes, smooth skin, and a fine widow's peak. His nose, like his name and his confident attitude, seemed to be Roman. He had grown to six foot three. He carried no excess fat, but was lean, and athletic. Despite all this, he was still a virgin, but quite unburdened by this.

His attentions had been diverted toward his sick pal. It seemed to him that his payment, his debt to Johan, would supersede anything he could ever feel for a girl. Subconsciously, he had accepted this in his youth, and nothing had happened so far to prompt him to consider an alternative. That remained so until, at an open-air circus on the beach during the throbbing annual carnival in Cádiz in the summer of 1932, he saw a young girl.

Twenty minutes or so into the event, a violent electric storm forced the audience, the crew, the animals, and the performers to move for cover, and hastily. Cicero stayed in his seat. He might well have been infected years earlier with Johan's mistrust of the misanthropic umbrella, which in turn had given way to a sizzling affection for warm summer rain. Or perhaps his childhood illness had made such extravagances so much more fun to him, amusements that the fools running for cover could (sadly) never comprehend. Johan left his protégé there, announcing that his older bones were suspectible to a chill and that he was going to a favored restaurant in the back alleys of the old town to watch the flamenco girls. He would meet Cicero there.

Cicero then closed his eyes. This accentuated the feel and sound of the rain. His enjoyment was intense, but was magnified beyond his imagination when, five minutes later, he opened his eyes to see high above him a girl on the swinging trapeze, performing for him and only for him. She remained there for twenty, maybe thirty exquisite minutes, at high risk, both of falling without a safety net and from the lightning. She managed to perform without a partner, and it seemed that she did so to perfection, thoroughly reveling in the heightened peril, all glittering and inspiring. Her backdrop was dark, which only highlighted the twinkling stars on her costume and the trail of a supernova she left in her sublime arcs high above Cicero. If one stares hard enough into the night skies, the planets may change color; it seemed this girl also did this that night in Cádiz: electric blue, fire red, burnt orange, Aztec gold, and the brightest of whites, which one suspects is the very same white of the light that leads us into death. Cicero felt privileged.

Eventually she shimmied down, and Cicero was there to meet her at the bottom of the rope. She made it very easy for him to talk to her, encouraging his initial shy mutterings until his pulse had calmed, but only back to the level of someone who had just fallen in love, and for the first time.

"You looked so happy up there."

"I might just be happier down here right now. My name is Veronica, though for their show the circus likes to call me Florita, the little flower."

"Cicero. Emperor."

"Emperor of where?"

"That is a secret. I might tell you one day, but I have to be on guard, you understand. There are treasonous plotters in our midst." He wondered if he was being an idiot, but her giggles and her gentle sways in front of him suggested otherwise.

"I completely understand, Your Highness. But why did you not take cover from the rain? You will catch your death of cold."

"It's impossible to catch cold if one enjoys the rain. I have often suspected that this was a marvelous secret, too, but I just watched you up there, and I know that you also know this. Maybe we could keep this secret between ourselves, though?"

"I would like that. I would like that very much, Emperor Cicero."

"Would you like to walk along the beach? We might then take a drink with a friend of mine, if you wish. He is waiting for me, and you might just like him. And he you."

"I am all yours."

And they walked along the beach, guided by the flickering gaslights. The rain hardened, and the swish of the tide caught their feet. Cicero told her that he had never had a girlfriend, for his hero was the Flying Dutchman, the mythical phantom sailor destined to sail his ghost ship on the high seas until he found his one true love, who would be willing to die for him. She suspected she might be dealing with a fine politician, and smiled.

Veronica pulled Cicero away from a collection of beach parasols bending threateningly in the persistent winds, and it was then that Cicero knew that Johan would simply adore her. They kissed.

When, soaked and smiling, they came into the restaurant where Johan was waiting, the aroma of apples came with them. Veronica needed not the artificial help of an eau de toilette, for her skin when mixed with the Cádiz air and the warm evening rain created something of true beauty. Johan nicknamed her Manzana.

* * *

The following night he took the couple to a picture house off the town square to see *Freaks*—the story of a circus of strongmen, midgets, characters with extreme deformities, and a radiant and beautiful trapeze artsist whose name was Cleopatra. They laughed throughout. The next afternoon, Veronica returned to see the film with her best friend, a bearded lady called

Gertrude, but Emperor Cicero was there to meet his very own Cleopatra after the film, with an armful of tuberoses.

Veronica's show that night made the audience gasp with delight, even more so than usual. Cicero was there, of course, and brought Johan along to witness the high pitch of her sublime art.

The next evening, Cicero asked her, "Would you, Veronica Florita Cleopatra Manzana, make the Emperor Cicero the happiest boy in Spain, and please marry him?"

She had more names than there had been days since they'd met.

"Only if you promise with all of your heart to tell me on our wedding night where you are emperor of. If you can do that . . ."

"I promise."

"I do say yes."

* * *

Veronica moved into the boys' *casita* by the beach of La Caleta, and Johan rented a second room for himself. She continued to perform at the circus until the winter break. Cicero watched every performance from the same seat. They were married in September 1932, when Cicero stood by his promise and told his bride that he was the emperor of that place in the east to which he now pointed, that birthplace of all the Universe's stardust and supernovas since the beginning of time. Of course, his finger was in the precise direction of Rome.

Johan's best friend was happy, and in this, Johan knew he should take solace. He adored Veronica, for she laughed a lot and she in turn worshipped the ground Cicero seemed (in her eyes) to float above, as serenely as she did for real each evening.

Johan spent all his days in the same way by the beach between the two wonderful ancient castles of San Sebastian and Santa Catalina. Without the diversion of upheaval, movement, and war, and remaining in one place, weeks and months passed by quickly. He attempted to live vicariously, through Cicero.

Johan joined the local library under the cover of yet another false name; this time it was Pedro Alvarado. Pedro, from his friend in Portugal; Alvarado, from the label of a rather decent bottle of wine he had with him for company. He spent most of his days reading alone in a small café on the promenade by the beach. He would frequently drop what he was reading and tap out a few words on his typewriter, though he wrote no new novels during these months. Cicero did, however, mail several piles of bizarre short stories and a few clunky poems to London under the title of *The Gospel According to Blanche de la Peña.* Her name was such that these were published and sold well. It was around this time that Johan came upon the following in the *Manchester Guardian,* by the critic Archibald DeWitt-Vultura, which made him chortle and Cicero snort with delight and pride.

THEY SEEK HER HERE; THEY SEEK HIM THERE

The mystery of the identity of Miss de la Peña has continued now for almost two decades. I suspect we shall all go to our graves unaware of her (or his) true identity. Last night, I heard chat at a dinner party that the Prime Minister is where some of the smart money may lie, violently afraid as he is since the Peking Summit to fully reveal his own born-again pacifism. Dorothy Parker's fingerprints are suspected, too, as she is allegedly still shuddering from that emetic bloodlust in Spain. Mrs Christie? Lord Buchan? The Duke of Gloucester? Mr Compton? Mr Niven? Mr C. B. Fry?

Rumours, allegedly emanating from around the environs of Bloomsbury, of Our Blanche having revealed herself (though not in the biblical sense, sadly) in the latest adventure of Rex-Foyle are (I may confirm here in these editorial pages) wide of the mark, and likely to have been a cunning stunt of that wily old Ludgate Circus book lord, Mr Tobias Kilz. The claim that her self-portrait might be found in a mystery locker at St. Pancras station is piffle, for no such trail of clues in the text exists.

She may just as well be that fusty old gent with the twitch and the monocle opposite you on the Northern Line right now, or some dashing Brylcreemed wing-half making his debut for Charlton Athletic on Saturday. He may be the leading man (Mr Roger Livesey) or his counterpart (Miss Wendy Hiller) in Mr J. Arthur Rank's upcoming moving picture of The White-Kilted Brigadier. *Or he might not.*

Surely someone reading this missive knows Miss de la Peña, either unwittingly or otherwise.

One thing that I may tell you for sure, however, is that the latest pulp instalment shall not disappoint. In fact, it could not be more exciting than if old Holmes himself had survived (or is he really keeping bees in Sussex?), returned to Blighty, and had, to an audience gasp as the credits played, revealed the grinning face of Jack the Ripper on the wireless.

Bravo, Blanche! Please just stay as unknown to us as you currently are, although you are most welcome to take high tea (or something ridiculously stronger) here at our offices on any day of any week. Your secret is safe with the Manchester Guardian, *and there is no need to use the code word. Three simple winks and to whistle the first four bars of "The Colonel Bogey March" shall suffice, Prime Minister.*

* * *

For companionship, Johan would engage in conversation with many of the tourists who stopped in for the café's well-publicized and quite delicious orange ice cream. He himself preferred the café's wine, and while he could be charming before the middle of the afternoon, he often became intrusive with his comments, which he alone seemed to find amusing, as the evenings approached. The old owner, Carlos-Ramón Kitríl, initially tolerated Johan, for he was his best customer. Latterly, Carlos-Ramón admired and possibly even loved him. He appreciated Johan's air of eccentricity, as well as his erudition. Carlos-Ramón, in his youth, had started the superbly colorful and rich local custom of the *chirigota,* the bizarre, even surreal, satirical musical troupes which circulate the artistic haunts of the Old City to this day. Johan, too, was very fond of Carlos-Ramón: his ever-present generosity, his wise, creased face, and his superbly spiced Moorish pork.

The beaches, the labrynthine old town (which made Johan think of Bascarsija), and the promenades made Cádiz a quite beautiful place in the early thirties. Its bizarre geography offered a further soothing comfort to Johan, for the city lies on a narrow spit, hemmed in by the Atlantic waters as they approach the warmer, calmer Mediterranean at British Gibraltar. Cádiz displayed with chest-out civic pride the signs of her successful resistance of Napoleon, her flourishing history under Moorish and Roman occupation, and her naval traditions, for it was here where Sir Francis Drake famously singed the King of Spain's beard.

Most evenings, Johan would dine with Veronica and Cicero, who would tell him of their days, her new routines on the trapeze, their adventures around the town or out on fishing boats. Johan was often quite tipsy at this point, and would soon be in his bed and unable to recall much detail. He was unable to recall anything of real note for Ernest until he told him that Veronica died swiftly in July 1936 after contracting typhoid.

Cicero buried her in a local cemetery. On her white limestone gravestone was engraved

VERONICA FLORITA CLEOPATRA MANZANA EMPRESS OF ROME

Cicero wept openly. Johan stared into space, but this did not mean he was not moved, for he was, and deeply so.

On the same day as her funeral, they learned that an errant right-wing general in the Spanish armed forces in Morocco, by the name of Francisco Franco, had declared a civil war. The renegades were marching up from the south and were taking all in their dusty-blood path as their own. The geography of Cádiz meant that Johan and Cicero had to move quickly. They backtracked eastward across Spain, staying in one-tavern towns. Cicero drove most of the way, with Johan stretched across the backseat, usually staring west, fully aware that the decay of his now beloved Portugal was all his fault.

Sadly, to Cicero, his logic did indeed seem to make sense.

*　*　*

"If I could not turn the clock back to Sarajevo in '14, then I would return to those warm days and nights of Cádiz. The sun and the lights of the city, the shaded back alleys and the worn mosaic tiles that cooled us into a blissful serenity. I would spend a day at Carlos-Ramón's with my friend, eating orange ice cream and drinking wine, waiting for Veronica and Cicero to appear at dusk."

Johan picked up another letter, and passed it to Ernest.

New York City, July 6, 1936

My dearest J.,

I am returning to Europe with Carl. I have promised to show him Paris, Athens, and London. We will also be in Sarajevo. I have a pair of rooms reserved in a certain hotel near Bascarsija, where he wants to read The Arabian Nights. *Oh my!*

I would hate to impose, but we might even consider visiting Argona so that he may perhaps meet his grandparents.

Carl is on leave from the navy. A pair of skinny pink doughboys from Arkansas told him he has an older doppelgänger living by the last lighthouse in Europe, in Portugal. He has a crazy notion it's you, and doggone, I think he has me convinced of it, too. Fascists be damned, we're on your trail.

Your ever-determined Lorelei xxx

Fourteen

The Girl in the Tatty Blue Dress

When therefore I have performed this, and have sealed to them this fruit, I will come by you into Spain.

—Romans 15:28

1937. Molina, Spain

By that summer, the fighting was closing in on them, though they did not know this. They had been continually assured that Franco's incursion would be a limited one. Month after month, however, it showed no sign of waning. Cicero had started to sense the fear in the locals as they passed through the dusty, neglected wastelands of Extremadura. That sense of foreboding increased as they headed across the plains into the morning sun.

They stopped in the small town of Molina for gasoline one glorious dusk, the type of evening that knows that trouble is on the way and that begs to be loved one last time. As they started off once more on their journey, there by the pumping station stood a creature of crazy beauty in a tatty blue dress. She had grime on her forehead, elevated cheekbones, and black, black hair. She was young, no more than sixteen. Her beauty was of Babylonian proportions. She clearly obeyed the moon. She held what appeared to be a section of a bedsheet with the words *No Aqui*—"not here"—daubed in motor oil.

There was only one thing for Cicero to do, for she was no quixotic mirage. He pulled the car up next to her and kicked a half-present Johan to speak on his behalf in Spanish. She took a seat in the back, and sat in silence, exuding a coy virginal air, but one that seemed to itch. She caught Cicero's glances in the mirror. He was convinced he saw her bite her lip, as if to suppress something, as they bumped off through the potholes. The way she had moved her young slim hips and her muscular, boyish buttocks in the ragged dress suggested she had more than an inkling of things. (Indeed, her hands had discovered new and undiscussed delights one day at the bullfight, watching the famous Manolete.) Cicero noticed the skin of her cheeks redden, and her neck blush. Her almond-shaped eyes dilated black on black. He silently named her Buttercup, and he thought of his love, Veronica, Cleopatra, the Little Flower, and how she smelled of apples.

Her name was Catalina Boadicea Rodríguez. *Catalina* means "pure." She was an orphan that late July day in '37, the youngest of seven living siblings, the rest all male. Her mother, María, had died during her birth.

María had often dreamed as a child of being rescued from the village by the ancient warrior and rebel queen from the north, Boadicea; hence her father, Jesús, had given his daughter that name. Jesús had inherited from a bandito uncle a dusty but well-located gas station, the running of which—at best—kept his young clan from starvation. Jesús was a hard man; the harsh Molina terrain simply demanded it.

Jesús had died in 1934 from a form of gangrene caused by an infection to an open wound in his foot, incurred while sleepwalking one night in the toxic earth around his plot. Catalina had warned him many times that the ever-present cigarette on his bottom lip would kill him, yet he had continued to smoke next to the solitary pump for decades. Indeed, it was a kind of gas that got him in the end. Gas gangrene (caused by *Clostridium*) is quick and very painful. Catalina, alone, had watched him die. The day he died, all of her brothers had preferred to go to a bullfight. She never really forgave them, though she did try.

Back in the village of her childhood, Catalina had dreamed every night for as long as she could remember of being rescued by an American cowboy.

* * *

Paris, August 17, 1937

My dearest J.,

In secret we met—
In silence I grieve,
That thy heart could forget,
Thy spirit deceive.
If I should meet thee
After long years,
How should I greet thee?
With silence and tears.

The very chance would be a fine thing, Johan Thoms! Dorothy arrives at the Cap d'Antibes from the Spanish foothills next week. I fear for her in that dreadful land right now, for Portugal was bad enough. We aim to have fun. I miss her.

Viens à moi! Baise moi!

With my heart, but I suspect you may already know that,

Lorelei xxx

Fifteen

She Had a Most Immoral Eye
(1937–1940)

You come from very far away. But this distance,
What is it for your blood, which sings without borders?
Necessary death names you each day,
No matter in which cities, fields, or highways.

—Rafael Alberti

July 21, 1937. Monreal del Campo, Spain

As they drove into the region, Johan saw the sign for Aragon. He thought he was back in Argona, sweated, and entered a trauma. They drove twenty miles more before stopping for the night in the village of Monreal del Campo.

They checked into a small hotel by the side of a main road littered with trucks and weaponry. Cicero procured the girl her own room and promised to bring her some food and warm milk within the hour.

He then shoved a pliable Johan into a cold shower next to their two-bunk room. This brought Johan around. He was ready for some grog. They shaved, put on their best shirts, and headed across to the bar, which resembled a scene from an old cowboy movie. The town was full of fighters, trying to do the right thing for freedom. They hailed from the world over, for the fight was a microcosm of the globe. American drawls, English accents, Russian, Czech, French, Spanish, Basque . . .

Cicero's first thought was to get the girl some food. Johan's was to get soaked to the eyeballs in booze.

They grabbed a table recently vacated by a couple eager for some privacy. Their waiter was far from prompt but, sweating profusely, gave the opposite impression.

Cicero ordered a bowl of paella and a glass of warm milk for the girl. Johan's eyes were flashing as if the clock had been turned back to the Old Sultan's Palace. The room held a strange energy. A large-necked, thick-wristed American, celebrating a birthday, was holding court at the teak bar. For a while his magnetism was unmatched. He chewed gum like a cow pulling its hoof out of mud.

In the bar, various cliques had evolved. The American had maybe a dozen in the palm of his bearish hand. There was loud talk of deep-sea fishing, catches broader than the American's own huge wingspan, of bullfighting, of the scraps in the Sierra de Guadarrama. There was a slight danger of mere mortals getting a syllable in edgeways, but only when the gobshite (as Bill Cartwright would have called him) slugged back his dark rum and shut up for a second.

"Ernie! Tell the one about the mermaid and the carrot!" and off he would go to the delight of the initiated and the intrigue of the uninitiated.

"The only reason they won't let me fight is because when I gave a piss sample, it had a fucking olive in it!" he bellowed.

With a table of eight by the front window sat a distinguished, angular-faced lady, her dark fringe cut as straight as a German smile across her clever brow, who kept all around her hanging upon her every word. Laughter cracked out every couple of minutes in competition with fat-pawed Ernie's mob.

"I'll have an absinthe. Absinthe makes the tart go fondle'er," she declared. Johan shuddered when he heard *that* drink mentioned. Brown-nosed guffaws followed.

"Dorothy, Dorothy. Stop it! You're killing *us*! Whoa!"

It was *her*, Dorothy Parker, Lorelei's old chum, the woman whose clever lines surely had a hand in bringing the two together. Johan remembered Lorelei quoting Parker on the lawns of the Old Sultan's Palace one magnificent June night almost a quarter of a century earlier. She spoke with an acerbic New York twang and seemed to know everything about everything. Her delivery was deadpan, her audience in raptures.

"There was nothing separate about her days; like drops upon a window-pane, they ran together and trickled away!" she continued. Johan wished he had thought of this line, but when he heard the baying pack howl and saw them even sway in unison, he took on instead the expression of a man with a dead mackerel for a tie. The sycophancy made him want to puke.

Among the packed crowd, only one other caught Johan's eye. At a table toward the back of the bar, by the swinging saloon door that led to the latrine, sat a lone gentleman in a grubby suit, jotting in an old note-pad. Thin, gaunt, yellowing, he did not utter a word other than when ordering food and drink.

Johan was strangely drawn to the mystery of this silent, scribbling character, for he seemed to have much to say through the privacy of his pen. Johan's own pen had been mainly still during this time; he could not write while he was in motion. They say that this is not uncommon.

A rowdy rendition of "Happy Birthday, Dear Ernest" was heard, but Johan's attention kept returning to the solitary polite gentleman, and when the sweaty waiter returned, he asked for a drink to be sent over to him, when the waiter had a chance.

Meanwhile, the crowd was spilling out onto the pavements as folk songs started to come from a character with a Spanish guitar. Ernest and Dorothy politely and unexpectedly clammed up and listened. Johan heard them referred to in the third person around the bar by strangers.

The thirsty pushed their way in for drinks to take to their weary, nervous compadres, outside in the hot Spanish evening. Between songs, they listened to the rhythmic drone of the crickets in the dust-bowl fields.

Eventually the skeletal stranger received his complimentary drink, and the waiter pointed out the purchaser. He laid down his pen and gestured a polite *"Gracias."* Then he offered the spare seat at the table to the strangers. The stench from the urinals was now obvious even from where Johan and Cicero sat, so Johan instead offered a spot at their own table, closer to the outside air, an offer which was politely accepted.

"Buenas noches. Y muchas gracias, señor," the man offered in an awkward yet adequate Spanish which suggested he was an Englishman.

"You are very welcome," Johan replied in English.

"Johan Thoms. Pleased to meet you. This is Cicero."

Cicero politely nodded.

"Ah! The mother tongue." The man breathed a sigh of relief. "Thank the Lord. That is if He hasn't completely forsaken this poor land and their people for good. Blair's the name. Eric Arthur Blair. Well, it used to be. Let's stick with it around here, shall we?"

They shook hands, though it looked for all the world that Blair's would snap if someone were to as much as sneeze near it.

Johan noticed the words Blair had scribbled in large letters on a piece of card:

I have always thought there might be a lot of cash in starting a new religion.

Blair caught him looking and smiled.

"How long you been here in the scrap, lads?" Blair wondered.

"Oh no," said Johan. "We aren't. We are here by chance. We were in Sagres and Cádiz for a few years. We are wandering, and it looks like we've wandered into something!"

"I'd say," Blair agreed, with the plummy accent of a distinguished English gent.

Johan noticed a nasty wound on Blair's neck, strangely reminiscent of Franz Ferdinand's neck wound, which Johan had surveyed from a similar distance. Blair caught him looking the second time.

"I took one in the neck from a Nationalist sniper. The mucky little blighter. They say I am lucky to be alive. I say it would have been a damn sight luckier not to be hit at all! Cheers, boys!"

Already Johan liked him more than Ernest. Cicero watched and listened.

"What brings an Englishman here to fight this battle, Mr. Blair? And the Americans, too? Here in Spain, I mean? I just don't get it," said Johan.

"What the darn Frenchies call a cause célèbre, old boy. You ever been to Paris? Just had two years there. Queer bunch. Anyway, this is not about countries or borders, my friend. It is something far bigger, far more important. It is an idea. An ideal. It is humanity versus, well, them . . ."

"Good versus evil, you mean?"

"Yes, exactly. But I did not want to say it. So, thank you for saving me the embarrassment," he teased. "We're just a ragged army of bayonet

fixers, and there are trenches full of poets. It is about as sad and as romantic, as dangerous and as astonishingly inspirational, as it gets. One
feels as exposed as a naked man in a slippery-tiled sauna surrounded by
a squadron of thugs with razor wire and cutthroat blades, and they are
moving in on one, emitting a wholly unpleasant tang of savory vapors;
each miscreant with his one half-decent eye displaying an intent of no
good, nothing but graceless mobs of pigs and boars, bullies and lackeys.
And there are no bladdy atheists in these foxholes. We know a god would
not have allowed this on his watch. Unless he was sleeping off a hangover. In which case, he becomes far more likable, but still rather shoddy
for a god."

"And you believe in something so strongly that you would lay down
your life for it?"

"I guess so. I am here, aren't I?"

Blair did not sound the least boastful.

"The pen may be far mightier than the sword. To use both could be
pretty damned intimidating to one's foes," he continued.

Blair leaned forward, so as neither to be overheard nor to emphasize
his point, which is exactly what he managed to do.

"Ernest and Dorothy are great friends with their pens, but not many
swords. Just hacks, though popular and talented ones!"

Johan's homeland, Bosnia, had remained largely untouched during the
Great War, but Serbia had taken a battering. Yet he could not even con-
template fighting on his own side, never mind someone else's. Cicero, he
noticed, was looking intently and admirably at the Englishman, in a quiet
and studied state of awe.

"Where are you from?" Blair asked. "And how come the magnificent
command of English?"

"I? Sarajevo," Johan answered, guardedly. "Cicero? The craggy wilds by
the Croatian coast. We've been cohorts for far too long, Mr. Blair. But we
don't know any different these days. Twenty-odd years. Twenty very odd
years. As for the English, I learned at school, reading, and from an old pal,
William Atticus Forsythe Cartwright of Huddersfield. Poor bugger did not
make it past lunch at the Somme. My fault!" Johan started to stare into
space and twitch. Cicero gave his shin a kick.

Blair looked confused, and changed the subject, though with hindsight he might have delved a little more into Johan's story, for it might well have interested him.

"See him? Ernest chap? Big-shot American writer. Hemingway. Even louder on his birthday, it seems. Not a bad scribe, actually. Her, too. Very good indeed. Miss 'I bladdy well know it all' Parker. The thing is, chaps, that she *does* bladdy know it all. It's wonderfully annoying. I know that they are both here supporting our cause, so I guess I should not be too harsh on them. He writes for an American newspaper, I believe. They say Dorothy is making a motion picture, writing a book. Who knows? I do know I wouldn't like to get into a fistfight with *her* in a trench."

"Dorothy Parker! Who would believe it?" Johan thought again of how Lorelei had quoted a poem by her pal and how he had quipped back with some smart impromptu retort about worms and ashes.

"Yes. The very same, old chap. Keep one's distance, if I were one. Damned smart, that girl." Blair had become even plummier after his latest drink.

"Is this a weird dream? For we have a mutual friend. Or I beg your pardon and my solecism, I really should say a 'friend in common.' Tell me now if it is a dream, Mr. Blair."

"I would fully understand if it were, Thoms," he answered, using his surname in an Eton sort of way. "Sadly and surreally true, old chap! Sadly and surreally true."

Blair's food turned up, as did, finally, the paella and an unappealing cup of milk for Catalina. Cicero excused himself to take it to her.

The two remaining men turned their attention to Mrs. Parker, who was on form, revealing a fine impersonation of Mr. Ivor Novello.

"This one is called 'The Lovestruck Lads of Manchester.'

> "*The bombardiers of Manchester say,*
> *They used to love Blanche yesterday,*
> *For she was a lass of quality,*
> *More than a match for that Dorothy.*
>
> "*The lads clamber to be as manly*
> *As Blanche's white-kilted man Stanley,*

For the brigadiers of Manchester say,
They loved to love Blanche yesterday.

"When the beck roars like a river,
Blanche comes to make soldiers quiver
As the teary lads of Manchester say,
They fought to love Blanche yesterday.

"From the wheelchair and the grave,
They strut like knight and knave;
As the lovestruck ghosts of Manchester say,
They dreamed of kissing Blanche yesterday."

The bar fell silent, as first the ladies seemed to think of their own Private Strutter, which was enough to make the boys ponder their own fates. It really did not take much to be reminded of one's own proximity to death. Meanwhile, Johan tried to reckon on the odds of Dorothy being such an acolyte of old Blanche herself/himself, and *here*. Was it even possible that he had been exposed? This, along with the grog, got him thinking of his own long-absent belle. He knew he had to communicate with Dorothy at some point in the evening. Her fondness for Miss de la Peña seemed, in his gut, to bring Lorelei closer. How and why, he did not compute immediately, but the answers would soon come, as most answers do.

* * *

When Cicero returned fifteen minutes later, he announced to the pair at the table:

"I am going to war. Cicero will kill *Franco bastardos.*"

He had heard enough to convince him. His mind was made up. Twenty years in a hut with Johan Thoms could do that to a man. What's more, since Veronica's death, he had needed a new purpose in life, before it was too late. And he was already well over two decades in credit.

"By George! Cicero!" Blair choked on his rioja.

Johan stared at his friend. "Are you drunk? Are you cracked, man? Have you gone round the bend?"

"I mean it, boss. I am on borrowed time. If I take a bullet, I have seen more than the sisters of Mostar could have imagined."

"My God, you are NOT drunk. Do not do this. You will be as handy as a pig with a musket."

Cicero turned away and looked into the other man's eyes. "Where do I join, Mr. Blair?"

"Be outside at seven A.M. I will meet you there. One would hazard a guess that the job interview should not prove to be an issue. Never known it to be, so far."

He stuck out a rickety paw to Cicero.

"Welcome aboard, Comrade Cicero," he said, a glint in his intelligent eyes.

The three talked into the night, discussing the fronts in Guadalajara and Brunete. They expected to be fighting in Belchite within the month. The Teruel mountain range would be vital in the struggle. Then Blair told tales of horror he had heard from Germany, forecasting dark days ahead. He spoke of another war to match, and if not, to dwarf that of '14–'18. "Do not be fooled by their moniker. Forget about the 'Socialists'—focus on the 'Nationalists.' This Hitler needs a bullet."

He foresaw a Europe in tatters, for Blair, it would turn out, had a knack of foreseeing the future.

Johan kept them in rioja, and they were all quite pie-eyed by the end of the evening.

Cicero's interest and enthusiasm grew with each glass he drank. His dark eyes glazed over before midnight, when he fell outside to throw up.

Johan finally felt he was encroaching when Blair attempted to leave for the third time. By the time Blair did depart, Johan, now alone at the table, was keen to engage Mrs. Parker, who he could now see was heading to the door.

"Mrs. Parkurr." He staggered toward her. His head rolled drunkenly forward. "Do you know . . . Mrs. Lorlee Ribeiro, the American emb-see?"

"Yes, sir. And so do the Sixth Fleet, with all their necks stamped by her mouth. Now leave me alone, for you need to bathe."

This was one of Dorothy's typical quips, which she liberally attached to even the chaste among her pals, few in number though they were. In fact, Lorelei had been faithful to Johan. Initially, her fidelity was born from her pregnancy (Bill would have put it down to the increased levels of oxytocin) and a belief that Johan would soon return. She had marked the end of the war as the time when he might appear once more. By November 1918, her love for him had not waned, as some loves do over time, and it did not wane thereafter. Conversely, the pain felt by Johan at having started this fire proved commensurate with the solidarity she felt for him. Had she experienced moments of fleshly desires? Yes, she certainly had. But these had been passing whims. She was not really alone, for she had his son, Carl, and for the years when these longings had been at their most bubbling, she had still banked upon her eyes (and her arms and her legs) locking with Johan's once more. When Lorelei set her mind to something, that was that, and though she would continue to leave grown men as helpless debris in her fragrant swathe, *temptation* was removed from her lexicon.

Dorothy Parker, having thus maligned her friend, stormed out to the street, with a swaying, stumbling Johan following behind, yelling, "Well, YOU damn well tell her I . . . That bluddy stoopid wer-man!" Hiccup. In his drunkenness, he was unable to keep up, and dropped to join Cicero on the ground.

Dorothy stopped, turned back to him. "What do you want with Lorelei? And who the HELL are you, anyway?"

Even with a shield of alcohol, he was still, it turned out, not brave enough to find out more about Lorelei's current situation. Boozy ignorance was bliss.

"I am no one and please don't tell her you saw me. And don't tell me a thing. I don't want to know. Don't need to know, thank you, ma'am! Good night."

"Jesus! What happened to him?" She nodded toward the new recruit, Cicero, sitting doubled over by the curb.

"Oh, he signed up. He's just dealing with it. Of a fashion."

"And you, too?"

"I'm only helping him deal with it." Hiccup.

Then she managed to do something Johan had never seen before in his life. A look of pride, a beam on the left side of her face, appeared, dedicated to Cicero. How she managed a simultaneous look of disdain for the cowardly Johan on her right simply defied logic. But Dorothy Parker pulled it off. He was clearly to be no friend of hers.

"Good luck, soldier, especially in the morning, when you will be nursing a hangover which ought to be in the Smithsonian Institute under glass. And farewell, you!" She then turned and said to Johan, "For as a source of entertainment, conviviality, and good fun, you rank somewhere between a sprig of parsley and a single ice skate! You are as yellow as a canary lacking moral fiber and have all the depth and glitter of a worn dime. Good night and good-bye, sir."

"Bye, Mish Parker," he slurred. "And how are your friends the worms?" he mumbled to himself. She half caught this. There was one other person for whom those lines spoke volumes.

She flounced off toward two rough-looking types, waiting eagerly for her across the street. Three was going to be company, not a crowd. "A ménage-à-bunch," Bill used to say. Partway across, she stopped and turned to face Johan.

"If I do see her, I will tell her I saw you, *Johan Thoms*," she said, with a superior smile.

He paused, and seemed to choose his words very carefully.

"Would you perhaps be so kind as to pass along a message from me, please?" he said. "And please do not tell me if she hates me as much as I miss her."

"You must be cracked, Mac! I refuse to abet your emetic murkiness. Why don't you tell her yourself if you possess a fraction of the courage of a less than averagely endowed man? I am sure that even you might find the words; I was led to believe that you have on loan half a brain. Even if the other half were jelly, you could easily work out where to find that most remarkable lady. I *dare* you, you graceless and unwelcome bonehead of a drunk."

Dorothy revolved through one hundred and eighty degrees and started to sing quite expertly, and as if she could continue until dawn, a well-known tune of the day, "The Lorelei." Her two friends joined in, and all, including its composers the Gershwins, seemed to taunt Johan with its ribald lyrics about a lust for sailors and a most immoral eye.

Johan hesitated like one o'clock half struck, mumbled, and slurred to himself:

"Mish Parker! You may shtew in your own jooshes." He then scooped up Cicero from the floor and helped him to bed, leaving a hip flask of warm, stagnant tap water next to his head for the pending horror which the following morning would inevitably bring.

* * *

By eight A.M., Cicero had signed up. Even his stale dog breath had passed the induction exam. The friends had always known the day would come when they would part, but the circumstances still surprised them both.

"Are you sure? It wasn't the booze talking, was it?"

"Are YOU sure you won't come with me?"

It was a rhetorical question, yet playful and friendly. How could it be anything but?

They parted quickly and without visible emotion, almost militarily, having agreed to meet on the first New Year's Day after the war had finished, at noon, in the Café de Paris, outside the casino in Monaco. Even in 1937, by picking a spot well outside Spain, Johan was subconsciously legislating for a Republican defeat.

Sixteen

Archibald's Four Horsemen
of the Apocalypse

To burn always with this hard, gemlike flame, to maintain this ecstasy, is success in life.

—Walter Pater

And then, and with zero fuss, for the first time in a long, long time, there was just one. Just one, that is, apart from the latest passenger, Johan's new traveling companion and nurse-in-waiting, the girl in the tatty blue dress. Catalina Boadicea Rodríguez. When Johan returned to the car, Catalina was sitting on it. She seemed genuinely sad when she heard that Cicero had gone to war. Johan was delighted to have the company and, after the previous evening's talk with Blair, fully aware that they both had to leave Spain, and soon. He was also now responsible for the welfare of another human being, which he had not been since Cicero had been a young (and quite sick) boy.

Johan drove Catalina east into France on the high, winding, treacherous roads of the Pyrenees. Their route then hugged the road along the Mediterranean through Marseilles until they reached the small coastal village of La Napoule, outside Cannes. There they took refuge in a wonderful old château on the waterfront, the young and roguish owner of which had fallen for Catalina as they took coffee in the town square. Catalina never encouraged their host, le Comte de Benoît-Benoît, nor did she respond to his frequent and often desperate advances. She suspected that she was in love with Cicero, and as the date of their supposed rendezvous approached, she confirmed this to herself many times a day. She kept her own counsel for almost three years, but without an outlet, she later confessed, this caused feelings toward him to magnify in a violently romantic Spanish way.

It was here in the crumbling majesty of the castle on the waterfront where Blanche began to write again, the latest a story of distant love which had as its pivot a young fool's moment in Sarajevo in the summer of 1914, followed by a weak man fleeing, a horrific civil war in Spain, a chance meeting with Dorothy Parker, and a secret begged from two readers in particular.

It explored the concept of a Jesus not related to any god, his being just a really good bloke. Its every detail, arc, and character was so close to the truth of Johan's adult life that Dorothy would be sure to recognize it as *his.* Johan had figured out a way of using the great and mighty Dorothy to accomplish a task that he really ought to face himself: to communicate with Lorelei.

Dorothy may have been swifter than he on those Spanish steps that night, and was likely a consistently vicious adversary, but his maneuver now reminded him of chess moves once made against him. The difference this time was that it was he, Johan Thoms, who was playing black, he who was closing in on an unlikely victory, he who was mouthing the single, doom-laden syllable, "Check!"

If Lorelei then wished to reveal Blanche's identity to the world and to tell of the man guilty of starting the Great War, then so be it.

But when Blanche looked up from her typewriter in the château, the swishing, cerulean Mediterranean just beyond through the stone arches, she saw in the ancient mirror in front of her a *man,* no longer a boy, called Johan Thoms. It was through Blanche, not Dorothy, that Johan, finally, would speak to Lorelei. *This* was not a game. Thereafter he would write to Lorelei, albeit from a great distance, through the scribblings of Miss Blanche de la Peña.

Before long, her latest work was the subject of idle chatter from

Bloomsbury dinner parties to tutorials in dusty college lecture halls and under preternatural tulip trees within earshot of a Cambridge punt. It was to prompt this from Blanche's friend Archibald DeWitt-Vultura the *Manchester Guardian*:

ARCHIBALD'S FOUR HORSEMEN
OF THE APOCALYPSE CHRIST AND BUDDHA;
BLANCHE AND A GRIM REAPER

My Darling-est Blanche!

Where does one start? You illuminate old Manchester with more fire and light than Mr. Hitler's Luftwaffe ever could! Hemingway, Parker, Orwell in the same room as a blasted grim reaper. Though perhaps not the grimmest of reapers, this chap seems intent on inducing his own personal Apocalypse, a mere microcosm of the larger version, as he might say. And all of this in the smoky-alleyed, trinket-rattling Sarajevo and my luscious, bubbling España, too! Were it that You were there also, My Most Obsidian of Angels!

I despise dream chapters; however, the passages where Christ and Buddha become supremely pie-eyed on bourbon should be read aloud in every school at the start of every term. How astonishing this planet would swiftly become if we all followed the hungover, bleary-eyed, crusty-tongued Buddha's example of politely refusing his new pal's immediate miracle cure. Yes, Christian Atheism is the finest of approaches and the most marvelous of concepts. My immaculate love for you is matched only by my firing desire to think of these blasted revelations before you do.

Yes to Christ. No to god.

I am away to purchase the lilac-est of paints to daub this nabbed slogan for a new world around this gray, gray citadel; a collection of dwellings lit up by you. And I shall grin and grin and grin as I do it, my Blanche, hoping that I shall meet you as you take in the gentle delights of your midafternoon flâneuseries.

Miss de la Peña, stop not what you do, we beg! However, I simply must stop before I fawn myself via the most wondrous hyperbole to a mere sublimate. Yes, a cheering, guffawing, and jackknifed-

from–joy sublimate, for you are unreasonably good. To burn always with this hard, gemlike flame, to maintain this ecstasy, is success in life.

* * *

Cap d'Antibes, August 24, 1937

My dearest J.,

You're alive! You're alive! You're alive! You made me cry with happiness today, you great cad! I spoke with Dorothy. Oh my, what the hell did you say to upset her? Anyway, I hope you leave Spain straightaway, my darling. She suggested you might be doing just that. Oh, let me see your lovely cowardice up close, Johan! Please! I am on the Cap d'Antibes at her place. I await you with the excitement of a schoolgirl. I spoke to Carl, and he is a happy man today. It is still not too late, my love.

I promise that we will find each other soon, for I sense we are in France together right now.

Yours, with a joyous and trembling hand,
Lorelei xxx

Ernest looked at Johan, who diverted his eyes.

"I didn't see this for almost a decade. Who knows what I would have done at the time? That France was about to fall might just have been the excuse I had needed not to go. And that, too, was *my* fault."

Seventeen

Then There Were Three Again

¡Decias que no y hasta la trompita alzabas!

—Mexican slang[10]

January 1, 1940

By the time Johan Thoms and Catalina did meet Cicero again, as agreed, in Monaco on January 1, 1940, Spain had been under the German-sponsored fascismus grip of Franco for nine months, the northern cities of Bilbao, Santander, and Gijón viciously bombed into a stubborn and brave submission. Guernica, too, had fallen to the Luftwaffe and the Stuka. Johan and Catalina did not discuss the possibility, which they both feared, that Cicero would not appear, that he would be dead, a skeleton on a scorched hillside. As the crescendo of that day neared, however, they thought of little else.

Europe was already four months into Blair's predicted second round. Soon the whole world would be in the game.

France would fall before 1940 was out. Britain would come within a hairsbreadth. Thankfully, she remained intact, for without that wonderful bridgehead, there would have been no D-Day landings in '44.

An estimated million Spaniards (and others) had perished in Spain at the hands of the Spanish (and others). Horror stories of mass slaughters of men, women, and children, of mass graves, abounded, bringing a terrifying new element to modern warfare. Add this million to the thirty-six million boys, women, and men from '14 to '18, and to the inevitable toll from the current clash ('39–'45), then imagine the twitching, blurting, babbling state of Johan Thoms.

Nonetheless, he and Catalina made it to the Café de Paris as the sun tried to poke through a belligerent mist like an old tangerine at the far side of a steamy Chinese restaurant kitchen. Cicero was already there. However, he had lost his left leg below the knee and the use of both eyes. He heard his old mate approaching, accompanied by the gait of a waifish young girl, whose steps he thought he recognized.

"Hope you're not here to play cards, boss!" he yelled into the approximate area of Johan.

"You silly boy!" Johan's relief to find him there outweighed the sadness of his best pal's injuries, but only just.

"Johan, you old sea dog. And is that who I think it is?"

Yes, it was who he thought it was, but he had not the ability to tell if she was still in a tatty blue dress. Catalina swiftly kissed Cicero on his cheek, and lightly ran off to the gardens to weep. Cicero sniffed the Spanishness of her skin, and then heard her tears, but presumed not the emotion with which those tears fell.

And yes, Johan did now resemble an old sea dog, as Cicero felt his way around that bulbous melon along the tramlines etched deeply into his pal's face.

"You're looking old, boss."

"Hardly surprising!"

"I know! I know! Not only do we folk hear better, but we know what people are going to say next. How do you say? *It's all my damned fault.* Stop feeling sorry for yourself. You're killing yourself."

Stoically, Johan changed the subject.

"What got you, Cicero?"

"A land mine, thirty miles out of Madrid in '39. Thought it was a windmill, my Quixote! Four days from the end! *Pendejos! Hijos de putas!*"

At least his Spanish was improving.

* * *

A blind man with one leg, a madman who still wandered naked in the night with a patch on whichever eye, and a blossomed beauty, no longer in a tatty blue dress (or at least, not that often): this unholy trinity planned to head out of Monaco and seek refuge where they could. Johan's psychotic (and in this case, quite accurate) sixth sense was telling him once again that he was being looked for, and so movement could only be a good thing. As the trio pondered a plan on the terrace of the Café de Paris over three martinis, Cicero made a very sensible suggestion.

"Let's go to England, boss. The Germans will be here soon, they say."

"Ah. Forget them. They are here every fifty years, like clockwork. You know they say the krauts even designed the wide boulevards and the tall trees of Paris themselves so that their troops could walk in the shade."

"Well, I am not so keen to meet them. Anyway, you love those English. You can go to your Stratford-in-Avon, afternoon tea at the Savoy." Cicero grinned, tipping an imaginary teacup to his lips, with his little pinkie pointing to the horizon.

An all-seeing two-legged Cicero could have wrapped Johan around that very same little finger pointing to Dover. *This* Cicero could do so even more easily. Johan answered:

"It's *upon,* not *in* Avon."

* * *

Cicero told Johan how the unity of the troops had initially convinced him he had done the right thing in joining up. However, he had questioned his decision within weeks of seeing action. By the middle of 1938, he was looking for a sign as to whether he should continue. This sign appeared in the most bizarre of circumstances.

Cicero had seen Eric Arthur Blair again in Albuixech, ten miles up the Balearic coast from Valencia, which within nine months was to be the final Spanish city to fall to Franco.

Cicero's battalion had dropped back to the coast after taking heavy casualties near Albacete against a pocket of supposedly suicidal Nationalists way behind enemy lines. A rumor had spread that a Mexican battle cruiser was anchored off the coast. Medical, military, and nutritional supplies were supposedly on offer. It was true. The *Guadalajara* had indeed dropped anchor there, and for those very reasons. Blair and Cicero recognized each other in the otherwise empty town square, for both were strolling in the rain while all others had taken cover. Cicero went to embrace Blair, which forced the Englishman to retreat. However, they walked and eventually sat together on the front steps of a once-fine old mansion, which seemed to have been deserted; the heavy front door was open and the tall arched windows had been smashed from the inside. They looked out to a gray sea and compared tales of the past year.

Cicero told Blair of an amusing but puzzling scene the previous morning as he had been sitting by the road out of town. He had witnessed a rowboat being dragged at high speed by a crazed horse along the dirt track heading north. What had made the spectacle all the more amusing yet also disturbing was that there was a naked man in the vessel, a man whom Cicero was sure he recognized. He thought he knew the slightly off-center eyes, the vast hands, the thick neck and wrists, and the ability to swear, with what Cicero was sure was an American invective.

Blair, ever the consummate storyteller, was able to fill in the vital and enlightening details. The evening previous to the horse scene had been a wild one in a local saloon. Blair likened it to the one when he had first met with Cicero and his strange friend, Johan Thoms. It was similar in another regard, for Ernest Hemingway was once again celebrating a birthday; it must, then, have been July 21, 1938. Ernie had spent his evening as he spent most of his evenings, although this one was more notable than usual for the presence of two quite luscious twins—identical not only in their fine, swaggering build and exquisite facial features, but also in their attire, which was the deep scarlet of the Gypsy flamenco dancer. However, their blood might have had a sapphire tinge, for they claimed to be descended from Mexican royalty.

"You look exactly like my third wife," Ernest had said to one of them.

"And how many times have you been married, you beast?" she had asked.

"Oh, just twice."

They laughed so hard, until the hot blood of the *gemelas* stirred with the wine and with Ernie's pirate stories. They promised to indulge his every desire if he took them to their compatriots' boat, moored out to sea—the *Guadalajara*. He accepted without negotiation. But after almost an hour of searching for any type of vessel, it seemed as though the American was not to have his birthday treat after all. Hemingway excused himself from the girls momentarily—to urinate in a ditch, they presumed. He returned with a horse, a fine, dappled beast of eighteen-plus hands. He hoisted himself aboard and pulled each of the impressed ladies up, one in each of his mighty paws, placing one in front of him and one behind. In his broken Spanish, he explained to them how they would find a boat far more easily this way. He lied, for he then tapped the animal in the ribs with his size-fifteen boots, and they powered first toward and then into the warm Balearic waters. Ten minutes later, they were next to a small rowboat tethered to the warship. The twins jumped in and then climbed the rope ladders into the ship. Ernie tied the horse to the rowboat. "This won't take long, I promise," he assured the rightly uncomfortable creature.

Sadly, it took longer than Ernie had expected. He stirred hours later to a nagging, rhythmic knocking and the searing glare of the early-morning Spanish sun, which had just that moment shifted into the line of his wonkier right eye. He had a girl (even more beautiful in the daylight) nestled in each arm. He wrestled himself free of their minimal weight, and as he moved toward the annoying sound, he realized its unhappy source. Wearing not a stitch and remembering his promise to the beast who had generously conspired and helped to secure his pleasure, he was galvanized into action. Ernie was down in the launch within seconds. He untied the naval knot and was soon rowing the frothing, panicked animal toward shore. Ernie was not stupid, but he had not fully planned this out, for when the horse's hooves hit the firm sands under the water, it tapped a fresh store of energy. The rowboat which had been pulling the horse was quickly spun through one hundred and eighty degrees then dragged along the stony, bumpy road in a dust cloud, and at top speed. This sight presented itself to not only Cicero on that open road, but also then to the congregation of an emptying church on that cloudless Sunday morning, and to a police chief inspecting his officers in the town square. They had all laughed, but this had only made them sad, as they realized, as one, that they had not done such a thing for two years and five days.

Out to sea around that time, the Mexican navy woke to a vision now firmly entrenched in the swirling magic and the fine myth of that sublime land. In fact, it is rare to find a Mexican sailor to this day without a tattoo somewhere on his person of two grinning twins in scarlet-red dresses, the scarlet of a Gypsy flamenco dancer.

Johan had always impressed upon Cicero that Mexicans were the finest judges of character in the world. This was the sign that Cicero had been looking for. He trusted the twins' instinct and therefore, by association, the magnetic American. Cicero fought on with all his might.

Ernie Hemingway and the horse, they say, became great friends.

* * *

They finished up their cocktails at the Café de Paris as the sun started to fall toward a building, hefty mistral.

"Best togs for tonight," Johan announced. "We celebrate our reunion. We dine in the Hermitage. We play the casino." He believed he had become telekinetic.

Best togs for Johan was his old Schneider's suit (though immaculately clean), eye patch on the left in honor of Cicero's fallen comrades. For Cicero, his proud olive-green fatigues from Spain. Catalina procured something suitable—deep turquoise, as it happened—from a boutique near Le Jardin du Roi within thirty minutes. The purchase of shoes took an understandable two hours.

Cicero found his way back to the Hôtel de Paris with an unerring sense of direction, his sticks clicking at each curb like a deranged woodpecker. He checked into his sumptuous chambers and launched himself onto a chaise longue. Then a hot, deep bath, lavishly laced with unknown oils, drawn by a sweet-smelling chambermaid, who Cicero estimated at a hundred pounds from the creak of the floorboards, twenty-two years by the pitch of her voice and single, from her invitingly flowered *cassolette* of gardenia and skin.

That evening they attended the Lermontov Ballet, ate the best crab the principality (probably) had to offer, and drank champagne overlooking the choppy Med, which hypnotized everyone, even a sightless but imaginative Cicero, with a half-moon's sharp white light.

The casino was half full. A seat was found for Cicero at the roulette table, and Catalina and Johan flanked their friend. They had agreed that the extent of their gambling was a single round of roulette each.

They studied the form for over twenty minutes.

Both Catalina and Johan went for red. A straight evens bet. A pile of green and royal blue chips was stacked to above Cicero's erstwhile-eye level.

Cicero chose black thirty-three. An understated single gold chip.

The dealer threw in the chunky ball bearing before declaring a rhythmic and somewhat bored *"Les jeux sont faits."*

Johan pondered the appropriateness of the statement.

The ball fell and spun madly.

"Noir! Trente-trois!"

"Well played, soldier," players murmured as polite applause spread. Cicero was rewarded with a hefty pile of riches that he heard drag across the tight baize cloth. Catalina blushed at his success. A couple of pretty local ladies eyed the quietly smug veteran.

Cicero collected his winnings and pushed them in Johan's direction to cash in, then stood up and had started to hop away when, to his surprise, the dealer gave a condescending "monsieur." Then Cicero remembered the etiquette of roulette: a second chip was to be left on black thirty-three. He thought he smiled at one of the girls (he did) and gestured for her to take the wager on his behalf.

Catalina and Johan winged their cohort and off they moved toward the green neon of the *sortie,* to a distant, unenthusiastic call of *"les jeux sonts faits"* from their simian-mannered host.

Pause for four, five, six seconds.

Shrieks of delight. The stingy arse made a mean, envy-laden announcement of *"noir, trente-trois,"* barely audible under the cheers.

Within an hour, the trio had taken a fine bottle of bubbly onto the white stone deck at the Hermitage, (two of them had) surveyed the clipped grandeur (and described it to Cicero), and (all of them) discussed England. Johan teased Cicero by telling him not to worry if he heard a newspaper vendor cry, "ENGLAND IN DANGER."

"It just means they are losing at cricket to Australia." They laughed, as they did at regular intervals for the next couple of hours, until they retired to their chambers. Cicero, though, was to have company. The two winning ladies of black, thirty-three paid him a visit, having tipped the concierge with a gold chip to find out the soldier's room number. They would still be there in the morning, exhausted and sated, as Cicero giddily one-legged it to Johan's suite to postmortem on the turn of events.

The dealer left the casino quite disgruntled.

All others involved in the evening's proceedings were, however, quite *gruntled.*

* * *

They decided against driving.

Instead, Johan had the concierge leave the faithful old car in a rented lockup. It is possibly still there today.

They caught the first available train to Paris, with three tickets, two trunks, an old kit bag, and a pair of crutches. They shared a comfortable sleeper compartment, for money was not a problem. The wonderful old benefactor and guardian angel Count Erich von Kaunitz still made annual deposits, hugely generous ones, into the account; they had as well the lucrative earnings from the casino.

Cicero, still savoring the goings-on of the night before, smiled all the way to Lyons, where he eventually drifted off into a slumber. Observing his young pal's sated expression, Johan was reminded of a glorious day (or so) he had spent in the countryside years before at Kaunitz's castle.

"When this one is over, I want to go back and see him," Johan said to himself out loud.

* * *

In Paris, news of the war engulfed them. Stories of the escalating conflict gave Johan heart palpations, narcolepsy, and incontinence. Newspapers were pushed under his hotel-room door; cinema newsreels yelled it out if he had decided upon a little escapism at the movies; conversations in bars, elevators, taxis, the *métro,* and finally his own head.

In his waking hours, he saw the corpses of Ferdinand and Sophie, Bill

Cartwright, a million unknown soldiers in trenches of mud, snow, shit, bones, blood, fields of quiet poppies . . .

He took to wearing a loincloth around his hotel suite, and then farther afield. He had stolen the garment from a fancy-dress shop in Pigalle, after entering an episode when he was convinced Lorelei had passed by him on a bus. From his vantage point between a rack of bad Napoleon outfits and ropy old skirts for Moulin Rouge chorus girls, he had seen the bus trundle by with what seemed to be a familiar face in a rear window. He grabbed the loincloth, bolted from the shop, and chased the bus for a mile, in a reversal of Zhivago and Lara. He commandeered a cab and ended up in the eastern alleys of Montparnasse, in a taxidermist's boutique. Montparnasse was a grubby, nasty quartier littered with cheap, dangerous *tabacs*. The better ones, with their ignored spittoons, were populated in the front by largely toothless sorts, while well-missed toilets dominated in the rear (if a hole in the ground could pass for a toilet). The lower-food-chain establishments were to be recommended even less. There were some things the Montparnassians, these rank-and-file soldiers of gracelessness, did remarkably well, Johan begrudgingly admitted to himself. A lack of bathroom manners was certainly a forte of theirs, and he was a firm believer that one should always be encouraged to play to one's strengths.

He barged in maybe three minutes after he saw her go in, only to be confronted by former gnus, ex–boa constrictors, and erstwhile gibbons, before tapping her on her shoulder by the platypus section.

It was not her, of course.

What would *she* be doing on a bus? In Paris? In *Montparnasse*?

He could only respond by blurting *"Qu'est-ce que fuck?"*

Mon Dieu! Zut alors! Tant pis!

Lorelei Ribeiro, however, *was* in Paris that day.

Eighteen

Music, Brigadiers,
and Marigold (1940)

What's the use of worrying?
It never was worthwhile,
So, pack up your troubles in your old kit-bag
And smile, boy, smile!
—George Asaf, "Pack Up Your Troubles in Your Old Kit-Bag"

Johan had heard that if one were to melt down the Eiffel Tower but keep the same base measure, it would be just three inches high. He was still preoccupied by this fact, and by the practical applications of shrinking and stealing the tower, as they took the train from the filthy Gare du Nord. They headed to the northern coast, to the equally scabby, rat-ridden port of Calais.

Within months, the messy, bloody evacuation of the British Expeditionary Force would be in full swing down the road at Dunkerque, but on this day, the Channel could not have been more serene. In Paris, Catalina had managed to procure a wheelchair for Cicero and a nurse's uniform for herself.

Across the English Channel on September 1, 1939, the airwaves of the BBC (television, not radio) had ceased to broadcast for fear of its VHF signals attracting the Luftwaffe.

Walt Disney's *Mickey's Gala Premier* had been the final broadcast before the scrap had begun. Laurel and Hardy, the Marx Brothers, Clark Gable, and Mae West made guest appearances at the Chinese Theatre as Pegleg Pete kidnapped Minnie Mouse. The poor critter was predictably rescued by Mickey. The hero squeaked Disney's vocal tones and was soon smothered in grateful kisses from Greta Garbo. Roll credits. Then the homely BBC voice-over of Mrs. Jasmine Bligh bade farewell to the nation. Then silence.

(Until June 7, 1946, when the same Mrs. Bligh returned with a calm and very English, "Now, then. As we were saying before we were *so* rudely interrupted." This brief statement was followed by, of course, a Mickey Mouse cartoon.)

The one-legged soldier and his nurse had no problem entering England. Johan faced only minimal fuss once he brought out his yellowed papers from 1914. Other passengers were herded into a pen by the docks in Dover, anxious but relieved to have clear, blue water between themselves and the German Wehrmacht. By late spring, that same army had taken Norway, Belgium, the Netherlands, and Denmark; it had already annexed its own lands from the Treaty of Versailles, the Sudetenland, and a now meek, powerless, and obliging Austria. By June, they would have added France. By September, Poland.

Johan's movements in escaping war often had left him just a weak buffer away from a front line. Since Sagres, he had found no peaceful enclave to escape the horror which he had personally set in motion. Once again the only talk, the only thought in the minds of the British, was of war, of defending the "sunlit uplands" and vanquishing the fermenting evil in the east. There would be no escaping the reminders, so in order to at least minimize them, he resolved to banish the trio to the distant English countryside. They became evacuees.

Once again, Johan's natural instinct was to head west, which led first to two lazy nights at the Savoy on the Strand (where, in the foyer, he doffed his cap to a gaunt and yellowy face which he later recognized to be Eric Arthur Blair). From there, they went to Paddington station in West London, then out to the North Somerset coast of the Bristol Channel and the rolling moors of Exmoor. Johan knew the geographical lay of the land from his books, as he had when he and Cicero had first landed in Italy. The Baskervilles had finally drawn in this old crackpot, this fine and silly deerstalker.

Their next stop was the quaint seaside town of Porlock, with its neat station gardens, lovingly manicured and kept by the stationmaster, old Clarence, who, when not trimming the lawns, was to be found scrubbing the frames of the advertising signs persuading all to nibble on Fry's Chocolate or to drink hot beefy Bovril. It was Clarence who told them, upon their arrival, that they could get clean, inexpensive rooms above the Duke of Wellington public house. The red-and-white stripes of the barber's pole, the bandstand with the band all off to war, the red postboxes were all so English. Polite, welcoming chaps in deep Brunswick-green army uniforms or the grubby gray-blue of the RAF frequented the pubs and chatted to rouge lipsticked girls under lamplights on foggy nights. Those lamplights were to be extinguished soon, when the Blitz scorched London, Coventry, and Plymouth in the summer of 1940.

All feared that invasion was imminent. This led Johan into trances that lasted for days on end. Cicero got hold of marigolds, but Johan had now become almost immune to the stuff. With instantaneous news from the wireless, his paranoia and psychosis overtook him. He could not maintain eye contact, and shuffled like he was packed with amphetamines. He could sleep no more than fifteen minutes without tossing, turning, yelling. He spoke of going home to Argona and Sarajevo, how things would be as they used to be. He spoke of Bill Cartwright as if he were still alive, of an American girl he used to know and a book he still had to return to a university professor. The number of deaths under the rubble in Britain, the casualties over the Channel and around the world, meant that Blanche was not at her most prolific. The scale of events had stifled her, as had their travels. She would soon return.

Johan sensed again that someone was trying to find him, and for protection, he purchased a shotgun from a drunken farmer for three of his English guineas. He was looking out to sea, daydreaming of Lorelei, when the gun fired, blowing a chunk of his right thigh in the direction of Minehead.

* * *

As Cicero negotiated a bed for Johan at a fine old hospital up on Porlock Hill (it resembled the setting of a Somerset Maugham novel), it occurred to him that life had come full circle. Cicero had made sure the hospital was first class. A wireless was placed next to his bed, where he would try to remind himself to listen instead to classical music.

"If this music can survive, endure, and hold her shoulders back, then so can I!" he would say. "Music, brigadiers, and marigold. Music, brigadiers, and marigold."

Cicero visited every day, and sometimes at night, often with Catalina, who was now showing public displays of affection toward her Roman friend.

One day, almost at dawn, Cicero awoke in his chair next to Johan's bed. He quietly wheeled himself away from his pal (after once again putting a heavy crucifix in his hand). He recalled a night more than a quarter of a century before when the two of them had stolen away into the darkness, to give Cicero his unexpected life.

As he wheeled himself out, it was still dark, but only just.

He sat, surrounded by ladybirds and dwarfed by the majestic twenty-five-foot wrought-iron gates of the old hospital (soon to be melted down to make munitions), high on the hill above the picture-postcard seaside town, and he wept, loudly. Soldiers marched down in the town to catch the dawn train to Bristol and then to London, then to Lord knows where. The rhythm and the stomp of soldiers' boots and the optimistic whistling mixed with a chorus from some young lads, still full of youth, going to do the right thing, overwhelmed him. The song was a well-known one of the day, and Cicero had heard it many times in the last few months.

Catalina had been waiting in the gardens. She put her hand on the back of Cicero's head and saw, when he lifted his sorry face, that he was crying. She didn't know if he was weeping for his pal, for his own sorry legless, blind state, or for the poor bleeders down in the valley, marching off to a premature death in a foreign field. In truth, it was for all three.

Catalina started to roll his chair down the road that led to the town. She hummed along until they reached the last line of the troops' ditty, when she joined in herself with a quivering.

"And smile, boy! Smile!"

This time, Cicero couldn't smile.

from "The Unpublished Diaries of D. Parker"

The journey from the Pyrenees along the Côte had been smooth. We arrived in Marseilles. The trail was cold, as was I. As would be the revenge when it was served. It had been a few months now. We knew this was not going to be easy, though I knew for my fellow passenger little else mattered. A Faustian score was to be settled, and I did not want to witness it. More than anything, I did not want to witness it. It would have turned my stomach if the descriptions of the intended merciless and brutal acts upon him were to be reenacted.

She meant business, all right. Lorelei was like that. I guess she really fucking loved that fool.

I had left her in Cannes. She had heard from a rude and disgruntled black-jack dealer at the Bel Otero Casino in the Carlton Hotel that Johan had indeed been in Monte Carlo. Personally, I had had enough. I loved Lorelei like a sister, but if I never smell another Frenchman, it will be too soon. I went back to Paris, then on to New York. I told her she was cracked in the head. That photograph of him, which she had taken from the saloon doors of a grubby tabac in Dubrovnik, never left her purse, it seemed, in her search for him. His face was recognizable. His head remained unusually large for his body. He was dressed as if for a bracing cold outside. Unsightly, foul locals in the background appeared to be mocking him. The other picture was a close-up in what appeared to be the same bar. He held a schnapps in his right hand and a pack of stubby French cigarettes in the other.

That man—Johan fucking Thoms—was unmistakably the cowardly wreck I had encountered on the steps of that bar on Ernie Hemingway's birthday in July '37 somewhere in the Spanish foothills. How dare that wretch Thoms bastardize my poems! The worm! Indeed!

Lorelei Ribeiro was very close to finding a quite oblivious and lost Johan Thoms. She was walking back to him, but on a road that was perhaps moving even more rapidly in the other direction.

Nineteen

It Only Hurts When I Laugh
(Part II)

By informing a man about to be hanged of the size, location and strength of the rope, you do not lessen the certainty of his being hanged.

—*5 Fingers* (1952 film directed by Joseph L. Mankiewicz)

This was to be Johan's third, and his final, stint in hospital. The wards on the brow of the hill were full of lads with local dialects from nearby platoons, shipped back to be near their loved ones, and of unfortunates with no family, who had holidayed around the region as boys and had put in a successful demobilization request to be near the sea, to be nearer to happier, more innocent times. Down in the town, local children in short gray trousers and grubby knees played soccer, or rudimentary cricket with a bald tennis ball and a plank of oak floorboard. They took on teams of evacuated urchins from the East End of London, who had been recently bused away from sobbing parents, themselves confined to the dusty, blitzed remnants of the big city. The kids reeked of the lethane shampoo used to kill head lice on regulation pudding-bowl haircuts. None of the poor little blighters had ever seen a banana or a steak, and each night was a night of tears in a strange bed. They were surrounded by strange voices and strange habits, and they feared they would never see their mums and dads again. Some of them would stay out there until the end of the war in 1945, as would Johan, Cicero, and Catalina.

* * *

If a girl's downfall is that she always becomes her mother, then Johan's only hope for redemption lay in his becoming like his father. Johan later admitted to Ernest that it had been the shade and shelter afforded to him by his delusions and his undoubted madness that had prevented a full-on breakdown and his being placed permanently under lock and key. Much of his time was now spent plotting Allied maneuvers across the Rhineland, or restructuring the Marshall Plan, as a favor to his new chum, Churchill, before a Marmite-splattered breakfast. After all, he had proved to be somewhat of a liability in 1914 with all his faculties intact.

As he healed, Johan started to take afternoon walks through the fields above Porlock, breathing in the freshest air since Sagres, unpolluted, straight from the Atlantic, without the stench of battle and gunpowder, crumbled buildings, limbs, and blood. A couple of miles down the rugged coastline, a Victorian school sat high on the cliff. When he discovered the school for the first time on a still, hot summer's day, he sat and stared at the sixty-foot goalposts, on what looked like a regular soccer field, wondering what sort of game this was. Was it played by giants? He pictured this field a hundred years before, and the generations of boys who had graduated from this patch of green turf to the bloody fields of Belgium. He imagined (for he had recently seen *Goodbye, Mr. Chips*) their spirits all trudging off at the end of each year's house match with the masters. They were carrying their muddied heroic skipper, the best boy, on their shoulders, after a rare victory. Johan managed to do all this without even knowing what the contest involved.

He felt a presence next to him, and looked up.

"Do you play?" asked a young chap in RAF blue.

"Me? God, no. I do not even know why the big goals."

The pilot chuckled.

"The posts, old thing. Rugby. *Rugger* to its chums and victims. My father once told me, old bean, that they are, simply, two *H*s. And the field in between represents everything in life. At one end"—pointing with his unlit pipe and a flick of the eyes to the distant H—"there is heaven . . . the ultimate goal, joy, ecstasy. At the other"—glancing to his right and frowning—"hell . . . despair, defeat, pain, horror. It should be up to us at which end we spend our meager but welcome existence. It should be. But it is not. That privilege is long gone. But I guess that is why we are fighting, what?"—brightening up with a stiff upper lip—"To get it back. Crack that rotter Jerry and get back to the rugger field. Reckon it won't be long now. Anyway, you cheer up, old chap. What have you got to look so bloody glum about?" The Tommy gave him a hearty slap on the back and skipped off toward the school, whistling an out-of-tune version of "We'll Meet Again."

Johan examined the goalposts. He reminded himself that he had once dreamed of being a man to stand on the shoulders of giants. Instead, he felt as though around his neck hung the millstone of a thousand ogres.

* * *

Back at the hospital, not-quite-whole soldiers congregated, shipped in from North Africa, the Far East, Italy, France, the Low Countries. Mangled RAF pilots from the skies above Kent or somewhere between Biggin Hill and Dresden or Berlin. Scorched seamen from the North Sea or the Atlantic. They had every permutation of ailment, injury, and body-part loss.

Cicero and Catalina visited Johan every day and also spent the rest of their days in Porlock together. As for Johan, he had fallen in love with the cinema, and constantly nagged the others to accompany him down Porlock Hill to visit the old fleapit picture house, set one street back from the hat stalls and the candy-floss huts bearing "Gone Fishing" signs. The queues for the showings usually stretched all the way beyond the post office and down to Fat Beryl's (currently fishless) fish-and-chip shop. Betty Grable and David Niven were Johan's favorites. It was a grubby excuse for a cinema, the deep tobacco-yellowed screen and the dense smoke offering a curious slant to glorious Technicolor. But he loved it.

* * *

When he was healed in April 1941, they rented one of the nurses' cottages on the grounds. Living up to her uniform, Catalina began working long days on the wards, without asking for or even expecting any recompense, and the boys loved to listen to Rachmaninoff, Brahms, and Bach on the wireless with the other men. Johan had bought a new set for a ridiculously high price from a spiv in a dodgy three-piece pinstripe down in Porlock town while Catalina and Cicero were enjoying a few too many gins, consumed in the smoky taproom of the cozy Old Red Lion with its coal fires, dartboard, and barely six-foot ceilings. That same night, Catalina determinedly seduced Cicero, and they began a love affair which was to be the one and only in Catalina's life, and Cicero's last.

Johan was delighted at the union of his two best chums.

"Could not have scripted it better myself. Let's go get drunk," he said.

As the couple understandably stole an increased number of hours alone, Johan became a very welcome guest and fixture around the hospital's hallways and wards and gardens. He would spend demented days with his wireless, in an anteroom by the manicured lawns dotted with monkey puzzle trees, their green baize set against azure sky. Memories of the university quadrangle flooded back, and he often saw Bill Cartwright approaching over the brow of the hill, which offered a magnificent view over the serene blue-and-flecked-white waters off Porlock Bay.

*   *   *

With the Battle of Britain won, Johan suspected that the tide of the war might be turning, and this even before Hitler turned on Stalin and Japanese hubris dragged the Americans into the conflict. The unlikeliest of victories in the skies helped to calm Johan to the degree where he might actually face his fear. A kindly young Scottish doctor named Torquil McFelly had encouraged him to seek out his demons and confront them. Johan had trusted him, and soon switched his wireless to the news updates from the BBC. It seemed to work, to a degree. He listened to hourly updates and magazine broadcasts. He soon came to love the beeps on the hour, and made an off-key noise along with them, every sixty minutes.

He became an expert on all matters military, from pivotal battles to the cunning strategies of certain field marshals. He admired Montgomery but held Monty's adversary in North Africa, Erwin Rommel, the Desert Fox, in even higher esteem. As did Montgomery, who knew that his enemy was a soldier and *not* a Nazi. As the invasion of Europe by the Allies progressed, Johan maintained a fluid mental map of the proceedings. (He remembered a globe of oranges, pinks, yellows, and blue, in his boyhood home, and his bizarre bedtime routine, which had sparked *all* of this nonsense.)

He tuned in to Churchill's speeches, and studied them. He realized that the vocabulary used in the "We Shall Fight Them on the Beaches" speech never once utilized any French, Latin, or German. Only *ye Olde English*. It was a stroke of genius, designed to work subconsciously on the very, very back of the British brain, to tickle its psyche in order to convince a nation to "Never Surrender."

"That's inspired!" he blurted out loud as he pondered the speech and twitched beneath his tartan blanket in a chair in the gardens at dusk. For it was the very antithesis of his own stupidity on June 28, 1914. It was his antidote.

He had Churchill's other speeches sent to him by Rawlings & Bennett, an antiquarian bookshop in the Charing Cross Road, and he marveled to find that this use of language was a common strategy of Churchill's speechwriters.

"The clever buggers!" he exclaimed in awe in a moment of clarity as he exited the anteroom with a sudden urge for an extreme bowel movement. He remembered Martin Luther. Then he was back to thinking of Churchill. How come he, Johan Thoms, had not thought of writing such diatribes for Winston?

Soon enough, buoyed by Churchill and perhaps feeling (relatively) settled in this corner of England, good old Blanche de la Peña was back at her typewriter. She was to embark upon what many at the time regarded as her masterpiece, *The White-Kilted Brigadier and the Resurrection of the Roman Empire.*

Within six months, Mr. Tobias Kilz of the Ruben-Wolfram Press in Ludgate Circus would be weeping with joy. Within a year, a growing band of readers would be doing the same. Across the ocean, with a fine view of the park in upper-ish Manhattan and very much within this burgeoning number, Lorelei Ribeiro was now almost joyful at knowing that these were missives to *her* and perhaps exponentially more powerful than the presence of a crumbling old man on her now solemn doorstep would be. Equally solemn were her bookshelves, which resembled a shrine to Blanche, though they lacked a certain formality lower down, replete as they were with scrapbooks of cuttings from the *New Yorker* and the *Times,* and even some by a lesser-known Manchester critic, a favorite of Dorothy's by the name of Archibald DeWitt-Vultura. Archibald was always flattered when he heard the rumors that he was a gritty northern nom de plume for Dorothy Parker in England. If one were to have seen him in his nicotine-stained garb each Monday at 7:30 A.M. at the editors' meeting, one would understand why it pleased him almost as much as it would have offended Dorothy.

* * *

One morning Johan spent an hour over his breakfast talking with one of the angels around the ward. He told her of his fear of the nuclear age and how he believed that the reach for happiness is akin to an atomic half-life, always being homed in on but by its very definition never, ever reached.

Outside the window, Catalina and Cicero had billeted themselves in the front gardens by the psychiatric wing under a weeping willow. In front of them, a young man of about thirty was tending to the garden. A pretty young woman in a nurse's uniform sat at the bus stop, waiting to be taken away from her shift. She eyed the young man, as if she recognized him. The chap approached her and began the mating ritual. Eloquent and erudite, he persuaded her to accept a date to go out with him on the weekend to the visiting fair of freaks and Romany Gypsies, with their bearded ladies and clairvoyants. (Cicero gulped back a tear.) The fellow was very impressive, making her blush and tickling her innocent fancy. The number thirty bus chugged up Porlock Hill, and she turned to meet it. Then, as the bus was about to open its doors, a hefty chunk of brick smacked her on the back of her head, making her stumble to the ground. She gathered herself and turned to see her new beau (known to the staff as "Mad Brains") being dragged away by three warders as he pleaded with them, "That's my future ex-wife, you bastards," and yelled to her:

"Don't forget Saturday night, will you?"

During this struggle, there fell from the chap's pocket a copy of *The White-Kilted Brigadier's Unadulterated Letters to the Most Brusque of Lady*

Politicians. It appeared that Blanche's supporters ran the gamut. When Cicero told Johan, this delighted Blanche no end. For what was the point otherwise?

*   *   *

The end of the conflict did not cease Johan's madness, but immersing himself in the news from the wireless had weirdly decreased its acceleration. Cicero feared there would be a crescendo, however, after the news reached his pal of two Japanese cities wiped out by just two bombs.

Even before the *Enola Gay* left with her cargo that August morning in 1945, seventy-six million or so had already perished in yet *another* war to end all wars. This meant a total death toll, since that first bullet had entered Ferdinand's neck outside Schiller's sandwich shop, well into nine (and nearing ten) figures, all on Johan's conscience. One billion, if one were to have counted the direct, the indirect, the secondary, the tertiary, and the more distant casualties, all relevant according to his massively engorged guilt gland. Gas chambers for women and children. From Burma to the hellish corners of Poland, where it seems to many visitors that to this day the birds no longer sing and the flowers no longer grow. (The fact that the über-horror is given few words here is not to underestimate the extent of the subhuman treatment of other human beings, for this is a story, which is, *in parts,* depressing enough.)

When he found out that one bomb killed hundreds of thousands in Nagasaki and then the same in Hiroshima, Johan could not digest the whole. If he had, he would have probably curled up and died. His mind, however, was semiprotected by its own defense mechanism.

Instead, he became addicted to the omnipresence of the global war, to knowing all, seeing himself as a chief of staff, but the friendly, quiet kind who does not insist on being on the payroll. He reveled in it. He became a bizarre and unconventional elder statesman. Unshaven, with hints of gray at his temples and in his beard, he muttered to himself and blurted out obscenities every couple of hours. With his patch on his left (or right) eye, he may have given more the impression of a fool. But this would have been to miss the mark.

"Never wink at a one-eyed man," he would observe with his patch lifted up to his forehead and a wicked glint in his eye, whenever Cicero and Catalina said good evening.

"Nor a blind one," Cicero would retort, to Johan's smile, which Cicero could hear.

For thirty years, there had been plenty of madness in Johan's method, but for once there was some method in his madness. He had perhaps missed his calling, and how strange; if he had stuck around Potiorek, it could have been a different story.

If if if . . . and he went off into quoting Kipling at length. His friends sat and smiled.

His knowledge of the battle lines and the tide of the Allies rising through Southern Europe had been updated hourly courtesy of the plummy voices from London. His mental map had, over recent months and years, morphed on a moment-to-moment basis, along with the dread that he was being tracked down. Now he realized it might just be safe for him to return home to his birthplace, to see his parents, Kaunitz, the old house . . .

* * *

And so, one August morning in 1945, the nurse, the wheelchair-bound blind veteran, and the bigheaded, besuited, bepatched, delusional, friendly kook were on their way again, this time into a postnuclear world. They would return to London, where they could hunker down and where they could more easily set about the bureaucratically arduous task of attaining the necessary documents and tickets to get to Sarajevo to return to the womb of Argona.

Johan wished the "Best of British" to some of the boys around the place with whom he'd become well acquainted in his haze. For although these young souls, some only fifteen, were battered, bruised, and half dead, with visions of dead brothers and comrades still fresh in their minds, they had saved the world. Johan always maintained that the war began to be won in June '44 but was destined not to be lost after the Battle of Britain in September 1940. No Panzers would roll down Sloane Street after that. These brave boys had rescued humanity itself from the nastiest idea ever foisted upon it:

Nazism.

This was their finest hour. The world was once again at peace.

But war is as war does, and Johan Thoms recalled the words of Eric Arthur Blair. He knew that he would be fooling himself if he didn't believe that it was again merely an intermission—a malicious intrusion, an illusion, a sick delusion.

from "The Unpublished Diaries of D. Parker"

So, what happened to Lorelei? you might be wondering. For months, I received a wire and a letter every week. I still feel responsible for much of this latest nonsensical traipse of hers. Should I have told her I had seen him in Spain? Anyway, in Monaco, two ladies had met him at the casino, and he was with his now blind and legless friend, Cicero, the poor, wonderful creature. It seemed the boys had female company tagging along, but Lorelei was not swayed. I could picture her eyes narrowing with determination at the prospect. She discovered that they had left a car in a lockup there, which meant they must have taken a train. Given their trajectory and Johan's undoubted desire to avoid Italy under Mussolini, this could only mean Paris. She went to Paris and of course to the George V (where else?). Johan had definitely been there, and acting unusually, according to the management. The trail then went somewhat chilly. Until, that is, she got chatting to some English author by the name of Orwell. (I read one of his books, set in Spain during the civil war, and he looks damned familiar. I must know him from somewhere.) She wrote that she was heading to England. To London. I often wonder if Lorelei would have been as determined had she not had to impart the news to her long-ago beau in person that three decades before, they had had a child. Well, now that child was to become a father, which was wonderful for Lorelei, but it was a wicked shame that the damned intolerable Thoms bloodline was to continue. And keeping THAT fucking secret about him is killing me! I know who he is! I know who HE is! I KNOW WHO HE IS!

Twenty

"Gawd Bless Ya, Gav'nah!"

This royal throne of kings, this scepter'd isle,
This earth of majesty, this seat of Mars.
This other Eden, demi-paradise . . .
This blessed plot, this earth, this realm, this England.

—Shakespeare, *Richard II*

August 1945

Catalina wore her tatty blue dress, as this few, this weird few, took an old steam train east from the tiny, picturesque stop of Porlock. They said their own farewell to the place, which had been good to them all. As they did this, Lorelei was checking out of the Langham Hotel in London.

Their train hugged the North Somerset coastline through the seaside town of Minehead, the hamlets of Watchet and Williton, over the Quantock Hills, past Burnham, and over the Cheddar Gorge before swinging over the August sun-drenched moors to Weston-super-Mare and on to Bristol. There they switched platforms in the dusty shade of the Temple Meads station and boarded the Great Western Railway (or as the locals rightly rebranded the GWR, God's Wonderful Railway) for the 11:59 A.M. to London Paddington.

* * *

They arrived at Paddington in the late afternoon. Johan hailed a porter to take their minimal freight to the waiting London cabs by the imposing southern arches. The platforms were dotted with khaki and camouflage, green and RAF blue—lucky men making their way out to the west of England and South Wales, to wives and mothers, sisters and fathers, rectories and churchyards, classrooms and libraries, pubs and subpost offices, village greens and old wiry Jack Russells, gardens and bedrooms as they'd left them.

The world had sunk to vile new depths in the previous six years, and it was this London, this island citadel, that had held back the evil. That was how Johan saw it, at least.

A black hansom cab pulled forward to meet them at the rank.

A cabbie alighted, and as he opened the rear doors for Catalina, he swayed from side to side on his bowlegs. Johan quoted Bill Cartwright with a whispered:

"He couldn't stop a pig in a passage."

Cicero and the girl chuckled.

"The Langham, please," Johan instructed the skinny driver, who looked as if he'd been driving all day and all night but who was chirpy.

"Gawd bless ya, gav'nah!"

"But would you first take us on a tour, please? What's your name?"

"Reggie, governor. Reginald Victor Windsor! No bleedin' relation, sadly, sir! And yes gladly!"

"Well, Reginald Victor Windsor. Please take us on a tour of the city, with a commentary for a blind man and a girl, for an extra half-a-crown tip! Deal?"

And off Reggie sped to tales of how his wife had run off with the milkman, Archie Pettigrew, to his relief.

Then of how the Hun would never be back for a third beating (nor would the milkman, Archie Pettigrew).

Of how he was looking forward to a real egg one day soon.

Of how the ravens didn't even think of leaving the Tower of London during the Blitz.

Of rumors of Harrods having a stock of bananas.

Of the proud widows with the clean handkerchiefs outside St. Clement Danes Church (later the official church of the RAF), on the traffic island in the middle of the Aldwych—the quietest and most dignified place in London, he swore, despite number-thirteen buses rattling past each flank every three minutes on their way to Whitechapel or Piccadilly. It defied bleedin' physics, he told them.

Of his favorite part of London on the steep meadow in Richmond looking down the bend of the Thames into the sunset and down toward Eel Pie Island and Ham House, where he would spend Sunday afternoons as a lithe and lissome young man of barely twenty.

Of the cheaply painted, happy whores of Soho.

Of a thousand myths and tales of VE Day around Leicester Square, Gloucester Road, and the Embankment. Bethnal Green, Highgate, and Brixton. Ealing, Notting Hill, and Westminster. Of hearing the self-satisfied clinking of teacups in the Ritz, Claridge's, and the Savoy. A hidden and off-key whistle of "We'll Meet Again" from under the wrought-iron gates guarding the dusty basements of St. Anne's Court. Of seeing urchins in short trousers in Dulwich firing imaginary and victorious bullets from their lumps of wood, liberated from the nearest bomb site. The kids then hid behind the sandbags in the yard, now home to a snuffling pig and three squealing piglets. There were the old dears in Borough Market praying that this be the last time. There were the spivs on Atlantic Road with nylon stockings on offer. Two strangers had hugged on the soggy cobbles of Grosvenor Estate as an old soldier smiled from the privileged balcony above. Of oblivious street dogs, who sniffed each other on the rubble of Peckham. Of sixteen of the twenty-four flagpoles above Selfridges boasting a royal crest, a Saint George, or a Union flag for the first time in five years. Of six German POWs in the George pub on Wardour Street, with half a platoon of Royal Bedfords, their camp commandant, and a truckload of procured provisions (stout and snouts, aka Guinness and cigs). Of these erstwhile Luftwaffe pilots singing "God Save the King" to their English friends. The boys from Stuttgart and Bonn and Mainz had been shot down in '40, and now they carried around the works of Milton and Conrad and had decided en masse to support Queen's Park Rangers. Of a solitary scuffle in the Black Lion on the Bayswater Road, before it was smoothed over as a misunderstanding and Bloody Nose/Torn Jacket from Hastings was buying Black Eye/Thick Lip of Muswell Hill a brandy and everything was as before. Of a sign in a window declaring E.M. WINKLE & SONS. WINDOW CLEANERS. *If you've got no windows, we'll clean your chimneys.*

Of three couples, all arm in arm, marching out of *The Picture of Dorian Gray* at the Rank picture house in Piccadilly Circus and whistling (with varying degrees of success) the tune of "Goodbye, Little Yellow Bird."

Of how he had been in the Uxbridge Arms at the back of the Coronet, sipping at a half of Guinness, when ace pilot "Cat's Eyes" Cunningham had spilled his and the Ministry of Defence's exquisite secret. Carrots had not afforded Cunningham and his RAF pals the gift of night vision and therefore air supremacy over the Hun; it was a new invention called radar. Carrot growers the world over have attempted to stifle this revelation ever since.

Of how a palpable municipal relief permeated the doors of an air-raid shelter in Pimlico and the mosaic steps of a tailor in Savile Row, spread from the tiles of Marylebone station and the steam baths of Ironmongers' Row to the smoky snugs in Kentish Town pubs and beneath the gaslights of Holland Park. Freedom and victory poured into every nook and cranny of the city in millions of simultaneously ecstatic and mournful moments. A proud Gurkha and a tipsy vicar sang in the stained doorway of the Green Man and French Horn pub off St. Martin's Lane. A couple kissed in the middle of Birdcage Walk. An impromptu street party broke out on the cobbles of Sheffield Street, where the reddy-black brick looked like it had been imported from the steel city itself. This gave an incongruous— but not unwelcome—northern industrial backdrop to the scene; the street tucking itself into snooty Holborn. Even the presence of a knife seller and a proper northern fish-and-chips shop only seemed to add to the feeling that the proprietors were there temporarily and that they were spying for the provinces. Simultaneously, London whinnied and quivered, vibrated and thrummed, with one word on the people's lips: victory. From the exuberant chat behind a grill in an Air Street bakery to the bum-filled deck chairs in Regent's Park. From the cool arcades of Knightsbridge and from the lush carpets of Belgravia, where the scarlet shag was deep enough for a larking boy or his thrifty old grandmother to lose a farthing, to a lone old soldier, now homeless other than the earth beneath his single foot, staring into space from a damp bus stop in Hammersmith, holding to his chest a book by Blanche de la Peña.

Reggie paused, almost choked with a quiet emotion, which was soon chased away by the omnipresent bulldog spirit of this island race who had done what was required and more.

It should never be doubted that Reginald Victor Windsor (no bleedin' relation) could (in the words of old Drago Thoms) "talk a pie off a shelf."

* * *

London, June 1945

My dearest J.,

I know you're here. And I suspect my daily scribblings are piled up in a post office train, somewhere in subterranean London, but they will get to Sarajevo one day soon. I hope that if you receive these thousands of notes one day, it will not cause you heartache, but make you happy; far happier than receiving nothing and believing you meant little or nothing to me. It's a tough call, but how can I break my sad habit now?

Wonderful news: Carl is now a father, my darling. I know we will celebrate this together soon. I once thought I would not want to see you as an old man, but still I desire little more than to have you and to have Carl home safe. He left for the U.S. Navy yesterday. The war in Japan has to be over soon, too, and I still pray for our happy ending.

I am at the Langham Hotel off Oxford Circus, for it seems like your sort of place. I have just bought Blanche's latest from a wonderful spot on Charing Cross Road called Rawlings & Bennett. They are quite the adorers of our friend in common, as you would have me say, you damned stickler. I shall close the world out tonight and meet you, robed in gardenia, on page one. I shudder.

As if it were still yesterday,
Yours, as always,
Lorelei xxx

Twenty-one

A Giant in the Promised Land

I saw a Puritan-one hanging of his cat on a Monday,
For killing of a mouse on Sunday.

—R. Brathwaite, *An Age for Apes*

As they pulled around Marble Arch, Johan saw a crowd and asked Reggie what was happening.

"Speakers' Corner, squire! Every psychopath, cuckoo brain, and nutter in England gathers there."

"We'll see about *that*!"

Reggie pulled up on the south side of the arch and the strange-looking quartet crossed into the park.

"They get on their soapbox, squire. It's where the saying comes from. It's the beauty of the English way. If you're mad, talk away, but don't ever be surprised if no one listens."

And so they entered the exquisitely bizarre fray.

"Blasphemers and infidels. Degenerates and heretics. What a joy!"

They headed toward the trees beneath which the orators gathered, on the wide pathway to Park Lane. A grubby, olive-skinned man, stood on the foot of a stepladder. His beard was so full, he looked like he was peering over a hedge. He was in the throes of asking his small but interested, amused, and growing audience about the Promised Land.

"And why, my friends, is it called the Promised Land? Because God promises it to anyone and everyone. Jews, Arabs, and bloody Christians alike! The lot. Anyone with a beard and a funny hat. Every religion needs a beard and a funny hat, if you can call a crown of thorns a hat. Which I do! No wonder there is such turmoil, my friends, when God has all the ethics of a spiv selling silks in Camden Town. Abraham, the father of these three clans! He hears voices and goes up a mountain to kill his son. They say he's a prophet. If my father, who is a decent and religious man, heard voices and took me onto Hampstead Heath to slaughter me, what would they do to him? Lock the man up, throw away the bloody key, and rightly so! But no, God *talked* to Abraham. I despair, my friends! I truly fucking despair!"

The speaker's eyes darted madly, pleased with himself as his entertained flock increased. Then this delightful man lost four of his disciples (Johan Thoms et al.), as they continued their fun sweep of the enlightened, the unstable, and the unwell.

They came next to a giant of a man who needed no soapbox, no stepladder. He was nearing seven feet tall in his odd-colored Wellington boots. His bald head was stained by a black-currant birthmark, his jaw was crooked, and one of his eyes appeared to have been gouged out. And he was reciting medieval English poetry. Throughout his rehearsed spiel of crazed but hypnotic poetry, his lengthy arms remained upright in what seemed to Johan to be an impression of the rugby posts on Porlock Hill.

"Is this Heaven or Hell?" Johan let out involuntarily.

"That is the smartest question I have *ever* been asked, good sir," the giant acknowledged. His crowd spun around to see from where the inquiry had come. Johan stood impassively for once, his mind on a different plane.

A sign behind London's tallest orator proclaimed the source of the loon's words:

RICHARD BRATHWAITE'S *AN AGE FOR APES*
DRUNKEN BARNABY'S FOUR JOURNEYS TO THE NORTH OF ENGLAND
1658

There was a serenity and a peace about the giant in his massive stained dungarees as he shared with the intrigued number the words of this Brathwaite character, seemingly his favorite poet:

"Inns are nasty, dusty, fusty,
With both smoke and rubbish musty.

Thence to Gastile, *I was drawn in*
To an alehouse near adjoining
To a chapel; I drank stingo,
With a butcher *and* Domingo,
Th' curate, who to my discerning,
Was not guilty of much learning."

"Doesn't sound like hell at all to me, chaps. More like damned heaven," said Johan, once again slightly louder than he had planned.

Giant threw his head back in ecstatic relief.

"Whoa! We have surely been joined by a savant, a seer, people. All this and, indeed, the heaven of which he speaketh, too!"

He then bellowed out what seemed to be his favorite Brathwaite couplet on a completely new train of thought:

"I saw a Puritan-one hanging of his cat on a Monday,
For killing of a mouse on Sunday."

Johan gestured to Catalina not to push Cicero on, but to stay and breathe in every part of every second. A fine calm had descended upon Johan Thoms for the first time in decades. For once, he was not in a rush. Time stood still, like it had once in the university quadrangle under the monkey puzzle trees, in the Old Sultan's Palace under the banyan tree, in Suite 30 of the Hotel President. Johan and Giant held eye contact as if they were best friends from a previous incarnation. They were certainly bound in union by their own deeply individual and articulate madnesses. But there was more. The perhaps unnecessary slaughter of the mouse was one thing; but to see the cat suffer, and in full view of the world, moved Johan, resonated deeply within him. Who would then slit this Puritan's throat?

When would the killing stop? Giant seemed to know that it was unlikely to stop anytime soon, but also that he would not be judging anyone, least of all the man he now faced. A smile touched upon both their lips as the world carried on around them in silence. Tonight Blanche would write of this scene, for she knew it would be appreciated by one of her Manhattan readers.

Suddenly Catalina broke their ethereal calm. Carefully measuring her English words, she looked at Johan Thoms and said, "But you, old man. You would NEVER wait for this. You would want to kill this poor mouse on a Saturday! Maybe even before, you old *stupido*!"

After so many years with the man, she was fully aware of his penchant for rushing ahead or dreaming of the past, of his inability to live in the present. She was still unaware, however, of Johan's secret, for Cicero had breathed not a word.

Cicero choked. He could only wholeheartedly agree with her beautiful, direct wisdom.

The crowd sniggered. Giant radiated silent joy, dumbfounded for the first time in more than four hundred visits to this unique spot.

Catalina then walked off on her own and procured a discarded soapbox. Giant politely gestured for his crowd to note this strange young woman.

Today, in her tatty blue dress, Catalina gladly accepted the crowd's attention. She clapped her hands sharply three times and proudly announced to the gathered delinquents, degenerates, and miscreants in something a little north of pidgin English:

"I would like you all know that I have something to say."

Giant looked at Johan but nodded toward the blind man at his side and mouthed the word *congratulations*. Johan cocked his head, still locked in eye contact with the erstwhile speaker. Their friendly glare was broken by her next, three-word declaration:

"I am pregnant."

She bit into her bottom lip in that way she did, motherly hands cupped underneath her belly, and looked at Cicero. "And *that* man there is the father."

A gentle ripple of applause spread from a six-year-old girl called Ivy, a stunned Johan, and their gracious driver, Reginald, through the crowd. Hats were thrown in the air. Many lined up to shake Cicero by the hand, but not before Johan had held him tightly and at length. The father-to-be was unable to find any words until Catalina embraced him, and then he simply said that he loved her. Giant drifted into the background, settling on his haunches by an oak and smirking happily to himself, as if the final part of life's jigsaw had just fallen into place. Johan thought that he saw a copy of *The White-Kilted Brigadier* in the pocket of Giant's dungarees.

Johan was blissfully confused. It was a surreal few minutes, but also beautiful and quite mysterious. Time did stop then. Or seemed to. He had never imagined being this happy again in his life. *This* was the feeling he had continually tried to capture. He recognized it without fail, although he noted, too, that he could never summon it himself.

A brief chorus of "For They Are Jolly Good Fellows" broke out among the crowd, then it slowly dispersed.

* * *

The mean concierge eyed the girl in the tatty blue dress suspiciously, and with some disdain, until she took over from Johan the reins of pushing a uniformed Cicero through the grand swinging doors of the Langham. A distinguished-looking (yet still glazed-over) Johan was at her side, having now removed his eye patch altogether in order to get a better view of the place.

They checked into two luxury rooms on the fifth floor. Their three vast arched windows sat below the belfry tower, which hosted the recently refired rouge neon of the establishment's name. Johan swished back the curtains, twenty feet high and of violet crushed velvet, to reveal to the right the curve of Regent Street and the still-regal (despite bomb damage) brown stone Church of All Souls, and to the left a white monolithic structure which he had seen many times in the *Times of London*.

"By George!" he blurted as he looked out onto the BBC. "Can this day get ANY better?"

He immediately picked up the house phone to the concierge. The chief of staff requested field glasses. Within five minutes, a pair of binoculars was delivered to the room, though this was never recorded in the Langham's official log.[11]

"Need to put names to faces!" He peered out through them happily, hoping to match the plummy voice from the six-o'clock news with the bowler-hatted and mustachioed figure twirling a dreaded umbrella by the front doors across the road.

Catalina and Cicero slipped into the adjoining suite.

from "The Unpublished Diaries of D. Parker"

August 6, 1945

I received an airmail letter from Lorelei today and this passage I relate unedited.

    D. I am tired. London has finally worn me out. After Mr. Orwell's suggestion of the Savoy and the Langham, I can find no clue. The embers are fading, though I sense I am close. The embassies are of no or little help. What priority may I demand in such times here? It is not their fault. I have even placed newspaper advertisements in London, Oxford, and Cambridge, but I fear they are lost in the sea of similar sad postings. I still write every day, even if it is one sentence. I wish I could find him for the sake of our son. I often fear that there is not much else to salvage, but for the boy, it is different. Carl has grown into such a fine man without his father, and he deserves this at the very least. I thought I was close, but I suppose I should take solace in my son and in Blanche and all that entails. It can be oh so confounding. We have a right to want more, but we must also remember when and where we are living.

    I ponder what will happen were I to find my Johan; yet I fear the alternative far more.

    I will be moving out of the Langham tomorrow.

    Then who knows?

I miss and love you,
Lorelei x

Twenty-two

Pepper's Ghost, Fluffers, and a Brief Encounter

Out of intense complexities, intense simplicities emerge.
—Sir Winston Churchill

During their stay at the Langham, Johan talked at regular intervals (every hour or so) about going home to Sarajevo. He developed the stare of a madman, and his episodes increased in frequency and exposed his madness to the innocent general public. Naked night traipses (oddly, very similar to Catalina's own father's) were his specialty, as well as relieving washing lines of their pieces.

Once, he was found naked in some opium den in Whitechapel, steadfastly refusing to smoke any more of the narcotic after having hot ash dropped onto his now red raw groin by a bucktoothed African goof called, of all things, Scottish Paul. The other smokers were too smashed to care about anything as dull as nakedness. The small Asian man on the front door was more interested in a half-crown tip.

On another occasion, in the Red Anchor pub in Covent Garden, he had left the tap bar, drunk, to piss in the gents', when the darkness fell, in a rare afternoon episode. Lost and confused, he wandered the labyrinthine corridors of the West End building. Fifteen minutes later and no closer to his release, he opened a door and walked straight out onto a stage in the middle of a period production of *The Importance of Being Earnest*. He settled on a mauve chaise longue for the majority of the third act, much to the befuddlement of Lady Bracknell and Algernon, and to the utmost enjoyment of the audience. He arose toward the play's close, passed wind loudly, and sauntered down the central aisle and out into the glaring afternoon sun. It was not the first time in his life that he left uproar in his slipstream. He (or as the reviewer called him, Pepper's Ghost, which refers to a Dickensian theater trick of making objects or people appear and disappear) received a fine, if slightly tongue-in-cheek, review in the following day's *Times*.

Johan also sleepwalked one night along the tracks through the underground system, ending up at Vauxhall station on a drizzly dawn with no clothes on. The stations were still kept open, ever since the nights five years before when a hundred thousand plus would sleep beneath the city to escape the Luftwaffe's fiery bombs and V-2 rockets. Compared to today, those were innocent days, when sabotage by one's own populace was an unimagined and unimaginable event. Johan was found by a team of those unfortunate hair collectors (known as fluffers) who had (and still have) the horrific task of trawling the tube network during the night for dry hair, dust, and other waste which, particularly in the summer, becomes a fire hazard. Two old, stooped Cockney characters kindly led Johan out of the tunnel between Vauxhall and Waterloo. All they were able to help with sartorially was a large plastic bag or two, which they were using to collect their hairy haul. Back at the Langham, the concierge, broadcasting absolute horror from every frown line, snapped his fingers for an underling to engulf Johan in a blanket.

* * *

In clearer moments, Johan loved to take Catalina and Cicero to breakfast at the Wolseley, by Green Park. Catalina happily went along with the boys' plans, still delighted by everyday surprises to be found in new towns, new faces, and new words. She was content to be soaking up every new inch of the world outside that piece of scrubland in the hinterlands of 1930s

Spain. Like her two friends, she was living on borrowed time; her sell-by date had been the day her village was crushed by Franco's tanks. She was quite a wonder, with a scarily sharp brain and a seldomly utilized scowl. Her dark eyes, sensual swagger, and blemishless Spanish skin were enough to stop strangers in their tracks, especially in the pale-skinned northern climes of Anglo-Saxon London.

*   *   *

Within a few weeks, they received notification from the Yugoslav ambassador that they could now return to Sarajevo. The travel documents were delivered to the Langham while Johan was enjoying a breakfast of kippers, English muffins, and Marmite. He then read the *Times*, spending a full half hour on the obituaries. ("It's where all the interesting people are to be found these days," he used to say.)

He had also carefully torn out a clipping from another paper for his own wallet.

A BRIEF ENCOUNTER

Last evening's Oxford Literary Awards Supper was made infinitely more bearable by the shortest acceptance speech in their controversial history; made even swifter and less bothersome by the nonappearance of the winner, as intriguing and perhaps revealing as that event might have been. After last year's dreary, syrupy, and tear-ridden effort (which was dragged out for eighteen uncomfortable minutes) by Miss Fanny Reiker (almost as frightening in person as her prose is on the page, though I would call it "typing," not "writing"), we were thankfully treated to just sixteen syllables, eleven words, four clipped sentences, one telegram.

Heresy, blasphemy, and bad taste shall endure. Stop. Thank you. Stop.

No! Thank you, Blanche. And if bad taste should prevail, then the Daily Telegraph *shall not count you in its unwelcome number.* Vive le Brigadier!

Mr. Valentine R. Beauchamps,

Daily Telegraph

Johan was going to miss this country and this city. They had been in London only a very short time, and in England for less than five years. If it were not for the desire to return to his parents and to see old Kaunitz, he would have happily stayed in England, and in London, for good.

Johan was now fifty-one. He shuddered when he thought of how different his parents would be. Kaunitz, too. Would they still be alive? Would they really not blame him for all the things for which he blamed himself? Would they really not see his trail of horror?

Part Four

Many of us crucify ourselves between two thieves—regret for the past and fear of the future.

—Fulton Oursler

One

"Everybody Ought to Go Careful in a City Like This" (1945)

Like the fella says, in Italy for thirty years under the Borgias they had warfare, terror, murder, and bloodshed, but they produced Michelangelo, Leonardo da Vinci, and the Renaissance. In Switzerland they had brotherly love. They had five hundred years of democracy and peace, and what did they produce? The cuckoo clock.

—Harry Lime in the film version of *The Third Man*

October 1945

They were to fly to Vienna in a military aircraft, leaving from the small RAF strip at Northolt. Even with the bureaucracy of the paperwork overcome, physical passage across Europe was still not easy. However, Johan and Cicero had engaged an aging cigar-puffing general by the name of Fannet-Holmes, with a belly like a bay window, in the bar at the Langham. Half a dozen gin and tonics later, they had been given a telephone number and a password in order to purchase air tickets to Vienna. From there they would take the train.

Cicero was fascinated by the general's knowledge of the war and of planes in particular, especially how the machine guns on a Spitfire were synchronized to fire through the aircraft's propellers. (If the General had been complete in his information, he would have attributed this technology to the Germans in the Great War, when the Fokker Scourge of 1915 gave Teutonic supremacy for almost a year. During this time, a British airman's average life expectancy was just eleven days.)

The slightly drunk general, however, was far more tickled by the fact that Johan Thoms's anglicized name was actually John Thomas.

("Oh, my word! John Thomas! How delightfully degenerate!" as Johan looked on with a puzzled crease in his forehead. The general continued, "I went to school with a Richard William Cock. He actually married a wee slip of a girl by the name of Fanny Hyman. What were the parents thinking of? And why would anyone by the name of Johnson not change his or her name? I ask you!")

They thanked the general for his help. The battle-weary general laughed as they said good-bye.

He was still laughing as they slipped through the great glass doors and out onto Langham Place.

* * *

They landed in the Vienna of Harry Lime, not of Lorelei Ribeiro. And yet it seemed that, despite two world wars and a heavily shaken kaleidoscope, Johan's papers and his bank accounts functioned as well in 1945 as they had back in 1914. Johan thought of his good friend Kaunitz, and how very deeply his ancient institutions must be rooted to have survived all *that* horror.

A train took them south through a land blistered and burned.

They had prepared for their arrival at the Sarajevo train station by pouring the lion's share of a bottle of vodka down Johan's throat en route. It was malice aforethought. As was Cicero's Republican uniform, which lubricated their entrance into the Communist quarter of Vienna. He even enjoyed a pat on the back from the Soviet guards before they ventured into Tito's new Yugoslavia.

At the station in Sarajevo, two porters lifted Johan into a waiting car. His wealth allowed this luxury over the train, which was still as uncomfortable as it had been in his youth, but was now also far more unreliable. He was briefly reminded of how the city had smelled in his youth. The air was full of memories, and an old, happy feeling seemed to pass by on the sighing wind. However, the less he saw of this particular part of his past, the better. He did lift an eye above the parapet for a split second when he felt he was in the environs of the Hotel President, but he slipped on his elbow and crashed back down in the rear seat, slammed his head against something hard, and groaned off into another temporary coma.

The driver was given the instructions which Johan had written down in Vienna: *To the outlying town of Argona. Please.*

from "The Unpublished Diaries of D. Parker"

That bastard! That damned bastard! If I ever . . . I took a telegram this lunchtime at the bar in the Algonquin. It was from London. It was Lorelei. Carl's ship has been lost off the Philippines. A second loved one of hers condemned to the bottom of an ocean. Let's hope that bastard Thoms is in a deep trench of his own somewhere. She is returning to New York City. Poor, poor girl. No Hollywood endings here, it seems. Maybe there is a God.

Two

The Return of Abu Hasan

Forget regret.
Or life is yours to miss.

—Jonathan Larson, "Another Day"

Dorothy's wish had been granted, for Johan Thoms was indeed in a trench. The deepest of psychotic trenches. He was in a self-induced, protective twilight world.

"Fuck!" he blurted out. Running away for thirty years had left him incapable of coping. His head felt as if it were in a vise as they walked the cobblestones of a town he barely knew. Argona had been scorched by war.

The ruthless Croatian Ustase[12] had been through here. The Serbs were gone, the Muslims cleared. Their houses were rubble. One-third of the enemy had been deported, one-third imprisoned, and one-third slaughtered. Their dogs, horses, and cattle were just bones.

This was the personal microcosm of his own self-induced Apocalypse. In 1945, he could not mentally piece the town back together, to how it had been in 1914. The school was only just there, as was the butcher's shop and part of the church. The remnants of a street corner where he had once played soccer.

He placed the palms of his hands to his face in horror. "Look around here. The town of my birth. Just rubble. This was a place. A beautiful one. Now look."

The car waited for them in a place that might have been the town square. They continued walking through the town, Johan straining his brain to trigger memories of innocence and boyhood, and of times, before it became necessary to forget. Most of the town had been destroyed by mortars and bombs, and the streets were deserted. He imagined that he would see his own house reduced to a pile of brick. He was even having trouble placing it geographically on streets he simply did not know anymore.

Minutes later, they were outside the old house, one of only two standing in a fifty-yard radius. It had a huge hole in the roof. He shuffled slowly toward it, memories now flooding onto the celluloid screen of the back of his eye.

The house appeared still on the inside, unlived in. The door was hanging off the hinges; a couple of the windows were cracked, a couple missing. Mucky mauve curtains blew inward, into what used to be their living room.

He inched inside. "Hello?" He banged on the loose wood of the door.

There were perhaps three seconds of silence. Then, in the kitchen at the back, a bell rang, and he heard muffled voices.

He moved through the hallway and down the two steps to the scullery. When he pushed the door open, he saw a figure sitting in a rocking chair by the old kitchen stove.

It was Elena. He recognized his mother immediately, despite the ravages of several decades.

"Mama! It's me, Johan!"

He dashed to her, and held her while she sobbed. Johan found it hard to blink, until an errant housefly hit his pupil.

Catalina and Cicero had remained outside. Slowly, fondly, she pushed him around any ground not littered with brick. Johan came out with Elena some ten minutes later and introductions were made.

* * *

Johan learned that his father had died when a German Luftwaffe Stuka had crash-landed on the roof. Drago was quite insane at this point, though still athletic enough to be on the roof during a heavy rainstorm. The plane hit the house as it spun out of control with innocent(ish) engine troubles. Elena cared for the handsome pilot until he was well enough to find work in the village bakery. He looked like a stunt double for the great Teutonic actor Hardy Krüger, insisted he was not a deserter, that he was still contributing to the war effort. The German would say it with such a straight face that some people thought he was being serious.

Meanwhile, mad Drago Thoms was buried in the back garden, which was no longer much of a garden, more of a postapocalyptic landfill with stubborn, battle-hardened hints of former azures. Drago left other thumbprints around the property, for Elena continued to find beans around for years to come.

They sat around talking into the night. Elena found a bottle of grog from behind the pantry door. After a couple of shots from the grubby cups, Johan asked if they were hungry (and they were) and went loping out into the street, in a weirdly similar stride, Elena thought to that of his father decades earlier. He would have made a conger eel look arthritic. Johan had not given his mother the chance to explain how unlikely it was to find anything to eat out there. He had also not hung around to explain how he had a fat wad of dinar in his back pocket to persuade some unscrupulous oaf to part with some nourishment.

To the old woman's surprise, he returned with a pot of stew, two bottles of wine, fresh bread, and a plentiful bag of provisions which had been liberated from the kitchens of the Langham and which he collected from the car.

Elena was tired, and eventually turned in, frail but smiling, still in shock, Johan believed. Her little boy, her own flesh and blood, was back where he belonged, where he had always belonged. Cicero passed out by the fire, the combination of wine and medication too much for him. Catalina pushed a chair next to his and curled into it, closing her eyes. Johan rose and walked outside to the back of the house. He sat on the steps, which faced the shack and the old gardens, where bluish flowers now poked through the rocks.

Johan Thoms was home.

The next morning Elena asked him to follow her into her room. From a closet, she removed several very large bundles, which she laid on her bed.

"Son, I want you to prepare yourself. This is not going to be easy."

Johan stared at her, and then at the parcels. He filled with fear.

"From *her*," Elena said.

Johan stumbled sideways and edged into the corner of the room. His legs buckled and he was down. Again.

On the bed were thousands of letters from Lorelei. Inside the cupboard, he saw more. They were piled waist-high and several feet across, a powder-blue hillock of desire and longing, dusted with virgin snow. Her bouquet passed teasingly beneath his nose, as if to torment him further. He took as much as he could into his nostrils and imagined that if he lost himself in her fragrance, he would transport himself back to another time. Here was the real birth of his attempts to conquer the space-time continuum.

Elena moved toward him, and he held her by her knees, his head to her thigh. They remained like this until Johan finally managed to speak. "Why now? Why not before? Why not *before*?"

"I am so sorry, my love. I only received them a few weeks ago. They were sent from the home of Count Kaunitz."

Johan said once more, "Why not *before*?" and then cursed with an invective so vile as to make his sturdy mother blush.

"Johan Thoms! You atrocious cunt!"

*   *   *

London, August 1, 1945

My dearest J.,

> *Oh, darling! The U.S. Navy called at the New York house this morning. I am returning to Manhattan immediately on the Cunard Line. I will write from there. I fear the worst for our fine son. My heart may finally be tiring. This room at the Langham reminds me of the President.*

> *The years may have beaten us. I truly gave it my best, Johan.*

> *It seems we are powerless to push time forward to get to where we wish to be, but we are infinitely more impotent to turn it back to where we were. If only . . .*

> *This might be it, though. This might be where the story ends.*

I'll see you soon in my dreams, and of course through our Blanche.
I am so tired.

Your one and only,
Lorelei xxx

Ernest was reading this letter to himself when Johan began to recite from memory its final sentences: "It seems we are powerless . . ."

"But why would you not go to her, even in '45?" asked Ernest.

"My stubbornness, my regret, my shame, the gulf of years, my fearing her reproaches, my fearing her no longer possessing the passion of her early letters. And then to lose a son in a war I started. And still I could have saved him. How could I look her in the eye? I had killed her son. Our boy. How could she ever forgive me of that?"

He paused.

"This is not yet the end of the story, though it certainly did feel like it.

"But do I regret not going to her then or even years before, if I had had the courage? Of course I do. It blights my every hour. Why do you think I now need to go back in time? Of course I might save millions of lives and veer a century away from hellfire, but it might also be for her. For us. To see Dubrovnik at dusk once more, tight on booze and just minutes away from our bed. I eventually got Kaunitz's letters—the ones he'd mailed to Portugal—when some kindly soul liberated them decades later and sent them en masse to the old hut in Vila do Bispo. I was long gone from the End of the World, but the Young Hooligans saw to it that they were sent here. The few letters that I had ever seen in Portugal made no mention of her or were meanly censored. Nine out of ten of these begged me to go to her."

"And if you had known that she had written to you every day for thirty-one years, what would you have done?" asked Ernest.

Johan struggled to emit the next words. "I have thought about nothing else some days and even more nights. For never was a story of more woe."

Ernest, who had previously felt an increasing impatience with and an uncomfortable urgency about the unresolved affair, was now filled with sadness. He sensed that in the shadow of Johan's mistake of June 28, 1914, there had taken root in him an even deeper unshiftable regret.

Three

The Brigadier's Au Revoir

How like a winter hath my absence been
From thee, the pleasure of the fleeting year! . . .
Or, if [the birds] sing, 'tis with so dull a cheer,
That leaves look pale, dreading the winter's near.

—Shakespeare, Sonnet 97

With the eye patch still present, Johan started to wear a long, black, hooded hessian cape and a helmet. He claimed, albeit with a chuckle, that it was a metaphor.

The trio moved into the house. Johan utilized his still-considerable cash resources to bring the property back into some sort of habitable condition, to attempt to restore it into the warm, cozy home he remembered having as a small boy. Elena had never seen such irresponsible spending, but she had not been exposed to the decadence of London, nor had a considerable fortune been siphoned off to her for the last thirty years. Nor did she complain.

The roof was soon fixed. The water was turned on, a ridiculously modern newly installed power switch flicked, windows mended, plentiful winter supplies of coal and wood delivered for the old kitchen fire and stove. The scullery was filled with food. Drago's old shack at the bottom of the garden was spruced up, for Johan saw it as a refuge and a reminder of his father. He resolved to plant more flowers outside amid the rubble in the next spring, but only bluish ones. Lilacs, violets, speedwells, bluebells, plumbago, ceanothus. The one after which he really hankered was the mythical Blue Rose of Forgetfulness, one whiff of which would erase his pain, his memory, forever. (He had heard it could, for sure, be found in a village by a river outside Baghdad, but this only made him think again of Abu Hasan.)

The old shack was thirty feet by thirty feet and had been Drago's tribute to horticulture, his Museum of Mother Nature. Low ceilings and just two cobwebbed windows, letting in meager shafts of unsure light, gave the place a weird feel. A litter of six tiger-striped kittens kept it mainly rat-free for Johan as he spent spring and summer days in a rocking chair Drago had left in it.

"R-r-r-r-r-at," he would blurt out, as if to instruct one of the young cats that it was lunchtime. He hated these rats and would now wage his own personal crusade against the belligerent squadrons and stubborn dragoons of the verminous critters. It was his new project; an ousted Winston Churchill no longer needed his help. The shack offered him a modicum of comfort in his perennial high tide of dementia, as did the time he spent on Blanche de la Peña's personal favorite, *The White-Kilted Brigadier and the Search for the Elusive Blue Rose of Forgetfulness.* It was his twenty-seventh novel, one for each unsullied day of June 1914. This, however, would have seemed a quite pessimistic tale had it been for a cathartic and pioneering twenty-eighth. An apologetic but big, brave, shoulders-back, chest-out, and chin-up twenty-eighth. Large parts of it had been written over the years, and now it needed only to be edited and stitched together to form the dénouement of the series. Catalina and Cicero were, as Drago would have been, so very proud indeed, but theirs was nothing compared to the pride felt by Elena. Johan intended this to be the final chapter of Rex-Foyle, though this would only be an au revoir; we would see his return on a different canvas.

While the old house was rebuilt day by day by hired laborers and became a hive of activity, the rest of the village fell away around them. Johan's mother, however, was soon able to bathe every day with fresh soaps and oils, in a new bathtub. She wore clean clothes, slept in clean linens, drank clean, fresh water, and became an expert baker.

Johan bought a battered old truck from one of the workers. It still had various farm implements and tools in it when the deal was closed. He asked why bloodstains covered the open back of the truck. The vendor assured him it was from the transfer of animals to market. Johan doubted it (as did Cicero's superkeen nostrils), but he reluctantly parted with a small pile of dinar for the vehicle along with a spare wheel (with a flat tire) and a half-empty tank of gritty gasoline.

Every Saturday morning around ten o'clock, he took his family off to the market in Sarajevo.

The old lady and her clutch of weirdos. A silent pregnant girl, a legless blind soldier in a foreign uniform, and a twitching, middle-aged son with a big head and odd gait, eyes flicking as if the nonexistent snipers knew he was there.

For obvious reasons, Johan refused to drive anywhere closer to Sarajevo than the old western boundary of Ilidža. Then they either walked or used the streetcar. They returned to the truck in a taxi, having met in Bascarsija at a designated point in midafternoon.

Having left his old wireless for the maid at the Langham, Johan bought a new black-market one in the bazaar one nondescript Saturday in November so he could listen to the BBC World Service, though perhaps it would have been better had he been isolated from the news. A newsmagazine arrived once a month or so from London. His theory (learned from Torquil McFelly in Porlock) was that if he turned away from the world completely, he would just presume the worst (he was used to it). Through this monthly gazette and his shortwave wireless, he now sought any story that did NOT involve death, destruction, horror, or hell; the additional absence of rape, pillage, and murder was a sick bonus to him. In the fact that the world had still not ended he might take solace. It was a strange kind of medicine. But then so was marigold, and that had worked for the longest time.

In early January '46, he procured a pair of ice skates from Bascarsija. They would have fit a child of six or perhaps seven. He told himself that Catalina and Cicero's child would wear them one day on the frozen Miljacka, where he now sat waiting for the others as some words from his past flashed through his dull skull.

Glide gently, thus forever glide.

He was convinced that his friends' coming offspring would heed these words better than he had in his sorry life. From the south side of the river, across the thick ice, came a scruffy lad, carrying a branch twice the size of his meager frame. The boy started for a section of the wall near to where Schiller's Café had been decades before, but thirty yards downstream Johan called him over.

"Will these fit you, boy?"—lifting one of the skates with his right hand.

"Yes, old mister." The boy stepped forward, sensing opportunity.

"Can you skate?"

"Better than you," he smirked, eyeing Johan's big head and small feet.

"Well, put them on and do me a favor."

The lad had them on in less than two minutes, despite his chilblained fingers and the stiff laces, frozen and black.

"What's the favor, Grandpa?"

Johan asked him to skate out a word in the ice for him to look at.

The boy looked confused, as any lad of his—or any—age would if befronted by such an odd character. After a couple of practice turns and sudden stops, he set about his task. Johan sat with his back to the ice and listened to the mesmerizing sound of blunt steel on Bosnian ice, while fish and very life itself were protected beneath by the frozen crust.

When the urchin had finished, he came and sat next to Johan, who was now shaking visibly from the bitter cold. The boy pulled off the skates and, seeing Johan's state, discovered his politeness, thanked the old man, slipped on his own excuses for shoes, and disappeared toward the town.

Almost an hour later, Johan turned round to see that the boy did not excel in spelling. The River Miljacka—in fifteen-foot, uneven letters— proclaimed in the ice:

LORE...LIE

Johan Thoms started to walk toward the Appel Quay, head down and confused.

* * *

Within the first two weeks of Johan's return, his mother seemed to lose ten years of wrinkles and worry lines from her face. The news of a child brought a faint odor of old times back, though they were always *just* out of reach. The smell of fresh bread, a man's laughter (usually Cicero's) in an adjacent room, or the sound through an open window of the clanking of cutlery and a kitchen being set for dinner and, just for a second, Johan felt as if the clock had been turned back to some innocent day in the past. For Elena, the realization that it hadn't been, and that it was actually 1946, brought a wry, knowing smile. For Johan, however, it meant a reminder of a billion corpses.

The peace and calm that had descended over the old house was fleeting.

* * *

Once the remains of the German fighter plane had been removed, Johan moved back into his old room. He spent his first afternoon there, laying out the vellum-bounded volumes of the *Kama Sutra* from his youth. He had pulled them from his old kit bag. He read some of them. He read some old letters to himself, too, and stared into Lorelei's old paperweight, which contained that message of few words. He smelled the old bottle of El Capitán cologne, extracting half a nostril of memory before it was gone. This was the first time he had been through the satchel in perhaps a decade.

* * *

One morning at breakfast in late January '46, Johan eagerly announced that he planned to go to see Kaunitz, for the Count would now have returned from his traditional wintering in Naples, Cairo, and Constantinople. Elena got up and crept to the sink, her gray head down, and told him what she knew. Kaunitz had been taken by the Ustase secret police. Johan had overheard whispers of their brutality, rumors of mass graves close to the village. The smell of rotting flesh rode in on the wind when it blew from the north. The Thomses had probably been spared this brutality by their Germanic surname, their light skin, and Elena's blue eyes. The Croats had stuck with their kraut friends for centuries. They still do.[13]

But Kaunitz was Austrian royalty. He was on their side, was he not?

Yes, but Kaunitz also wore cerise pink, windmilled his arms (at least it looked that way to the quixotic Johan), flustered flamboyantly, had a limp wrist and a reputation worse than the Catholic priests. No amount of royal Wagnerian influence from the Aryan north would have been enough to save him from the evils of the Ustase, their torture, their death camps, their mass graves. Johan asked his mother for details of what had happened to the Count. Elena would not say.

"Don't even bother going to the estate. They ransacked it. Even killed his cranky old butler. Ate ALL the deer in one go, they say."

"Well, thank God *for that* . . ." Johan replied, seeming to hold back tears. But he did not cry. Kaunitz was dead for sure.

He shuffled off to his room, to be alone. He locked the door and did not come out for ten days. They heard him drink from the tap in the room from time to time and they saw him urinate through the window. The wireless blasted out more news, more horror, more guilt.

His veil had fallen again.

When he did reappear, he was unshaven and he smelled awful. His mother led him straight into the bathroom and dumped him unceremoniously into a hot bath, immediately, and with no discussion. He may as well have been five years old.

Four

The Veil

To give birth is a fearsome thing: there is no hating the child one has borne even when injured by it.

—Sophocles

It was Johan Thoms's birthday, in February 1946. Catalina, seven months with child, was walking Cicero before breakfast. Elena had set off on an early-morning walk in the opposite direction to buy bacon from the nearest farmer, a mile away. The three of them left the house at the same time.

As she walked back from her stroll with Cicero, coming down the short but steep hillock on their usual lap around the property, Catalina slipped on black ice. Right onto her belly. She lay screaming next to a ditch. The trench was serenely littered with early, yet very dead white orchids, themselves having caught cold, surprised by the night frost and preserved in their ice. The orchids were the last things she saw before she blacked out.

Cicero rolled down the hill in his wheelchair into the freezing brook, cracking his head on a rock. The would-be father was left unconscious, the crown of his head in the frozen ice, warm blood pouring into the crystal-cut waters.

A short while later, from his warm slumber up in the house, Johan heard Catalina's distant screams. At first, he placed it as part of a dream, a former lover's climactic shrill giving him an early-morning erection. He stirred to recognize the actual source, and a quite different emotion. He ran down the stairs and out into the cold February morning of his birthday just as naked as the day he was born, in that selfsame house on that selfsame date.

Nature's weird symmetry.

* * *

He collected her in his arms and took her toward the truck.

Catalina mouthed one word as she peeked out above the parapet of her inevitable and pending coma: "Cicero!" She gestured with rapidly glazing, rolling brown eyes and the slow flick of a finger. He helped her into the passenger seat. The keys were always left in the truck, so off they drove. Johan was still naked. Catalina was hemorrhaging from her jackknifed center. Johan saw Cicero's wheelchair as they swept down toward the bottom of the lane.

He found his old pal next to death in ice-cold water. His stump stuck out skyward. His black hair collected ice from the brook, and the freezing north wind coagulated the frozen blood in the thick mop on his head.

As Johan picked up Cicero and sat him next to Catalina in the front of the truck, his eye caught his cape in the back of truck and he threw it around their shoulders.

Off he sped toward the city, desperately pulling at the rudimentary dials on the dash for some heat from the engine. Outside, the crap and the mud on the windscreen of the van was an inch thick in places, and made it almost impossible for him to see out on the potholed road. The wipers did not work.

"Put your arms around him, keep him warm," he urged in panic. "And yourself."

Catalina did not speak, nor did she move.

When they arrived at the hospital less than twenty mad minutes later, his greatest friend was dead. Catalina was unconscious, her midriff a mass of clotted and still-weeping blood. A pair of orderlies, outside smoking, took the injured pair inside. Johan Thoms stayed motionless outside in the truck. Still unable to sob. The cape had fallen from his friends inside the car as they had been transported in.

The hospital was poorly equipped and did not really deserve the name. There was a nurse, however, who cared (of course), and Catalina was placed in her care. Johan recalled those nurses, those angels who had shown him love and generosity of spirit through his life. They always appeared to be there when they were most needed. And they were needed now.

* * *

The wipers were still not working. He cursed the truck.

"Fucking piece of shit," he blurted.

He threw the cape around himself, raising its hood to protect his identity and himself from the cold. He crept out of the truck's cabin and around into the back. From the pile of farm tools and digging implements, he improvised. The farmer's old scythe was the nearest he could find to a windscreen wiper.

Johan Thoms—the Angel of Death—walked to the front of the truck, which dripped blood and had just released a corpse or two (or three) from its front seat. Outside the morgue-ish hospital, naked from the shins down in a long black cape with the hood up, carrying a bloody scythe, he started to clean the windscreens.

At the busy windows, the collected ill and dying and the inmates of the attached asylum gasped. They saw only the Grim Reaper, the Eternal Footman, the Spoiler of Worldly Mansions, the Dark Minister of the Graveyard, who, still faceless, caped and holding his scythe in his left hand, slowly crawled into the driver's seat and smoked the single cigarette which lay on the dashboard. He sat up, turned the keys in the ignition, and drove off. When Catalina ever so briefly came around, she had to be sedated.

This time, Johan did not run. He parked around the back of the hospital and went inside. He sat with Catalina and held her hand. She drifted in and out of consciousness, though Johan continued to speak to her regardless, fondly. From the ghostly pale complexion of her exquisite face, framed by the deep red blood on her forehead, cheeks, and chin, he suspected that she was falling away rapidly into the unknown realm now occupied by her beloved blind soldier. A young doctor attended to her with a vigor beyond the capacity of a loved one. On the stroke of eleven, Catalina died. Johan screamed a guttural and desperate scream that could not have been matched by those grim of mind and loose of faculty down the hallways in the asylum. Then his raw yells were matched by those of a newborn, a new life released from the confines of a dead mother's womb. A girl.

This unreasonably dark cloud might yet reveal a lining of unfathomably bright silver, though at that exact moment, Johan could think only of his lost friends—Catalina, the girl in the tatty blue dress, and Cicero, that great senator. They were runts, rescue cases, and as rich and as intriguing and as astonishing as they had been, both had finally overstayed their welcomes.

Having seen the sorry, shambolic state of Johan, a nurse offered to take the child and look after her, either temporarily or on a longer-term basis. Johan was having none of it. He reached out for the baby in the style of the Reaper, arms seemingly extending a preternatural length to scoop back his loved ones' spawn.

This girl had lost her mother but had taken from her with that last breath a gift of vitality so rich and potent that she would burst upon Johan's gray world as soon as his veil would allow it. Some might say that she even lifted it all by herself.

*   *   *

New York City, September 1, 1945

My dearest J.,

   It seems our son was lost one week before the Japanese surrendered. Our grandson looks just as his father did at the same age. One day, I hope to tell him about his father, and, of course, his grandfather.

I can write no more.
   Good-bye, my darling.

Always,
Yours, Lorelei xxx

Johan took the letter from Ernest.

"This was her final one. I never saw her again. I have never met my grandson. Now you know why I must return. Why I shall soon return . . ."

He smiled. He had to be thinking of a June night in Sarajevo. Or of that smoky old bar in Dubrovnik.

Five

A Blue Rose by Any Other Name

Non que non tronabas pistolita.

—Mexican slang[14]

Spring 1946. Bosnia

For a while, Elena was nursing two children. She doted over the baby, who had already developed the proud and distinctive widow's peak of her father, and who possessed the black-marble, obsidian eyes of her mother. The girl's absolute will to live was a joint parental gift.

Meanwhile, Elena poured liquids into her son's mouth, force-fed him mashed-up foods. Even on his best days, he resembled a forlorn street dog. Then, gradually, he began to emerge from his semivegetative state to notice the new life before him.

"Mother! This child may be the key to our survival," Johan said one afternoon, watching the two of them.

"She shall be. She is a miracle. But we cannot continue to call her 'this child' and 'she.' You need to name her."

"I know. Her nerve reminds me of someone close to me. I shall name her after this formidable lady, a previous savior of mine. The girl will be known as Blanchita."

"That is beautiful!" said Elena as she set about playing mother, a role that delighted her beyond words. "And will she be a Thoms?"

Johan's answer was based not on a (perhaps) subconscious desire to distance the poor girl from his darkened past, but on something far more visceral.

"Blanchita, like her father, shall have no surname, for she, too, is unique.

"The Queen is dead. Long live the Queen."

* * *

Just as he had once nursed the girl's father, Johan discovered again his paternal instincts. And so Blanchita grew up, nestled in a loving home, amid the rubble of *his* destruction, the source of which she remained blissfully unaware.

In the fall of that year, Johan recalled Portugal, and visited the remains of the school in Argona in an attempt to found a local chapter of a certain chess club. After all the children had left for the day, he met a teacher in a corridor. That hallway made him tingle with memories. The professor was in his early sixties, and approached Johan with caution.

"May I help you?" he asked Johan.

"I believe so. But I do not know where or how to start without you thinking me a madman, a charge to which I gladly and proudly confess. There are different kinds, and I am the type that means no harm. I promise you this much as an opening gambit. Do you play chess?"

The teacher was sure he was indeed dealing with a madman, but he indulged this character, for there was something in his manner that reminded him of someone he had once adored in this very place. Before he answered Johan's question, he paused and then posed one of his own: "You're Thoms, aren't you? You are. I remember you. You nearly beat old Pestic at chess. And I certainly remember your father, that much is assured. I adored him. We all did, for he was a fine man. And yes, I do play. *He* taught me. I am Vrbicek. Please come with me and we may talk in comfort."

Vrbicek held out his hand to Johan, who took it and replied, "Johan. You know the rest."

The pair walked into the dim light of the staff room, where Johan was offered a comfortable battered chair. Vrbicek pulled a flask from his pocket, took a swig, and offered it to Johan, who thanked him before also glugging the cheap grog.

"Tell me what you want. If it is in my power to facilitate, then you shall have it," said Vrbicek.

"Thank you, my friend. It is a tale that starts in Portugal many years ago. With a bunch of boys about the same age as the ones who eagerly ran out of here a few minutes ago. I shall make them want to stay until way past dusk each night, and not go home. But then to go home when they are asked and to adore each minute they have with their parents. Please indulge me and let me tell you the story of the Young Hooligans' Chess Club at the End of the World, and how I taught them how to *glide. And gently so . . .*"

Vrbicek settled into a comfortable chair of his own, lighting a pipe and showing the early signs of a wide, handsome grin.

* * *

Johan soon had a Portuguese flag shipped to him from Vienna, flew it above the school on the evenings when the club met, and ordered a silver trophy bearing the Young Hooligans' coat of arms.

The boys and girls (whose company soon included a growing, blooming Blanchita) learned to say "hello" and "you're welcome" in many different languages, along with a cheeky, saucy one-liner guaranteed to bring a broad smile to the face of a particular foreigner. *Non que non tronabas pistolita.* The difference between *may* and *can* followed. They all soon knew the absolute ease and marvelous effect of a well-intentioned "please" and a well-timed "thank you." The others developed a deep sibling love for Blanchita; she grew up surrounded by the smiling faces of the chess-warrior-hooligans. Their parents were continually delighted, as Drago Thoms would have been, too.

When the Young Hooligans in Portugal found out in their annual letter from Johan that Cicero had died but had left a daughter (and one named Blanchita at that), they offered (of course, they did) to send all of their book royalties to her. Johan replied with a compromise to split them:

one-third to each of the clubs, and one-third for Blanchita. This made sense to Johan, as Kaunitz's generosity was no more.

For many years, Johan continued to make a regular pilgrimage to the Count's old estate, to remember his dear friend. He would sit on that same old stone bench by the lake and try to dredge up images which seemed so near, yet so distant that it could well have been a different life, or maybe a movie he had once seen in the old fleapit cinema in Porlock.

One year, a ten-year-old Blanchita swore she had seen a deer in the woods, but Johan pulled her quickly toward him and changed the subject. It was around this time that he started to call her Bandita instead. She loved this the first time she heard it, giggled loudly and at length, and playfully rubbed her face on his stubble, as he himself had once loved to do with Drago. He thought he had heard her call him *father*. He thought of her real father, and wished that he were there that day with them; the bravest Roman for many a century.

Most evenings ended for Blanchita with stories of Catalina and Cicero. On her eleventh birthday, he gave her a sturdy silver crucifix which her father had once (or twice) placed on Johan on a hospital bed.

Blanchita's genetic clash of Spanish beauty and bristling Roman courage was quite the sight to behold. Her accentuated, elevated cheekbones only just managed to mask a fury and a desire for a scrap. So well measured was this disguise that the full, lurking wrath rarely had to be unveiled. Johan was convinced that her beauty and potency had helped her win several closely fought chess battles, too. Blanchita sensed that some went out of their way to avoid playing her, and so she also took up a solitary pursuit: the piano. She taught herself, with the aid of a baby grand rescued from the University of Sarajevo, a gramophone from Bascarsija, and a regular stream of vinyl discs, which would arrive with a Belgrade, Prague, or Budapest postmark. Johan could not think of bad things when he heard her play, nor could he be distracted by any pain when he met her on the chessboard. He knew this was close to the ultimate anesthetic he sought.

"A Blue Rose by any other name . . . ," he would say as they began each game.

* * *

And so, Johan and his keen and starry-eyed protégés traveled one night on a potholed track to another school, where the old man had almost had his moment of glory decades before. This time he took his mother with him, but on the return home, he had the same vision as before.

Once again, Johan fell asleep in the cart on the dirt track back, waking from time to time with images of a chessboard on the lids of his eyes, opening them to see the image transposed onto the stars in the clear night sky.

Once again, Mars was his rook, the moon his queen.

Once again, he saw an army of a thousand pawns in the celestials, which made him wonder (once again) why *he* was allowed only eight.

He hugged Blanchita tightly, and wondered if she saw the same thing.

Six

Dragons, Confucius, and Snooker

Be not ashamed of mistakes and thus make them crimes.

—Confucius

1958. Sarajevo.

Johan's writing, sporadic through Blanchita's early years, began to gather steam once more. There would be no immediate return to Stanley Rex-Foyle however. Instead, Blanche picked up a thread from her first novel, almost three decades before.

In the *Dragon in Chains* series, Blanche tells the story of Ming of the Red Mist, a military officer forced into early retirement by the loss of a kneecap and an eye, and Qi Chu, the renowned Saintly Abbot from the White Cloud Monastery. The unlikely pair meet in the hills outside Chengdu, Sichuan Province, in 1898. Their train has stalled and they are forced to overnight in their carriage. They become firm friends after they discuss at length their shared love of (the much-quoted) Confucius and snooker. They travel on to Peking together and plot their futures.

There the following spring they open a small, luxurious, very expensive, and somewhat secretive hotel called Typhoon Hill, which is to become the favorite haunt of visiting ambassadors, dignitaries, presidents, prime ministers, princes, and kings, and famously to host the Peking Summit on the lawns in its walled Xing Garden.

By this time, Ming and Qi Chu are the purveyors of the land's finest unadulterated opium, and they introduce (or reacquaint) many of the guests to her charms and delights.

Dragon in Chains is a term used to describe the urge to satisfy one's addiction, which, in this case, is wonderfully utilized by our heroes to set the world in the direction of a Nirvana and a Shangri-la where war and inequality are actively discouraged and our leaders, it would seem to a confused onlooker, in unison start to act like reasonable, rational, caring human beings.

Dragon in Chains: How Opium and Confucius May Yet Save the World, Part One went to the ever-reliable Tobias Kilz in Ludgate Circus, and sold out across London bookshops almost immediately.

It was dedicated to LR, as was each of the subsequent books in the series. A fuming Dorothy Parker would not be seen for days afterward. The publication of this volume prompted a single powder-blue envelope with a New York postmark. In it, Lorelei expressed her utter delight at this mischievous, revolutionary, even angry side of Blanche. It made Johan smile to know he had not totally abdicated his responsibilities to *her*.

The book was received as "decades ahead of its time" and "superbly militant and deliciously subversive" by Mr. Archibald DeWitt-Vultura of the *Manchester Guardian*. Of course it was, though the review had been penned from a well-intentioned and comfortable Cheshire asylum. The column had been heavily edited down the road in the grubby city, but Archie had squeezed in some Baudelaire which the censor had not the heart to cut. *"Laissez-moi respirer longtemps, longtemps l'odeur de tes cheveux."*

* * *

Meanwhile, Miss de la Peña continued to ponder how, if absinthe, guilt, and stupidity had brought her down, then opium, deep breaths, and intelligence might yet save her.

More volumes and literary acclaim followed. Meanwhile, she tried every day to remember Ming's Confucian wisdom.

"Be not ashamed of mistakes and thus make them crimes."

* * *

Johan kept his wireless on. People have been known to learn languages by keeping a radio on during the night. Leave on *Süddeutscher Rundfunk* through two years of gentle slumber and it is feasible that one may converse with the good folk of Stuttgart as one of their own. Well, Johan kept up-to-date with his trail of unique destruction in very much the same way, via the BBC.

Yugoslavia (literally "the land of southern Slavs") had turned to Tito and communism when the Ustase were hounded out, and Moscow gripped the whole region. Stalin (harboring the enmity and distrust of capitalism from the Johan Thoms–inspired Treaty of Versailles) had turned his back on the West amid the seedlings of a new war (the BBC was calling it a "cold war"). Communism was the new threat. The communism of the Soviets and the Chinese even conceived a bastard baby in Hanoi. The Chinese were mobilizing. They limbered up by slaughtering tens of millions of their own. War kicked off first in Korea, and then came the horror of Vietnam. Clashing ideologies flourished in rice paddies, surrounded by fat snakes and pissed-off spiders. Another few million for Johan to endure and file away.

American paranoia about communism spawned the evils of modern-day U.S. foreign policy—the CIA with their fingers in Iran, Chile, Peru, Iraq, throughout the fifties, sowing seeds of revolution and destruction of anything remotely resembling a democracy. A few more million.

* * *

In early 1963, Elena died from pneumonia. She was ninety-four. They buried her next to Drago in the old gardens, which were soon to be a mass of varying blues once again.

Johan sobbed, too, for the first time in his life. Now quite the young lady, Blanchita held him closely, protecting him, as they had done for each other for the past seventeen years.

A few weeks later, Johan accidentally set fire to the old house after having fallen asleep at his typewriter and knocked over a flickering church candle. Blanchita had seen the smoke on her way back from the village.

The upstairs was gutted, but Blanchita was still able to live comfortably in the downstairs.

Johan had already moved some of his old things into the shack, where he now isolated himself from the world. Some old books, his typewriter and manuscripts, his wireless, a kit bag, an old Schneider's suit, a sublime paperweight carrying just five words, letters, an empty bottle of cologne, old sepia photographs, bits and pieces. He was repatriated with his old globe, which had played its part in starting this whole saga.

News kept coming through from the BBC, opposite his old room at the Langham. More deaths in Vietnam. The Cultural Revolution in China. Genocide in Cambodia—Year Zero and Pol Pot. Johan could trace the conflicts fought around communism back to the Treaty of Versailles, and hence the Great War, and hence himself. Up the road in Hungary, deaths of children from Russian bullets. East Timor. Iran. Argentina.

All this continued to permeate Johan's consciousness overnight out in the shack. The months slipped by with the occasional visit into the house to rant or to sleepwalk in the nude. Blanchita could sometimes hear the expletives from his pain from across the expanse of bluish flowers at dusk or dawn, or during the nights.

Blanchita was the exquisite best of Catalina, Cicero, Drago, Elena, and Johan. She was fire and music; scarlet and turquoise; crimson velvet and pirates' blood. From her evenings with the Chess Club, she easily made the transition into schoolteacher, in which position she mainly taught the piano. She was still a teenager, but she appeared to be far, far wiser. Her skill had already alerted the University of Sarajevo and the Sarajevo Chamber Orchestra. Blanchita played regularly with them, without pay, always with her eyes closed to accentuate the delights and the definition of the music, and in honor of her dead, blind father. The orchestra toured regularly, including internationally, but she did not want to leave Johan. She insisted that she was happy to remain an amateur, and always explained that the word came from the Latin verb for "to love." However, Johan demanded that she play a minimum of three recitals outside of the country each year, and being a Young Hooligan at heart, Blanchita simply had to respect her elder. This little girl would be very much *seen* and *heard*.

* * *

The exposure allowed her to fully soak in the wondrous delights of the world from the comfortable base camp of six-star hotels, for the orchestra had of late provoked the interest and generosity of a mystery benefactor. This cushion of luxury inevitably led to love affairs and to the breaking of many young men's hearts. She gladly dipped her toe, and enjoyed each of them for what they were. She was *very* Spanish, after all.

* * *

The mass of blue disappeared. It returned. It went again, as legions of new readers read the words THE END in *Dragon in Chains: How Opium and Confucius May Yet Save the World, Part Two*.

In England, Tobias Kilz and the Ruben-Wolfram Press had become supremely rich from the scribblings of Miss de la Peña. Kilz could now fund many new young writers. The plentiful earlier royalties soon seemed insignificant in comparison to those from the *Dragon in Chains* series, for opium and Confucius were indeed a supreme combination. I guess there is a deep seam of interest in having the world saved, especially by such magnificent methods as those employed by our fine, unassuming Eastern heroes, of the Red Mist and the White Cloud Monastery.

Blanche took exciting and enthralling liberties with plotlines, while Ming and Qi Chu quietly, and to an impressive degree, pushed their luck, too. Meanwhile, governments covertly and overtly searched for Blanche, in attempts to charm her. In other days, the possessor of Blanche's typewriter might have sweated profusely at the thought of such pursuers. The irony was not lost on him/her when he/she received coded updates from his/her protector, Tobias Kilz. The publisher was no longer of Ludgate Circus, thanks to the kerfuffle started by his wonderful scribe. Kilz had been inspired by Conan Doyle, Holmes, and latterly Archibald DeWitt-Vultura and actually done it; yes, he was keeping bees in Sussex, though he was at pains to point out to anyone who inquired that it was not against their will.

Dragon in Chains continued with *Ming of the Red Mist and the Scented Squadron of Mata Haris* (1965).

The title of *Who Shall Slay the Bothersome Elite? Perhaps Qi Chu and I Shall* (which was translated into many languages; almost as many as there are words for "butterfly," pondered the author, minutes before she saw a pair coquetting above the blue wilderness) was stenciled and sprayed, etched and painted, whispered and yelled across the burning cities of Europe (and beyond) in 1968 (and beyond).

The revolutionary sixties then shot their bolt as subtle subterfuge, high-waisted suits, sweating and handkerchief-dabbing Sydney Greenstreet types, tinny gunshots and femme fatales returned in *Qi Chu and the Hurricane That Lasted for the Illegal Fortnight* (1971). The book was closer in spirit to *Key Largo* than it was to the *Brigadier*. Bacall, Bogart, and Barrymore would all have approved. The "Illegal Fortnight" is a rowdy and unruly time in Peking, when the city is struck by a weather pattern never before seen. No sane person thinks to leave his or her residence during the violent storm; one has to remain where and with whom one was when the tropical cyclone landed. Cabin fever takes hold, and large swathes of the city resort to total reliance on the opium that is delivered by the only two men with the courage and the knowledge to take on Mother Nature. Ming of the Red Mist and Qi Chu, the Saintly Abbot from the White Cloud Monastery, are able to sense safe corridors in the tornado, as well as when the epicenter (which swirls around the metropolis for twelve long days, refusing to leave) is directly above them, allowing them secure passage in whichever direction the malicious and devilishly persistent storm is heading. Many thousands of Pekingese would feel a lull in the winds before the politest of knocks on their door. Shortly after the departure of the pair, bliss would be inhaled and ecstasy would beckon. Blanche thought of that blue rose, just out of reach. Once people are liberated, apocryphal and exaggerated tales of the duo's exploits during the siege spread.

As the title suggests, 1979's *The Torrid Fibonacci*[15] *Sequenced Orgy on the Untarnishable Xing Lawns of Typhoon Hill* exquisitely pushed boundaries of taste and decency, incurring the censors' wrath in many of Kilz's territories. He could have kissed them, for his presses rarely rested in supplying public demand, nor did the translators, who sometimes risked their freedom and that of their families. May the blind and determined fools generously continue to determine such dubious tidemarks for us, Kilz happily concluded of the censors. The numbers involved in the Fibonacci bacchanalia are not only vast, but supremely arranged to mathematical perfection, as if Ming of the Red Mist and Qi Chu, the Saintly Abbot from the White Cloud Monastery, are conducting their orchestra from above with a perfect plan view and the minds of calculus professors in a stream of consciousness. Qi Chu waves his baton. It is a thing of beauty.

Those who were lucky enough to witness the superbly debauched events at Typhoon Hill either are purged, rise to power within the party, or are still out there somewhere, spinning out of control and flying the flag for the cowards who just read or heard of their exploits.

Meanwhile, a whooping Archibald DeWitt-Vultura met the release of the *Fibonacci* hot potato with the following exhalation of camp honesty in the *Manchester Guardian*.

CAREFUL, MY DEAREST, MOST IMMACULATE BLANCHE.

They, the miscreants in our midst and in your crosshairs, usually end up crucifying your sort. If I were able to knock the nail into my final hand, I would gladly die on the cross next to you, but only after having taken down as many of those who would deny you as possible. Excuse my lower Danish, for it is indeed quite rusty: THE BASTARDS!

I fawn for no other, and never have. Never shall.

Come and make friends in person, for mine are dying off at such a rate these days that I am actually quite shocked, and invariably delighted, if they make it through luncheon. They have promised to let me out if I stop the lilac graffiti. I have conceded to this wish, for I dream of stumbling into you in either this or another realm, you High and Dark Angel of Mischief. Together we shall slaughter the intolerant.

Archibald.

DeWitt-Vultura was out and looking for Blanche, as harmlessly as one might imagine.

The royalties were routinely sent by Mr. Kilz to Blanchita and to the two accounts of the Young Hooligans' Chess Club. He had researched the recipients of the monies, and had guessed that a fine (albeit eccentric) philanthropic spirit was behind Stanley Rex-Foyle et al.

* * *

Johan's physical appearance began to concern Blanchita at times. She devotedly delivered his breakfasts, lunches, and suppers on the stroke of nine, twelve, and six. Many remained untouched. Johan started, at age eighty-five, to resemble one of those poor bastards in the pictures from the liberated death camps, which he believed that he had personally instigated. His large skull was now old, a home to sallow, heavy bags under his eyes, a full head of scraggy gray hair, gray stubble, and gray beard. He shuffled around the cabin like a lifer in prison. His eyes, though, remained as azure as those glorious waters off Split he'd looked into back in 1914.

He wrote more prodigiously but his thoughts became increasingly scattered. It would be another seventeen years before Kilz received his penultimate package from Blanche.

The Year the Opium and the Marigold Failed (1996) warned of a vicious world without heavy drug use. Movie deals were offered to Blanche via Kilz, but there was never a chance that the rights holder would agree to the bastardization of her work. Perhaps if Gene Tierney, Sydney Greenstreet, or David Niven had been attached to the project, things might have been different. She preferred to remember the tobacco-yellowy silver screen at the bottom of Porlock Hill during the war.

In 2001,

God's Troika of Stardust
When Ming and Qi Chu Entertained the White-Kilted Brigadier in the
Smoky Gallery of the Mirrored Buffoons
An Unretractable Apology

was published. Blanche's heroes all came together in the style of one of those monochrome classics from the thirties, where the Wolfman meets Frankenstein meets Count Dracula; Chaney, Karloff, and Lugosi to boot. Naturally, Stanley Rex-Foyle is hugely drawn to Ming of the Red Mist and Qi Chu, the Saintly Abbot from the White Cloud Monastery, for, although Stanley had not tried opium or read Confucius (that is, at least not until thirty pages in), he is an avid and reasonably competent snooker player. It is on the green baize that their friendship is formed. The Brigadier wagers his belongings in games with the pair until he has only his white kilt as leverage. He then loses on the black ball, due to the numbing and quite blissful effects of the narcotics. He is stripped naked after his defeat, but wakes two days later, fully dressed, kilt and all, with his wallet stuffed with banknotes. Ming of the Red Mist and Qi Chu, the Saintly Abbot from the White Cloud Monastery, have spent those two days in the Gallery of the Mirrored Buffoons, laughing almost continually through a plume of thick opiatic smoke. At midnight on the second night, Qi Chu tells Red Mist his ultimate secret: how it was he who drove a car on June the twenty-eighth, 1914, and how his momentary lapse of concentration started the Great War. And with it comes an apology which remains unretractable to this day; unretractable for it was accepted by his friend with a gentle, manly kiss on the forehead. And that was the last we would hear of our three friends.

Blanche had no qualms in stealing her opening line for the final story from a German[16] whom she had always much admired. It was a warning which remains as apt as ever.

> Don't rejoice in his defeat, you men.
> For though the world stood up and stopped the bastard,
> The bitch that bore him is in heat again.

We all knew this was an adieu; and a fine one at that.

* * *

He had convinced himself that there was a way back in time, a vortex, a portal, a wormhole in the space-time continuum, a loxodromic magic carpet ride through the decades. He would stare at the objects around his shack, mementos of his life which he was convinced were his passport. He was determined to return to 1914 and do things—well, just one thing—differently. There had to be a way. The vellum tomes, the letters stamped from Vienna in 1913 and 1914—something would transport him back if he concentrated on it hard enough at the right moment in time. There existed a mathematical equation which would give him the formula, the key. He scribbled for days on a yellowed heavy-stock, embossed tablet of writing paper lifted from the President, back when things had been good. Integration, differentiation, heavy mind-bending calculus. Sigmas and dy/dx's.

He pictured himself reappearing as a youth in the old library. The still-cream-bound volumes of the *Kama Sutra* were spread out in front of him on his study desk. He imagined looking down at his veinless youthful, smooth hands, those of a young man, a boy, a student, flourishing, thriving with the world at his feet. He looked up and caught a glimpse of his reflection in the glass casing of the philosophy section, a boyish complexion, a creaseless face, lean-jawed and handsome. He breathed in the smells of youth: of dewberry on girls' necks, of ylang-ylang in the summer air at the Old Sultan's Palace, of gardenia on his pillow. The window was open on a spring afternoon, and he heard the sound of a piano. It was the *Gymnopédies* again. He forced himself to reappear there. To squeeze through that vortex and to go back, in order to put things right.

His concentration was broken by a rat scuttling over his foot. He was back in the shack, old, creased, mad, smelly, decaying rapidly, not long for this world (he was past his one hundred and ninth birthday).

"Fuck!" he blurted. "I was nearly fucking there. Fuck. Fuck. Fuck. F . . . U . . . C . . . KKKK!"

Agony overtook him, and he passed out onto the floor.

* * *

He came round a few hours later, with a phrase on his lips.

"I am the Resurrection.
And I am the Life . . ."

But whom was he trying to convince?

He had been responsible for two billion deaths and had touched the lives of everyone on the planet, so why could he not do this one single thing? It made no sense. Instead of turning time back, he was hurtling forward through it at great speed, for he had now been back in his homeland for fifty-seven years, and forty of those had been spent in this shack.

Johan heard a noise behind him again. A face peered in through the cobwebbed pane, framed amid the mass of lilacs, speedwells, and ceanothus. But no Blue Rose of Forgetfulness. Not quite yet.

It was a face he did not fully recognize, but it resembled someone he thought he knew. He beckoned the visitor in through a door which had never been locked.

"Welcome to my humble abode," Johan said with an English accent which would have been more than acceptable on the World Service. "Please come in."

Seven

"I Know Who You Are!"

An autobiography is an obituary in serial form with the last instalment missing.
—Quentin Crisp

And so my grandfather, while on a supposedly innocuous trip to find a new twin town for Goole, had stumbled across the one man in the land whose story he'd only *dreamed* of finding.

At six that evening, a delivery of food arrived from the remains of the big old house across from the hut, and Ernest met Blanchita.[17] She promptly returned with a healthy portion of stewed meat and cabbage for the rare visitor, along with a mug of claret. It was delicious, apparently—as was everything which Johan's adoring lady friend brought to their door at the stroke of nine, twelve, and six for the next four days.

Johan knew full well that he would feel better after he had got the whole tale out of his decrepit system.

When he neared the very end, he paused for lengthy, comfortable gaps, and Ernest felt it was more than appropriate for him to add an opinion. Johan listened, too. He listened enough that Ernest went one step further and actually interrupted Johan's diatribe. The elder man was aghast, for Ernest's words echoed those of a very dear man he used to know.

"Oh Christs and blimey! Get a grip, old boy! It is *true,* my friend. That war would have started anyway. It was a fait accompli. June the twenty-eighth was just the excuse the bastards were desperate for. The powers that be had determined it long before you conjured up your nicely perverse image of Lorelei and a powder-blue plume and then veered off down a cul-de-sac. There would have been another spark; that much was inevitable. As sure as night follows day. Any historian on this continent would back me up. I wish instead that some foresighted critter had brought Queen Victoria's troublesome young grandsons and that other damned cousin together for a Sunday lunch at Buckingham Palace, and then, after their rhubarb crumble and custard, put them all in a boxing ring out on the back lawns. Let them sort it out there, rather than buggering a poor continent. They were, in aggregate, impertinent snobs—and, in detail, unmitigated ruffians. The wicked little sods needed their legs slapped and to be sent to bed with no supper."

Ernest was referring to George V, *der Kaiser,* and the Czar, though his intonation, his vocabulary, and his belief in his words were so reminiscent of another to Johan that he put his face close enough to his new friend's to once again feel each other's breath.

Ernest's heart skipped a beat.

"I know who you are, young Cartwright. There can be no mistaking *him,*" said Johan, smiling. "Your father was a wonderful man. God, I love him.

"And you are right, I know. It maybe was not all my fault. I believe I *suspect* this now, but I wish I had *known* this earlier. Anyway, I say place down a marker for reality and then another for one's worst fears. Any bothersome, snaggletoothed braggard who has not left a chasm there through which to fly a Lancaster bomber is a better man than I. I do know that my good pal, your old man, would call him a gobshite."

And so, although countless others had plowed this same furrow for many years, it took William Atticus Forsythe Cartwright's own boy (and the continual and dependable reinforcement of the BBC World Service) to finally assuage the majority of Johan's guilt. As he said this, he passed to Ernest another small pile of envelopes, recently scrawled upon. They had been addressed to both of the Young Hooligans' chess clubs, to the Marigold Society of Southern Europe, to the Chirigotas of Cádiz, to the Dorothy Parker Society, to the Family of Carlos-Ramón Kitríl, to his Blanchita, and two to his grandson, one of which had been originally made out to Lorelei Ribeiro. Each, it seemed from his words to Ernest, would contain an apology for his actions and his weaknesses. He had written that he had finally started to realize that the war would have started anyway. It was not all his fault, but for decades he had not known this. This was a large part of his downfall, and had he been braver and stuck around in 1914, he would possibly have known this far earlier.

He also addressed one to the editor of the *Times of London,* and marked it *Obituaries.*

Blanche de la Peña

I was born on June the twenty-eighth, 1914, in the land of the Slavs. My life has been a blessed torment. I have known deep love and true friendship. I have known absolute horror, for I believed that I had caused absolute horror. I may yet return to change this. I may yet return to change history. I am sorry for the deaths I know I have caused. I apologize to an archduke and his princess. And their children, born and unborn.

My hours are now short. Bill, Cicero, Catalina, Manzana, Kaunitz, Mother, Father, Carlos-Ramón: I doubt I shall see you soon, but I guess there is a minute chance. Archibald, I shall miss you, as I shall miss your delightful lilac mischief.

And you, fine Hooligans, be blessed! Go grab and rattle the world, for she needs grabbing and rattling by your tender hands! And remember to nod at the altar of your Spanish friend and my Roman namesake. Her piano, purity, and beauty shall endure.

If my plan works, I will see you, Lorelei, on the jade lawns of a bright, white palace in a distant and immaculate June. I am close, my single love.

Adieu or au revoir? We shall soon see . . .

Signed: Blanche de la Peña

Even in the third millennium, this apparent confession of homosexuality would cause such consternation at the *Times* that the proprietor was consulted and had the casting vote on whether to censor or even not publish at all. But the rich old man on the paper's masthead was (bizarrely, in many eyes) one of Blanche's greatest admirers, and laughed off any suggestion that it would not be printed. Indeed, he went further, and had it published on the front cover in both the early and late editions. Sales across the country set a record for the paper (when not announcing the declaration of a war or a victory over evil, the sinking of a large boat by an iceberg or a man walking on another celestial sphere). Some, however, suggested the proprietor's motives were simply financial.

It was still not the obituary of Johan Thoms, for this you hold.

Eight

The Death and Life of a Grim Reaper

Let us not unman each other; part at once; all farewells should be sudden.

—Lord Byron

Easter Monday, April 21, 2003

On the Monday evening, Ernest got up to urinate in the makeshift latrine at the back of the now-darkening hut. After he zipped up and pushed open the old door, he saw that Johan had prostrated himself on his scabby old mattress.

Johan's voice grew weak, as if his last burst of energy, his fifth wind, had been exhausted. There was nothing left in him. He believed in his delirium that he'd had his catharsis.

The vision of Bill had absolved him. Johan could live the rest of his time (relatively) unburdened. He then started to mumble, in tongues.

Ernest told me that Johan spoke of a Yorkshireman called William Atticus Forsythe Cartwright, slaughtered on the morning of July 1, 1916, on a French field called the Somme, within hours of the start of the battle. He said of Bill, "A shadow can never claim the beauty of the image." There were silences during this tale, but they were never uncomfortable.

He remembered the smell of a thousand ancient books in a cool, dark library in 1913 as the summer sun tried to melt the Southern European roads outside.

He remembered playing chess as a seven-year-old against a supremely talented old fleabag.

He remembered a sick, young boy with dark-ringed eyes giving him a crucifix, somewhere near the Adriatic.

He remembered a dog, emanating very ripe smells and bouncing out a furry welcome on an Italian beach; just a fraction of a memory of an irretrievable past.

He remembered a Portuguese friend, brave men and women in Spain, and waking up naked on a London street.

He remembered his best friend, a blind, legless soldier, dying in an icy stream, and a beautiful Spanish girl facing death next to the whitest of white orchids.

He remembered Franz and Sophie, their bullet holes, and the realization in some sick, spluttering wretch's crossed coffee-brown eyes of the error of his ways.

He remembered his mother. His father. And smiled.

He remembered a line he had once read, and spoke it aloud.

"When I despair, I remember, that all through history, the way of truth and love has always won. There have been murderers and tyrants and for a time, they can seem invincible. But in the end, they always fall. Think of it always!" [18]

He remembered searching for the Blue Rose of Forgetfulness, even as he realized that he was just seconds away from finding it, which made him smile more.

He remembered angels in stiff white cotton floating around his white starched linen, saving him once, twice, thrice. He imagined their tears when he had broken free with a reincarnated, dark-eyed, skeletal, ex–Roman emperor and fine future foot soldier against evil. He remembered Cicero again, this time as a two-legged youth with vision.

He remembered being in a cart with his mother, staring at the stars, pondering a game of chess that he should have won.

He remembered Blanche and her pal Stanley, and how they had helped him to survive with their benediction, generosity, and love. Ming of the

Red Mist and Qi Chu, the Saintly Abbot from the White Cloud Monastery, too, of course, the degenerate and quite marvelous planet savers and drug fiends.

He thought of his beloved Bandita across the blue shrubs.

He remembered having lost the love of that one woman. The smile turned at a tangent.

"There but for the grace of God . . . goes God," Johan Thoms whispered.

Ernest recalled hearing the words *heretic, blasphemer, infidel,* and *degenerate.* And then: "What a joy!"

"It's time I went, my friend," Johan Thoms mumbled to my grandfather. "Out of my way, spirits!" His right hand went to grab the creamvellum tome one more time, in one ultimate attempt to find his portal back to a time when he could change it all.

In doing this (and this was his undoing), he seemed to be in a hurry, and succeeded only in knocking an old glass paperweight, perhaps over a hundred years old, from the top of the pile of books down onto the bedside table. It shattered into what seemed to be a million or more shards around the old man's right hand. That same right hand which had not been able to find a reverse gear had committed one last crime.

Thus, close to his last breath, Johan Thoms destroyed his one true portal. It had been there all along. The wormhole opened. Then it closed.

- Still in a hurry.

- Still fucking up with his right hand.

- Still unable to see things as they really were.

A trinity of flaws to take down ANY man.

Johan had even rushed into his own death, a fraction of a second before his portal would have finally been exposed to him.

Then Ernest saw an old man death-rattle through his final breath.

Silence fell, minutes long. Ernest did not move until, finally, he picked up the leaf of paper that had been freed from the paperweight. It had been swept away on a released thermal, had slowly fallen, and had floated to the grubby deck, like a burnt-orange maple leaf on a way-too-late bruised October afternoon.

Johan was now gliding on his own magic carpet ride toward a light as white as an orchid. He was inhaling the Blue Rose of Forgetfulness for the first time, breathing in the ecstasy of knowing no pain. The smile of his youth returned to his face.

His beloved Blanchita sensed this, and screamed his requiem from within the remnants of the house, where the now dead, yet finally contented man, had been born, grown up, which he had deserted, returned to, rebuilt, and then partly destroyed.

My grandfather squinted and checked both sides of the message on the paper. He thought he should be finding more than was initially apparent in the gathering blue gloom.

The scrap of paper, however, contained just five words, the final resting epitaph of Johan Thoms.

GLIDE GENTLY.
THUS FOREVER GLIDE . . .

Epilogue

I now have the cream-vellum volumes of the *Kama Sutra* which once sat in the University of Sarajevo. Their beauty is a rare one. I have some old sepia photographs, a kit bag, an empty bottle of cologne on which the words *El Capitán* are subtly embossed. Those possessions from his golden time of 1913 provided the focus for Johan Thoms's mind; objects procured later in his life would not have landed him far enough back in time to take a different path. These earlier objects were Johan's supposed wormholes in the space-time continuum, his portal, his vortex to a magic carpet ride through the ages. But the old man never did master the intricacies of the reverse gear.

My grandfather swore to me, though, that at two remarkable points, one when discussing an old love and the second when Ernest, clearly and without nuance, forgave and absolved his new friend for the death of his father, William Atticus Forsythe Cartwright, Johan had looked twenty-five years old again for a brief, supernatural moment. It was dusk and the blue light was playing tricks—devilish, mean, and quite wonderfully malicious tricks.

I also have a trunk. It seems to have spent time on the ocean floor; it has a lilac *P* painted on the side, and fish scales, which weirdly smell of warm butter. It is the sort to have once held Spanish gold, but today it holds thousands of powder-blue envelopes and an ever-fading hint of ylang-ylang.

There is a separate letter from Lorelei's grandson, which informs of her death in 1963 from throat cancer.

* * *

It has now been a month since Ernest died. I have been busy with the knowledge which he left me.

Tomorrow, I shall leave his blown ashes and England, for I have an air ticket to Faro, Portugal.

From the airport in the Algarve, I am to be taken to Vila do Bispo.

I am to stay in a small hut there in the village, the hut where *those boys* once lived. I know in my mind what it looks like; it has already been tinged by the prismatic blue, turquoise, scarlet, lilac, and lemon-yellow hues of Johan's generous memory.

I will visit the old school, where it shall be a great honor to meet with representatives of the two Young Hooligans' chess clubs.

It is quite possible that, to this day, Portuguese boys by the sea where oceans meet are drilled with precision by their grandfathers in walking on the outside of their belles; in switching positions in the middle of the street to always face the oncoming traffic; in never referring to their wives as *she,* always pointing with two fingers instead of one, and never waiting to start on a meal delivered warm, so as not to offend the chef. Not one of them would ever wish to carry or even to own an umbrella, nor would they ever consider using red ink to write. Not only that, the technicalities of en passant may have been engrained into, and the Oleg and Luzhin Defenses may well have found favor with, the fine, fertile minds of the wonderful young chess hooligans of southwest Portugal and of Sarajevo. Indeed, despite his resounding error way back when, Johan Thoms may have left one or two rather positive thumbprints around Europe during his days there.

Cicero, too, for it may also be quite possible to dig just a couple of feet down on those expansive banks above the beaches and find there the oceanic treasures left by the young man on those days between the wars when Alfredo was still young and Johan Thoms sat above on the vast hill, tapping on his typewriter while he tried not to ponder his unique trail of destruction. And how he might deal with it.

One chess club member allegedly holds the honor of possessing a map to and the knowledge of the fine oceanarium of spewed wonders known as Museu de Cicero, which I shall be shown.

Other guests at this memorial to Lorelei and to Johan include the Chirigotas of Cádiz, Blanchita, and an American gentleman, also in his midsixties, whom we should all surely recognize from the pictures I have of his grandmother Lorelei Ribeiro and his grandfather Johan Thoms, and which will be posthumously published in the modern-day edition of the final installment of *The White-Kilted Brigadier*. If any further help is required in identifying him, we shall apparently know him by the Dorothy Parker autobiography under his arm and the extra-large Panama hat tilted on his head. His name is Johan Ribeiro.

The delicious genes of Catalina Boadicea Rodríguez, William Atticus Forsythe Cartwright, Cicero Emperor of Rome, Lorelei Ribeiro, and Johan Thoms shall be together there.

The meeting shall fulfill a promise I made to my grandfather in his final hours.

There is even talk of a game of chess or two, but we have been warned to watch out for the killer instincts of Blanchita, Mr. Ribeiro, and those fine Young Hooligans from several generations and from two countries, whose flag shall be flying proudly.

Dr. S.P.E. Cartwright
PTSD Unit,
International Red Cross

Notes

1. Ernest toured the world as a conductor, as junior partner to (Sir) Thomas Beecham—alongside Leonard Bernstein, the greatest musical talents of their age. From Covent Garden to the Café de Paris, they turned the stale, staid world of music on its head. A self-taught master of music, Beecham had been the first in the British Isles to perform Wagner's *Mastersingers of Nuremberg*, Strauss's *Elektra*, and the magical, mythical *Salome*. Beecham was *the* iconoclast. With a stashed family fortune from the production of laxative pills and cure-alls, he had formed the London Philharmonic Orchestra in the summer of 1932 in Covent Garden. In the ensuing years, Ernest had understudied the genius of Beecham, who later in '47 established the mighty Royal Philharmonic. Together, in their rebellious early days, they had championed English music, particularly that of Frederick Delius, whom they brought to Covent Garden society. Sibelius and Handel had been other favorites, played in wonderfully personal and very inventive arrangements to stunned audiences. They were instinctive and enthusiastic. Their productions of Bizet's *Carmen* were legendary.

   It was Beecham who had once famously said that "the English may not like music, but they absolutely love the noise it makes." His remarks and witticisms became the center of much fun and interest within society. At an event for the well-to-do, he found himself chatting with a lady whom he was sure he recognized.

"How are you?" he asked.

"I'm very well, thank you, Sir Thomas, although my brother has not been well of late."

"Oh yes. Your brother. Is he still doing the same job?"

"Oooh yes, he is still the King."

Beecham and Ernest eventually went their separate ways professionally but remained firm friends for the rest of their days. (Ernest had met his wife, Betty, at this point. From a family of moneyed Cape Town piano dealers, Betty was also a member of the South African tennis team, a more than proficient show jumper, and a bright young bureau chief for the London *Daily Mail* in Africa. Thankfully for me, off they went to make babies—three, to be exact. (Now all sadly scythed down by booze.) With his mentor, Beecham, Ernest left a legacy of musical revolution. The landscape would never look the same again. The old guard and the establishment had been left cowering, muttering their disbelief behind their evening programs.

On his deathbed, Beecham reckoned that the best advice he could offer to anyone was, "Try everything once, except incest and folk dancing."

2. *Idi u kurac:* Literally, "Go inside the cock." Less literally, "You are a fucker."

3. *Tizi pizdun:* "You are a pussy."

4. *Merkin:* a pubic wig.

5. Quotation by Jean Rostand.

6. The royal visit: The Austro-Hungarian Empire (aka Hapsburg Empire) constituted a powerhouse in Europe, akin to the British throne. Geographically, the area it covered was immense. In the time of Charles V, it had stretched from Castile and Aragon to pockets of the Netherlands, Sardinia, Sicily, and Italy, south of Naples. The main landmass included modern-day Austria, Hungary, Croatia, the Czech Republic, Poland, and Bosnia.

From the Middle Ages to the beginning of the twentieth century, the Hapsburgs were central to European politics and power.

Although harshly referred to as a "prison of nations," their empire offered a shelter to far-flung regions to protect against stronger, local cultures. As the landscape of Europe shifted and entered the industrial age, the Hapsburgs, however, did not evolve.

Nestled next to and, crucially, upon the powder keg of the Balkans, the empire was despised by the fiercely nationalistic and expansionist Serbs. They saw the Hapsburgs as occupiers of land which had once constituted Greater Serbia. Key to this dispute was the province of Bosnia.

The dream of Greater Serbia was to include the lands of Kosovo, Herzegovina, Vojvodina, Bosnia, Serb Krajina, Macedonia, and of course Serbia itself. Ever since the region was freed from Turkish slavery and the Ottoman Empire, this had been the goal of the typical Serb. The Serbs desired a seaport for the landlocked homeland. It would be hard to find tougher, more ruthless people, and if there was ever an equally psychotic bunch of villains and gun-toting, ax-wielding homicidal, wild-eyed genocidal lunatics, it was their neighboring foe, the Croats. The third ethnic group in the region, the Muslims (there as the result of ancient Byzantine expansionism), were held in equal disdain by both.

The Serbs and their historical brethren of Russia were set against the Croats and their friends in Germany, creating a microcosm of the struggles within a wider Europe. "Ethnically Serb, territorially Serbia" was their aim.

7. Marigold is believed to be the most useful and multifunctional of all plants. Yet, like other weeds which have been adopted into cultivated gardens by horticulturists, the marigold is so aesthetically pleasing that its practical uses and beneficial properties have become largely ignored.

Its healing properties were once legendary across the Mediterranean, from the Iberian Peninsula to Mesopotamia. It contains querticin 3-0-glucoside for cuts and bruises, volatile oils for antiseptics, and salisylic acids for external anti-inflammatories. When taken internally, it relieves headaches and extreme nervous conditions. It heals warts and relieves fever. Marigold leaves cure scrofula (a form of TB of the bones and lymph glands) in children. Delayed menstruation, heart murmurs, and skin diseases yield to the marigold. Bad circulation, varicose veins, chilblains, eczema, measles, and digestive disorders, too.

The fabulous weed is a styptic, which means it can stem bleeding by forcing tissue to contract. It was first used in this way in the American Civil War by nurses and medics, and later in the Great War. Indeed, as Johan was picking the flower, the famous English gardener of the day, Gertrude Jekyll, was only months away from having to send millions of bushels from her Sussex estate to the field hospitals in France and Belgium, where they were to be used for dressings.

8. While the old bells of Shrewsbury Church sounded out the news of the armistice, a crooked and elderly Mrs. Owen noticed that a telegram had just landed on her front doormat. It took her a minute or two to reach it as she

wiped her ancient-looking hands on her fastidiously clean apron, then another to find a knife to cut open the correspondence. The telegram told her of the news of the death of her only son, Wilfred, just four days before, in Belgium.

9. *Henslow* was from John Henslow, the Cambridge professor, who had given up his place on the *Beagle* to a spiky fellow by the name of Darwin.

10. *Decias que no y hasta la trompita alzabas*: "You say you don't want to, but your lips are pursed."

11. Binoculars had officially been banned to the public by the 1915 Defence of the Realm Act. The act (DORA to her friends) was responsible for a whole range of freedom-limiting moves, including England's somewhat archaic licensing laws.

12. The Croat militia, the Ustase (literally "insurgent"), had taken control of Yugoslavia in April 1941 and were allies of Hitler. Even though the Croats were seen as substandard to the Aryan model, this was a convenient geographical bedfellowship for Berlin. A conservative estimate of lives lost in the concentration camps, such as Jasenovac, Gospić, and Pag, was one million. Six more noughts for the total. The Ustase had traditionally had close links to the Catholic Church. The Ustase leader, Anten Pavelić, was actually smuggled to Argentina after the war disguised as a Catholic priest through a network which became known as the "rat channels." Pavelić had been famous for always having in his presence a basketful of Serbian eyeballs. The Ustase had been brutally cleansing the countryside of Jews, Romany Gypsies, and Serbs. Muslims were often, however, bizarrely included in the Ustase, regarded as Croats of the Muslim faith, even having their own mosques in Zagreb and Split. No doubt more than a few of the militia would have been exposed to more than one Catholic priest with dubious, yogurty activities on a hot sticky Sunday evening by the sea in Dubrovnik or in the privacy of a rainy Wednesday afternoon in a cloister in the suburbs of Mostar. Their vengeful anger toward sodomites would have had known no bounds as far as the poor old Count was concerned.

13. The Balkan bloodbath of the 1990s was started, arguably, by the Germans, at the behest of the Croats. After Tito's death, out of Yugoslavia's old racial tensions and hatred rose the ugliest head of all. Europe and Brussels were desperately trying to push through the Maastricht Treaty on European unity. The Germans had the power of veto and wished to see their business interests and their cousins thrive free of Serb interference in a land free now of communism. A free market was going to mean cold hard cash. The Germans agreed to sign the treaty on

the proviso that their Croat cousins were granted autonomy by Europe and independence from the rest of Yugoslavia. Brussels relented, keen to realize its own bureaucratic goals, myopic to, and probably not even giving a distant damn about, the powder keg, into which it was throwing a lit match. Another round of genocide ensued—Srebrenica, Milošević, Tudjman—and the only thing we learn from history is our bloody-minded refusal never, ever to learn anything from it. Sarajevo was to rightly re-earn its tag as the Lebanon of the Balkans, repeatedly the innocent and unwitting venue for someone else's fight.

14. *Non que non tronabas pistolita:* No literal translation; "bit by bit, one can explode a mountain with a small pistol." The suggestion is that if one perserveres, one can do absolutely anything, despite the odds.

15. Fibonacci sequence: There are infinite numbers of Fibonacci sequences where the next number is the sum of the two previous ones. It is a common misapprehension that there is one: 1, 1, 2, 3, 5, 8, 13 . . . Any procession of numbers may display the sequence's properties—5, 7, 12, 19, 31, 50 . . . Or 3, 90, 93, 183, 276 . . . Johan was fascinated by this, as he saw the parallel in his taking the blame for an event for which many should equally be fingered.

16. Bertolt Brecht, from *Der aufhaltsame Aufstieg des Arturo Ui* (*The Resistible Rise of Arturo Ui*). The word *aufhaltsame* is not used in German. *Unaufhaltsame* is "irresistible," and the fact that Brecht used *aufhaltsame* merely underlines his belief that it had been possible to prevent Hitler's rise to power.

17. When in the future (1992) evil returned, the rest of the world turned its negligent, mean-spirited, and ruthless back on Bosnia. Blanchita then found her father's olive-green fatigues from 1937 and joined the fight. Her pianist's hands helped to dig the famous tunnel which seams below the landing strip of the international airport to this day. For three years, the single underground track offered the only way of delivering water, electricity, and food to the besieged citizens and when the burrowing was finished, she continued to work with the men at great personal risk from the shells bombarding the innocent citadel. When the shelling eventually stopped, she quickly reprised her roles of teacher, pianist, and chess assassin. Johan's guilt from the past and concern for *her* present were outweighed by his vast now-paternal pride, but only just. On Johan's hundredth birthday, the irony was not lost on him that his beloved Sarajevo was under siege from malice, and that it was the generous and spirited flesh and blood of Cicero that had tunneled a lifeline to it.

18. Quotation by Mahatma Gandhi.

Acknowledgments

For their generosity or inspiration or both, the author wishes to offer thanks:

IN ENGLAND, TORONTO, LOS ANGELES, SYDNEY,
elsewhere, or in my memory:

To my beautiful children, Laszlo and Clementine, and to their mother, Heather Gordon, who saved my life and has been each day since, "light of my life, fire of my loins."

To my late mother and father, Val and Rob Thornton, whom I miss beyond measure, and without whom *nothing* would have mattered. To the rest of my family, Carl and Darren Thornton, Rache, Jack and Hannah Kenny, William Alan Thornton, Ernest Reid-Smith and Betty Darter. I say a huge thank you for the guidance and the access to your food cupboards; the wisdom and the love. I wish some of you were still here for a chat over a gin and tonic or a snooker table. I wish, too, that my brother Carl had been blessed with a portion of my good fortune so that I (we) could have known him.

In the seven years it has taken to bring this book to fruition, there have been many periods of fallow activity. This has meant that I have leaned on friends beyond their call of duty, and I am lucky and grateful that those of whom I had always thought the most highly were the ones who remained around to be there for me. You all gladly gave me keys, a bed, food, drink, and/or generous portions of love and patience. Your number is vast, but that does not devalue any one of you: Charles Kittrell; Roger and Maryum Malik; my oldest friends, Marie and Kevin Chappelow (and their children, Antonia, Saffron, and Elliot); Karl, Nikki, and Louie Domonkos; Neil and Sam Wilson; Chris Mould and David Chambers; Todd and Mari Stevens; Chris Fletcher; Torquil, Debbie, and Molly Macneal; Claire Best; Debbie Mason; Duncan James and Penny Lamanna; Sarah Polayah; and Nathon Gunn, who also helped to crack open the case of the search for a literary agent. This book was made possible by you.

To the artists who have inspired me and who took me away from the offices, the sales meetings, the telephones, and the strip lighting that would likely have seen me dead by the age of forty: Michael Powell, Emeric Pressburger, Anton Walbrook, Deborah Kerr, Roger Livesey, David Lean, Orson Welles, David Niven, Joseph L. Mankiewicz, Dorothy Parker, John Kennedy Toole, Jon Stewart, Jake Thackray, John Lennon, Joe Strummer, Sydney Greenstreet, Ricky Day, Tom Waits, Arthur Lee, Chris Morris, Peter Cook, Stephen Fry, rock god Steve Genn, and Miguel Maropakis. To Jon Snow at Channel 4 News for your generous encouragement in the early days of scribbling in Costa Rica. To Stephen Patrick Morrissey and George Harrison.

To the late Chris Gunn and all those from my previous incarnation in the international television market who made those years such a ride; Tony Mendes, Orsalye Valde, Cecilia Hazai, Tim Brooke-Hunt, Theresa Plummer-Andrews, Sharon Ward, Mark Hurry, Barbie Holloway, John Campbell, Erik Pack, Suzanne Gutierrez, Lan Mainville, Moving Pictures, Susannah Morley Wong, DCH, Adam Black, Chris and Margaret Wronski, Chris Hainsworth, Phil Nelson, Jerry Diaz, and David Jenkinson, and all at C21 Media.

To Tina Egerton, with much love. And to her boys. And to Hilary, Tony, Wendy, Hazel, and Christian.

To Nicole Vrbicek for reading the manuscript as you said you would. And by the next day. And then a later version as well for good measure.

To the other crazy Croat, Illyria Pestich, for getting me out on the tennis court, for translating Serbo-Croat curses, and for making me smile.

To Michelle Kass, Harry Bingham, and Paul A. Toth for their early advice. To the preeminent Dr. Arthur Molinary at the College of Psychic Studies in South Kensington for his unerring insight and frighteningly enlightened encouragement. To Meredith Duncan for offering me both work and friendship. To Howden Library, Goole Bookshop, and the top fella that is Ray Adamson, my inspirational German teacher at Howden School, for being there in the sticks and fighting the good fight. To Nick Gaughan for being a true gent and a pal, and to his family, Finley and Kirsty. To Dr. James Burton and George Hespe for their friendship back in the days of the class of 1989 at Sheffield University and since.

For staying in touch and for being as genuine as I ever could have wished them to be, the fine and smiling couple Gina and Walis Williams and the thoroughly unique and remarkable lady that is Sandy Santino.

For individual cases of friendship and generosity that need not be elaborated upon: Jeremy Gawade, Elizabeth Radford, Elena Stepantchenko-Efremova, Kirill Efremov, Philipa Davies, Laetitia Tetart, Lorraine Kent, Vicky Cavallero, Marcie Phoenix, Martin "Tetley" Smith, Solange Ribeiro, Chris Podge Day, Pierre Doisneau and Justin Quirk at Soho House, Malik Meer at the *Guardian*/G2, Jagg and Petie Carr-Locke, Carl and Katy Liddell, all at the Football Factory in Toronto, and my particular strain of Aidan Butterworth, Nic Jones, Tom Wood, Irish Carl, and Darcy Richards. To Marta Radasova, Leroy Samuel, Kathy Nelson, Tim Cribbens, the late Jane Tomlinson, Roma Khanna, Dr. Tom Axworthy, John Andrew, Alison Digges, Hayley Gould, Justin Morris, Boston Hommel, Alexandra Park Cricket Club, Karen and Jamie Dunwoody, Ted and B. J. Maude, Asem Azar, and John Mamajek, Martin Sainty, Dr. Stephanie Merrifield, Louise Wilson, and to Dove House Hospice. To Fabienne Fourquet and Isabelle Hen-Wollmarker. A massive thank you to Shelley Ambrose of *The Walrus*.

To my amazing Canadian family: Jim Gordon Sr. and Simone Gordon, Christine Gordon and David, Susan Gordon and her supremely intelligent daughters, Madelyn and Shannon, and "The Boomster" Jim Gordon Jr.

To all at the Compton Cricket Club and Paul Smith, the Hayes and Cazarez families, Anna Kowalski, Charles Brotherstone, and Howard Lewis.

To Nick Compton and Geoff Boycott for their help and generosity with www.everyday-counts.org

To two fine teachers of the old school who left their mark, the late Paul Howarth and David Lucas. And to others at Howden School, Anne Robinson, "Rupert" Robinson, Keith Green, Sue Butler and Diane Meyers.

To the late and very great Don Revie and Billy Bremner, for invaluable lessons in running through brick walls.

To my darling goddaughter, Princess Nina Wilson.

To all of our armed forces past, present, and future, and to their loved ones. And to the decent folk of Sarajevo.

In Costa Rica:

Ati, el Gordito Edgar Villalobos-Esquivel, Mami, Papi y todo la familia Villalobos-Esquivel a Taberne Pariolis en Alajuela. Iancito, Lolly, Guapa Marjerie, and to My Friend who convinced me that the answer is indeed blowing in the wind.

Rest In Peace, man to the unknown Costa Rican boatman who rescued my manuscript from a thieving spider monkey in Cahuita. To "de two badman" Bobby and Winston in Trenchtown. *La Paz y Jah Rastafari.*

In Mexico:

To Stephen M. Joseph for his patience, encouragement, friendship, and guidance in editing the manuscript in the early days. To Danny Blue and all at the Metro House in San Miguel de Allende: Pedro "Cantinflas" Alvarado, Sam Seaman, Sam-illo Oliver, the one and only Shamana Mexykana, Klaudia Oliver, the Lebanese Cowboy Simon el Habre, Nenita, and Cappu. *Paradis continuas, cabrón!*

And finally . . .

To Lien de Niel, Carolyn Forde and Whitney and Bruce Westwood at Westwood Creative Artists in Toronto for their trust and confidence in signing me to the finest agency in the land: of this I am sure. To Vadim Perelman and Christian Grass for their decency and the comforting proof that all is NOT lost in the film industry. And, of course, to the preternatural abilities and generosity of my editor, Barbara Berson, whose rare talent transformed a rambling, ill-disciplined manuscript into something more. And to Stephanie Fysh for her thoroughly illuminating line edit. And then the final pieces of the jigsaw: to Simon&Schuster in Canada for so lovingly taking my publishing virginity and to Marginesy in Poland for giving me the thrill of their becoming the first to translate *Johan*. And of course to the maverick brilliance of Scott Pack and his team of Rachel Faulkner and Cicely Aspinall at The Friday Project / HarperCollins in London. Sometimes ignorance is bliss, for had I known in advance how difficult the postwriting bit can be, I might well have given up. But finding on the other side of this brutal, fantastic, and unrivaled adventure the final and shining treasure of those named in this paragraph forces me into the broadest of grins and has done every day since I heard the news, of which every delusional scribbling nutcase dreams.

I could go on, but I do not wish to fawn myself into a sublimate in the style of Archibald DeWitt-Vultura. I hope you will stick with these pages long enough to meet him. And the others.